THE
ALL-STAR
ANTES
UP

THE ALL-STAR ANTES UP

WAGER OF HEARTS
♥♣ BOOK 2 ♦♠

NANCY HERKNESS

Text copyright © 2016 Nancy Herkness

Published by Montlake Romance, Seattle

www.apub.com

Amazon, the Amazon logo, and Montlake Romance are trademarks of Amazon.com, Inc., or its affiliates.

ISBN-13: 9781503935464
ISBN-10: 1503935469

Cover design by Eileen Carey

Printed in the United States of America

In loving memory of my father, who was my biggest fan.

PROLOGUE

Luke Archer picked up his cut-crystal glass and winced as the motion tweaked the bruises from yesterday's game. He switched hands before bringing the glass to his lips. He'd been sacked once, but those aches and pains didn't faze him. Some ice, some work with his trainer, and he wouldn't notice them by Friday's practice.

What he didn't want to think about was how in the last seconds of a hard-fought battle, he'd thrown an interception. He'd been set up to pass one way but had seen a better opportunity downfield, so he'd redirected his throw. It was something he'd done a thousand times before, but this time pain had seared through his shoulder like a branding iron. The shock spoiled his aim and sent the ball spiraling into the hands of the enemy.

Then the pain was gone, like it had never been there. He hadn't told his trainer because Stan would be all over him to get it checked out by a doctor. Luke didn't want to admit, even to himself, that it was anything other than a misthrow.

Luke grimaced at his glass. Maybe he should have ordered tequila instead of water. The alcohol might ease the sting of the memory. However, even alcohol couldn't dull the agony of losing to the Patriots, so Luke swallowed his water and stretched out his legs under the brass-topped bar table. His motion made the light from the wall sconces glint off the patent leather of his tuxedo shoes and sent more twinges of discomfort jabbing through his stiff muscles.

The perfect emptiness of the Bellwether Club's bar was spoiled as another tuxedo-clad patron with an almost military posture strode through the big mahogany door to settle at a table across the room. His air of command brought a waiter instantly to his side. After the new arrival ordered scotch, he ripped off his bow tie, which made Luke think the fellow was settling in for some serious drinking.

The man seemed familiar, but then Luke had met most of the members of the Bellwether Club at one time or another, because there weren't that many of them. Membership required a net worth in ten figures, and all of it had to be earned, not inherited. Hell, if Luke hadn't invested in the BankBuddy start-up as a favor to a friend, he wouldn't be a member here himself.

He let his chin sink forward onto his chest. It wasn't really the muscle aches or even the loss that had sent him to the bar instead of home to his New York City penthouse. It was the party he'd just been to, a charity gala honoring all-star wide receiver DaShawn Williams's retirement from football.

That and the fact that Luke's brother, Trevor, was waiting for him back at his place.

As a cloud of gloom settled itself on his shoulders, the door swung open again. Glad for the distraction, Luke glanced up to see a tall, lean man with disheveled dark hair stagger in, also wearing a tux. The man threw Luke a long stare, and Luke gave him his well-practiced polite but distant nod. The man nodded in return before hoisting himself onto a bar stool and ordering a bourbon straight up. His face nagged at Luke's memory more strongly than the first man's, but he couldn't place it, either.

When the newcomer had been served his drink, he turned and made a sweeping gesture around the room with his glass. "To my fellow late night tipplers. Bottoms up!"

Luke lifted his glass and took a swallow of water while the other man polished off his bourbon in one gulp. He was pretty sure the drinker at the bar had recognized him. Thank God the man hadn't tried to start up a conversation. He didn't want to talk about the game.

That was one reason he liked the Bellwether Club. The members were all at the top of whatever field they were in, so they respected the desire for privacy. Still, even CEOs of multinational corporations had opinions on football.

Which brought his thoughts back to DaShawn.

They had played and roomed together in college, forming a bond so close that the other players claimed they used mental telepathy on the field. Their partnership had been pivotal in the three NCAA championships they'd won for the Longhorns. The NFL draft had broken up their partnership on the field, but their friendship had stayed strong.

Now DaShawn was leaving the game.

He and Luke had talked about the decision for hours the night after the Empire beat DaShawn's team, the Seahawks. DaShawn had looked Luke in the eye and said, "I can feel myself losing just one microsecond of jump at the snap. No one else knows it, but I do, and that's enough. I want to go out at the top of my game, bro, not as some washed-up old guy who won't let go of his glory days."

DaShawn had paused before continuing. "The thing is, I've lost my passion for playing. When I'm on the road, all I think about is Marcy and my kids." His friend smiled in a way that sent a strange hollowness echoing through Luke's chest. "I don't know why the hell Marcy married me, but she's the center of my world. I need her like water."

DaShawn had gripped Luke's shoulder, his left one. "It's different for you, man. You've still got the hunger. You're still going for the gold."

Luke shifted in the leather chair again. The irony was that he had helped make it possible for DaShawn to retire by advising the wide receiver on how to invest his contract money. Luke had watched too many fellow players get drained by greedy family members and bad managers, or just spend their money as though they were going to keep playing football for fifty years.

So he'd started taking them aside and offering basic financial advice. At the beginning it was just his friends, but word got around, so teammates began to seek him out. During the off-season he spent time with his own money manager, augmenting his knowledge of the markets. It gave him something to think about as he powered through the punishing grind of the training required to keep his thirty-six-year-old body in top condition.

Luke rolled his right shoulder, feeling the ghost of the brief, excruciating pain that had burned through it.

He couldn't argue with his friend's decision. DaShawn had a wife and two sons, and a powerful dedication to the foundation he'd started to help kids from disadvantaged backgrounds go to college.

Luke had football.

"At this hour of the night, I'm betting it's a woman."

Startled, Luke looked up, but the man at the bar was talking to the quiet drinker on the far side of the room.

"I know what *his* problem is." The man on the stool jerked his head toward the corner where Luke sat. "He threw an interception with five seconds to go against the Patriots."

It was inevitable. Pissed off, Luke locked his gaze on his glass.

"So am I right?" the barfly asked the other man.

"I don't see that it's any of your business."

Luke gave the scotch drinker kudos for refusing to play the game.

The barfly laughed. "Everything's my business. I'm a writer."

Luke raised his eyebrows. The fellow must be one hell of a bestselling writer if he belonged here.

"What do you write?" the other man asked.

There was a moment of silence. "Novels," the writer growled.

The connection snapped into place in Luke's brain. He'd seen the author's photo on the back of his paperbacks. "You're Gavin Miller. I read your Julian Best books on planes." The fast-paced spy thrillers helped him unwind after games. Miller made a half bow from his stool in self-mocking acknowledgment. "When's your next one coming out?" Luke asked.

"My original deadline was three months ago." Miller turned a humorless smile Luke's way. "I missed it. My deadline extension was today. Missed it, too. Writer's block."

That explained why Luke's assistant hadn't been able to find him a new Julian Best novel for the past six months.

"So what happens when a writer misses the deadline?" the other man asked.

"The same thing that happens when a quarterback throws a bad pass. The coach isn't happy. And I get no royalties." Luke kept his face impassive as he mentally cursed the novelist up, down, and sideways. Miller gulped some more of his drink. "But there's nothing they can do about it, because I don't have a backup."

"No ghostwriters?" the other man asked.

"Don't think I haven't considered it, but I have enough respect and gratitude for my readers to believe I owe them my own efforts." Miller shook his head. "The truth is, I could keep myself in style on the residuals from the Julian Best movies for the rest of my life and beyond, but good old Julian has become a small industry in his own right. The editors, directors, actors, film crews—hell, even the movie theater ticket takers—all depend on him."

Luke felt an unexpected flash of sympathy. He carried the same burden every week of the season.

"So we've established who two of us are. What about you?" the writer asked the third man.

"I'm just a businessman."

"Not if you belong within these hallowed walls." The writer tipped his glass at the fancy paneling, which had come from some English manor house that was being torn down. "Frankie Hogan doesn't allow 'justs' in her club."

The other man gave up dodging Miller with a shrug. "Nathan Trainor," he said.

"Computer batteries," Luke filled in.

Miller gave Luke a mock salute. "So you're not just a dumb jock."

Anger surged again like hot lava, but Luke quashed it. Miller had clearly had too much to drink even before he'd arrived at the club.

He dismissed the writer by turning his attention to Trainor. This was a man he wanted to talk to. "I'm considering an investment in Trainor Electronics stock," Luke said. "No one has ever figured out how to make a computer battery as long lasting as yours."

"We've diversified," Trainor said. "Just in case they do." He took another swallow of scotch, as though the idea made him unhappy. Then he gestured to the table where he sat. "Why don't you all join me? That way we won't have to shout at each other."

The writer slid off his stool with a slight wobble, saying, "Don't mind if I do."

Luke considered the idea. Trainor didn't seem interested in football, and Miller was too drunk to be much of a problem. So he hauled himself out of the chair, his muscles protesting, and carried his water glass across the room. Miller had dropped into the only other chair at

Trainor's table, so Luke spun one around from a nearby grouping and eased into it.

"It's the beginning of a bad joke," Miller said. "A writer, a quarterback, and a CEO walk into a bar."

Luke waited, expecting something sharp and funny from a bestselling writer. Miller just sat there, staring into his empty glass. "What's the punch line?" Luke asked.

Miller shook his head. "I have writer's block, remember? That's why I missed my deadline."

In Luke's world, blocks involved huge, violent men wearing cleats and pads. No one was standing between Miller and his keyboard. Annoyance put an edge in Luke's tone. "What does that mean, having writer's block? You can't type?"

Miller slashed a look at him. "Why'd you throw a pass nowhere near your wide receiver?"

Because his shoulder had betrayed him. "It's harder than it looks," Luke said. He resettled his shoulder against the cushioning of the chair.

"Exactly," Miller said with a short laugh. "You must have some major endorsement contracts to be a member of this club."

Luke couldn't fault him for the thought, since he'd had a similar one about the novelist. "I've had some luck in the stock market. It's a hobby of mine." And he'd had a friend who needed funding for his electronic payment company, which had gone stratospheric in its success.

"Luck, eh?" Miller said. "Maybe I'll buy some Trainor Electronics stock, too." The writer turned his attention back to the CEO. "So, a woman?"

Why the hell was Miller so determined to ferret out Trainor's reason for being here? He must be some sort of obsessive drunk.

Trainor seemed unbothered by the writer's persistence. "Maybe I just learned that my competitors invented a better battery." He slanted a sardonic smile at them. "Which means you might want to rethink that investment."

Luke wasn't fooled. The man was reputed to be a genius at electronics development.

"It's after midnight and you're wearing a tux." Miller's eyes were half-closed as he tilted his head back against the chair. "You weren't jilted at the altar, because it's a weekday. Maybe you caught your wife in bed with another man."

Miller really was an asshole.

"Is this a way of trying to break your writer's block?" Trainor asked.

"Are you married?"

"No." The tinge of amusement on Trainor's face vanished. Maybe Miller was right about the woman thing.

"You wear an expression of cynical disgust, so her motives were less than pure," Miller said.

Luke thought of all the football groupies he'd encountered from high school on. He'd been flattered until he realized they just wanted to be seen with "the quarterback." Or sleep with him. It had only gotten worse when he started making big money in the NFL. He tilted the last of his water down his throat. "Good luck finding a woman without ulterior motives when you qualify as a member of this club."

Trainor flagged down the waiter and turned to Luke. "What are you drinking?"

"Water." He'd given up alcohol during the football season a few years ago. It took too much work to overcome the effects of liquor on his body now that he was over thirty.

Miller snagged Trainor's bottle of scotch. He splashed a generous serving of liquor into his own and Luke's glasses. "If we're going to discuss women, you need something stronger than water." The writer slapped the empty bottle into the waiter's hand. "Bring us one of bourbon and another one of scotch. And some nuts."

Luke picked up the glass of single malt, inhaling the smooth, smoky aroma. He stared at the clear, golden liquid and decided, *What the hell.* The first sip was pure heaven.

"Attaboy," the writer approved before he went back to poking at Trainor. "Did she break your heart or just injure your pride?"

Trainor thought for a moment. "How can you tell the difference?"

The writer gave a snort of laughter. "Now that is an excellent question. When my fiancée dumped me, I believe she broke my heart. But I was new to Hollywood back then and quite naive."

"Hollywood?" Trainor asked.

"She's one of the actresses in the Julian Best movies," Miller said. "I met her on the set."

Luke enjoyed the movies, too, so he mentally scanned the cast. "Irene Bartram," he decided. "She plays Samantha Dubois, the double agent." Irene seemed like Miller's type. She was hot and hungry.

Miller inclined his head in acknowledgment. "A true fan. My thanks."

"You don't have a lot of women in your books," Luke said. That was partly why he found them relaxing.

"There's a reason for that," the writer said.

Trainor grunted in agreement before looking at Luke. "So, Archer, how do you handle women?"

During the football season, Luke focused on the game. On the occasions he sought out female companionship, he prided himself on keeping expectations realistic. "Full disclosure and keep it short. I don't have a lot of free time."

"None of us do," Trainor pointed out.

Miller was intrigued by a different point. "Full disclosure?"

"No strings, no rings," Luke said with a shrug. He never raised false hopes, and he always carried condoms.

"No gifts?" The writer raised his eyebrows. "I hear Derek Jeter gave them signed baseballs."

The women Luke knew generally weren't interested in sports souvenirs, but occasionally one would request something for a father or brother. "If they ask for a football, I'm happy to oblige. Seems kind of arrogant to assume they want my signature, though." Except maybe on a check.

Miller gave him one of his provocative stares. "I would think arrogance went with the territory. You're a quarterback."

Luke met Miller's look with one of those smiles that made defensive linemen take a half step backward. "I've got plenty of arrogance on the field."

That stopped Miller's jabs. He returned to Trainor. "So have you figured it out yet?"

"You're damned annoying," Trainor said, but there was no heat in his voice. "All right, pride. She played me and I'm pissed about it."

"What are you going to do?" Miller asked. He leaned back in his chair, his eyes glinting. Luke poured himself another glass of Trainor's scotch.

"Nothing," Trainor said. "I don't care enough to expend the energy." The truth of it showed in the flatness of his tone.

"Disappointing," Miller said.

Luke disagreed with the writer. You couldn't let them know you were hurting. "It's the only way to go."

He wished he'd kept his mouth shut when Miller swiveled toward him. "Have you had your heart broken?"

"Half a dozen times," Luke said. "I got over it." The last time was in college.

"Ah, yes, the stoic, monosyllabic jock." Miller was amused. "If I wrote you in a book, you'd be too much of a stereotype and my editor would complain."

Luke had learned silence at the home dinner table, letting his family's academic debates rage around him as he mentally reviewed plays for the next game. It had turned out to be a useful skill because it kept people guessing. He let his gaze rest on Miller.

The writer shifted in his chair and blew out a breath. "Since we agree that women are nothing but trouble, maybe we should play cards. It would distract us from our problems."

"Cards? Where the hell did you get that idea?" Trainor snapped.

"Don't they say, 'Unlucky at love, lucky at cards'?" The writer gave them a one-sided smile. "Although it's hard to predict who will get the good luck in this group."

Luke took a swallow of scotch and leaned forward. "I don't buy it." The two supremely successful men drinking with him didn't get into the Bellwether Club by sitting back and just waiting for good things to happen. "Everyone at this table knows you make your own luck. We wouldn't be here otherwise."

"Luck is the residue of design," Trainor said with a nod.

"We're all big on quotations tonight," the writer noted.

Luke had a flash of insight. DaShawn looked forward to retirement because he had someone to share his future with, someone to give him a focus and purpose, someone who needed him.

Luke faced retirement with profound dread.

He slashed his hand down to silence Miller's blathering. "How important is finding a woman you want to spend the rest of your life with?" Trainor took a sip of his drink while Miller lounged silently in his chair. "Pretty damned important," Luke continued. "How much effort has any of us put into the search?" He gave Trainor and Miller each a hard look.

Trainor shook his head. Miller shrugged. Luke went on. "I'm guessing not a lot. We see the same women at every event. Friends or colleagues fix us up. Maybe we even get a napkin slipped into our pocket and call that number."

He wasn't proud of that, but he'd done it when he was younger and the woman was hot.

"Speak for yourself on that last one," the writer said with a smile that was part envy, part amusement. Trainor chuckled.

Luke didn't let Miller throw him off stride. In fact, not much threw him off stride, including women. But maybe the time had come to change that policy. Maybe he needed a Marcy. That way, he wouldn't feel so goddamned depressed about his best friend leaving the game. "Our problem is lack of focus. We aren't making it a primary objective in our lives, so we're failing." When you were on the field with bodies, voices, and refs swirling around you like a dust storm, having the primary objective in mind made all the rest fall away.

"So we should be wife hunting instead of running a business or winning football games or writing the next bestseller?" Trainor shot back. "If you're that desperate, hire one of those executive matchmakers."

Luke dropped the temperature of his stare to frost level. "That's like using a ghostwriter."

He got a belly laugh from the novelist.

"At least the transaction would be honest," Trainor said, an edge of cynicism in his voice.

Luke leaned in, resting his forearm on his thigh. "How badly do you want a wife and family?"

Trainor swirled his drink around in his glass as he considered the question for several seconds. "I'm listening. Miller?"

"Hell, yes, I'm still looking," the writer said. "What's the point of all this if you've got no one to share it with?" He swept his free hand around the bar where just one leather chair cost more than a scalper's ticket to the Super Bowl. Miller turned back to Luke. "And, of course, you need a passel of sons to toss footballs with in your white-picket-fenced yard."

"I'm hoping for daughters," Luke said. He didn't want any of the ugly competitiveness that had gone on between him and his brother. "But, yeah, I want kids. So what I'm saying is, we need a plan."

The writer hummed softly under his breath, then held up his hand. "I have a better idea." Miller's eyes gleamed with unholy glee. "Gentlemen, I propose a challenge."

A challenge was interesting.

"We go in search of true love. We keep looking until we find it."

Luke sat back in disgust. "This challenge is a load of garbage. How do you prove you've found true love?"

"A ring on her finger." Miller gave him a barbed smile. "Sorry, Archer."

Luke remembered when DaShawn showed him the engagement ring he'd bought for Marcy. His friend was lit up like a kid at Christmas as he opened the velvet box. "I didn't get her the biggest diamond," DaShawn had said, flipping the box back and forth so the stone caught the light. "But I got her the most perfect diamond, because she's the perfect woman for me."

"A ring doesn't prove anything," Trainor said.

"I've spent—what?—half an hour with you gentlemen," Miller said. "And I am confident you would not put a ring on a woman's finger unless you believed you would spend the rest of your life with her." The writer sat back in his chair.

Luke gave Trainor an assessing scan. Miller was right. Something about the CEO said he had integrity. Maybe it was that straight-up posture or his clear gray eyes.

Trainor thought about it before he shook his head. "You've had too much to drink. And so have I."

The two nearly empty bottles on the table suggested that maybe they'd all had too much to drink, but that didn't change the magnitude of the goal. This was a game changer, so it required a concrete incentive to get everyone's attention. "I say we make it a bet," Luke said. "We need to stake something valuable on the outcome."

"The stakes are our hearts." Miller sounded depressed.

"We need to bet something more valuable than that," Trainor said, the edge back in his tone.

"All right, a donation to charity," Miller said.

Luke shook his head. "Too easy."

Miller lifted a hand for silence, and Luke caught a spark of slyness in the writer's eyes. "Not money," the writer said. "An item to be auctioned off. It must have intrinsic value, but it must also be something irreplaceable, something that would cause each of us pain to lose."

Now Miller was talking.

"Who chooses this irreplaceable artifact?" Trainor asked.

"You do." Miller waited for their reaction.

"So this is an honor system," Luke said as the gears whirred in his brain.

The writer placed his hand over his heart in an exaggerated gesture. "A wager is always a matter of honor between gentlemen."

Luke snorted. He'd seen plenty of wagers that had nothing to do with honor.

"A secret wager," Trainor said. "We write down our stakes and seal them in envelopes. Only losers have to reveal their forfeits."

"I think we require Frankie for this," Miller said. He turned in his chair to get the bartender's attention. "Donal, is the boss lady still awake?"

The bartender nodded. "Ms. Hogan never sleeps, sir. I'll call her."

"Miller, it's well after midnight," Trainor said. "Leave the woman alone."

Luke nodded his agreement, but Donal was already speaking with his boss. He hung up and said, "She'll be here in ten minutes."

Miller asked Donal to bring them some stationery before he swiveled back to face the table. "I've done a lot of stupid things when I was drunk, but this may be the most ridiculous one." He skimmed a glance over Trainor and Luke. "We can cancel this right now before it goes any further."

"I'm still in," Trainor said, his voice taut.

"You backing out, Miller?" Luke asked. The writer had started this.

"Pardon my moment of sanity," Miller said, shaking his head before he drank a slug of bourbon. "Gentlemen, I suggest we ponder our stakes."

Luke knew exactly what he was going to wager. When you needed the win, you left everything you had on the field.

Trainor sprawled in his chair, frowning as he tapped his fingers on the arm. After a few moments, his expression changed. The CEO had made up his mind.

"That's a downright unpleasant smile, Trainor." The writer had also sunk deep into his chair. Luke was ready to catch the glass dangling from Miller's lax grasp.

"I've decided on my wager," Trainor said, his smile broadening.

"Are you sure it's something that would draw a high bid?" Miller asked.

"I guarantee it."

The writer switched his focus to Luke. "Have you made your decision?"

"Made it five minutes ago." He decided to up the ante to see if Miller would stay in the contest. Pulling a pen out of his pocket, he lifted his glass off its napkin and wrote a large number on it. Spinning the napkin around so his fellow bettors could read it, he said, "Just to sweeten the pot, we should add a significant monetary donation to the charity."

Trainor raised his eyebrows but said, "Done."

Luke gave the CEO credit for committing without hesitation. He'd picked a number that could make even a billionaire think about it.

Miller read the number and nodded his agreement.

Luke sat back. He'd made sure they all had their heads in the game.

The big paneled door swung open for a third time, and Frankie Hogan strode into the bar. Her silver hair caught a gleam from the brass chandeliers, and her dark blue blazer and white blouse reminded Luke painfully of the Patriots' uniform colors. As she approached their table, all three men rose to their feet, dwarfing the tiny Irishwoman. Luke's knee popped. He winced and hoped no one else had heard the sound.

"Gentlemen, I understand there's illicit gambling going on in my establishment." Her rasp of a voice reminded him of a referee at the end of the fourth quarter, except for the Irish accent. "I want a piece of it."

Miller chuckled. "Frankie, we're wagering on matters of the heart, and you haven't got one."

The Bellwether Club's founder gave a snort of laughter at the insult. "Clearly, I can feel pity, because I let you join my club."

Frankie Hogan was Luke's kind of person. She didn't take crap from anyone. When she'd made her massive fortune, she'd applied to some fancy clubs and been turned down, probably because she was new money, Irish, and a woman. In his eyes, that made her achievements more impressive, not less, but the old-money snobs didn't think so. So she'd turned the tables on them by starting her own club and shutting out the people whose only accomplishment was having rich parents.

She settled into the chair Trainor held for her. "You're famous for your honesty and your ability to keep a secret," Trainor said as they all sat, and Donal brought over paper, envelopes, and Montblanc pens.

"Along with ruthlessness, cunning, and sheer cussedness," Miller interjected.

Luke added his glare to Trainor's, and the writer shut up. Trainor continued. "So we're entrusting you with the personal stakes in our wager, sealed in separate envelopes. Each one of us can win or lose individually, but it takes the agreement of all three to declare someone a winner."

Frankie considered his terms before saying, "I'll want to read them to make sure they're legit."

When Trainor looked at him, Luke nodded. Miller did the same.

"What's the time frame?" Frankie asked.

"One year," Luke said. He had to get through the rest of football season before he could focus on the wager. "Anyone who hasn't claimed their stakes back by then is declared a loser."

"A long-term game," Frankie said, her voice carrying a hint of surprise.

Trainor nodded. "One year. Miller?"

Miller didn't miss a beat. "Agreed," he said. Was the man simply too drunk to know what he was consenting to? The writer met Luke's gaze steadily and with a gleam of amused intelligence in his eyes. He knew what he was doing.

"I'll lock them in my private safe," Frankie said. "Who's going first?"

Miller threw Luke a challenging smile as he grabbed one of the shiny black Montblanc pens and wrote his name on an envelope. He slid a sheet of heavy paper to his side of the table. "I'll trust my fellow bettors not to read over my shoulder," he said as he wrote down several words before holding it out to Frankie.

The club's owner accepted the sheet and glanced down at it. As she folded it and slipped it into the envelope, she leveled an assessing gaze on the writer.

Luke didn't bother with the ceremonial pen. He used his own to record his stakes in bold capital letters. Frankie read his wager and gave a low whistle. He allowed himself a tight smile. He wasn't going to lose.

It was Trainor's turn. When Frankie read the paper he handed her, she frowned. "Are you sure?" she asked the CEO, concern in her Irish lilt.

His answer was bald and definitive. "Yes."

Frankie sealed his bet into the envelope. "You'll inform me anytime someone is approved as a winner, or else we will meet in my office in one year's time." She tapped the envelopes into a neat stack on the table. "I certainly hope whatever you win is worth what you all might lose."

"It will be life changing," Trainor said.

Luke hoped he was right.

"That explains the stakes," Frankie said, picking up the envelopes before rising. "Good night, gentlemen."

All three men came to their feet as she made her exit. Miller scooped up his glass, lifting it high. "To our wager of hearts. May we be guests at each other's weddings."

If Miller had to be on the guest list, Luke just might elope.

Chapter 1

At 8:45 a.m., Miranda Tate's desk phone buzzed.

"I need you in my office now." Her boss's voice held an undertone of glee, which meant he believed he'd caught her in a mistake.

She should have known something was up when Orin came in half an hour earlier than his normal day shift. The head concierge at the luxury condominium never worked an extra minute if he could avoid it.

"I'll be right there," she said, keeping her tone neutral.

She slipped her feet into the black high-heeled pumps she'd kicked off under her desk and stood. Smoothing her slim, charcoal wool skirt down so it touched the tops of her knees, she moved to the mirror hanging on the back of her door. There she checked that her long, dark hair was still neatly tucked into its low ponytail.

After straightening the collar of her blouse, she opened the door of her office and strode across the lobby's granite floor, her heels clicking on the stone. The Pinnacle had been built with the finest materials, but this gold-and-gray floor was her favorite, reminding her of hot desert sand swirling around cool river rocks. Sometimes she still couldn't quite believe she worked in such a spectacular building whose residents were on every A list in their respective fields. It was a far cry from milking cows in upstate New York, but she'd worked darn hard to get here.

Her boss, Orin Spindle, had chosen his office for its impressive size rather than its convenience, so she had to hike down a lengthy hallway to reach it. Although Miranda was an assistant concierge, the small, elegant office she shared with her fellow assistant Sofia Nunez was much more accessible to the building's tenants, which meant they tended to come there first. Depending on his mood, that either irritated or relieved Orin.

His door was closed. Not a good sign. Miranda knocked lightly.

"Come in." Her boss nearly sang the words.

She braced her shoulders and turned the knob. Once inside, her first impression was that Orin's capacious office was crowded. The impression resolved itself into the presence of two very tall men seated in the black leather armchairs in front of Orin's desk. Since there were no chairs left, Miranda walked to the side of the desk. "Good morning," she said with a polite smile.

Dismay clenched a fist in her chest when she recognized the men as the Archer brothers.

Almost anyone in the New York metropolitan area would be able to identify Luke Archer, the superstar quarterback of the New York Empire, winner of four Super Bowls, and a media darling for his blond hair, blue eyes, and laconic charm. He lived in the building, but she rarely saw him since he was either training, playing, or at his ranch in Texas during the off-season. And his penthouse had its own private entrance. He made very few requests of the concierge service, partly because he had a full-time assistant and partly because he was showered with invitations to every exclusive event in the New York metro area without having to ask.

His brother, Trevor, was a different story. She'd heard that he had a PhD from Harvard, but he didn't seem to have done much with it. He had the same blue eyes as his brother, but his hair was light brown, and his physique was lanky, rather than superbly muscled like the athlete sitting next to him. When Trevor visited his brother, he availed himself of the concierge services with gusto. In fact, she'd had a problem with him last night, but she couldn't imagine Orin calling her in about that.

Luke Archer surged to his feet, towering over her. "Morning, ma'am," he said, his Texas accent making it sound friendlier than he probably intended. "Please," he said, gesturing to his chair.

"Thank you, but I'm fine," Miranda said with a quick shake of her head. Orin would be angry if she took a client's chair.

Trevor looked somewhere to her left as he nodded in her general direction.

Luke didn't return to his seat. Instead, he folded his arms and leaned against the wall near her. She was used to celebrities, but Luke Archer was beyond that—he was a living legend in New York. She couldn't help slanting a quick sidelong glance to take in the breadth of his shoulders under the pale blue T-shirt and the swell of his thigh muscles under well-worn jeans. He exuded a coiled energy that must explode on the playing field. It certainly made her breath come a little faster.

"Miranda, I am concerned about a complaint from Mr. Archer that you would not accommodate his request last night," Orin said, his voice oozing with false courtesy.

Trevor shifted so the leather chair creaked. Miranda dragged her attention away from Luke. "I explained to Mr. Archer that honoring that kind of request is against our policy in this building."

Orin flicked an uneasy glance at Trevor. Was it possible Trevor hadn't revealed what he'd asked for?

"We are dedicated to making sure our residents and their guests lack nothing here at the Pinnacle," Orin spouted.

"However, we have certain boundaries," Miranda said, feeling her way into the discussion.

Trevor's fingers beat an uneven rhythm on the arm of his chair. "I might have been unclear about what I wanted," he said. "This is just a misunderstanding."

She felt the air move beside her as Luke Archer pushed off the wall and leaned forward to brace his hands on the arm of his vacant chair. "What exactly did you ask for, Trev?" His drawl made the question sound almost casual, but there was steel beneath the leisurely cadence. Miranda was glad he wasn't addressing her.

Trevor turned toward his brother briefly before looking back at Orin. "Nothing I haven't asked for before."

Sweat beaded on Orin's forehead, and Miranda wound her hands into a knot in front of her. Her boss really didn't know what Trevor had requested.

Either Orin had been too awed by Trevor's connection to his illustrious brother to probe, or he had been so thrilled to catch her in a supposed mistake that he'd leaped at the chance to make her look bad in front of Luke Archer. Or both.

It didn't surprise her that another concierge had broken one of the rules of their building, but it cast Orin in a bad light, since he was the owner of the concierge service. He would make her life even more miserable now.

Orin picked up a pen and clicked it open and shut as he spoke. "It seems there has been a misunderstanding between Mr. Archer and Miranda. I would like to offer my sincerest apologies, Mr. Archer. Miranda, you may return to your office."

"Just a minute," Luke Archer said, his voice carrying the edge of command he must use to direct the giants of the offensive line on the field.

He took a step backward as Miranda turned away from Orin's desk, so she ran smack into him. She bounced off, tottering on her stiletto heels as the sudden contact with his body sent sparks arcing through her. Luke's hand shot out to grasp her elbow in a grip that felt like sun-warmed iron. As he held her steady, she had the sense that he could lift her off the ground with just that one hand.

"Thank you," she gasped. She, who prided herself on never losing her composure, sounded like a breathless teenager because a blond football god had touched her elbow.

Then he unleashed a weapon so powerful she had no defense against it. He smiled. The ice in those intense eyes melted, his teeth flashed brilliant white, and the famous single dimple put a rogue's brand on his left cheek.

There was no need for Photoshopping on all those billboards and clothing ads. Luke Archer looked exactly like his pictures, only better, because she could feel the heat of his hand through her silk sleeve, watch the expansion and contraction of his chest as he breathed, and inhale the scent of clean, warm male.

"You're welcome," he said, and released her before turning back to his brother. "Trevor?"

It took all her powers of concentration to recall the question Luke had asked before. She needed to get her inappropriate reactions to the quarterback under control or she would have even bigger problems with her boss than she already did.

Trevor leaned back in the chair with an air of unconcern that Miranda didn't buy for a second. "I just wanted a little company, and I asked her to find me some." He shifted away from his brother's gaze. "Just make a call to an escort service. Nothing illegal about that."

Luke's smile evaporated and all the warmth leached out of his eyes, leaving them the pale blue of a glacier. "*That's* what you asked her to do for you?" He hissed out a sound of disgust. Miranda watched him settle himself with an effort of will before he pivoted to meet her gaze. "We owe you an apology, ma'am. If I'd known what—" He shook his head. "Well, I'm sorry my brother asked you to do something so distasteful, and even sorrier he complained about it to Mr. Spindle here."

Miranda tried to keep her smile from appearing forced, but all the apologies in the world weren't going to fix her already precarious relationship with Orin after this. "Don't mention it, Mr. Archer," she said. "I won't, either."

His gaze traveled over her face like a laser beam, scanning and assessing. She felt a wave of heat flush her cheeks and then spread lower and deeper. Luke turned to Orin. "Mr. Spindle, I just want to make sure that Miranda will not be held at fault as a result of my brother's actions. Trevor never should have made that request." He turned a hard look on Trevor, who was now slumped in the chair, staring at his knees.

Trevor hunched a shoulder. "This meeting was Spindle's idea, not mine."

Miranda watched Luke's big hands curl into fists. She'd heard him called the Iceman because he never showed his feelings on the field or off it. However, his brother seemed to have gotten to him. She considered her own family and how they could push her buttons. Without thinking, she flashed the quarterback a smile of understanding.

For a split second, surprise registered on his face, and she regretted her impulse. A man like Luke Archer didn't need her sympathy. In fact, a man like Luke Archer didn't want anything from someone like her. She was just a country girl trying with all her might to act like a city sophisticate.

"We'll talk about this later," Luke said to Trevor, jerking his head toward the door.

Trevor unfolded himself from the chair and stalked out of Orin's office. Luke started after him before turning back. "My apologies. Let me know if you'd like tickets to Sunday's game."

Orin lit up. "That's very generous of you, Mr. Archer." Miranda was sure he would sell them to one of their other clients for a hefty price.

"I'll have my assistant call both of you," Archer said, turning away.

Miranda felt bad that the quarterback had been put in this situation by his brother. She didn't want him to feel obligated to give her compensation for it. "You're very kind, but I have to work on Sunday." It was a lie, but she couldn't gracefully refuse the tickets after her boss had accepted them. She was counting on the fact that Orin didn't know the weekend schedule for the assistant concierges, since he never worked then.

Archer looked over his shoulder with the dimple in evidence again. "Would you like a signed football as a substitute?"

Her brother's son would love that. And it would make Orin's greed less obvious, so maybe he wouldn't punish her for refusing the tickets. "Thank you. I know someone who would very much appreciate that. My nephew is a huge fan." She added a smile.

For a moment Archer seemed to freeze, and she wondered if her smile had revealed a little too much of the warmth he had sent sizzling through her. Or maybe she shouldn't have taken the ball. It seemed fairly insignificant compared to tickets. She was trying to think of a way to back out when he nodded. "It will be in your office later today." Then he was gone, his absence leaving a curious flatness in the room.

"Are you aware of which assistant concierge called an escort service for Trevor Archer recently?" Orin's nasal voice was harsh.

Miranda shook her head. "Someone must have done it without realizing there was a rule about it."

That was the sad part. Concierges often called escort services—and worse—for their clients. The first time she'd gotten such a request, she'd been openmouthed with shock. Growing up on a dairy farm in the boondocks of upstate New York hadn't prepared her for the shamelessness of vice in the big city. She'd been relieved when the Pinnacle's owners had instituted the policy after a resident had sued because he caught an STD from the escort. She had always refused to handle those requests, even before the rule was put in place, but she was in the minority, since the gratuity for arranging that kind of service tended to be large.

Orin nodded. "I'll make sure the other assistant concierges are aware of the policy." He shuffled through a pile of papers and pulled out the week's schedule. "You aren't working Sunday, so why did you turn down the tickets?" He skewered her with his "I'm your boss and I want answers" glare.

She pretended surprise. "I must have gotten my weeks mixed up. I thought I was on duty this Sunday." Giving him a conspiratorial smile, she said, "I'm not much of a football fan anyway."

"So the ball is really for your nephew?" Orin appeared unconvinced.

"Yes. Theo thinks Luke Archer walks on water."

After shooting her one more skeptical glance, Orin dropped the schedule back onto his desk and turned to his computer monitor. "Mrs. Belden wants you to book her massage because she says you always send the best people." There was a note of peevishness in his voice. Mrs. Belden was a big tipper, and Orin tried to reserve that kind of client for himself.

"I'm so glad she liked the last one. I mentioned to Mrs. Belden that he was from a spa you'd recommended," Miranda said, crossing her fingers behind her back at the lie. She needed to stay in Orin's good graces just a little longer so he would give her a reference for the head concierge job at a new apartment building going up in Midtown. Expecting a glowing recommendation was unrealistic, but at least he couldn't give her a *bad* review without real evidence.

Or even worse, fire her. Since the Pinnacle's owners contracted with Orin's concierge service for their building, her boss had sole discretion over who worked there. She would have no recourse if his simmering dislike of her boiled over into something more serious.

"And Mr. Saperstein needs a new dog walker," Orin said.

Miranda mentally rolled her eyes. Mr. Saperstein needed a new dog walker at least once a month, since he always found some reason to fire his current one. It was becoming difficult to find anyone who would agree to work for him, because word had gotten around the dog-walking community that he was unreasonably demanding. Sticking her with the task was Orin's revenge for the Archer incident.

"I'll take care of both requests," she said, even though it was nearly time for her to go home. She had pulled the night shift this week. Generally she was fine with that, because the residents who required services in the middle of the night compensated her accordingly.

Unfortunately, last night had been quiet and routine except for the unpleasantness with Trevor Archer. Win some, lose some.

That reminded her of Luke Archer and the way the air around him seemed supercharged. She had felt as though lightning was flickering right beside her. The memory made the tiny hairs on her arms tingle in a weirdly delicious way.

"You may go," Orin said, his eyes on his computer screen.

Miranda exited his office as fast as she could without running. Most of the time, she loved her job. Getting her clients exactly what they wanted while making it look effortless was a point of pride for her. Which was why Trevor's request had distressed her. She wanted him to be happy while he was at the Pinnacle, but she had been unable to make it happen without breaking the rules and, even worse, venturing into territory that bordered on illegal.

When she recrossed the lobby, Luke Archer walked out of a shadow by the elevators and came toward her. As he strolled through an early-morning sunbeam shining through the plate-glass window, his hair turned to molten gold, and the muscles of his forearms were outlined in light and shadow. He moved as though he knew how every part of his body worked most efficiently.

The sheer beauty of the man made her gasp out loud, her body reacting without conscious thought. She tried to turn the sound into a cough, but she caught a flicker of something in his face that meant he'd caught her response. So much for her facade of cool sophistication. Of course, Luke Archer was probably used to the effect he had on women.

He stopped in front of her, his hands shoved into his jeans pockets. "I owe you more than a football for putting up with Trevor's crap. Tell me what I can do to make it right with your boss."

Even with her high heels on, she had to tilt her head back to meet his gaze. She felt delicate and feminine when she stood so close to him. It wasn't unpleasant.

"Everything's fine with my boss," she lied. "It was just a misunderstanding."

Archer shook his head. "I didn't read it that way."

One thing Miranda was not going to do was involve this prominent resident in a work squabble. "Mr. Archer, I appreciate your concern, but there's nothing to worry about."

"Call me Luke," he said. The honey of his drawl poured through her, kicking up little flares of sensation. As the silence drew out, she realized he was waiting for her to use his given name.

"Thank you, Luke." And she would never address him that way again. She had to remember he was a client.

He gave her another one of his appraising scans. "You let me know if something becomes a cause for concern."

"Of course, Mr.—er, Luke." So she had to use his name one more time.

"You take care," he said, giving her a nod of farewell before he headed back to the elevators.

She couldn't resist watching him walk away. His jeans fit him almost as tightly as his football uniform pants, which gave her an excellent view of a tight butt and rock-hard thighs. The cotton of his shirt draped over a magnificently contoured back. Something seemed to melt low in her belly, and she shook her head to break the powerful spell.

Even if Luke Archer hadn't been a client, he was miles out of her league in every other way.

She was just bowled over that he'd stayed behind to see if he could fix things. Her brother always claimed that the great quarterback was a decent guy, not a prima donna. Maybe his image wasn't just a skillful public relations campaign.

She shook her head again. No one that famous and that good-looking could be a normal human being.

Chapter 2

"Trevor, what the hell is the matter with you?" Luke stalked into the kitchen, where his brother sat eating cold pizza. "You're a married man."

Trevor looked up. "Seriously? You think that stops me from wanting some fun?"

Luke raked one hand through his hair, making his head throb. Too much scotch from last night at the Bellwether Club, and now Trevor. And that damned wager.

"Have fun somewhere else. Don't involve some poor concierge, who's now in trouble with her boss because you complained." Although he hadn't minded at all when the concierge had run into him so he could feel her soft curves crushed against his chest. He was human. "And don't drag me into a meeting without telling me the truth."

"I told you the meeting was Spindle's idea." Trevor took a bite of pizza and chewed. "You didn't have to come. I could have handled it myself."

"I live in the building. You're a guest." When Trevor had texted him about the meeting, he should have asked more questions and controlled the situation, but he had a morning appointment with his coach.

Furthermore, he got the feeling Spindle had had his own agenda for getting them all into his office.

Trevor tossed his half-eaten pizza on the plate. "Look, Jodie's nagging me up, down, and sideways about finding another job because I didn't get tenure. All I hear is, 'Why don't you finish your book? Why don't you write a scholarly article? Maybe you'd have tenure if you did, and we could have a baby.' So she doesn't exactly put me in the mood for sex right now."

"Christ, Trevor, that's enough about your sex life."

Luke agreed with Jodie's logic, even if her methods weren't effective. Trevor had been passed over for tenure at the small liberal arts college where he was a professor of philosophy, so he'd come to New York to drown his sorrows. Or dump them on Luke. Personally, Luke thought his brother should be in his office finishing the book he'd been working on for the last three years. Wasn't it publish or perish in academia? Even Luke knew that, and he was as far away from Trevor's world as it was possible to get.

"Don't judge me," Trevor said. "I remember the stories you told about the football groupies and some of the wild stuff you did with them."

"I was a lot younger and stupider then," Luke said. "But even more important, I was single. No strings, no rings," he repeated, remembering last night's conversation at the club. He didn't add that he'd never had to pay for sex.

Nor did he mention his concern about the press. The concierge—Miranda—had said she wouldn't mention it again, and concierges probably needed to be discreet. However, if her boss gave her a hard time and she got miffed, she might talk to a reporter. Luke didn't want Jodie or his parents hearing about Trevor's little escapade from the media.

As he thought of Miranda, he remembered the sympathetic look she'd given him and the genuine warmth of her smile. There had been real understanding there, but also some intriguing banked heat in her big brown eyes. Both had caught his attention because they were unexpected.

She'd turned down football tickets, too. No one did that. He knew her boss was going to sell the ones he'd accepted—he could see it in the way the man refused to meet his eyes. But Miranda, who was the injured party, had rejected his first peace offering. He suspected she had accepted the football just to appease him and Spindle.

He'd waited for her afterward to offer his assistance because he could tell that her boss was unhappy. She had put him off then, too. It was interesting.

So was the fact that behind that serene mask she wore, she had reacted to him. Most women didn't try to hide that.

Trevor picked up the pizza and ripped off another bite. "Yeah, well, I didn't have a chance to do wild stuff when I was young and stupid."

Luke's hangover made his stomach heave at the sight of the congealed pizza, so he took his brother's plate and tossed the rest of the pizza in the garbage. "At least eat something healthy."

Trevor stood up and leaned forward so his face was just inches away from Luke's. "I don't have to eat healthy, because I don't make my living with my muscles. I use my brain."

There it was. The one weapon Trevor could use to jab at his overachieving older brother. Luke stepped back to avoid the bits of pizza Trevor was spewing.

"I spend hours reading and researching and analyzing and writing and discussing ideas. It's exhausting. Up here," Trevor said, tapping his temple. "You don't understand that."

Luke crossed his arms and thought of the hours he spent watching video and reading scouting reports, pinpointing his opponents' strengths and weaknesses, devising plays with the coaches, memorizing and running them with his teammates. It was exhausting, too, but that's what it took to do his job to the absolute best of his abilities.

Trevor had always been the smart one. Their parents had been so proud when he had been the salutatorian of his high school class and gone on to Harvard for undergrad and his doctorate.

Luke, on the other hand, had taken the courses he had to in order to play football. His parents had been stunned when Luke received the National Football Foundation's High School Scholar-Athlete Award, one of five given in the entire country. Their baffled astonishment when he'd told them about the luncheon at the Waldorf Astoria in New York City had been both gratifying and hurtful. They'd accompanied him, of course, but had spent the afternoon looking at the professional football stars attending the event—people he hoped to emulate—as though they were aliens.

Luke pushed that memory away. "I have a meeting at the Empire Center."

"Go ahead!" Trevor shouted. "You with your helicopter waiting on the roof! With the groupies panting for your attention! With the view of the Statue of Liberty!" He waved his hand at the sliding doors that opened onto the penthouse terrace, where Lady Liberty's torch showed above the railing. "You've got it all, and I've got nothing."

Anger boiled up inside Luke, but he slammed the lid down on it. "You have a wife who loves you," he said in a flat tone. "That's worth more than all the groupies in the world."

Shock silenced Trevor for a moment. He stared at Luke with his mouth opening and closing before he said, "You could have any woman you want."

He'd had a lot of women he'd thought he wanted.

Thirty minutes later, Luke faced Head Coach Junius Farrell across his huge oak-and-chrome desk. "With all due respect, Junius, I think we should keep the play as is. We can change it up for next year after we have time to work on it in training camp. But reconfiguring it in mid-season is going to cause a lot of confusion on the field."

He'd been through this with the coach before. It was Junius's first time as a head coach, and he wanted to put his stamp on the Empire, so he kept trying to fix things that weren't broken. As the veteran quarterback, Luke got the job of running interference to keep the new coach from screwing up the current season. That's why he was at the Empire Center on a Tuesday when every other player had the day off.

"But if we run the pick, it would free up Marshall," Junius said, jabbing his finger against his desk authoritatively.

"You're right," Luke said. "But it's tricky and we haven't had time to practice it often enough. If we try to run it this week, we'll have the guys tripping over each other at the forty. How about using it against the Colts?"

That game was in three weeks. By then, the offensive line could probably learn the new scheme well enough not to screw it up completely. In addition, it would work better against the Colts than either the Cardinals or the Buccaneers.

"I'll consider it." Junius swiveled to face his computer screen and clicked on his mouse a couple of times. He wasn't a bad guy. He just didn't realize he'd taken over an organization that had the talent and momentum to carry him to the Super Bowl if he'd get out of the way.

As long as Luke's shoulder held out. He had to stop himself from rubbing at the phantom pain that had appeared out of nowhere and disappeared just as fast. No one knew why he'd thrown that interception, and he wanted to keep it that way.

They discussed some personnel changes and some strategies for Sunday's game before Junius thanked Luke for coming and let him go.

Luke walked down the carpeted hallway. It wasn't empty, because the massive moneymaking machine that was an NFL football team ran at full speed from the beginning of training camp until the team's last game—and then some. But the office staff members were smaller than the players, so they didn't take up as much room in the corridor. Luke nodded to a couple of the PR people he passed. He didn't envy them their jobs. There was always some problem that had to be hushed up. Or spun for the press, if it couldn't be squelched.

Luke hoped that Trevor's little incident wouldn't end up on their radar. It was pretty tame—a nonevent, in fact—but Luke's image had been scrubbed clean because it was less distracting that way. However, the press would love to have some dirt sticking to him. He got it: scandal sold papers and drew viewers. He just didn't want to answer questions about anything other than the game.

His head was throbbing again. Damn Gavin Miller anyway. He'd tempted Luke with the seductive forgetfulness of single malt. And talked him into that ridiculous wager. He considered calling the writer and telling him the bet was off. It wouldn't surprise Luke if Trainor had backed out already, since the whole thing had been hatched in a drunken haze of one-upmanship. Who the hell bet on true love?

He pulled out his phone, found Miller's number, then put the phone away. Luke had never welshed on a bet in his life. Let the other two call it quits. He could wait them out, because he was going to put it out of his mind until the end of the season and then show them how to run a courtship.

He headed for the cubicle pen where his assistant, Doug Weiss, worked, along with a battalion of other staff members who handled everything from ordering supplies for the locker room to cutting the players' paychecks. It was a hive of activity. When Luke leaned into Doug's cubicle, the tall, skinny young man pulled his telephone headset off and fluffed his mop of frizzy red hair. "Hey, Boss Ice, what do you need?"

"I need two good tickets to Sunday's game with a signed football. And I need four VIP box tickets and the works."

"The works?" Doug whistled. "Is this for some charity auction I don't know about?"

"No, it's for someone my brother dumped on."

Doug grimaced at the mention of Trevor and spun around to his computer, his hands poised over the keyboard. "Let me have the info, boss."

Luke gave him the two concierges' names before adding, "Check on Miranda Tate's schedule, and have the VIP tickets and the works delivered to her personally." He didn't want Spindle horning in on his apology gifts to Miranda. "You got the list of who else needs tickets for the game, right?"

"All taken care of," Doug assured him. "And you saw the addition of the table at the gala next Thursday night on your schedule, right?"

Luke didn't curse, but he wanted to. "Remind me whose idea that was?"

Doug's freckled cheeks reddened. "Um, Kathy Middleton's. She's in PR."

"I see." Kathy Middleton was a hot brunette Doug had a major crush on. Luke lowered his voice. "Have you asked her out yet?"

Doug shook his head, making his hair flop. "She wouldn't go out with someone like me."

"You just got me to go to her gala. She'll be positively disposed toward you."

"Seriously?" Doug's eyes were wide. That was one of the reasons Luke liked his assistant; the kid didn't take advantage of his access to a celebrity.

"Try it. I'm betting she'll say yes."

His assistant took a deep breath. "Okay."

"Keep me posted," Luke said.

Back out in the corridor, he debated whether to watch some video or go home. Instead, he shrugged into his leather jacket without zipping it and jogged across a couple of vast parking lots to the stadium. Swiping his security badge into the players' entrance, he cut past the locker rooms and headed out into the big shell of the arena.

A couple of maintenance crews worked on the field, their black fleece jackets contrasting with the emerald green synthetic turf. A gust of wind pushed chilly air through the cotton of Luke's shirt, but he kept walking until he was right in the middle of the Empire logo on the fifty-yard line.

He performed his weekly ritual, turning slowly in a full circle to imprint the empty seats and near silence on his brain. On game day he would use this image to overlay the roaring, heaving crowd of spectators so he could block out everything except the players on the field. His college coach had taught him the technique after his first game freshman year, when he'd been distracted by all the commotion on the sidelines and beyond.

Luke had always had natural field vision, the ability to see how a play was developing and what patterns the players were running. This visualization was one of the ways he'd honed it to a precision tool.

"Hey, I figured I'd find you here." Stan Gatto jogged up to him. The older man had been Luke's trainer since day one at the Empire. "We gotta talk."

"About what?" Luke folded his arms across his chest.

"You know about what. And let's do it inside. It's colder than the hair on a polar bear's butt out here." He looked at Luke. "I know they call you Iceman, but you don't have to take it literally."

"Seriously, Stan? I've played in blizzards." Still, Luke started walking back toward the tunnel.

"That's different. The adrenaline keeps you warm." As they passed through the big doorway, Stan glanced around and lowered his voice. "So what happened on that last pass on Sunday?"

"It got intercepted." Luke kept walking.

"Yeah, even that moron announcer Chris Hollis could figure that out. What made you throw a pass that got intercepted? You could have connected with Marshall with your eyes closed, but you threw it right at the Patriots' cornerback." Stan put his hand on Luke's nonthrowing shoulder and pulled him to a stop. "Talk to me."

"In the training room," Luke said, nodding toward a door farther down the hall.

Stan jogged beside him as he strode along the corridor and into the empty room. The trainer closed and locked the door behind them before he turned to Luke. "Well?"

Luke allowed himself to roll his shoulder. He should have known he couldn't fool Stan. "I was cocked to throw to Rob when I saw that Marshall was wide open. I tried to make the change when this pain just ripped through my shoulder and arm. It came out of nowhere, and then it was gone again. That's why I screwed up the throw."

"Sit down," Stan said, pointing to a chair. He came up behind Luke and started probing his shoulder and upper arm. "Does it hurt now?"

"Only when you jab your fingernails into my skin."

"Smart ass." Stan jabbed especially hard. "Answer my question."

"No, it doesn't hurt now. It hasn't hurt since after I made the throw." But it might in the next game.

The trainer took Luke's arm and moved it through various positions before he stepped back. "There's no damage that I can find. But we should get the doc to run an MRI to be sure."

"No. This stays between you and me." Luke met Stan's eyes with a hard look. "It was just a twinge because I tried to change directions too fast. Give me some exercises to stretch and strengthen my shoulder."

"I can give you all the exercises in the world, but neither one of us is getting any younger." Stan patted Luke on his left shoulder. "You gotta watch the sudden moves."

That wasn't what Luke wanted to hear.

That evening, Miranda walked back into her office for her next shift. After her encounter with Luke Archer, she'd gone home to her apartment in Jersey City, fallen into bed, and slept for eight hours. Her dreams had been shockingly vivid encounters between herself and the quarterback, minus the T-shirt and jeans he'd worn that morning. She'd awakened feeling restless and unsettled.

The one task she'd accomplished that made her feel good was sending in another payment on the loan for her brother Dennis's cheese-making equipment.

The Tate family dairy farm had been struggling until Dennis read an article about turning the milk he produced into artisanal cheese. Miranda had been a little skeptical, but her brother had rented a trailer equipped to make cheese and started experimenting. Much to their delight, New York City chefs and gourmet shops loved the concept, and the flavor of Dennis's handcrafted cheeses. She'd even been the one to introduce Dennis's products to some of the chefs at the multistar restaurants where she sent her clients.

The farm was already carrying a heavy load of debt, so Miranda had offered to finance the purchase of the equipment. It assuaged some of her guilt about leaving her parents and Dennis behind when she'd headed for New York City as soon as she graduated from community college.

None of her family had understood her dream of living in the Big Apple. Her father pushed her to join the 4-H club. Her mother wanted her to date the local boys so she could find a nice, solid husband. They shook their heads in bafflement when she saved up her babysitting money to subscribe to *New York* magazine so she could pore over the reviews of Broadway shows and restaurants. They said such things were only for idle rich people. Even Dennis felt that way, although he was more diplomatic about it.

Nowadays the guilt lay heavier on her because her brother carried all the responsibilities of the farm since her parents had moved to Florida. He had shouldered them willingly—being a dairy farmer was what he wanted to do with his life. But because it wasn't what she wanted for herself, she felt as though she'd abandoned him in some way.

Hanging her coat on the coatrack, she sat at her desk and started clicking through the e-mail requests that had come in since she'd left that morning.

"Miranda Tate?" A man in a royal blue tracksuit with some sort of logo on the sleeve stuck his head in the door.

"Yes, I'm Miranda. Do you need me to sign for a package?" Usually the doorman took care of that, especially this late, but maybe it was something unusually valuable.

"You don't have to sign for it, but I have a delivery for you." The man ducked back out before returning with a hand truck stacked with three cardboard boxes.

Miranda came around her desk as the deliveryman picked up a manila envelope off the top box. "The message is that you should open this right away. Compliments of Mr. Archer."

She took the envelope and glanced at the label. Sure enough, her name was typed on it underneath the whooshing blue-and-gold *E* of the New York Empire. "I don't understand. I was supposed to get a football."

"Oh, there's a football in one of these boxes, I guarantee you," the man said. "There's also authentic Empire jerseys, posters, towels, polo shirts, T-shirts, baseball caps . . ."

"Okay," Miranda said to stop the flow. "But it can't all be for me."

"Yup." The man nodded emphatically. "Doug—that's Mr. Archer's assistant—said you get the works. Where do you want me to put 'em?"

"In that corner, I guess." She pointed to the only space where the pile of boxes would fit. She hoped no one stopped by her office tonight, since the look wasn't in keeping with the luxurious decor.

The man waved away the tip she tried to give him, saying, "Mr. Archer takes care of me."

Once he was gone, Miranda opened the envelope, spilling the contents onto her desk. Four tickets fell out, along with a note scrawled on a sheet of Empire stationery.

Dear Ms. Tate,

A football wasn't enough to make up for my brother's unfortunate request. Enjoy the game, or at least the food in the VIP box.

Luke Archer

A flush of heat coursed through her. Embarrassment or arousal? She wasn't sure, but she had to stop it now. He was a client.

She looked at the tickets, which were embellished with shiny gold borders. She sat down and read the note again. On top of being gorgeous, famous, rich, and talented, the quarterback had a sense of humor, a rare attribute among most of the celebrities she had dealt with. Somehow, by going so over the top with his gifts, he had turned this into a charming inside joke.

It looked like she would be rooting for the Empire from now on.

That reminded her of her nephew, Theo, who was the ultimate Empire fanatic. She glanced at the shiny tickets she still held in her hand. Theo would love to go to the game. Maybe she could convince Dennis to take a day off and bring his family to see the Empire play. It was less than two hours' drive from the farm, but Dennis didn't like to leave his cows with the hired hand.

She picked up her cell phone and hit her brother's auto dial. "Are you okay?" he asked, sounding alarmed.

"I'm fine. Why?"

"You never call after nine because you know I go to bed then."

"Sorry, I forgot." She'd been thinking about Luke Archer, not her brother's working hours. "But you're awake now, and I have a treat to offer you and Patty, and most especially, Theo. I have four tickets for a VIP box at the Empire game on Sunday. With free food." That might get him there.

"On Sunday. I don't know." She could almost hear her brother worrying about his cows.

"I have all sorts of Empire stuff for Theo, including a football signed by Luke Archer."

"How did you get that?" Dennis knew she could get tickets, but sports collectibles didn't usually come her way.

"I just might have met Luke Archer himself," she said with a note of triumph. And another shimmer of remembered pleasure.

"You met Luke Archer?" Awe rang in Dennis's voice. "Did he shake your hand? If he did, don't wash it until Theo gets to touch you. I also might want to."

Miranda laughed. "So will you come?"

"Whatever it is, he'll come." That was Dennis's wife, Patty, shouting into the phone. "He needs a day off, and so do I."

"Hey, give me that," Dennis said. Miranda waited as sounds of a tussle over possession of the phone floated into her ear. She heard a muffled exchange of conversation between husband and wife before Dennis came back on, saying sheepishly, "I guess we're coming to the game. Thanks for the offer, sis. Patty's right. I haven't taken time off in a while. And Theo got a great report card, so this will be his reward."

"I have four tickets, so you can bring someone else if you want to."

"Wait, aren't you coming?"

"Me?" Miranda hadn't even considered it. "I'm not a football fan."

"You're a Theo fan and he's a fan of yours, so we'd all like you to come. If you're not working." Dennis paused for a moment. "We haven't seen you in a while, and I'm not saying that to make you feel guilty or anything. It would just be nice."

She knew Dennis meant what he said, but guilt elbowed her just the same. She didn't go home to the farm much. Her time off was spent cultivating contacts at new restaurants or previewing hot Broadway shows. If she wanted to be a competent head concierge, she had to be able to get whatever her clients wanted—within the law. "Of course I'll come. Thank you for inviting me."

"I'm pretty sure you invited us," Dennis said.

"You know what I mean."

"Does Luke Archer live in your building? I swear I won't tell anyone if he does. Not even Patty." She could hear his wife snort.

Dennis knew how seriously she took the residents' privacy concerns. However, it was common knowledge that the quarterback lived in the Pinnacle, so Miranda could admit it. "Yes. He doesn't usually ask for anything because he has his own assistant, and everyone showers him with freebies anyway. However, his brother is visiting and needed some help, so Mr. Archer gave me the goodies as a thank-you."

"Heck of a thank-you," Dennis said. "Wait till I tell Theo. He'll be over the moon."

"We're not telling him until Saturday." It was Patty again. "Otherwise he'll drive us crazy."

Theo could be a bit obsessive. "I won't mention it if I talk to him," Miranda promised. Sometimes her nephew would ask his parents to dial her up so he could check in with her, which she considered a huge compliment. "I'm at work, so I'd better go. We'll work out logistics later."

After Miranda hung up, she decided she should write Luke a polite thank-you note. Pulling out a piece of the Pinnacle's elegant cream notepaper, she picked up a pen.

Dear Mr. Archer,

He could make her address him as Luke to his face, but not in writing.

Thank you very much for including some additional gifts with the autographed football.

She liked her little dig of understatement there, but then she got sincere.

You've made my nephew a very happy boy. My brother might be an even happier man. In fact, I have caught Empire fever and will be attending the game myself.

She hoped he wouldn't remember she'd claimed to be working on Sunday.

In all seriousness, you gave us more than just tickets. You gave us a wonderful family outing. We all appreciate that.

Regards,

Miranda Tate

She reread the note and addressed it to Luke Archer's apartment. She would give it to the building's messenger to hand deliver.

Now it was time to deal with all the messy requests Orin had dumped out of his in-box and into hers.

Chapter 3

The next morning, Luke sat on a stool at the counter in his big, open kitchen, drinking a protein shake and rereading Miranda Tate's note. She was a class act, that lady. What really got him in the gut, though, was the image of Aunt Miranda with her nephew, the Empire fan. Luke had no idea how old the kid was, but he put the concierge in her late twenties, so the nephew could be about the age of DaShawn's nine-year-old son.

Luke looked forward to Trevor starting a family so he'd have a nephew who cheered on the team, no matter whether they won or lost.

The imaginary nephew left a hollow ache in Luke's chest, so he grabbed Miranda's note and slid off the stool to head for his home office. As he stepped through the door, a slant of early sun caught in the jewels of his Super Bowl rings arrayed in their glass case and threw a confetti of light onto the opposite wall. He kept most of his trophies and memorabilia at his ranch in Texas, but his rings, his second Heisman Trophy, and the congratulatory letter from Joe Namath came with him to New York for the season as his good luck charms.

He stopped in front of the rings. A hell of a lot of pain and effort had gone into earning them. Not just on *his* part, but from the whole team. His fourth Super Bowl win had been a brutal contest against the Patriots, with too many players from both teams getting driven off the field on stretchers. Some never came back to the game.

Trying to shake off his gloomy mood, Luke dropped into the ergonomic chair behind the glass-and-chrome desk and clicked on the Pinnacle's staff e-mail list to find Miranda Tate.

Dear Miranda,

He figured it was time to move to a first name basis. In fact, as he remembered it, he'd asked her to call him Luke. He tipped back the chair and stared at the sparkling rings as he debated what to say next.

A picture formed in his mind of the sophisticated concierge with the hot simmer behind her eyes wearing his team's jersey instead of her conservative silk blouse. He'd like to see that, although it would be even better if she wore nothing underneath the jersey.

His mind started to drift in a dangerous direction, and he pulled himself up short. She worked in the building where he lived, and he had a football season to focus on.

But it wouldn't hurt to go see Aunt Miranda and offer an extra treat for her nephew so he could find out how that Empire jersey suited her.

Manny, her favorite doorman, walked into Miranda's office as she was putting on her coat to leave after a quiet night shift.

"The roses for Mrs. Anglethorpe are here, and I think you better take a look at them," the doorman said.

She dropped her coat on her desk and followed him into the lobby. An annoyed-looking deliveryman stood at the reception desk, on which rested an enormous vase of white roses.

Miranda gasped. She had ordered the flowers herself, specifying peach-colored roses and then reconfirming the color yesterday. Mrs. A's husband sent her the same shade of roses every year on her birthday because his nickname for her was Peaches. The gift would be ruined if the wrong color had been delivered.

"There must be some mix-up," she said as she hurried over.

The deliveryman pulled a wrinkled sheet of pink paper out of his back pocket and checked it. "Says here the white roses are for Mrs. Anglethorpe at the Pinnacle."

Miranda took the delivery order to read it herself. The word *peach* had been crossed out and amended to *white*.

"I'll call your boss and straighten this out," Miranda said with an apologetic smile. "In the meantime, I'm afraid you're going to have to take these back and bring peach-colored roses." She hoped the florist had them. It wasn't a high demand color, so it often had to be specially ordered. She foresaw a whole series of phone calls ahead of her as she tried to locate the proper colored flowers.

The deliveryman picked up the vase with ill-concealed annoyance. "Joe ain't going to be happy."

Maybe not, but Mr. and Mrs. Anglethorpe were her clients, so she was far more concerned about them. As she dashed back to her office, she worried about how much time the new delivery would take.

She was surprised by the error, because she used Richmond Florals regularly and Joe had never gotten anything wrong before. Dialing the number, she checked the order again, noticing that there was handwriting at the bottom. Because hers was the third page of a three-part form, the note was too faint to read.

Joe himself picked up. "Miranda, I just heard from my driver that you sent back the white roses. What's going on over there? You and Orin can't make up your minds?"

"Orin?" Miranda was too confused to be diplomatic.

"He called yesterday afternoon to change the order from peach roses to white. I had to steal them from some wedding centerpieces I'm working on."

Miranda sat down hard. This was sabotage of the worst kind. Orin must be out-of-his-mind furious about yesterday's meeting if he was willing to upset a client to make Miranda look bad.

"I wrote a note at the bottom of the order," Joe said. "Didn't you see it?"

"It didn't come through on the copy." She would have to take a hit on this one. "Bill me for both bouquets, but please tell me you have peach roses to send over ASAP." She tried to inject a smile into her voice, even as she shuddered at how big a chunk the extra flower charge would carve out of her paycheck. Any mistakes made in orders had to be absorbed by Orin's employees so her boss could keep his profits high.

"No problem with that. I already had the peach ordered, so they're here." The slight edge of exasperation in Joe's voice was gone. "I won't charge you for the white roses because I can use them for the wedding flowers. But I'll have to bill you for two deliveries."

"Of course." Miranda could handle that. She debated a moment about her next statement, but she couldn't be at the Pinnacle twenty-four/seven, so it needed to be said. "The next time Orin changes an order I've placed, would you just drop me an e-mail? That way we can avoid future confusion."

"Sure." He sounded puzzled, but Miranda didn't care. Orin had crossed the line on this one.

After she hung up, she braced her elbows on her desk and massaged her temples. The amount of damage Orin could do if he kept this up was mind-blowing. She couldn't double-check every order she placed with every vendor she worked with, and she certainly couldn't meet every delivery that came in.

She opened her desk drawer and pulled out the cow-spotted stress ball Dennis had given her for Christmas, saying it would remind her of the farm. It was surprising how often she used it these days. She clenched her fist around it and squeezed.

When she'd applied for the position at the Pinnacle, she'd heard that Orin was difficult to work for, but this went beyond that.

She didn't understand why he had a problem with her. She was good at her job, which should reflect well on him as the owner of the concierge service. Yet he seemed to resent the fact that certain residents came to her on a regular basis rather than routing their requests through him. It wasn't uncommon that people got to know and trust a particular concierge. She wondered if some of the clients who now worked only with her might have once dealt with Orin.

She was going to have to find another job sooner than she'd expected. And it wouldn't be easy without a reference from her boss. She wouldn't go to her clients directly for references, but maybe she could tap some colleagues.

She would have to be careful in her job search. The concierge community was tight knit. A lot of back-scratching and favor trading went on, and Orin was well connected.

As the complexities of her situation loomed large, she crushed the ball until her nails dug into her palm. Maybe she should just resign from the Pinnacle now to cut her losses. She could find temporary work at a lower tier hotel. It meant giving up on her dream job at the new building, but it might be better than second-guessing everything she did here.

Or maybe she should grovel to Orin. He might take pity on her. The thought of it made her feel like she'd swallowed a rotten egg.

No matter what her decision, she was going to have to speak with him about the roses. And she would have to pretend that it was all just a misunderstanding.

Anger and frustration boiled up, and she hurled the foam stress ball at the wall. It ricocheted off just as Luke Archer walked through her door and caught the projectile in his left hand, his long fingers closing around the spotted ball.

Those ice blue eyes did a quick scan of her face, and he frowned. "I've come at a bad time."

She froze.

He didn't look embarrassed or uncomfortable. He looked concerned. That surprised her and kicked her brain back into gear. She gave him a rueful smile, even as images from her dreams sent a guilty awareness prickling over her skin. "I was just practicing." Cupping her hands in a mute request for him to throw the ball back, she added, "My nephew says I have a weak arm."

He tossed it exactly into the center of her palms with a motion of such pure grace that it made her breath hitch. "Looked pretty impressive to me," he said.

"Now I can brag that I caught a ball thrown by Luke Archer." She dropped the toy back into the drawer, knowing that she would forever remember his powerful hand wrapped around it. "How may I help you?"

After a moment's hesitation, he lowered himself into the moss green chair in front of her desk, the breadth of his shoulders completely covering the upholstered back. Pushing the chair a couple of feet farther away, he stretched out his long, denim-clad legs.

"Your nephew sounds like someone I'd like to know," he said, his drawl once again pouring into her ear like sweet molasses. "If you can wait for about forty-five minutes after the game, I'll have someone escort your family to the meet-and-greet lounge. Your nephew and your brother might enjoy some of the folks they'll see there. I'll be stopping by myself."

Disbelief and excitement made her heartbeat speed up. She knew she shouldn't allow Luke Archer to do this. It went beyond generous. But the thought of Theo getting to shake the hand of the quarterback he worshipped was too tempting. And she wouldn't mind spending a little more time with Luke Archer herself. "You just made me the best aunt in the universe. Theo will be thrilled."

He gave her a whole different kind of smile from the last time they met. This one was slow and deliberate, bringing the dimple into view gradually. The way it creased the plane of his cheek sent a shudder of appreciation through her. "One of the unexpected benefits of my job is making kids happy just by showing up."

Oh, dear God, this man was too perfect. No wonder supermodels drooled over him.

Before she could say anything, he locked that laser gaze on her again. "I appreciate the fact that you didn't talk to the press about Trevor."

So this was just more insurance that she would be discreet. She tried not to sound insulted, but she couldn't keep her feelings out of her voice. "I would never discuss a client with the press."

"Hey, I didn't mean to imply you would." He held up his hands in a gesture of surrender. "But it's happened before. Not in this building," he added. "That's why Trevor is supposed to go through my assistant when he needs something."

She gave him a sideways look as she mentally berated herself. He hadn't come to her office because of her fascinating personality.

He shifted in his chair and the dimple vanished. "By the way, my assistant wouldn't have made that call, either."

So his brother was a total sleazebag. Which made her wonder about Luke, who had endless opportunities for sexual partners. She needed to keep that in mind, especially given that her few, brief romantic relationships didn't exactly qualify her as experienced in that department.

She pressed her folded hands hard onto her desk. "You don't need to thank me for doing my job."

She expected him to give her another well-rehearsed smile, unfold that gorgeously muscled body from the chair, and depart.

Instead, he crossed his long legs at the ankle. "I guess you get some strange requests."

Seduced into honesty, she snorted. "You have no idea."

His chuckle came from low in his throat. "Too bad your concierge code won't let you tell me about them."

She pressed her lips together and shook her head. She couldn't speak because his laugh was still vibrating through her like a hot, sexy riff on a flamenco guitar.

"You know, I liked your note. Not too many folks take pen to paper these days." He rose from the chair in one swift, fluid motion. The full impact of his height still startled her. How did a human being that large move with such speed and precision?

"I have to get to practice," he said. He tucked his hands into his jeans pockets. "I'll see you after the game." He gave her a wink and was out of her office in a single stride.

Miranda slumped back in her chair and considered fanning herself. It was impossible not to respond to Luke Archer's magnetism. He exuded alpha maleness from the very tall top of his blond head, down over those chair-spanning shoulders, through his washboard abs, and along the hard, curved muscles of his thighs to the big feet encased in high-tech running shoes. And that damned dimple. A man with ice blue eyes should not have a dimple. The contrast made him far too fascinating, like a contradiction that needed to be resolved.

Not to mention his comment about kids. Miranda rolled her eyes at herself for falling under his spell. It had sounded sincere, but it had to be canned. No one who had been as famous as Luke Archer for as long as he had could still be surprised by a kid's reaction.

Well, at least, he had taken her mind off Orin for a few minutes so she could get her temper under control.

She glanced at her watch. Her boss should be in by now. She would go beard the lion in his den.

Miranda struggled to be diplomatic as she sat in front of Orin's desk. "I'm concerned about the mix-up in Mrs. Anglethorpe's roses. The peach roses got switched to white ones. Fortunately, I caught the problem before they were delivered."

Her boss swiveled away from his computer screen. He laid his hands on his desk and fixed a cold gaze on her. "So I will credit your alertness for catching the mistake. Well done." There was nothing complimentary in his tone.

"Someone from our service called Richmond Florals and requested the change." She wasn't about to accuse Orin of placing the call, no matter what Joe said. "I'm sure they meant to change a different order. However, the mistake would have made both of the Anglethorpes unhappy and ruined the birthday celebration."

Orin's jaw went tight and his lips thinned. "If Joe can't keep his paperwork straight, maybe you should find a different florist."

"I'm just wondering how we can make sure something like this doesn't happen again." Miranda waited. Orin liked to think of himself as a problem solver.

"You have brought the issue to my attention, Miranda. Since I am the CEO of Elite Concierge Services, it is, of course, a priority for me to make sure this problem does not occur again." Orin smacked his palms on the desktop, making Miranda start. "You need not concern yourself further."

As she left his office, Miranda let out the breath she'd been holding. She'd made her point and he hadn't fired her.

Still, she would polish up her résumé when she got home.

Luke settled on the leather seat of the limo and wondered what had Miranda Tate so riled up. She didn't seem the type to throw things—even balls. He had a suspicion that Orin Spindle was involved, and guilt nagged at him again. If Luke hadn't had that god-awful hangover from drinking with Trainor and Miller the night before, he wouldn't have let that whole situation get to the point it did. He owed it to Miranda to fix it. But she had made it clear she didn't want him to fight that battle for her.

Which surprised him.

So many people expected him to help them out.

He'd get a better idea about her at the meet and greet. He wanted to see her outside her professional persona. Bring out that genuine smile again, the one she'd given him when Trevor had pissed him off. Find out if that smooth, satiny voice ever took on an edge, or her sleek, shiny dark hair ever looked mussed. Like someone had run their fingers through it. See how the spark of temper he'd caught in her brown eyes might be turned into a different kind of heat.

He felt a stirring in his groin. Where the hell had that come from? One brush of her breasts against him and he wanted the whole package?

Luke straightened on the seat and began to run through the Empire's playbook in his mind. One of his signature moves was not using a wristband with plays listed on it. He kept a mental file instead—it made his decisions on the field easier. And it intimidated his opponents.

Football was a physical game, but it never hurt to mess with your enemy's mind, too.

Chapter 4

"This is awesome," Theo said, his hazel eyes the size of saucers. They'd just been escorted into the VIP box.

"Awesome is right," Miranda agreed. She was startled to discover that the box was decorated like someone's large, elegant living/dining room, except for the wall of glass that overlooked the outdoor seating and the brilliant green of the football field. She'd gotten tickets for people to sit in VIP boxes more times than she could remember, but she'd never actually been in one herself. She'd imagined they would be decorated with team logos and neon beer signs. This suite boasted oak paneling, tan leather sofas, and plush russet carpeting.

"Mr. Archer got you one of the nicest boxes, and you have it all to yourself," Heather, their young hostess, said. She'd met them at the VIP entrance, wearing a skirt and jacket in the now-familiar Empire blue, and whisked them up to their luxurious suite in an elevator.

Dennis whistled. "Four flat-screen TVs."

"Hot dogs and pizza." Theo inspected the contents of the chafing dishes laid out on the marble countertop.

"A private bathroom," Patty said, sticking her head in the door. "With real towels, not paper ones."

"Anything you want, just ask Milt here. He'll be taking care of you." Heather introduced them all to a wiry older man dressed in black slacks and a white dress shirt with a black necktie. "I'll be back after the game to take you to the lounge."

"You folks want something to drink?" Milt asked. "Anything we haven't got right here, I can get for you."

Theo ran to his mother and beckoned for her to bend down so he could whisper in her ear. She listened and then nodded. "Yes, but after you eat."

The boy raced over to Milt and skidded to a stop just in front of him. "Mr. Milt, do you have milk shakes?"

"Chocolate, vanilla, or peanut butter?" Milt asked with a smile.

"After I eat"—Theo threw a glance at Patty—"may I please have a chocolate one?"

"You got it, young man." Milt looked at the adults.

"How about a beer?" Dennis asked. As Milt recited what he had on tap, in the refrigerator, and what he could get from the lounge, her brother's face lit up almost as brightly as Theo's. The circles under his eyes and the lines of fatigue etched around his mouth disappeared. Patty had been right—her brother needed a day off.

Patty and Miranda both opted for white wine, much to Dennis's disgust. "You don't drink chardonnay at a football game," he scoffed good-naturedly.

"So far, I don't feel like I'm anywhere near a football game." Miranda sipped the crisp chilled wine.

"Yeah, well, let's change that." Dennis gestured for Miranda and Patty to follow Theo past the televisions and the sofas to the glass wall. Tall bar chairs were lined up along a countertop positioned so one could watch the game from inside while eating and drinking. Theo pushed open the frameless glass door, letting in a burst of brisk autumn air.

"Want your coats?" Milt asked.

"No, no, we're fine," Miranda said. "Just exploring before we eat."

The brilliant sunshine made the green of the synthetic turf and the royal blue of the Empire logo blinding. Clumps of early spectators dotted the giant arcs of seating, most of them sporting blue jerseys, but a few stood out in the dark red of the opposing Cardinals.

"We're on the fifty-yard line," Dennis murmured in a tone of awe. He turned to Miranda. "Just what did you get for Luke Archer's brother?"

"You know I can't answer that."

"Yeah, that was rhetorical," her brother said with a wry smile. "It must have been really something, though."

Miranda was a little overawed herself, especially because Luke had reserved a box that probably accommodated twelve people for their exclusive use. This was far beyond what she'd expected, especially when she considered that she'd received all of this by *refusing* to get Trevor Archer what he wanted. Luke was trying to buy her silence in a big way.

"Can I have my Empire stuff now?" Theo asked, tugging on Miranda's elbow.

"Of course, sweetie." She'd sorted through the boxes and selected jerseys and hats for all of them to wear at the game, packing them in the tote bag she'd brought with her. She also had the autographed football and a fancy commemorative booklet that she figured Theo could get more autographs on after the game. The rest she had shipped to the farm.

They trooped back into the suite, where Miranda distributed her goodies. Father and son handled the football with equal reverence. "We're going to put this in the china cabinet and never play with it," Dennis said. Theo nodded as he held the ball by its pointed ends and stared at the scrawl of Luke Archer's name slashed in black Sharpie across the pigskin.

"Yeah, it will add a nice touch beside my grandmother's Royal Doulton." Patty smiled indulgently at her husband.

Dennis returned the smile but with some extra heat. Miranda sighed inwardly. Patty and Dennis had the kind of love that seemed to grow stronger through their struggles with the farm's finances, the difficulties of conceiving and bearing a child, and the stress of Patty's mother's protracted illness and death while she lived with them.

They still used every excuse to touch each other, looked forward to their date night once a month, and indulged each other's interests, like Dennis's love of football and Patty's of square dancing. At an exhibition dance she'd attended, Miranda had been impressed with how light on his feet Dennis was on the dance floor, even as he threw a long-suffering grimace at her.

She tossed everyone a football jersey, which they pulled on over their shirts. "All of a sudden I feel underdressed." Patty glanced between their fan apparel and the elegant suite.

"Look at the back." Miranda turned around in front of Patty.

"Oh, my God, the jerseys are autographed," Patty said, trying to look over her own shoulder. "Luke Archer touched my jersey."

"I think he touches a lot of jerseys," Miranda said.

"Not as many as you'd think," Milt spoke up. "He prefers to donate his autographed items to charity auctions rather than selling them. But he's happy to give his friends his John Hancock." He winked at Theo, who looked down at his child-size jersey with new admiration.

"Hmm," Miranda said. That was an unexpected side to Luke. Since he'd been so generous to her, she'd assumed he had stacks of the signed stuff in a warehouse somewhere.

"I'm hungry," Theo said.

Right on cue, Dennis's stomach growled, making them all laugh as they attacked the buffet.

Three hours later, the Empire were down by two points. All four of them were standing outside, yelling at the top of their lungs as the Empire drove down the field in an attempt to win the game. Milt had brought Theo a giant blue foam hand with the index finger raised, which the boy waved over his head with enthusiasm, occasionally whacking someone in the face.

Miranda found herself tracking Luke's number nine jersey, whether he was on the field or on the sideline. Every time the quarterback got hit by a hulking lineman, she gasped and winced. Luckily it didn't happen too often since, according to Dennis, his teammates did a good job of protecting him. "He's tough and almost never gets injured," Dennis explained, "but he's getting older, so they have to step it up a notch."

"Older?" Miranda thought of the power and energy the quarterback radiated. "He can't be all that old."

"He's in his midthirties. That's old by football standards. He's coming to the end of his career."

"He sure doesn't look like it," she said as Luke threw the ball like a bullet to a receiver on the fifteen-yard line for a first down.

"Yeah, he's still got an arm."

On the next play, disaster struck. Once again the quarterback dropped back into what Dennis called the pocket, the football in his hand. Luke looked like an island of calm in the midst of a swirl of colliding bodies as he scanned the field for his intended target. He cocked his arm back and sent the ball riffling toward one of his teammates. An opponent blasted into the air as the ball was midflight and came down with it in his hands.

A collective groan went up from the stadium as the opposing player began to zig and zag in the other direction, gaining several yards before he was buried under a pile of Empire players.

Miranda looked back at Luke to see him standing with his hands on his hips, his posture expressing pure frustration. It was a fleeting moment, because he turned and walked off the field without any further reaction.

"That's the second time he's thrown an interception in the last five minutes of a game. He never makes that kind of misjudgment." Dennis sounded upset. "Please tell me he doesn't have a shoulder injury."

When the Cardinals' offense took the field, they all sat down and leaned forward on the edges of their seats, hissing in distress every time the opposing quarterback connected with his receiver for a first down, and cheering when the Empire's defense stopped their advance.

Then the Empire got a major break when the Cardinals fumbled the ball and an Empire defender recovered it.

Luke Archer jogged back on the field. The giant screen at the end of the stadium showed a close-up of his eyes in the helmet's opening. They burned with ice-cold intensity. "He's going to win this," Miranda said.

Dennis gave her a smile. "Turned into a football expert, have you, sis?"

"You could see it in his eyes," she said. "Want to make a bet on the outcome?"

"No way! I would never bet against my team. Or Luke Archer."

A dropped pass and two running plays advanced the Empire to the forty-five-yard line with a fourth down and two.

"Kick the field goal," Dennis muttered under his breath.

"No, Dad, it's too far. Archer's going to put them away with a touchdown," Theo said.

"I don't think so, Theo." Dennis was so engrossed in the game that he didn't even glance at his son. "That's too risky."

All of a sudden the players stood up, and Luke trotted toward the sideline. "Time out, Empire," the announcer called.

Miranda could see Luke's helmet tilted at an attentive angle as the coach held his clipboard in front of his face to hide whatever they were discussing. The helmet bobbed a couple of times as Luke said something emphatic in response. The dialogue went back and forth a couple of times, and then Luke nodded and headed back onto the field.

"They're not gonna kick it," Theo crowed.

Dennis dropped his head into his hands briefly before he lifted his eyes to watch again.

So not kicking must be a bad idea. Miranda held her breath as Luke got into position behind his offensive line and shouted whatever it was that quarterbacks shouted at their teammates. A couple of players moved to different locations, and the ball was snapped.

Luke dropped back into the pocket with the ball still in his possession.

"He's going to throw!" Dennis sounded incredulous. "Who's open?"

Miranda tensed as a mountainous Cardinals player shook off two Empire linemen and charged toward the quarterback. "Oh, no, I can't watch," she whispered, closing her eyes.

"Brooks is open!" Dennis was screaming. "He's throwing to Chaz Brooks."

Miranda peeked through one eye just as Luke drilled the ball down the field right into the hands of number twenty-five.

"He has it! And he's got a clear field!" Her brother was on his feet.

Miranda stood, too, watching as the blue-shirted ballcarrier extricated himself from the grip of another gigantic Cardinals defender and took off toward the goal line.

"He's gonna score!" Theo squeaked with excitement. "Touchdown!" He threw his arms up and smacked Miranda in the face with his foam finger, but she didn't care.

She was screaming along with the rest of the Empire fans as Chaz Brooks did a dance in the end zone.

"Oh, no, Archer is down." Patty's voice cut through the celebratory racket.

Miranda scanned the field to find a ring of players and trainers standing around a fallen player. She checked the big screen to see a close-up view of the top of Luke's helmet resting on the turf behind a wall of cleats and ankles.

"Is he conscious?" she asked, concern extinguishing the thrill of victory.

"I can't tell," Patty said. "Oh, yeah, there. He moved his foot."

Suddenly, one of the standing players bent down and offered his hand to the quarterback. The player straightened and brought Luke to his feet.

Cheers and applause filled the stadium again as the clot of players followed Luke off the field.

"Is he limping?" Miranda asked, trying to distinguish Luke from the crowd of blue jerseys surrounding him.

Patty was watching the big screen. "I can't tell. Dennis?"

"I think he's okay," her husband said, his attention locked on the sideline, where activity swirled around the quarterback. "They'd have a lot more trainers working on him if he wasn't."

Luke had taken off his helmet, making it easy to spot his matted blond hair. Miranda flicked her gaze back and forth between the sideline and the big screen, which was focused on the quarterback as he sat on the bench, drinking Gatorade and talking to one of the staff members. If he was in pain, he gave no indication of it. Relief washed through her. Muscles she hadn't realized she had clenched suddenly relaxed, and she sat down hard.

She barely registered the successful kick for the extra point and the running out of the clock for the Empire's win.

Theo whooped and danced on his seat, while Dennis gave his wife a hug that lifted her off her feet. He held up his hand to Miranda for a high five.

"Your boy did it," he said, shaking his head. "That was a frozen rope he threw to Brooks."

"A what?"

"A really good pass," Patty translated.

"So he's not at the end of his career, after all?" Miranda asked.

Dennis shrugged. "At least not until the next interception."

Chapter 5

Back inside the suite, the televisions were tuned to the postgame show.

"I can't believe Archer went for it," one of the commentators said.

"You can't tell me that was Coach Farrell's idea." The second one shook his head.

"No, that was all the Iceman," the third commentator chimed in. "Archer had that play in his back pocket and was just itching to pull it out when the Cardinals weren't expecting it."

"He had something to prove today after throwing interceptions in back-to-back games," talking head number one said.

"I guess that puts to rest the rumors about a shoulder injury," the second man added. "You don't throw like that if you're hurting."

Miranda had never in her life paid any attention to sports commentary, but she found herself enthralled by the discussion of Luke Archer's performance and health. Her interest faded when they moved on to an analysis of the Empire's defensive brilliance, so she accepted the glass of wine Milt brought her with gratitude.

"I never knew watching football could be so exhausting," she said to Patty.

Her sister-in-law gave her an appraising glance. "So how well do you know Luke Archer?"

"I've probably spent a total of fifteen minutes in his company. But you get kind of invested when you know one of the players."

"He's not just one of the players, honey," Patty said. "He's a superstar. What's he like in person?"

"You'll find out soon enough."

"No, I mean when he's not being Mr. Football Player."

Miranda considered her impressions of Luke Archer. Other than the ones she wouldn't talk about. "Well, he's surprisingly low-key. Or as low-key as someone who looks like a combination of the gods Thor and Apollo can be."

Patty grinned and fanned herself. "You said it, sister."

Miranda didn't want Patty to think she only cared about Luke's impressive physical attributes. "He gets involved when his brother needs help, and he was very generous to me with all of this." She waved her hand around the suite. "And that's about all I can say."

"You're as bad as a lawyer with all your confidentiality rules," Patty said, but she was smiling.

"Hey, ladies, they're interviewing Archer." Dennis drew their attention back to the television screens.

Luke's sweat-darkened hair clung to his skull. He wore some sort of athletic undershirt that hugged his muscular shoulders, and his chin bore a smear of what looked like dried blood. Yet Miranda wished she were the one standing close to him as the quarterback bent his head to catch the reporter's question.

"So I guess that final touchdown pass proves all the rumors about a shoulder injury wrong," the willowy brunette reporter said.

The quarterback's attentive expression didn't change. "I don't know how the rumors got started."

"They started because you've thrown interceptions at critical times in two games," another reporter pointed out.

Luke flashed that self-deprecating smile Miranda had become familiar with. "Well, you know, sometimes an interception is just an interception."

The reporters chuckled. With one answer, Luke had turned the tide of the interview. She watched him field a few more questions, his expression varying from that dangerously disarming smile to grave consideration. His eyes never changed, though—they retained the same ice-cold focus.

"He's good." Miranda admired his strategy because she often used similar methods with her more temperamental clients.

"In so many ways." Patty gave an exaggeratedly languishing sigh.

Dennis nudged her. "Hey, I'm right here."

After a few more minutes, Milt opened the door to admit Heather. "Time to go meet some players," she said to Theo. "Do you have your program with you?"

Theo scrambled off the couch and grabbed the commemorative booklet. "Yes, ma'am."

They gathered up their coats, thanked Milt for the great service, and reluctantly left the luxury of the VIP box.

"Well, it was nice to live like a rich person for a few hours." Patty threw a wistful glance backward.

"Those luxury suites are fantastic, aren't they?" Heather said. "When they built the new stadium, they paid serious attention to the details."

As they sailed down in the elevator and followed Heather through a labyrinth of hallways and doors, Dennis and Theo peppered the hostess with questions about the players and the stadium. By the time they reached the lounge, Heather and Theo were fast friends. Theo's wide-eyed enthusiasm, combined with the good manners Patty insisted he learn, had that effect on people.

"Oh. My. God . . . goodness," Dennis said as he halted and looked around the spacious room.

At first, Miranda didn't understand what he was so impressed with. The carpet was blue, of course. The walls were decorated with photos of football players and the Empire logo. The sofas, chairs, and tables were standard high-end office furniture, also in the Empire's blue with accents of gold. Clumps of people dotted the room. She could identify the players because they wore stylish suits or blazers and stood head and shoulders above the fans, most of whom were dressed in team jerseys and baseball caps. She scanned the crowd but could not find Luke. He must still be trapped in the locker room.

Dennis remained where he'd stopped. "I can't believe the amount of talent in this room," he said.

"Oh, so that's why your mouth is hanging open," Miranda teased.

"Dad, that's Dante Rogers." Theo pulled on his father's hand. "Can we go meet him?"

"I'll introduce you." Heather started toward a gigantic man with magnificent dreadlocks.

"Go ahead," Miranda said to Patty. "You know who these guys are. I would just embarrass myself." She didn't want to interfere with any true fans getting to talk to their favorite players.

Patty followed in Theo's wake. Miranda smiled as the huge man grinned and bent down to scrawl his name on the little boy's program. Dennis said something to him and they shook hands.

A charge of excitement ran through the room. Miranda glanced around to find Luke Archer walking in through the players' door. His blond hair was still damp enough to show neat comb marks, and he wore a perfectly tailored charcoal gray suit with a white shirt and an Empire blue-and-gold tie. Miranda could barely catch her breath.

Half the fans abandoned the other players and surged toward him. A couple of men in dark suits stepped forward to flank him and control the crowd, much like the linemen who protected him on the field.

He chatted and signed several autographs before raising his head to sweep his gaze over the milling throng. When his attention seemed to lock on someone near Miranda, she turned to check behind her. There was no one else standing near her. As she swiveled back, she saw he was walking straight in her direction. He was coming to talk to *her*.

Her heart did a little cha-cha of excitement.

As he strode across the floor, several people tried to waylay him, but he just smiled, nodded, and kept walking until he stood in front of her. The air around him seemed to glow with energy, an energy that pulsed through her own body as he got closer. His minions had fallen back a pace and were subtly keeping the other fans away.

"I knew you'd look good in an Empire jersey," he said, his dimple flashing. "Did you enjoy the suite?"

At the sight of his smile, Miranda's mouth went dry, so she had to swallow before she could form words. "It was fantastic, but I enjoyed the game even more. Congratulations on your win!"

His response was automatic. "It was a team effort." He looked around. "Is your nephew here? I wanted to make sure to say hello."

"I'm here." Theo slipped past the suited guardians and raced up to Luke. "You were awesome. I was afraid you were hurt."

Luke knelt in a fluid motion so he was at eye level with Theo. The powerful athlete in his custom-tailored suit bringing himself down to look a small boy in the face socked Miranda somewhere right around her heart. "No, I just got the wind knocked out of me. Rodney D'Olaway has sharp elbows." Luke winked. "And I can't take all the credit. The whole team was awesome."

"This is Theo Tate," Miranda said to Luke. "I think he already knows your name."

"Nice to meet you," Theo said, belatedly holding out his hand. When Luke shook it, Theo looked down and said, "Wow, I just touched the hand you throw the football with. It's cool that they let you shake hands. I mean, what if one of your opponents squeezed your fingers really hard on purpose?"

Luke chuckled. "Don't suggest that to the Cowboys. They might try it."

"Thank you for the football and the jersey," Theo said. "Would you sign my program, too? I'm kind of collecting everyone's name."

"Sure thing." Luke pulled a pen out of his breast pocket as Theo turned to the page with Luke's photo on it. The quarterback signed his name legibly under his picture.

"Awesome," Theo said. "I mean, thanks."

"You're welcome." Luke gave the bill of Theo's cap a friendly tap and rose to his spectacular height. Miranda caught a spark of warmth in his pale eyes. So he genuinely liked kids. Odd that he didn't have any of his own. There must be thousands of women who would volunteer to have his babies. The heat dancing through her urged her to join the willing egg donors.

Patty and Dennis joined them, and Miranda once again made the introductions. Dennis spouted some football jargon that Miranda didn't understand, while Luke responded in the same language. Patty just stood there with a look of pure bliss on her face as she let her gaze rest on the quarterback.

"I have more autographs to sign," Luke said with a wry glance toward the waiting crowd.

"Thank you for a truly memorable afternoon," Miranda said while disappointment rippled through her. She wanted to soak in the golden glow that seemed to surround Luke. "I am now an enthusiastic Empire fan."

"You mean you weren't already?" He shook his head in mock disappointment. "Well, that's how we build ticket sales, one fan at a time."

Miranda felt the tug of his charm in all the places she shouldn't. "Judging by the noise in the stadium, you're running a pretty successful campaign. Now go greet the rest of your admirers. We've taken enough of your time."

He nodded, and she was pleased to see his eyes still held some of the warmth she'd noticed with Theo. Then he stepped forward and was engulfed by the waiting crowd, leaving her feeling bereft. All she could see was his gilded hair above the sea of blue jerseys.

She sucked in a breath, trying to shake off her shockingly intense awareness of the man.

Dennis and Theo went off in pursuit of more autographs, but Patty stayed behind with Miranda.

"Good Lord in heaven!" Patty said. "He saw you and walked right across the room to talk to you."

"He was looking for Theo," Miranda said. But she had felt that searing rush of exhilaration at being singled out for his attention.

"Girl, he only wanted to meet Theo because of you."

"He promised to stop in to see my nephew. That's all," Miranda said, trying to fix that thought in her own mind.

"Well, you should have heard people trying to figure out who you were," Patty said. "They were divided between an actress and a model."

Miranda burst out laughing. "That's just because they couldn't imagine Luke Archer dating any other kind of woman."

"That's not true. You're beautiful," Patty said with more loyalty than truth. "You've got gorgeous, thick, glossy hair . . . when you let it down out of that ponytail. And those big brown eyes make men want to fall into them." Patty sighed. "I wish I had your figure, too. My waist will never be as small as yours again."

Miranda hugged her. "You're blind, but I know it's because you love me."

They plunked down in two armchairs and watched Theo and Dennis circulate among the other players. But Miranda never lost track of Luke Archer as he moved through the room—greeting fans, signing shirts, hats, and programs, and accepting congratulations. With his tailored suit and flashing smile, he reminded her more of a presidential candidate or a movie star than a football player. She said so to Patty.

"He's a little of both, Miranda. That man carries hundreds of millions, if not billions, of dollars on his broad, gorgeous shoulders. He's the face of the franchise, so he *is* a movie star. And think about it—he can practice endlessly, but he doesn't know what his costars' lines are going to be. It's all improv, kind of like a political debate. He has to be a pro, on and off the field."

"That's a lot of pressure for one person."

"Well, if anyone can handle pressure, it's the Iceman."

Miranda wondered, though. Could anyone be that impervious to the responsibilities placed on him? She thought of him in the office with his brother. Trevor was another of his obligations.

Heather came over with Theo and Dennis in tow. "The meet and greet is wrapping up. I have some goodies for you in my office."

"Oh, gosh, we already have plenty of goodies," Miranda said, feeling a pang of distress that she wouldn't get to say good-bye to Luke. "You've been a terrific hostess."

"Mr. Archer told me you're a concierge." Heather pulled a business card out of her blazer pocket and held it out to Miranda. "If you ever need tickets or something special for your clients, just give me a call or drop me an e-mail. I'll make sure they get taken care of."

"That's very generous of you." Miranda rummaged in her purse and found one of her cards. "The same goes for me if you need theater tickets or a restaurant reservation in New York City." It was the least she could do, because having Heather as a contact was going to make her professional life much easier during football season.

"Hey, thanks!" Heather said, tucking the card away. "Okay, let me get you to your car."

As Dennis drove to the station so Miranda could catch the train back to her apartment, Theo paged through his book. He ran his index finger over the autographs from the players as though he couldn't quite believe they were real. "Aunt Miranda," he said, turning his face up to her, "you are the most awesome aunt in the whole world."

Miranda thought her heart might swell right out of her chest. She put her arm around Theo's thin shoulders and hugged him against her side. "And you are the most awesome nephew in the whole world."

"She's the most awesome sister in the whole world, too," Dennis chimed in, throwing Miranda a laughing glance over his shoulder.

"And sister-in-law," Patty added.

But it was Luke Archer who was truly awesome. He had provided the tickets and the collectibles. He had made a point to meet a small boy, an encounter Theo would probably talk about for the rest of his life.

Unlike many of the wealthy, privileged clients she worked with, he had done his best to make up for the problem his brother had caused. She felt a squeeze of regret that she wouldn't have any further dealings with him. It had been a surprise to find a streak of genuine decency behind the polished facade.

Not to mention experiencing the full force of that famous dimple up close and in person. As the memory of her breasts crushed against the muscled wall of his chest lit up her insides, she decided it was fortunate that she wouldn't see him again. She was a struggling assistant concierge from Smalltown, New York, and Luke Archer was a superstar as well as a client.

But none of that mattered anyway. Luke would go back to his penthouse far above her little office and never think of her again.

She just prayed Orin never found out about the VIP box.

Chapter 6

By the time the PR director released him from the meet and greet, Luke was sweating from the agony in his side. In case someone was watching, he strode down the hall to the trainers' office with his usual smooth stride, but it took all his willpower to do it. Reaching the door, he swung it open, stepped through, and slammed it behind him before he sagged against it.

"Jesus, it hurts like a son of a bitch," he said as Stan hurried around the desk to help Luke to a chair.

"It could be a cracked rib," Stan said. "Where's the worst of the pain?"

Luke pointed to the place where D'Olaway had connected with his rib cage. "I can't have a cracked rib. Not now."

Stan gently prodded at the spot, making Luke wince at what felt like daggers slashing into his flesh. The trainer shook his head. "You have to get an X-ray for this. If there's a broken bone in there, it could slice through a blood vessel or puncture a lung. You don't want to die for football."

"Maybe I do," Luke said, trying to get comfortable in the chair. "Go out in a blaze of glory."

Concern clouded Stan's eyes. "What's going on, son? Why are you talking crazy?"

Luke scrubbed his palms over his face, sending another bolt of agony into his side and making him hiss. "I'm not crazy. Just tired and pissed off that I let Rodney get to me. Davis was out of position, and I was so focused on making the pass that I forgot to check my blind side." In fact, he'd been coddling his shoulder so he didn't tweak it again with a misthrow, and that's why he'd neglected to keep an eye on his opponents. That pissed him off even more.

"If you don't get an X-ray, I'm going to sic Doc Tyler on you, and then Junius will know about your injury." Stan lifted a hand when Luke opened his mouth to object. "The X-ray is nonnegotiable. We'll find a private doctor who won't rat on you."

"Where do we find a doctor like that on short notice?" Luke asked. "Your closemouthed buddy Colangelo retired, and I'm not exactly hard to recognize."

"Let me think. I used to know another guy who would keep his mouth shut for cash, but I think he moved to Florida."

Luke started to lean back in the chair, but his side spasmed again. He gritted his teeth. Then he remembered Miranda Tate. Concierges had connections everywhere, so she might know a doctor who could keep secrets. Furthermore, discretion was her religion.

Except today was her day off, and she was with her family. Not to mention that he had no idea how to reach her. Maybe Doug would know, since he often worked out of the condo at the Pinnacle. Luke gingerly eased his cell phone out of his jacket pocket and hit Doug's speed dial.

His assistant answered instantly. "That was a major pass, Boss Ice. You are the man."

A smile tugged at Luke's mouth. "Thanks, buddy. I had to make up for losing to the Patriots."

"Ha! The Pats caught a lucky break with that one."

"You're not biased or anything," Luke said. "Listen, I need to get in touch with Miranda Tate at the Pinnacle. You have any idea how I can do that?"

"Was there a problem with the works? Sheldon swore he delivered everything to her personally."

"No problem at all. She brought her nephew to the game today. The kid had a blast."

"That's cool." He could hear the relief in Doug's voice before his assistant said, "I think you could reach her through the main concierge desk. Let me check out the listing online . . . yeah, here it is. I'll text you the number and her extension. The website says it forwards to her cell phone if she's not in the office."

"Thanks, buddy. You deserve a raise," Luke said, amused by the young man's cheerful energy, even as it made him feel ancient.

His assistant laughed.

"I'm serious, Doug. We'll talk about it tomorrow."

"You don't need to do that. It's an honor to work for you."

"Never tell your boss that. It undermines your negotiating power."

Luke disconnected and swiped to the text screen. Should he ruin the rest of Miranda's day? He looked at Stan's expression of implacable resolve and dialed the number.

Lulled by the rocking motion of the train carrying her home to Jersey City, Miranda drowsed in her seat while images of her amazing afternoon spun through her mind. Of course, most of them involved a broad-shouldered, blue-eyed quarterback with a dimple that sent waves of desire surging through her.

When her cell phone rang with the tune that indicated it was a concierge call, she sighed. Sofia was on duty today, and she wouldn't bother Miranda unless it was either a problem or a special request.

"Miranda Tate. How may I help you?" It was hard to inject her usual warmth and enthusiasm into her voice because she wanted to go back to daydreaming about Luke Archer.

"Hey, it's Luke Archer."

Miranda gasped and sat bolt upright on the bench seat. "H-hello."

"Look, I'm sorry to bother you when you're with your family, but I have a problem that I think you might be able to solve for me."

He was laying the Texas drawl on thick and slow, which made her want to fix everything that was wrong in his life. Not that there could be much that needed fixing. "I'll do all I can to help," she said with total sincerity.

"I got hit at the end of the game, and my overanxious trainer thinks I might have a cracked rib." She heard a squawk of protest in the background before Luke continued. "I need to get an X-ray on the QT. Since discretion is your middle name, I'm hoping you can help me with that." His voice held a smile, and she could easily picture the dimple that went with it.

Luckily, this was an easy assignment. Clients often needed to keep health issues confidential, so she had a trustworthy concierge doctor on call at all times. He had an office outfitted with the latest in medical technology, charged astronomical prices, and kept his mouth firmly shut. "Not a problem. Dr. Cavill's office is in the city."

There was a short silence. "I just want to be one hundred percent clear on this. Dr. Cavill will not tell anyone, not even his wife, that he saw me." Steel laced his words.

"The doctor has a clear understanding of privacy issues. He expects payment commensurate with that."

When Luke spoke, there was admiration in his voice. "Where do you keep your magic wand?"

Pleasure washed through Miranda. She'd impressed a man who had people waving magic wands for him all the time. "In my purse. It's safer than in my pocket, where it sometimes would go off accidentally and burn a hole in my clothes."

He gave a low, rumbling chuckle that made tingles of delight dance over her skin. "Give me two hours to get to Cavill's office."

"I'll confirm with the doctor and call you back."

She disconnected and hit Cavill's speed dial, arranging the meeting and stressing the need for secrecy. The doctor whistled when he heard who his visitor was. He had many wealthy, prominent patients, but Luke Archer's name impressed even him.

When Miranda dialed Luke back, he answered on the first ring. "Can Cavill do an MRI, too? My worrywart trainer wants to be sure there's no danger of further damage."

"He has a fully equipped office, and he's a very skilled doctor. He'll take excellent care of you."

"If you recommend him, I have no doubt of that." His tone turned serious. "I owe you, Miranda."

She thought of how she'd like to collect on that debt before she pushed away her fantasy of Luke's bare chest under her hands. "No, you don't. You're a resident of the Pinnacle, and the concierge service comes with the building. Frankly, this was easy."

"You have an interesting job," he said with a dry note in his voice.

"Interesting doesn't begin to describe it," she said with equal dryness. "But it has its perks, like introducing my nephew to the football player he idolizes."

"He's a cute kid. Nice manners, too." A pause. "The young fans are my favorites. They don't critique my on-field decisions." The smile was back in his voice, evoking a heart-fluttering vision of the dimple.

The train entered a tunnel with a whoosh of changing air pressure, and regret thickened in Miranda's chest. She was flattered that Luke seemed to want to prolong their conversation. "My train is about to pull into the station, so I'd better go."

"And I have to get to the doc. See you at the Pinnacle."

Since she'd only caught brief glimpses of him before the meeting with Orin, that seemed unlikely. However, a girl could dream.

"You can put your shirt on," the doctor said, stepping back from the examining table where Luke sat. Cavill had run three different kinds of imaging machines over and around Luke's torso, as well as doing a manual examination that had the quarterback clenching his jaw in order not to groan. The man was nothing if not thorough.

"The good news is that no ribs are cracked. The bad news is that you have inflammation of the cartilage, as well as periosteal and intramuscular bruising. It's going to hurt like hell for a week or so, and that's if you rest it. Which I understand may not be an option." The doctor's eyes held a hint of ironic humor. "So it's going to be pain meds and ice for you."

"How deep's the bruising, Doc?" Stan's forehead was creased with concern.

"Deep. What hit you? A Mack truck?"

"Rodney D'Olaway, which is about the same thing," Luke said, wincing as he gingerly slid his left arm into the shirtsleeve. He was stiffening up. "I guess you don't watch football."

The doctor shook his head. "All I can think about is the damage being done to the bodies on the field, which makes it unpleasant." He walked over to a standing desk and started typing on the computer there. "I'm going to give you a prescription for the pain, instructions on icing, and a thorough write-up on your condition with all the medical jargon. I will also recommend that you stay away from the field for ten days, but I imagine you will ignore that."

Stan snorted in agreement.

Inserting his right arm in the shirtsleeve was slightly less painful, but Luke decided to leave off his jacket. As he buttoned his shirt, he scanned the doctor's office. The room itself was decorated more like the Bellwether Club than a medical facility, while the extensive array of equipment was cutting-edge. Cavill must do all right with his practice.

The doctor himself was about Luke's age, which initially had been a concern, but Cavill wore his crisp white lab coat with the kind of confidence that arises only from skill, knowledge, and experience. Not to mention that Miranda had recommended him. Luke had come to trust her so completely that it surprised him.

The doctor stopped typing, and a printer began to spit out pages.

"You don't have a sign outside, so how do patients find you?" Luke asked, buttoning his cuffs.

"My business is all word-of-mouth," Cavill said, picking up the printed pages and inserting them in an electric stapler. "And it keeps the paparazzi away if they don't know where to stalk me."

"So does Miranda Tate send you a lot of patients?" Luke planted his feet on the floor and eased off the examining table.

Cavill slanted Luke a look. "I can't tell you that."

"Okay, so can you tell me about Miranda Tate?"

"She's very discreet and very good at her job. And a nice lady."

"You have a mutual admiration society." For some reason, that annoyed Luke. "What about her boss?"

"Her boss?"

"Spindle."

The doctor's expression altered subtly. "I don't deal with him."

"Don't or won't?"

Cavill gave Luke another of those assessing looks before he said, "Both." He held out the printed papers.

Luke's feeling about Spindle had just been confirmed. The man was a weasel. Luke took the sheets from the doctor and folded them in half.

Cavill raised his eyebrows. "Don't you want to review the instructions?"

"Stan knows more about this than I do." Luke handed his trainer the papers. "Bottom line is pain meds and on-field decision making don't mix."

"Let me emphasize one point," the doctor said as he pulled his stethoscope off and stuffed it in his coat pocket. "Severe pain can cloud your judgment almost as much as the meds do. If you don't stress the muscles for a few days, the pain will be less when you start playing again. So you might want to give it a rest in order to play better."

The doctor was right. This kind of pain made him avoid moving in certain ways, and that limited his options. Not to mention that the press was allowed to come to the Thursday practice. Some of those reporters had been around football players longer than Luke had been alive. They could spot an injury a mile away. Better to admit he was taking time off after D'Olaway's hit than to have the newshounds speculate he was covering up something more serious.

Not that he would stay away from the Empire Center. He could watch film and work on the new plays Junius wanted to institute with his teammates.

"You've convinced me, Doc," Luke said. "I'll take a couple of days off."

"A couple is better than nothing." Cavill grinned, which made him look younger. "I don't think I had anything to do with your decision, though."

"How do I take care of payment?" Luke asked.

"The paperwork goes to Miranda, and you pay her," Cavill explained. "Another layer of discretion."

And she would add her commission. That's how it worked with concierges. Luke didn't begrudge her the payment. She'd saved him from a lot of official crap that the league required team doctors to go through when a player was injured. All he had to do now was have a chat with Junius and tell the reporters he had some bruising from the tackle.

He thought of the twinge in his shoulder. If it happened again, he was coming back to see Cavill.

In the limo, he and Stan worked out their strategy for Farrell. Stan was going to call the head coach and express his concern about Luke's condition, without mention of the visit to Dr. Cavill. He would advise Farrell to convince his quarterback to take some time off. Farrell would call Luke to tell him he needed to rest. Luke would object before agreeing. That way the head coach would credit himself with persuading Luke to let the bruising heal.

The limo pulled up at the Pinnacle's private entrance. Luke ducked out of the car, which headed on to New Jersey to drop Stan off. As Luke stepped into the elevator to his penthouse, he dialed Miranda's number.

"Miranda Tate. How may I help you?" she answered.

There was something about her voice. It poured smooth and rich out of the phone, like heavy cream, and made him picture the perfect, pillowy curve of her lips.

"It's Luke Archer. I wanted to thank you for setting me up with Dr. Cavill. He's a great guy."

"I'm glad you were pleased with his service." That was her professional response. Her tone changed to a more personal one when she asked, "Are you all right? Or is that top secret?"

"No cracks, no breaks. Just bruising. It'll heal quickly." That was *his* professional answer. He added, "Here's the secret part—I'm taking a few days off to speed up the process."

The elevator door opened into his entrance hall, and he wedged his foot against it to keep it that way.

"That sounds wise. If you need anything while you're resting, let me know." With ringing sincerity, she added, "Thank you again for a truly memorable day."

He wanted to have done something real to earn her gratitude. "You're welcome. And that's the last word on it."

"If you say so." He heard amusement in her tone, and then she disconnected.

He stepped out of the elevator and walked into the living room. Trevor was sprawled on the couch in front of the flat-screen television, his bare feet propped on the glass top of the coffee table. Beside his feet sat a bottle of Gran Patrón tequila, a dish of salt, a plate of limes, and two shot glasses, one of which held a few drops of clear liquid.

Trevor pointed the remote at the set, muting the sound before he turned to his brother. "You were quite the hero in the last minutes of the game, bro. Such poise and precision. But then, you're the Iceman. Nothing shakes you out of your cleats." He leaned forward to pick up the bottle of tequila, filling both glasses. "We should celebrate your win."

Anger spilled through Luke so fast and hot that it shocked him. He swallowed it back down. "Thanks, Trev, but you know I don't drink during the season."

His brother gave him a look of exaggerated surprise. "You were pretty loaded on Monday night, so I thought you'd loosened up on that rule."

The anger simmered. "That was a mistake." In more ways than one.

"So you can drink with two strangers, but not with your brother. The hell with you." Trevor pinched up some salt to sprinkle on the back of his hand. He licked the salt off and tossed back the tequila, finishing up by sucking on a wedge of lime. He slammed the shot glass onto the table so hard that Luke thought it would break. Miraculously, both table and glass stayed intact.

Luke combed his fingers through his hair as guilt pricked at him. "How about we take the party out to the fire pit?"

The guilt jabbed even harder when Trevor's face lit up. "Now, that's more like it. You gotta celebrate the good times in life." Luke could hear the slurring in his brother's voice now. He checked the level of the tequila and figured his brother had had several shots already. Luke needed to get some food into him.

"But you can't drink tequila without salsa and chips. And maybe some quesadillas." Luke headed for the kitchen. His housekeeper made fresh salsa for him, and he could throw together chicken and cheese on a whole wheat tortilla.

Trevor followed him, bouncing off the door frame into the kitchen before he plunked down at the table. "You know, there were two *SI* swimsuit models in the box with us," Trevor said. "Man, their legs just go on forever."

Luke winced as he rummaged around in the refrigerator. He hadn't known who else had tickets for the box he'd put Trevor in. He should have been more careful after the incident on Monday, but his brother had never been such a letch before. "Yeah," he said, setting out quesadilla ingredients. "They're paid to have long legs."

"Probably paid by the inch," Trevor said, snorting out a laugh. "You ever dated one of them?"

"Once or twice, maybe." In those heady early days of fame, he'd dated actresses, models, and the daughters of very rich men. None of them had interested him as much as football.

"That's as often as you date anyone," Trevor pointed out. "Once or twice. Have you ever made it to three times?"

"Not in a while." Luke shrugged. "I have other things to focus on."

"And I don't?" Trevor's tone was bitter.

"You're married, Trev. You found the right woman."

"Sometimes I'm not so sure." Trevor stared down at the shot glass in his hand.

"What's going—" Luke's cell phone rang. He dropped the cheese grater and pulled out his phone. It was the head coach. "Damn, I've got to take this. Be back in a few."

He swiped "Answer" and walked toward his office. "Hey, Junius."

"Stan called." Junius's voice was brusque. "He says you got more banged up by Rodney D'Olaway than you let on."

"It stiffened up on me." Luke kept his tone easy. "It's just bruising, though. I got it looked at."

"I want you to give it a rest so you can heal faster."

Now Luke had to read from the script. It was easy, because he'd said the same things before when he meant them. "I'll heal fine without any rest."

"You're taking the week off, including the game."

Shock ripped through Luke like a barbed wire fence. "No way, Junius. It's a bruise. I've played with worse." He was no longer faking his objection.

"When you were younger and less valuable. I can't afford to have you get seriously injured because you've been slowed down by this one."

Well, at least Junius had called him valuable. But old.

The coach continued. "We're playing the worst team in the conference, so it's a good time to give Brandon some game experience."

It was hard to argue with either point. Brandon Pitch was the backup quarterback—a young, talented, but inconsistent player whom they'd drafted in the second round a year ago. He needed some game exposure. It might settle him down.

Luke cursed mentally. "It's your call, Coach, but I'm capable of playing right now. How about I take two days to rest and practice on Wednesday?"

"Luke, we have a chance at the Super Bowl, and I'm not going to risk it by playing you against a crap team when you're hurt. I don't want to see you on the field or in the weight room for a week."

"Yes, sir." Luke heard the note of finality in Junius's voice. In fact, he found it in himself to admire the new coach for overriding him. "What are we going to tell the press?"

"That I'm resting my star and giving my rookie some seasoning. The reporters will fill in the blanks about what team I'm playing my rookie against. They won't suspect anything else, especially after your postgame appearance today. No one guessed you were hurt." There was disapproval in the statement.

"Because it's not serious."

Junius hung up.

Luke walked into the living room, picked up the full shot glass, and tossed back the tequila before he threw the glass into the fireplace. It shattered with a satisfying explosion of glass shards.

"Holy shit, what was that?" Trevor came to the kitchen door and stared at his brother.

"I've been benched."

Chapter 7

At six thirty Monday evening, Miranda slumped back in her desk chair, thankful for a lull in her noon-to-ten shift. Mondays were always busy because everyone woke up and decided they needed to get their week planned. It generally took them until noon to figure out what they wanted to do, and that's when the phone started ringing. She loved this shift, because she only overlapped with Orin for a few hours, and it was lucrative when it came to commissions and tips. All money that could be put toward the loan on her brother's cheese-making equipment.

But it was exhausting. She grabbed her water bottle and gulped down a couple of mouthfuls. She still had to get theater tickets and some dinner reservations for next weekend, but those could be taken care of later when the phone was less demanding.

She groaned as the ringer went off again. She couldn't even pretend to be busy and let someone else pick it up, because it was coming through on her direct line. Sitting forward, she checked the caller ID. *Luke Archer.* She grabbed the phone.

"I thought I told you no more thank-yous," he drawled in that disarming Texas accent.

She had sent him a note as soon as she got in that day. "My conscience wouldn't rest until I'd written a proper note." And she'd hoped it would induce one last encounter with the gut-meltingly gorgeous quarterback. Even his voice on the phone was enough to make her breath quicken.

"A conscience can be inconvenient." He paused, which gave her time to wonder which part of his life he referred to. "But I don't get a lot of handwritten letters, so I appreciated it."

Again, she felt the fizz of gratification. She'd given something unusual to a living legend. And it was such a little thing. "Then it has done its job."

Another pause before he said, "I want to take a tour of New York. Tomorrow. See some cultural stuff."

All these years of living in the city and he hadn't had time to see the sights? Football was a demanding mistress.

"Of course. Are you interested in art, performances, or historical landmarks?" She was already flipping through her mental guidebook.

"Not landmarks. I've seen the Statue of Liberty and the Empire State Building. How about museums?" He sounded oddly tentative.

"Absolutely. I can set up lunch and dinner and add a show of some kind. Just let me know how many people will be accompanying you."

"Only one."

"Any food allergies or ethnic cuisine preferences?" Miranda had her stylus poised over her tablet.

"I'll eat anything. How about you?"

"I'm sorry?"

"I need a tour guide, and I'd like to hire you."

The stylus clattered onto the tablet's screen. "Me?" she squeaked as a mixture of shock and excitement rippled through her.

"I'd like you to show me the things I've never had time to see before."

"But I have to work tomorrow." She tried to think of how she could get out of it. Turning down a whole day with Luke Archer would be downright painful.

"I'll call Spindle and tell him I consider this part of your job as a concierge. And I'll give him VIP box tickets this time."

"I'd have to get someone to cover for me."

"Let your boss deal with that. It's his responsibility."

That was a little high-handed, but he wasn't wrong. She went back into her professional concierge mode. "Well, of course, I'd be happy to accommodate you, as long as Orin approves it. Shall I send you a list of possibilities to choose from?"

"No, surprise me."

That didn't make her job easier. "Shall I arrange transportation?"

"I have a limo. What time do we start?"

"Generally, museums open at ten."

"I'll see you then."

Miranda hung up. The most famous quarterback in the world had chosen *her* to show him New York City. She wanted to do a jig around her office. Instead, she forced herself to sit with her hands on her desk and breathe normally.

This was nothing more than a client availing himself of the concierge service. She shouldn't feel this bubbling elation, and she certainly couldn't let Luke Archer suspect that his request made anticipation burn through her veins.

She forced herself to pick up her tablet and stylus, and then the nerves hit her. What on earth would a superstar quarterback want to see?

As Luke started to shove his phone back in his pocket, it rang again. Gavin Miller's name appeared on the screen. Luke frowned at it for a moment. His mood had shifted from restless to anticipatory, and he didn't want to screw with that.

But he might as well find out what the writer wanted.

"Archer, I hear that hit knocked the stuffing out of you."

"Just some bruising. Nothing serious."

"Is that why you're sitting on the sideline for Sunday's game? Some bruising?" Miller sounded skeptical.

Luke clamped down on his annoyance. "Coach wants to give Pitch some real game seasoning."

"I thought I'd check in on your progress with our little wager."

Leave it to Miller to use every possible irritant. "No progress. I have a football season to get through first."

"Let's see, if you make it to the Super Bowl, you'll have used up roughly four of your twelve months. You're a confident man."

"I don't like to split my focus."

"All football, all the time, eh?" Miller chuckled. "You must be a dull date. Except perhaps for a cheerleader."

The writer knew where to aim. "I can talk horses and cattle, too."

"So you're looking for a country gal. That would go with the white picket fence and the sons. No, I remember now . . . you want daughters."

"I want to be left in peace is what I want," Luke snapped.

"Well, since we're talking nothing but football, should I bet on the Empire to go all the way?"

That was familiar territory. "You're big into gambling."

"A little risk keeps life interesting."

Luke decided to dish out some of what Miller was giving him. "How's the writer's block?"

There was a tense silence before the other man said, "It's breaking my back, boyo. It's strangling my spirit."

While Luke didn't understand writer's block, he knew how he was feeling about being benched, so he cut Miller some slack. "Sorry to hear that."

"By the way, I think Trainor is ahead of us. He's already showing signs of being frustrated by a woman."

For a moment, Luke's competitive streak reared its head, giving him a shot of negative adrenaline at the thought of being beaten by the CEO. "Sounds like he already had a draft pick in mind."

"I don't believe so. At the Bellwether Club, he seemed like a man who was disillusioned with the entire fair sex."

That reminded Luke of what was required to win the wager, and he decided he was well out of it for the time being. "I wish him luck."

"Speaking of luck, what's your answer about your team's chances for the Super Bowl?"

"We're going all the way."

Miller made an exasperated sound. "Dispense with the sports clichés and give me a real answer."

"I. Just. Did." Luke put steel into his voice.

Miller whistled softly. "I'll be placing my money on you for the win, then."

The writer hung up, and Luke tossed the phone onto the sofa, grimacing as the careless motion sent pain slicing through his side. Miller had turned his mood sour with the crack about being a dull date. No one had ever complained, but Luke didn't kid himself about what most women wanted from him. It wasn't sparkling conversation.

His expedition tomorrow was aimed at more than just getting his mind off the fact that he couldn't play football for the next week. He was tired of having people like Trevor and Miller make him feel uneducated. He could learn culture the same way he had learned football.

Spending the day listening to Miranda Tate's silky smooth voice talk about whatever she would be talking about seemed like a pleasant way to ease into the project. He pictured her curvy body next to him on the leather seat of the limo and again felt a flash of arousal. Nothing wrong with having that bonus to add interest to the tour.

And she would keep his secret if he revealed his ignorance about whatever paintings she showed him.

The prospect of Miranda's company put a smile on his face. He walked back out onto the terrace, where his brother sat by the fire pit, drinking a beer.

"Thank God," Trevor said.

"What?"

"The smile is a major improvement. You've been as pissed off as a castrated bull since you got benched."

"Maybe you shouldn't remind me about that if you want me to keep smiling." Luke lowered himself into an armchair. If he was careful, the bruises did nothing more than twinge.

"So why are you smiling?"

"I found something to do tomorrow."

"Hey, I'm sorry I set up my meetings for tomorrow," Trevor said. "If I'd known . . ." He trailed off.

He *had* known. Tuesdays were Luke's day off. And neither one of them had expected Luke to have every day this week off.

"It's okay, Trev." Luke leaned forward to grab his water bottle, and agony wrapped around his rib cage. "Oof!"

"Still sore?" Trevor asked. "Have a beer for medicinal purposes."

"I'd need something stronger than beer."

"There's always tequila." Trevor grinned. "You used to put that away like a champ."

"If you get up and get it, I'm in," Luke said.

Since he was forced to take the week off, he might as well take advantage of it.

Chapter 8

On Tuesday morning, Miranda waited by Luke Archer's private eleva-tor, listening for the hum that would signal its descent. She tapped her toe against the granite floor and mentally reviewed their itinerary one more time, debating whether she should swap out the Frick for the Museum of Natural History. But he'd said he wanted culture, so she was going to give him culture. If he got bored, she could adjust.

She'd changed her outfit three times before she'd decided on a peach silk top that hugged her hips, slim-legged taupe trousers, and taupe leather wedges that were comfortable for walking. Over it, she had added a cashmere tweed blazer in soft beiges and grays, one of those splurge purchases she'd never regretted. She had tried to strike a balance between her professional service persona, which required blending into the background, and her desire to look pretty while spending the day with a gorgeous man. After all, she was only human.

The elevator kicked into action, and nervousness tightened her throat. What would Luke expect of her? Did he want information or conversation? Would he like the restaurants she'd chosen? The biggest question of all: Would he think she'd lost her mind when he heard what she'd booked as the conclusion to his day of high culture?

When the elevator doors opened, she had to swallow her gasp. The waves of his hair caught the lighting of the elevator in a way that made them glow gold. Dressed in worn jeans, a maroon T-shirt, and a black leather jacket, he looked more like a model than a football player. His cool blue eyes warmed slightly when he caught sight of her, and that slow smile brought out his single dimple.

Speech deserted Miranda as every nerve ending in her body yearned for the man in front of her.

"Mornin'," he said, pulling a Yankees baseball cap out of his pocket and fitting it over the gleaming hair.

"Is that—" Her voice was a croak, so she stopped to clear her throat. "Is that your disguise?"

His dimple deepened. "I have Ray-Bans, too."

She let her gaze roam over the height and breadth of him. "It's going to take a lot more than sunglasses to make you incognito."

He grunted. "I gave up on anonymity a long time ago."

She understood. That's why he lived at an exclusive place like the Pinnacle, used a helicopter or limo to travel around the city, and had a full-time assistant. It was impossible for him to lead a normal life here, so he used his money to buy some privacy.

"Well, people won't expect to see you at the Metropolitan Museum of Art, so maybe they'll leave you alone."

His smile disappeared, and she saw a muscle tighten in his jaw. What was it about her innocuous comment that bothered him?

He put on his sunglasses, making his expression even harder to interpret. "So that's our first stop?"

She started toward the door. "Yes, we're doing a whirlwind tour that includes Van Gogh, Degas, Henry the Eighth's armor, the Temple of Dendur, the Chinese Garden Court, Tiffany windows, and the Frank Lloyd Wright living room." As he held the door, she smiled up at him, hoping to coax his dimple back. "Because those are my favorite things at the museum." And she thought he would like the variety.

The corners of his lips turned up slightly, but all she could really see was her reflection in the lenses of his dark glasses. "Is that going to take an hour or all day?" he asked.

"However long you want it to," she said, nodding to the limo's chauffeur, who had opened the car door for her. She'd already given the driver their itinerary. She started to slide across the backseat, then swiveled to sit on the seat facing the rear of the limo. It seemed more conversational and businesslike that way.

Until Luke bent to enter the limo, his shoulders filling the doorway and blocking out the autumn sunlight. He slid onto the seat carefully, reminding her that he was injured. Settling with a creak of leather against leather, he stretched out his legs so they slanted diagonally across the space between her seat and his. It was the only way he could fit comfortably, but it emphasized the physical presence of the man. The interior of the limo suddenly felt very intimate.

He removed his sunglasses and baseball cap and massaged the bridge of his nose.

"Would you rather postpone the tour?" Miranda asked, noticing circles under his eyes.

"No." His reply was sharp. He gave her an apologetic look. "Trevor and I knocked off a bottle of tequila last night."

She debated whether to bring up the public speculation about the possibility that a secret injury was keeping him out of the next game.

He stared out the window and answered her question for her. "Being benched doesn't sit well with me, so I decided to deal with it the wrong way."

She'd wondered how Luke felt about not playing. "I hope Dr. Cavill didn't do anything he shouldn't have."

He turned back to her with a rueful grimace. "No, I brought it on myself." He shrugged and winced. "My backup needs some seasoning, and this is a good time to give it to him."

Miranda was relieved that she hadn't contributed to Luke's unhappiness. "Does it hurt a lot?"

"No, it's just—" He stopped and shook his head. "Yeah, even though it's just bruised, it hurts like a gore from a steer's horn when I move in certain ways. I couldn't give my best when I feel like this, so the coach isn't wrong." He looked her in the eye. "This is all just between you and me."

"Of course." He'd decided to trust her with sensitive information. That sent warmth seeping through her. "Is there anything you can do to help it heal?"

"Go on a cultural tour." He smiled, but it didn't reach his eyes.

So the subject was closed. She pulled her tablet out of her gray Kate Spade knockoff tote. "You have some choices about what museums to go to. I wasn't sure what kind of culture you were interested in. Would you prefer the Museum of Natural History or the Frick Collection? The Frick is as interesting for its building as its art, since it was originally Mr. Frick's Fifth Avenue mansion."

"Let's go for art all the way."

"Okay." Miranda blew out a breath and considered the schedule. She didn't know how long he would want to look at each work of art, so she'd booked lunch reservations at three different locations. Now she could cancel the one near the Museum of Natural History. She swiped around on her tablet's screen to take care of that.

When she looked up, he was watching her with a faint smile. He said, "You look as nervous as a rookie the morning of his first NFL game."

"I'm more a behind-the-scenes kind of person. I've never taken someone like you on a guided tour before."

"Someone like me?" He raised his eyebrows.

"You know—" She waved her hand vaguely.

"You mean a jock who doesn't know anything about culture?"

Surprise zinged through her. Was that how he saw himself? "No, that's not at all what I meant."

He waited.

She wasn't going to explain that he was so spectacular it was hard to draw in enough oxygen when shut into an enclosed space with him. "I meant that you are practically a national treasure, so it's a little intimidating to be responsible for your entertainment for an entire day."

A shadow crossed his face. "I was born with a certain talent for throwing a ball and taking a hit. I'm not curing cancer. I'm not feeding third world nations. I'm just an entertainer."

That word didn't fit him. "Frank Sinatra was an entertainer. You're more like a gladiator."

That made his eyes glint with amusement. "Okay, a gladiator, but they were just there to entertain the Romans."

"And you give a lot of money to people who cure cancer and feed third world nations," Miranda said. She'd spent far too much of her limited free time googling Luke Archer.

"I have enough money to *buy* a couple of third world nations, so that's no skin off my back." He leaned forward so she could see the scruff of blond beard he hadn't shaved that morning and the tiny squint lines at the corners of his eyes. "I put my pants on one leg at a time, just like everyone else."

"Yes, but you probably don't lose your balance," Miranda murmured.

Luke gave her a raised eyebrow, but she saw the corners of his mouth twitch. However, he didn't let her stop him from making his point. "I'm just another client, and you're just doing your usual excellent job."

She heard the compliment through a haze created by the scent of his lemony aftershave, the nearness of his sharply sculpted lips, and the breadth of his shoulders filling her entire field of vision. She wanted to shift forward just two inches so she could brush back the gilded lock of hair that fell onto his forehead. It would feel like silk, she was sure.

Instead, she hugged her tablet to her chest. It would be blasphemy to touch a legend without his permission. "Thank you. I hope you'll enjoy today," she said. Clichés were always useful when your brain refused to function.

He also settled back in his seat and crossed his arms, making the muscles in his chest shift under the fabric of his T-shirt. Now she wanted to flatten her palms against that wall of pure power, as he said, "Since my life is on the Internet for anyone to read, tell me something about you. Where are you from?"

Miranda felt a slight flush climb her cheeks as he mentioned the Internet, but his question was innocuous enough. "I was raised on a dairy farm in upstate New York."

"You?" His gaze skimmed over her body. She felt it almost as a touch. "On a farm?"

"Yup, I can milk a cow in nine minutes flat." But she knew why he was skeptical. She'd worked hard to fashion a veneer of city sophistication over her rural upbringing.

He looked at her neatly manicured hands. "When was the last time you milked a cow?"

"Last year. I like to keep in practice, just in case." Theo had challenged her to a milking contest since he also didn't believe his fancy aunt Miranda had ever milked a cow. Even she was surprised at how quickly she'd found the rhythm of it again. She'd let Theo win, of course.

"Just in case what?" His dimple was starting to show.

"Oh, I don't know, an apocalyptic failure of the power grid or something. I could survive on milk and cream."

"Or trade it for eggs."

She nodded, glad he was entertained by her whimsy. "So what would your survival skill be in an apocalypse?"

"Huh," he said, dropping his chin to his chest as he considered her question. "I could probably throw a spear to bring down game."

She had a vision of him dressed in a wolf skin, the muscles in his shoulders and arms flexing and rippling as he sent a spear streaking through the air toward his unsuspecting prey. "Okay, with that talent, you're invited to join my postapocalyptic enclave."

He huffed out a chuckle. "Does your brother still live on the family farm?"

She nodded. "It's not an easy life, but Dennis and Patty like it. I worry about Theo, though. The school up there isn't very academic, and he's a bright child."

"My parents are teachers, and they've always said that a kid can get as much education as he wants, no matter what school he's in." Luke fiddled with his sunglasses as he said it.

"That's reassuring, but it's not so much the teachers I'm concerned about as the kids. When I went to school there, it wasn't cool to be smart. I don't want him to hide his intelligence in order to fit in."

"Is that what you did?"

The man was far too perceptive. "No, but I'm female, so I didn't mind being considered a nerd." Well, not too much. There had been times when she'd longed to be part of the popular group, but she hadn't been willing to change who she was just to belong.

"So you weren't a cheerleader." He sounded almost approving.

She shook her head. "You probably knew a lot of those." She had discovered from her research that he'd been a standout athlete from high school on. Picturing him with a buxom cheerleader on each arm provoked a misplaced stab of jealousy.

"Yeah." There was no enthusiasm in his response. The jealousy evaporated.

"You're from Texas." She gave in to the urge to know more about him than just the facts everyone read on Google. "Do you miss it?"

"I go back summers, so I satisfy my taste for wide open spaces then."

"Is space what you miss the most? I can see how New York wouldn't give you much of that."

"One of the reasons I bought the condo at the Pinnacle was because it looks out toward the Statue of Liberty and the Verrazano Bridge. Makes me feel like I have some room."

She'd seen his presence on a football field, the way he dominated the swirl of bodies around him. He probably did feel the need for space. "It's a beautiful view."

He gave her that long, assessing look of his. He focused every ounce of his attention on her, and it was a lot to bear up under, but it also made her feel as though he believed she was worth it. It was probably a well-rehearsed trick of his, and she needed to resist the illusion.

"I want you to talk to me straight," he said.

"What do you mean?"

"That comment about the beautiful view. That's concierge-speak. Just talk. Like I'm your friend." He softened his command with a wink.

She felt weirdly disappointed at his request. Even friendship with this man was a gift beyond any normal expectation. What more did she want?

She opened her mouth and then shut it again when she realized she was about to spout a cliché.

He unfolded his arms and held out his hand to her. "Friends."

As she put her hand in his, a little shiver of heat sizzled through her. His skin was warm and dry. His grip was strong but not overwhelming. He probably muted it when shaking hands with mere mortals.

"Friends." She returned his grip and found herself wanting to hold on because his strength was so reassuring. If you needed him, he wouldn't let go of you. That had to be another one of those illusions he created. As a quarterback, he needed people to trust him.

The car glided to a stop, and he released her hand. The driver's voice came through the speaker. "We're at the entrance, Ms. Tate."

Luke slid his sunglasses back into place.

"You shouldn't need those," Miranda said. "I arranged for us to come in a back entrance. I figured that would lessen the chance that a photographer would spot you going in."

"Thanks," he said, but his voice held a tinge of disappointment.

"Would you rather go in the front? We can."

He shook his head. "You're right."

The driver opened the door and stood waiting. Luke shifted his legs out of Miranda's way and offered his hand for support.

She kept her hands on her tote bag as she scooted sideways on the seat. "I'm not going to aggravate your injuries."

"You'll aggravate me more if you don't take my hand."

She gave in and laid her hand in his, savoring the way his long fingers wrapped around hers. But she kept her weight balanced away from him, stooping to back out of the door so he didn't have to twist in his seat.

A cloud of annoyance scudded across his face, the mirrored Ray-Bans adding to the formidable effect. "That's called a pass fake," he said when she tugged her hand away.

As soon as she stood up, he swung his legs out, planted his worn tan cowboy boots on the pavement, and unfolded his body with a grunt.

"That's why I didn't lean on you," she said.

"When it's you doing the leaning, it feels good." His drawl was like molasses, slow-moving and scrumptious.

"Do you always flirt with your friends?" she asked, struggling against the slide of his seduction.

"When they're pretty."

Miranda didn't buy that. He was accustomed to stunningly beautiful. "Well, let's keep this on a friends-only basis." Otherwise she would fall completely under his spell.

He covered his gleaming hair with the Yankees cap again. "We'll see how it goes."

She choked on thin air as his implication sank in. Her body wanted it to go one place, while her brain knew it had to stay in another. But she'd handled flirtations from clients before. It shouldn't make her feel this flustered.

Marching briskly to an unmarked door, she punched in the temporary security code she'd been given by the museum's PR director. Luke reached around her to pull the door open, so the sleeve of his jacket brushed her shoulder, and his big body angled close to her. If she leaned a little to the right, she would come up against his muscular chest.

She practically ran through the door.

Luke followed her into an empty, utilitarian corridor and looked around. "How'd you get access to this?"

"Oh, I've arranged enough VIP tours of the museum that the PR director trusts me." In addition, she might have hinted that Luke would make a donation if he enjoyed his visit to the Met, as some of her other clients had.

She pulled up the map she'd been e-mailed and started in the direction that would lead them to the Temple of Dendur. He strode along beside her, his boots thudding on the commercial-grade carpeting. She tried hard not to notice the subtle creak of his leather jacket, or the way the worn denim of his jeans outlined his thigh muscles.

They passed through a catering kitchen used to serve the parties that took place in the venue and emerged on the stone platform beside the ancient Egyptian temple. She felt bad that Luke couldn't approach it from the front to get the full effect of the dramatic setting, but this offered less risk of him being recognized and bothered.

Still, the huge exhibition space with its vast ceiling and curtain wall of glass made a strong impact. Luke stopped and whistled softly as he took in his surroundings.

"The big pool of water surrounding the temple is supposed to represent the Nile River," Miranda said, drawing on the research she'd done. "The decorative carvings on the base of the temple are stylized papyrus and lotus plants."

Luke started walking toward the front of the temple.

"It was built in 10 BC under the rule of Caesar Augustus," Miranda continued. As they came around to face the entrance with its two tall columns, she said, "The winged disk is—"

"The symbol of the sky god Horus," Luke finished for her. He gave her a slanted smile. "As a kid, I got interested in the Egyptians. Some of it stuck."

"And you let me babble on about it. A *friend* would tell me to shut up." Miranda worried that she had sounded patronizing with her mini lecture.

He sauntered into the first room of the temple, his gaze skimming the carvings of pharaohs making offerings to the gods Isis and Osiris. "I don't know anything about this temple. I just recognize some of the symbols. Like that one means *pharaoh*."

"Which is more than I knew."

He shoved his hands into his jeans pockets and looked down at her with a gleam in his eye. "Well, the truth is, I like to listen to your voice."

"My voice? What do you mean?"

"It's all smooth and soothing. It just kind of washes over you."

There he went, nudging things past the friendship line. She didn't know whether to flirt back or try to keep things on a client-concierge basis. It would be easier if the molecules of her body didn't do a jig every time he smiled at her. "You mean my voice puts you to sleep."

He shook his head. "No, it makes you want to sort of bathe in it, like a hot shower."

A totally inappropriate picture of Luke standing naked under a showerhead sprang into her mind. He would rival any of the perfectly muscled statues in the European sculpture gallery. Heat cascaded through her, and she thrust the thought away. Better to keep the flirting to a minimum before she did something she regretted. "Thank you. I think."

She turned away to drag her mind off her fantasy of Luke's nude body and noticed that a couple of people were casting speculative looks at him and whispering to each other. He was either oblivious or ignoring them, because he continued to examine the bas-relief carvings on the temple walls.

"We'd better get moving," she said under her breath. "I think some adoring fans have spotted you."

Resignation cast a cloud over his face. He nodded and walked out of the temple. "Keep walking," he said, taking her elbow to propel her forward. She forced her attention away from the delicious power of his touch. "It's when you stand still that they get up the nerve to pounce."

"I want you to see it from the front, though," she said, veering toward the huge reflecting pool.

He let her guide him to a vantage point that showed the entire vista of seated statues on the edge of the pool, the temple's entrance gate, and the temple itself. She loved the stark majesty of it.

"You're right. It's worth the risk of getting ambushed by autograph hounds," he said. His face was alight with the kind of wonder she'd hoped to evoke. She let him stand there, drinking it in, as she kept an eye out for fans. The people who'd been staring at him in the temple were coming closer, so she tugged him gently in the opposite direction.

"We're going to duck into another side door and head for the Astor Chinese Garden Court," she said. "That ought to shake them off."

She got him through the door and into the staff elevator. "How did they notice you so fast?"

He shrugged with that gleam in his eye. "My charisma."

She took a step away from him and tilted her head. He had his shoulder propped against the elevator wall, and one booted ankle crossed over the other. He had more than charisma. He made her want to run her hands over every inch of his body. "I guess there is something there," she said, letting herself respond in kind this once.

The elevator slowed, and he pushed off the wall to look down at her. "Too bad the elevator ride wasn't longer."

The pale blue of his eyes no longer looked like a glacier. Now they burned with the scorching flame of an acetylene torch as it sliced through metal. Miranda felt the sear right down to her bones. Their flirting had taken on an unexpected edge that made her nervous. Because despite the city-girl facade she'd built for herself, she didn't have much experience with city men. She just didn't have the time. And she had a feeling that her romantic encounters with community college boys hadn't come close to preparing her for someone like Luke Archer.

As the door slid open, she held up her hand like a stop signal, hoping he didn't notice its slight waver as her blood pulsed hard in her veins. "Flirting again."

He laid his big, square palm against the doorjamb to hold it open for her. Miranda sidled past him and pulled in a shaky breath before she resumed her tour guide duties. "The Chinese Garden Court is modeled on a seventeenth-century courtyard and features Ming dynasty wooden furn—"

He took her wrist and pulled her to a stop in the hallway. "You're ignoring me."

"That would be impossible," she said.

"Okay, you're ignoring what I said." His thumb was stroking across the fragile skin on the inside of her wrist, which sent shivers of sensation dancing up her arm.

She could barely think straight, so she blurted out an honest answer. "I don't understand what you're doing. I'm supposed to be your tour guide and your temporary friend. I'm not your . . . your date."

"Why can't you be all three?" he asked.

Chapter 9

She stared at him like he was speaking a foreign language. He guessed he couldn't blame her. It was just that when they'd been closed up in the limo together, he'd become more and more conscious of how sexy she was. There was that smooth, creamy voice, but she also had shining dark hair that he wanted to bury his hands in, brown eyes that held a softness he found rare in this city of hard edges, and a lush mouth that made him want to taste it.

Not to mention the curves outlined by her fitted pants and silky top. Although her clothes led his mind in interesting directions, he had to admit there was nothing suggestive about them. She wasn't showing cleavage or midriff, as did so many of the women who sought him out.

He liked to watch her dodge and weave, especially when she decided to give some sass back to him. And if she stopped dodging, the day might get very interesting indeed.

For now, he released her wrist, regretting the loss of her warm, soft skin under his thumb. "Okay, back to friendship. For now."

She gave him a beaming smile that held equal parts relief and regret. The second one was promising. He followed her through the circular moon gate and into a serene oriental garden. She led him around as she pointed and talked about imperial kilns and yin-yang principles.

Spotting a bench standing in a sunbeam, he took her elbow and tugged her toward it. "Let's sit down for a minute and soak up the atmosphere."

"I thought you had to keep moving," she said.

"This doesn't look like the kind of place football fans hang out," he said, settling on the hard stone bench.

She perched a good foot away from him, her tablet balanced on her lap. The ramrod-straight line of her back set up a nice contrast to the gentle curve of her bottom. He imagined how it would fit in the cup of his hands and felt a twist of tension between his legs. So he pulled his gaze upward. He liked that she'd let her hair flow loose, not in the ponytail she wore at the Pinnacle. He missed the softness of women during the season.

"I'm not a football fan, and I would still recognize you," she said.

"But would you want my autograph?"

"For Theo, I might. People will dare a lot of things for kids." She scanned around the quiet space for a moment before tilting her head back slightly to bask in the sunshine.

The bared line of her throat drew his eyes, and he followed it down to the swell of her breasts. Those would rest in his palms quite nicely. His body reacted again, more strongly, so he turned away to take in the courtyard.

This was Miller's fault. He wouldn't be thinking about his tour guide this way if the writer hadn't proposed that damned wager. It was his coach's fault, too. He'd be watching film if Farrell hadn't benched him for the week.

Just then, the single-mindedness of his life hit him like a 350-pound linebacker. Here he was in the company of a beautiful, cultured woman, surrounded by great art. Instead of taking pleasure in the response of his senses, he was assigning blame.

Hell, he couldn't even enjoy his summers at the ranch anymore because he was so focused on getting in shape for the next season. He didn't allow himself to rope cattle or play pickup basketball games with the ranch hands, because he couldn't afford to get hurt.

It was a life with narrow horizons, and right now he felt like busting out of them.

He examined the courtyard with closer attention, noticing the pattern of the stone walkway and the tiles on the curving roofs, as well as the strange, contorted rocks. "So tell me about the kilns again."

His gut tightened when Miranda's velvety brown eyes lit with eagerness. "The Chinese reopened an old imperial kiln so the ceiling and floor tiles would be authentic. The workers pressed the clay into the frames with their feet. Everything was built by hand." He realized he was staring too hard at the shapes her lips were forming when she halted and dropped her gaze to her tablet, saying, "It's time to go see some paintings."

He pushed himself up from the bench, ignoring the complaints of his stiff, bruised muscles.

"It may be a little risky, but we're going to head through public spaces to get to Van Gogh," she said. "Maybe you should put on your sunglasses for this part of the tour."

He was used to being accosted every time he appeared in public. It went with the territory. But he slipped the Ray-Bans on to ease her concern. And to hide the hunger in his eyes.

Since walking didn't seem to bother Luke's bruises, Miranda set a brisk pace as she led her companion through a procession of galleries to the nineteenth- and early twentieth-century European section.

She didn't know how to respond to the blatant desire she had caught in his gaze. She'd never struggled so hard not to cross the line between professional and personal, but Luke turned her body into a mass of pure yearning. Just his touch on her elbow sent an electric shock zinging around inside her.

He is a client. He lives at my place of work.

But it was more than that. Luke Archer existed at a level she couldn't even imagine, with his prodigious money, talent, and fame. She had no business wondering what it would be like to kiss him. Even though she was sure virtually every woman in America wondered the same thing.

She cast a glance sideways to take in the way he moved beside her, the muscles in his long legs flexing under the denim, his big hands casually shoved into his pockets, and that perfectly carved face unreadable behind the mask of his dark glasses. His gilded hair curled out from under the dark blue of the Yankees cap, making her want to feather her fingers through the waves.

Who wouldn't be flattered to catch this golden god's interest?

She called on all her mental discipline to quell her unprofessional reactions, even as several women slanted long, admiring looks his way. Fortunately, no one seemed to realize who he was. Yet.

The painting galleries were going to be tricky, because the Van Goghs drew crowds of tourists. However, she didn't want to bypass them. Somehow the boldness of the brushstrokes and colors seemed meant for Luke Archer.

She made a couple of sharp turns that landed them in front of Van Gogh's *Wheat Field with Cypresses*, her personal favorite.

He took off his sunglasses and stood for a few long moments. "That's a heck of a sky," he finally said. "Reminds me of Texas."

She decided that was a compliment. "There's another wonderful sky in the next gallery. Along with his famous self-portrait, his early sunflowers, and irises."

"I remember one of his sunflower paintings from my junior year trip to Amsterdam," he said. "Always liked the guy's work. It's strong and a little crazy."

She nodded, feeling connected to him by the way he responded to the art. He didn't just glance and pass on. He got caught by the brilliance of Van Gogh's masterpieces. Sharing beauty with him set up a happy little hum inside her. It gave them something in common.

They walked side by side to the next gallery. He spotted the painting with its swirling sky and crescent moon and headed straight for it. "It's like the moment after the center hikes the ball," he said. "Everything is in motion."

"Luke Archer?" A middle-aged man wearing an Empire sweatshirt was towing his reluctant wife in their direction.

The whispering and staring started, and Miranda looked up at Luke to catch a fleeting expression of resignation cross his face. Regret pinched at her. She'd hoped to avoid this.

As the man approached, the quarterback plastered on a pleasant half smile and nodded.

"I knew it!" the man said to his wife. "We're huge fans. Watched you win all four Super Bowls, and we know you're going to bring home the Lombardi Trophy this year."

"It's a long season," Luke said, his drawl pronounced. "But thanks."

"Marilyn says I shouldn't bother you, but our son would be so excited to have your autograph." The man fished his wallet and a pen out of his pocket, thumbed out a twenty-dollar bill, and handed it and the pen to Luke. "Here, you can use my back as a clipboard," the man said, turning around. "My son's name is Chris."

Luke pulled out his own pen and signed the bill. "Would you like me to sign your sweatshirt, too?"

The man practically vibrated with excitement, nodding over his shoulder. "Oh, yeah, that would be great."

Luke wrote his name on the gold *E* insignia.

The man swiveled forward again and held out his hand. "It's an honor."

The quarterback shook his hand, and the man backed away, grinning and staring at the signature on the money.

An older woman approached more tentatively, opening her Chanel handbag. "I'm sorry to interrupt you, but I couldn't help overhearing that you're Luke Archer. My grandson thinks you are the cat's pajamas. Would you sign a dollar bill for him?"

Once again Luke smiled and signed the proffered bill. By then a small crowd had gathered around him with people lifting cell phones to take pictures and holding out various pieces of paper for his autograph. Miranda got edged aside, but she noticed that the fans kept a respectful space around Luke. No one shoved in to have a photo taken with him unless they got his permission. They knew they were in the presence of a star.

As people began to stream in from other galleries, Miranda cast around for a way to extricate the quarterback from his fans. Just then, a young man dressed in a slim-fitting dark suit and wearing a Metropolitan Museum ID badge strode up to the growing clot of people. "Mr. Archer, Ms. Tate, come with me, please."

Luke shot a questioning look at Miranda, and she nodded. Someone on the Met's staff must have noticed the situation and sent a rescuer. She offered up a silent thank-you as the crowd parted for them, and they followed the young man into the next gallery. When they passed through a staff-only door, Miranda breathed a sigh of relief and said, "Thank you so much! I wasn't sure how we were going to get out of there without causing a riot."

"It happens with celebrities all the time," he said. "Security notified me."

At Miranda's request, the young man led them through the back corridor to the Degas gallery and left them there with the assurance that he would intervene again if necessary.

"Why Degas?" Luke asked as they stood in front of a pastel of ballerinas rehearsing onstage.

Miranda took a deep breath. "Because I got tickets to the ballet for tonight." She watched Luke's face anxiously. "I've heard that pro athletes go to ballet classes to improve their flexibility."

"The ballet. Huh."

"The dancers are superb athletes, just like you. I got tickets to the New York City Ballet because the program is pure dance rather than a story. I thought you might like that because the choreography stands out more."

He continued to stare at the painting for a few moments. Then he slanted her a wry smile. "Sugar, you're trying to make a silk purse out of a sow's ear."

Miranda looked at the dazzling blond sports hero standing beside her. "Wait, you're calling yourself a sow's ear?"

"When it comes to this stuff." He gestured toward the ballerinas.

"You knew more about the Egyptians than I did!"

He shrugged. "That was just a kid's interest." He glanced to the right, and suddenly his arm was around her waist like an iron band, and he was moving her swiftly toward a door. "Someone spotted me," he explained. "I'm not going to put you through fending off another autograph session."

She was having a hard time keeping up with his long stride, so he pulled her more tightly to him and swept her along with her feet barely touching the ground. His strength made her feel weightless, while being pressed along his warm, muscular side from her shoulder to her thigh wrapped her in a haze of sensory overload. Every step thrust them into closer contact, so the hard planes of his body moved against her, sucking the oxygen out of her blood and replacing it with licking flames.

For a minute she gave in to it and let him carry her along. Then she realized she needed to direct them. She tried to wriggle out of his grasp so she could look at her tablet, but he didn't release her or slow down.

"Stop fighting me," he said. "You're making my bruises ache."

"Oh, dear, I'm sorry," she said with a jab of guilt as she fell into step with him again. He hid the pain so well that she'd forgotten he was hurt. "Do you know where you're going?"

He glanced down at her without slowing, his eyes gleaming. "No, but I'm enjoying getting there."

Did he mean because she was plastered against him? What else could he mean? "Um, I think you need to make a right here," she stammered.

She felt every point of contact. His long fingers were splayed over her hip, covering so much that the tips grazed the top of her thigh. It was much too close to the spot between her legs that was pulsing with heat in response to his touch. She struggled to focus as a hot, sliding sensation rippled through her.

"Left," she gasped.

"Where are we going?" he asked, slowing down but keeping his arm around her.

"Arms and armor. Downstairs."

He glanced at a sign and steered them toward the elevator.

"I'm not sure the elevator's a good idea. You can't escape if someone recognizes you."

"Trust me, they won't." He halted and let the doors close on a half-full car. "We'll just move to the back of the next one."

When the next elevator's doors opened and the crowd flooded out, he headed straight for the far corner, wedging his shoulders against the wall. "You're going to provide screening," he said, turning her to face him, so he was looking down into her eyes, the bill of his baseball cap nearly covering his face. "Now say something really interesting."

"What?"

"I need to have a reason to keep my eyes locked on you." His dimple was showing. "Or I could kiss you."

"I can do interesting." Although she hankered to know what it would be like to have his mouth on hers, his hands roaming up and down her back, his rock-hard thighs pressing against hers. Desire coursed through her like a stream in flood. "Um, the armor we're going to see was worn by Henry the Eighth in battle, probably in his last campaign, which was the siege of Boulogne in 1544. He was overweight and unwell, but he still led his troops. I thought you would be interested because you wear armor and lead your troops in battle, too."

In the shadow of his cap, his eyes blazed and his smile turned hot. "I like the way you define me. Gladiator, warrior, king."

She needed to lower the heat or she would combust. "Ballet-goer."

He threw back his head and laughed, a full-throated, husky sound that drew fingers of delight up and down her spine. Fortunately, the elevator doors opened, because everyone in the enclosed space turned around to stare.

Somehow she guided him through the last three stops at the Met and headed for the limo. As they walked back through the staff corridor, Luke took her hand, lacing his fingers with hers. "I enjoy touring with you," he said. "It's like a highlights reel."

Two kinds of pleasure danced through her: gratification at his praise, and the sensual thrill of having his large, warm hand around hers.

They scooted onto their opposite seats in the limo, the driver shutting the door and enclosing them once again in that dim, intimate space. Miranda felt a sense of loss as she had to let go of his hand, but it was for the best.

"You are incredibly generous with your fans," Miranda said. His unfailing courtesy and patience with his admirers, from Theo to the Chanel lady, had the effect of making her heart go soft. He curbed all the power and arrogance of his field presence in deference to his loyal followers. It was like watching a prince walk humbly among his subjects.

"They pay my salary," he said with a shrug and a grimace.

"Is your side hurting you?"

"Only when I move wrong. Don't worry about it."

He clearly wanted to brush it off, so she went back to her original topic. "I work with some other famous people, and they don't interact with their admirers the way you do. In fact, some of them are downright rude."

Luke stared out the window. "Those fans spend money on jerseys and programs and tickets. Money they work just as hard as I do to earn. The least I can do is write my name on their memorabilia." He looked back at her. "It's a powerful thing to be able to make another human being happy with just your signature."

With great daring, she leaned forward to touch his knee. "But it costs you time and privacy."

He covered her hand and held it against the denim of his jeans. She could feel the flex of tendon over bone under her palm, and a shiver of awareness ran up her arm. "When I want those, I can have them," he said. Picking up her hand, he tugged on it. "Come sit beside me. It's friendlier, and you can show me what we're seeing next on your handy tablet."

Nervous excitement vibrated through her. They were playing a game where she was the rookie. Now he was pushing the boundaries, watching her and waiting for her to pull back or go forward. She should just hit the correct icon and hand him the tablet. "I, uh, okay," she said.

As she transferred to the backseat, his weight compressed the springs so she slid up against his leather-covered side. He laid his arm along the back of the seat behind her shoulders so she could feel it brushing against her. He smelled of lemon, leather, and male, a potent mix.

She stared down at the screen and inhaled sharply, which merely intensified the heady aromas that enveloped her. Then she tapped the Morgan Library button.

"A library?" Surprise laced his voice. "I thought we were doing art."

"Books can be art." Relief muted her nerves as she returned to being a concierge. "Pierpont Morgan built it as his private library and stocked it with the most incredible treasures. The library has not one, not two, but *three* Gutenberg Bibles, the earliest books printed with movable type, and the most in any single collection. Can you imagine buying three Gutenberg Bibles for yourself?"

She glanced up at him to find that the easy smile had disappeared from his face. "You get mighty excited about books," he said, the angle of his jaw tight.

"The technology of movable type eventually opened up reading to the masses. It transformed the western world." She didn't know what had changed his mood, so she tried a different tack. "Who's your favorite author?"

The smile he gave her was humorless. "It used to be Gavin Miller, but I might rethink that."

"The Julian Best thrillers? Those are terrific. So are the movies. Why are you changing your mind about them?"

"Because I met Miller about ten days ago. He's a troublemaker."

"What kind of trouble could he make for you?" She was baffled.

He huffed out a short laugh. "You have no idea."

"Then I won't buy his books anymore."

He weighed her words. "I appreciate your loyalty."

"In my line of work, you can tell a lot by how people treat those who work for them," she said. "You're one of the good guys."

He turned so his pale eyes met hers. "Just remember, you've only seen me on my day off."

Chapter 10

At the Morgan Library, Miranda was less concerned about Luke being mobbed, so they went in through the front door. A couple of patrons cast appraising glances at him, but no one approached.

"Let's go to the original library first," she said, starting across the sun-drenched glass atrium that now joined J. P. Morgan Jr.'s former residence with his father's library. Luke reached for her hand as he looked around, letting her lead him into the magnificent Italianate palazzo. The easy familiarity of his gesture sent heat prickling through her. She could get addicted to the feel of his palm against hers.

They strolled through the beautiful rotunda with its marble surfaces, lapis lazuli columns, and gorgeous mosaic panels. "Now this is nice," he said.

"It's just the entrance. *This* is the library," Miranda announced in a whisper of awe as they stepped into what might be her favorite room in the world. "Close your eyes and inhale," she said, taking her own advice. "That's the smell of centuries of knowledge and music and culture."

She opened her eyes and tilted her head to see what Luke's reaction was. His nostrils flared, so he had at least inhaled, but his gaze was angled upward at the three tiers of walnut-and-bronze bookcases. "So this is what rich men did with their money in the old days."

"They still do it. The Robert Lehman wing at the Met was built just to house his private art collection when he bequeathed it to the museum."

"Huh," he said, echoing his comment in the Met. His face had gone sharp and focused as he continued to look around. "It's impressive." He brought his gaze back to hers, and she felt the weight of his concentration. "Let's see those Gutenberg Bibles."

"There's usually only one on display at a time." She led him to the glass case, where a large tome was opened to show neat columns of bold black Latin words. Beautifully colored and gilded leaves and vines swirled up one margin. "The decoration was done by hand," she said.

He stared down at it before sliding her a sideways glance. "Can you read any of it?"

"No, but isn't it amazing how clear it still is, so if I could read Latin, I would be able to?"

"For something that's over five hundred years old, it's in good shape." His grip on her hand tightened for a moment, and a bleak expression crossed his face.

"What is it?" she asked.

He shook his head. "Just thinking about the difference between my career and Gutenberg's."

"What do you mean?"

"His work is still important five hundred years later. Mine is—" He shrugged. Suddenly, the circles under his eyes were evident, and lines appeared around his mouth.

It hit her then. Here was a man who had reached the absolute top of his field. Her Internet search had led her to many discussions about who was the greatest quarterback of all time. About half a dozen names got thrown around, but Luke Archer's was always on the list, even if someone occasionally ranked a different player higher. He had won the greatest honors in his sport. Fans adored him—he was the face of the Empire franchise.

Yet other discussions she had read were about his age and when he was going to retire. Would he go out on top, or would he keep playing until his body betrayed him? Would he stay with the Empire to the end of his career, or would they trade their longtime star to another team as he aged?

All that work and talent would fade away, leaving nothing behind but old game footage being rerun during the off-season. It must be hard for someone as driven as Luke to face the slow slide into oblivion.

"Your work has brought incredible joy to millions of football fans," she said. "Remember what you said about making people happy? Parents and kids bond over your games." She gestured toward the Bible. "As cool as this is, I'm pretty sure it doesn't provide the same experience."

The tension in his jaw eased, and his dimple appeared, as did his drawl. "I like to think you and I have bonded over this Bible, sugar."

The potency of his dimple and his drawl left her breathless. The sudden glimpse of his vulnerability made her heart twist.

It was a dangerous combination. She pivoted on her heel and headed toward another display case, babbling, "Do you like classical music? Because there are some amazing manuscripts by composers like Mozart and Beethoven. There's something cool about knowing their hands touched those pages."

Luke followed her. She watched in fascination as the quarterback focused all his attention on the artifacts. His big body was angled over the display case, his gaze locked on the manuscripts. Every now and then he would straighten and glance around the room with the same laser stare he used on the football field.

She wondered if he planned to start his own library.

"Mr. Archer?" A bald man in rimless glasses and a tweed jacket approached them.

Luke nodded.

The man looked relieved. "I thought I recognized you. I'm Richard Brown, one of the curators here." He offered his hand and Luke shook it. "Is there anything in particular you're interested in seeing?"

"We came for the Gutenberg Bibles, so the rest is just icing on the cake." Luke gave him one of his aw-shucks smiles.

"I wonder if I might make a request," Richard said, his manner somewhat hesitant. "We would be honored to have an artifact of significance to your career in our collection. Perhaps a letter or a contract of some sort? I'm not very familiar with your sport, so I'm not sure what to ask for." His eyes twinkled behind his glasses. "My wife would know better. She's the football fan."

For the first time since she'd met him, Luke Archer appeared to be at a loss for words. It lasted no more than a second before another smile twitched up the corners of his mouth. "You want something about football for the Morgan Library's collection?"

Richard nodded.

"Well, I'll be damned." Luke's smile spread wider, the sheer joy of it lighting up her own mood. "Beg your pardon on the language."

"We value documents of cultural significance," Richard said. "And as Justine informs me after every Empire game, you are an iconic cultural figure."

Miranda could tell that Luke was enjoying himself, because he was laying on the Texas accent thick as he said, "I'll go through my papers and find you the best darned document I have. Please thank your wife for her kind words."

"We appreciate that." Richard shook Luke's big hand with both of his.

After the curator left them, Miranda and Luke headed to the library's restaurant for lunch. As they sat in what had once been the private dining room in the Morgan family's nineteenth-century brownstone, Luke still wore his dazzling smile.

"You look like the cat that ate the canary," Miranda said, basking in his happiness. "I may go blind from the reflection on your teeth."

He leaned back in his chair, making it creak alarmingly. "The next time you visit the Morgan Library, you might see my first contract displayed right beside Mozart's symphony."

She understood now. He'd been validated in a place he didn't expect to be. "Is that what you're going to give them? Your first contract?"

"Maybe. Or I have a letter from Joe Namath, congratulating me on signing with the Empire, which would be a double score for the Morgan. However, I need to hold on to that a little longer. It's a good luck charm." She noticed his Texas twang was muted now that he was talking to her about business. "I'll definitely send along an autographed jersey for Justine."

"Another autograph for another adoring fan." Miranda looked up from the menu with a teasing smile.

"Well, here's the thing. As part of my contract, I have to sit in a hotel room and autograph jerseys, photos, posters, footballs, and other crap that the NFL then sells at jacked-up prices. It's boring as hell and gives me writer's cramp. Which is why I only do it in the off-season. Don't want to damage the valuable tool." He held up his right hand, fingers splayed.

Miranda could see the power in that big square palm and those long fingers. She remembered the heat and strength of them and felt an exquisite shiver run across her skin.

He dropped his hand. "They glue on a sticker that says whatever I signed is authentic. My opinion is that it's more *authentic* to sign things for people I actually meet."

A waiter bustled up and took their orders. Miranda had felt safe bringing Luke here, where the clientele was almost entirely ladies of a certain age wearing expensive designer suits and even more expensive jewelry. However, she saw the waiter walk up to one of his colleagues and say something as he cut his eyes over toward their table. She sighed inwardly. To the young man's credit, he did not say a word until the very end of the meal, when he simply expressed his admiration for Luke's play. Of course, Luke signed the check for him.

"It's no wonder your hand stays so strong," Miranda said. "You're always using it to autograph things."

He just laughed and draped his arm over her shoulder as they walked out to the waiting limo. It was a moment of easy camaraderie that she hadn't expected from this intense man. She felt good about giving him time off from being Luke Archer, celebrity quarterback.

After touring the Frick and the Guggenheim, they had dinner at a quiet restaurant near Lincoln Center, discussing the art and artifacts they'd seen. Miranda had spent most of the meal mesmerized by the way the candle flame gilded the slash of Luke's cheekbones and cast a profound shadow in his dimple as it came and went.

When they headed toward the theater, she began to have second thoughts about their destination and came to a stop on the sidewalk. Moving in front of him, she watched his expression as she said, "Tell me the truth. Do you want to go to the ballet?"

He flicked her cheek with his finger. "Sure do. Who knows? They might invite me up onstage to do a pirouette."

"Do you know how to do a pirouette?"

She watched in amazement as he dropped her hand, braced himself a moment with his arms held out at shoulder height, and then spun into a turn on the ball of one foot. She caught only a hint of a wince as he landed. It wasn't exactly a pirouette, but it was both athletic and graceful.

A little glow of wonder spun in her chest. "You truly can do anything."

He gave her a roguish look. "You have no idea, sugar."

She laughed because she'd decided to just go with the flirting. It wasn't going to lead anywhere, after all.

At the theater, they walked in the front door like average audience members, had their tickets scanned, and headed up the steps. Luke eyed the oversize marble statues of plump women situated on the promenade. "They look like wrestlers, not ballerinas," he said. Since Miranda had always thought the same thing, she stifled a chuckle.

"Let's get you into your seat before anyone recognizes you," she said.

"I don't think this crowd will know who I am." His tone was dry as he looked around the big open space with its gray stone floor and tiers of walkways.

"You didn't think they'd know you at the Morgan Library and look what happened."

As Luke settled into his red velvet orchestra seat on the aisle of the vast, modern theater, he removed his baseball cap and slid down so his knees nearly hit the seat in front of him.

"No one will bother you while you're sitting," Miranda whispered, "so you don't have to slouch."

He slanted her a smile. "I'm being considerate of the person behind me."

She looked at the difference between his eye level and hers and muttered, "Oh, right." It was one of those small, courteous gestures he kept surprising her with.

Opening the program, she pointed out the write-ups about the three pieces they were seeing. "Just forget about the tutus, and watch the dancers' bodies. I think you'll be impressed by what they can do."

"Do you like the ballet?" he asked.

"It was one of the things I most wanted to see when I left the farm. The first live performance I came to, I kept getting distracted by this soft tapping sound. It took me a while to realize it was the hardened toe boxes of the ballerinas' shoes hitting the stage floor as they danced. On television, they edited that out, I guess."

"So the reality was a disappointment."

"Oh, no! It made it so immediate. I knew I had really made it to my dream city."

"You're an interesting person, Miranda Tate," he said, shaking his head.

The lights went down, and Miranda spent the whole performance sliding her gaze between the stage and Luke's face. He watched with a slight frown, his focus absolute.

When the first piece ended, he applauded with apparent enthusiasm.

"Well?" she couldn't help asking.

"You're right about the dancers. They have incredible balance and flexibility." He gave her a devilish look. "But they don't have half a dozen three-hundred-pound men trying to knock them off their toes."

"The famous dancer Mikhail Baryshnikov always said he admired athletes because they didn't have choreography to follow. They had to improvise within chaos."

"I like the man."

The lights dimmed, and Luke once again locked his attention on the stage for one of George Balanchine's famous leotard ballets. Miranda was glad Luke could see this because there were no sets and no costumes. He would be able to focus entirely on the dancers and their athletes' bodies.

When the lights went up, Luke stood. "Let's get a drink."

As they joined the stream of people heading out of the theater and toward the lobby bar, Miranda caught the telltale glance and whisper of recognition from a couple beside them. She blessed the city mind-set that required sophisticated New Yorkers to be too cool to bother celebrities.

Luke escorted her to the bar on the promenade, took one look at the champagne on offer, and handed the bartender a folded bill. "Is there someplace we can get the good stuff?" he asked.

The bartender pocketed the bill and deserted his colleague behind the busy bar. "Follow me."

As they wove through the crowd to a door set in the hallway that gave access to the orchestra seats, Miranda said under her breath, "That must have been a heck of a tip."

"If you're going to poison your body with alcohol, you should only do it with the best," Luke said.

Their guide swiped his ID card through a slot beside the door and led them into a lounge with a sleek black bar at one end and plush, modern furniture at the other. Several clumps of expensively dressed patrons were scattered around the room. The bartender led Miranda and Luke to the bar, murmured a few words to his counterpart, and turned. "Matt will take good care of you, Mr. Archer."

So he'd recognized Luke, too.

Luke shook hands with the young man, who practically bowed his way out of the room. By that time, the VIP bartender had poured them two flutes from a bottle of Krug Vintage Brut champagne.

Luke took a swallow. "Now this is worth drinking."

Miranda sipped it and had to admit that it tasted like heaven.

Luke picked up the plate of chocolate-covered strawberries the bartender offered and led her to two chairs tucked in a corner.

"How did you know they would have 'good stuff' somewhere else?" Miranda asked. "You've never been to the ballet."

"Where donations are needed, there's always a VIP room." Luke pushed the strawberries toward her on the low table.

Miranda took a bite of a strawberry, enjoying the pleasure of ripe fruit and rich chocolate on her tongue. Luke lounged back in the chair, his eyes disconcertingly fixed on her face. That blue flame flared in them again. She took another bite of the strawberry and felt awareness ripple through her when she realized he was staring at her mouth.

Luke raised his glass in a toast. "Here's to you eating strawberries."

There was something different in the air between them that made her shift in her chair. Maybe it was the fire in his eyes scorching over her body. "You should have a strawberry," she said. "They're yummy."

"I can tell by the way you're enjoying them."

She cleared her throat and left the rest of the strawberries on the plate. "Yes, um, the next ballet—"

He shook his head and stood up. "It's time for a different kind of dancing. Wait here."

He strode over to the bar and had a short conversation with the bartender, who nodded. Luke passed him money again before he pulled out his phone and tapped at the screen.

Miranda couldn't help feeling a small thrill when a couple of designer-clad women cast her an envious glance as Luke sat down next to her. "This time there's going to be audience participation," he said.

"I have no idea what you're talking about, but I'm not getting onstage."

He laughed and tossed back the rest of his champagne before standing up and holding out his hand to her. "We're leaving."

"To go where?" He pulled her to her feet like she weighed nothing. She noticed his brief grimace of pain and flinched in empathy.

"A friend's," Luke said, taking the large shopping bag the bartender brought over.

He led her out onto the promenade, where the ballet-goers were streaming back to their seats. The crowd seemed to part magically for him as he plowed through them going the wrong way. "Too bad your opponents aren't as easily cowed," she said, following the path he cleared.

He glanced back to lift an eyebrow at her but kept going all the way out to the waiting limousine. The driver opened the door, and Miranda scrambled in while Luke gave instructions that she couldn't hear.

Then Luke was sliding onto the seat beside her and plunking the shopping bag down on the carpeted floor between his cowboy boots.

"Why the rush?" Miranda asked.

"Because it's my day off." Luke's eyes lit up. "And I'm damned well going to take advantage of every single minute."

Chapter 11

Luke shrugged out of his jacket and reached into the shopping bag, allowing Miranda to survey the beautiful musculature of his arms. His skin was dusted with golden blond hair that glinted in the passing lights, and the muscles and tendons flexed and shifted as he pulled out a bottle of the same Krug they'd been drinking. He twisted off the cork with a subdued pop, not spilling a drop. "Flip open that compartment and there should be some champagne glasses," he said to Miranda, nodding to a padded console on her side of the big car.

She found them, neatly packed into the compartment, along with various other barware. "You keep a well-stocked limo."

"My teammates sometimes join me," he said, filling the glasses she held. Reaching into the bag, he pulled out a plastic container of chocolate-covered strawberries and flicked open the top. Instead of offering the box to Miranda, he picked one up by its leaves and held it in front of her mouth. "For you."

She started to put down a flute to take it, but he shook his head. "From me."

Miranda looked from the strawberry to his face and found his eyes blazing with an intention that was not anywhere near friendship. Heat spiraled through her, and she shifted her gaze back to the proffered treat.

"Take it, sugar." His drawl went rich and slow.

His voice vibrated straight into her bones. She leaned forward and bit into the juicy sweetness. A piece of chocolate broke off and started to fall, but he raised his other hand to catch it in a lightning reflex. He popped the stray piece into his own mouth, bringing her gaze to his lips and their clean, sculpted lines.

She leaned back abruptly, splashing a few drops of champagne on her trousers.

"Champagne doesn't stain," he said with a slantwise smile as he dropped the top of the strawberry onto the plastic lid. "I've had enough of it sprayed on me to know."

Her laugh came out with a nervous edge. He was so close that she could feel the heat of his body and smell the citrus of his cologne clinging to his T-shirt. It made her want to rub her face against his chest to feel the soft cotton on her cheek, to inhale the insanely male scent of him, and to hear his heart beating through the wall of skin and muscle. She lifted her glass and drank half the champagne in one gulp.

But the champagne couldn't douse the skyrocketing heat in her body. She put down her glass and started to shrug out of her jacket. The backs of Luke's fingers brushed against her neck as he helped her slide it off her arms. It was a surprisingly sensual touch for such a simple gesture. Tiny shivers arrowed along her spine as she pivoted forward again.

He tossed her jacket on the seat across from them before he refilled her half-empty flute. "Another strawberry?" His tone was soft, but his gaze was a challenge.

"S-sure," Miranda said.

He chose the largest berry and shifted on the seat, bringing him even closer to her. He brushed her lips with the chocolate-covered tip before she could open them, watching with his eyelids half-lowered.

She took a bite and closed her eyes to shut out the intensity of his gaze while she chewed and swallowed.

When she opened them, he smiled as he brought the juicy berry to her mouth again. "You don't need lipstick when you're wearing strawberry juice," he said, touching it to her lips. "I'll bet it tastes as good as it looks on you."

She had enough time to stop it, but not enough willpower. He moved closer, and she let her head fall back to meet him. When his lips brushed hers, she forgot about who he was and just let the sensation of his mouth on hers take over. He leaned in, so she flattened her palm against his chest, feeling the fabric, the muscle, and the heat, as she'd wanted. Then he flicked at her lips with the tip of his tongue and made a low humming sound in his throat, as though he liked the taste.

The warmth and slight roughness of his tongue sent flickers of delight dancing through her veins. One of his hands slid up the back of her head, his fingers twining into her hair and angling her head so he could bring his mouth down at a more demanding angle. She was caught between the solid barrier of his chest in front and the iron bar of his arm behind her, and she reveled in it. Her hand holding the flute was curled against his chest, the cool glass chilling her palm while the heat of his body warmed the back of her fingers. The contrast added to the sensations ricocheting through her.

But it was his mouth that was the focal point, slanting against hers, his lips hard one moment, softer the next, his breath with the fizz of champagne on it. He didn't force, he persuaded, and she tilted in to him to taste and feel more when she allowed his tongue between her lips.

He slid his other arm around to pull her in closer, and suddenly a sluice of cold wetness ran down her back.

Luke swore and released her, righting the glass of champagne he'd just tipped down her blouse. "Smooth move, Archer." He dug around in another compartment of the limo to produce a white linen napkin. "Turn around and I'll dry you off. My apologies."

"It doesn't stain," she parroted. As she pivoted on the smooth leather seat, Miranda didn't know whether to be relieved or frustrated by the interruption. With her back to Luke, she raised a hand to her mouth, touching her swollen lips in wonder, while her body fizzed and sparked with longing. Luke Archer had kissed her. Like he meant it. She could feel the outline of his big hand against her back as he carefully blotted the champagne from her blouse.

"I'm sorry, sugar. I forgot I had a drink in my hand." He moved the napkin to press against a different spot. "You should take that as a compliment."

"Oh, I will," she said. Wherever he touched her, those dancing ripples of pleasure radiated over her skin.

"I hope it's okay if I do this, but it's going to be a mite sticky if I don't." He slipped one hand under the back of her blouse to swipe the napkin over her damp skin.

She closed her eyes and shivered in delight when the rough tips of his fingers brushed over her shoulder blade. "It's fine," she breathed in a husky voice.

"All cleaned up," he said, withdrawing his hand. She could feel him pull her blouse away from her back and flap the fabric slightly to dry it.

"It's fine," she repeated, turning so he would let go of the blouse.

"Where were we, sugar?" he said, reaching for the glass in her hand.

She clasped it against her chest. "We were someplace we shouldn't have been."

He'd spooked her, going too fast, but her mouth had tasted of sweet berries, rich dark chocolate, and sparkling champagne. And innocence. He wanted to taste more. But he had learned the virtue of patience on the playing field. So he settled back in the seat and gave her an inch of extra space. "Sugar, I was happy with our destination."

"Friends, Luke," she said firmly, but he saw the rapid rise and fall of her breasts under that pretty silky top.

"Maybe we've gotten to know each other as friends and we like what we've found out."

She scooted six inches away from him, and he sighed.

"That was unprofessional of me," she said, her voice tight.

He turned on the seat and skewered her with a look. He wasn't going to have her job dragged into this. "You are officially off the clock. I'm *your* tour guide from here on out, so just sit back and relax."

He demonstrated what he wanted her to do by stretching out his legs and crossing them at his booted ankles before he swallowed the rest of his champagne. Grabbing the bottle for a refill, he offered it to her, and she nodded.

But she didn't change her position. "I'm not used to sitting back and relaxing."

"Truth is, I'm not, either." That's why he'd decided to make this a memorable day off.

She looked thoughtful, although her cheeks still held the flush of their kiss. He didn't want her thinking. He wanted her feeling like he was. Hot. Bothered. Needing more of that sexy body pressed against him.

"Don't you relax in the summer at the ranch?" she asked, the movement of her berry-stained lips pulling at his gut.

He forced himself to think about the twice-a-day workouts in the ranch's gym, the early-morning runs, the hundreds of laps in the pool. "The older I get, the harder I have to work to stay in shape. It's a year-round project."

He felt her gaze like a physical touch as she skimmed it down his body. "Well, you're doing a good job of it," she said, her flush intensifying.

His groin tightened. "Thanks, sugar."

So she felt what he did, even though she tried to hold on to her professional persona. Must be something about the code of concierges.

He nudged the strawberries toward her. "Don't let them go to waste."

She picked one up and bit into it. She did that thing again where her eyelids fluttered closed for a split second as she savored the taste. She liked sensual pleasures, whether she wanted to give in to them or not.

The limo glided to a halt, and she swallowed the bite of berry.

"Okay, time for audience participation." He boosted her toward the door, although it was really an excuse to fold his hands around the curve of her waist. The flash of pain in his side didn't dampen his pleasure one iota. She grabbed for her tote, but he kept moving her. "You won't need that or your jacket. We're going straight in the door, and everything's on me."

She squeaked a protest, but he knew how to use leverage and momentum, so she was out before she could stop herself. His bruises grabbed at his ribs when he followed her, but he ignored the hurt. They stood in an alley in front of a stainless-steel door lit by a single purple light.

She eyed the blank door. "Where are we?"

"A friend's place." He knocked and looked straight up at the security camera that was concealed in the light fixture.

The door swung open, releasing the pounding sound of dance music into the night. "Mr. Archer, a pleasure to welcome you to Cleats. Mr. Greene will be delighted to see you." The bouncer waved Luke and Miranda into the back foyer.

Luke took Miranda's hand and started down the dark hallway toward the music. She pulled him to a stop. "This is a friend's place?" she said, her gaze accusing.

"The club belongs to my friend Larry Greene. He played on the Empire for a few years before he retired and bought the club." Luke had financed his teammate's purchase and been repaid with more interest than he'd asked for or wanted. Larry welcomed all football players, former or still in the game, and gave them a break on the drinks but demanded that they behave. It turned out to be a winning combination, because the football players drew fans . . . and beautiful women.

Tonight, though, Luke was here for the music. On the dance floor, he could hold Miranda close to him again. He might pay for it in pain, but he'd played with worse.

"I'm not much of a club person," Miranda said.

"I went to the ballet. You can go to a club."

She absorbed that and squared her shoulders, almost as though she were bracing for a tackle. He grinned at her. "A little dancing never hurt anyone."

"It might hurt *you*," she pointed out.

"You dance. I'll watch."

She started to protest.

"Just joking, darlin'. This will be easier than a pirouette."

"Okay, Baryshnikov," she said with a wry smile.

As they walked into the VIP room, the full volume of the music crashed into them, and he felt her hesitate. Putting his arm around her waist, he swept her through the crowd to the dance floor. Taking her fragile little wrist in one hand, he pulled her arm up over her head and twirled her around to face him.

That motion cost him a burn of agony. He placed her hand on his shoulder and moved her close as he picked up the beat of the music. A slow dance. Luck was with him.

She stood on tiptoe and spoke over the music. "I don't want to hurt you by moving the wrong way."

"Follow my lead and it won't be a problem," he said, drawing her in closer.

For the first time in his life, being injured paid off.

Miranda had a hard time finding the flow of the music with Luke's nearness and touch setting off little explosions of sensation all through her body. His hands were wrapped around her waist, holding her so close that the fabric of her trousers and his jeans brushed every time they moved. He had lifted her hand onto his shoulder, where she could feel the ridge of muscle shifting under his T-shirt. She held her other hand awkwardly at her side. If she tried to put it on his shoulder, she would have to move even nearer to him because of his height.

As another dancer bumped against them, Luke ended her debate by pulling her in so her thighs were between his as they swayed to the insidiously seductive beat. She gave in and raised her free hand to his shoulder. That put her nose almost against his chest, another awkward position. She allowed herself to do what she had wanted all evening, turning her head to rest her cheek against the cotton of his T-shirt. It held the warm, male scent that was simply Luke. She could feel his breath riffling the hair on top of her head, making her scalp tingle.

Enveloped by the heat and power of his body, her own throbbed with awareness. He surprised her by being completely in sync with the music, his movement and the sound amplifying each other. The room was dark, lit only by colored lights along the walls, and they were surrounded by couples locked in each other's arms. No one was paying any attention to them, so she relaxed, letting his body carry hers into their own private rhythm.

He responded by moving his hands to press against the upper curves of her behind, sending ropes of heat searing through her. They coiled low inside her, stoking the growing ache of arousal. She sucked in a breath as she willed him to move lower, to cup her with his hard, warm palms.

Instead, he rubbed his thumbs in circles over her lower back in time with the music, so the yearning within her pulsed with every movement.

It was a strangely primitive end to what was supposed to be a day of high culture. Maybe this was what he needed to balance it, something wholly physical.

The thought made her stiffen, and he flexed his fingers into her flesh to bring her more firmly against him.

She let go of her resistance. She hadn't been held like this by a man in too long. In fact, she'd never been held by a man like Luke Archer.

After all, they were only dancing.

And then he shifted so that one of his knees drove between her legs, his thigh hitting just where her yearning was most concentrated. She gasped against him and dug her fingers into his shoulders as a shock of hot desire ripped through her.

Feeling rather than hearing a vibration in his chest, she dropped her head back to look up at him, trying to hear what he said. Another wave of arousal flooded her when she met the blaze of his eyes under their half-closed lids. The planes of his face were taut with tension, and his hold on her grew almost harsh as he shifted his thigh against her again. The friction sent her arching back against his hands.

His mouth came down on hers, his tongue stroking her lower lip in time with the music. The same rhythm was repeated in the thrust of his thigh between hers and the glide of his thumbs on her back.

She tried to change the angle of her hips to reduce the friction, but Luke gave her what she'd wished for. He moved his powerful hands down to grip her bottom and bring her in hard against his thigh. The extra pressure detonated the arousal that had been building inside her all day, her orgasm exploding in a blast of heat and sensation. She jerked and shuddered in his arms as the delicious shocks rolled through her, her groans swallowed by his mouth and the relentless sound of the music.

As the spasms subsided into tiny rippling quivers, she turned her head away from his kiss and buried her face against his chest in embarrassment, hoping he would mistake her climax for a new dance move.

Pleasure still throbbed low inside her, and she wanted to fold up into a boneless heap on the floor.

Instead, she felt him moving them both toward the edge of the dance floor. She didn't want to look him in the eye right now, so she kept her face plastered against his T-shirt and tried to slow their progress without being obvious about it. All too quickly, however, they were in the dimly lit hallway through which they'd entered the club.

Luke took her shoulders and peeled her away from his chest, so she straightened her spine and raised her eyes to his. If she'd thought his gaze was hot before, it had become positively blistering.

"Was that what I think it was?" he asked.

She could feel the blush radiating over her neck and cheeks. She swallowed. "I . . ."

"Did you just come on the dance floor?" His fingers tightened on her shoulders, and he stepped into her, sandwiching her between his body and the wall. She could feel his erection against her stomach as he leaned in, his mouth closing on hers. Her breasts were so sensitized that the pressure of his hard muscles against her nipples sent streaks of fire through her as he teased her with his tongue.

He pulled away an inch to say, "That was the hottest thing I've ever seen."

"I couldn't stop it," she managed to murmur, inhaling as he slid his hands between the wall and her behind, curling his fingers to pull her even closer. He bent his knees and flexed his hips, making her moan as the ridge under his jeans pressed between her legs.

He huffed out a laugh that sounded almost like he was in pain. "We need to leave. Now." He stepped back and spun her against his side, holding her there as he headed for the exit at a near jog.

Nerves and longing twisted together in her gut. How could she feel shy about being alone with him in the limo when she'd climaxed in the middle of the dance floor?

The bouncer opened the club's back door for them, telling them to have a good night. Luke jerked the door of the limo open before the driver could straighten away from the hood, where he'd been having a smoke.

"Take us home," Luke called out before helping Miranda onto the leather seat with a courtesy that contrasted with the devouring hunger in his eyes. He lunged in beside her and hit the button that closed the privacy screen between them and the driver. His gaze was locked on her face, and the set of his jaw showed tension. "You didn't expect this. I didn't expect this. But I say we go with it. Come back to my place," he said in what was more a command than a request.

She hesitated as the implications of what he wanted sank in. He dated the most beautiful women on earth. And the most sexually experienced. Miranda had slept with exactly three men in her life, and two had been at college. She couldn't begin to imagine what someone like Luke Archer would expect in bed.

Before she could respond, he angled his head downward and kissed her—this time with a slow, sensual touch. In the closed, private space of the limo's interior, he could have overwhelmed her with his big, powerful body, but he touched her only with his mouth, giving her room and freedom. Or the illusion of it. His mouth was mesmerizing, robbing her of the last shreds of sanity. She whimpered and grabbed a fistful of his T-shirt to draw herself into him.

That was all the answer he needed.

He seized her hips and lifted her off the seat and onto his lap, so she straddled his thighs. She thought she heard him grunt in pain, but his movements were smooth and sure. "I want to touch your skin." He slipped his fingers under the hem of her top at the back of her waist and pushed them up under the fabric until they were splayed across her shoulder blades.

The feel of his palms against her skin made her breasts grow heavy with longing. Shocked at her own daring, she leaned close to his ear and said, "You can unhook it."

Her bra came loose immediately, and he slid his hands around under the silky knit of her top to cup her breasts. She let her eyes close as she pressed herself into his touch. He groaned and rolled her nipples between his fingers, sending pure electricity sizzling down into her core.

"Yes, Luke," she breathed, tilting her hips so she could rub herself against his erection. All she cared about was finding some relief from the rekindled burn of arousal inside her.

He released her breasts and seized her hips, holding her still. "Slow down, sugar. You deserve better than a quick screw in the back of a limo. We've got all night to—" His expression went from hot anticipation to irritated frustration. "Oh, crap—Trevor!"

It took her a moment to clear the sex haze from her brain enough to remember who Trevor was. The sleazy brother who was staying with Luke. She did *not* want Trevor to find out about this.

Luke's eyes lit up again. "I know how we can get around that."

"How?"

He moved his hands back to her breasts, gently brushing his thumbs across the hardened peaks. "My private gym. It has a separate entrance for my trainer." His dimple appeared in all its seductive glory. "There are a lot of interesting ways to use exercise equipment."

Chapter 12

Miranda followed Luke out of his private elevator and into an elegantly paneled and carpeted hallway. This was the floor below his living quarters and accommodated his private gym, lap pool, and media room.

"I'm pretty sure Trevor won't be using the gym at this hour," he said. "But just to make sure, you wait here."

The thought of Trevor doused some of the fire smoldering inside her. But then Luke brought her up against him and took her mouth in a potent kiss before he strode away down the hall. She drank in the rear view of wide, rippling shoulders, well-muscled butt, and mile-long legs before she sagged against the wall and tried to pull herself together.

After a steamy ride in the limo, he'd backed her up against the wall of the elevator and practically made her come again before they'd reached his floor. Now that his enthralling presence had been removed, cold sanity seeped into her brain.

He'd said this was unexpected and she deserved better than sex in a limo. But she didn't kid herself—she was no more than a diversion for him because he'd been benched.

Was being with him worth the risk that someone at the Pinnacle— like Orin—would find out? Or that Trevor would interrupt them? Or even just the awkwardness of seeing him around the building after she became a notch on his bedpost? That last wasn't fair. He would treat her with unfailing courtesy after tonight . . . if she ever encountered him again.

"The playing field is all ours." Luke came toward her with that ground-eating stride of his. As she let her gaze drift over the shimmer of his golden hair, the burn of his blue eyes, and the hard male perfection of his chest and thighs, all her concerns evaporated like morning mist on a sunny day.

She wanted to peel off his T-shirt and jeans, trace her fingers over the lines of muscle and tendon, and feel him moving within her.

She trotted down the hall to meet him halfway. Running her hands up under the fabric of his T-shirt to feel his warm skin, she murmured, "Make me stop thinking."

Hunger flared in his eyes. "Inside," he growled.

He spun her around, swept her through the gym door, and turned to lock it. She took a quick survey of the room. Only one row of the overhead lights was on, casting a low-level glow over various machines constructed of stainless steel, metal cables, and black vinyl cushions.

He did a brief scan, too, before he grabbed her hand and led her to a massage table, also covered in padded black vinyl. Before she could move, he had grasped her waist in his big hands and lifted her onto the end of the cushiony table. If the effort hurt him, she saw no sign of it.

Then he was pushing her knees apart to stand between her thighs. "I want your skin," he said, as he pulled the hem of her top upward. "Lift your arms."

She obeyed and felt the soft fabric skim up her arms and over her hands before he flung it away. He snaked his hands around her to flick open the hooks of her bra again. "Practice makes perfect," she said, trying to counteract the intensity of her reaction to his touch.

He threaded his fingers under the straps and slowly pulled them down, his focus locked on the curve of her breasts as he uncovered them. "So beautiful," he muttered and then snatched the bra off and tossed it into the corner, too. His hands went back to her breasts, and she nearly forgot what she wanted as his palms pushed against the sensitive nipples. But she wrapped her fingers around his wrists, feeling the unyielding power in them as she tried to pull them away from her. "I want skin, too," she said, giving up on trying to move his hands, and reaching for the hem of his shirt instead. She tugged upward, exposing the rippled planes of his abdomen.

"Just like the statues," she said, with a sharp inhalation. As she pulled the fabric farther upward, she saw the spread of dark bruising. *But human and vulnerable to pain.*

"Fair's fair," he said, releasing her. He crossed his arms, grabbed the bottom of his shirt, and yanked it up over his head, leaving his hair delightfully mussed. The shirt followed her clothes, and then he bent to take one of her nipples in his mouth, making her forget about his injury.

The hot, moist friction of his tongue sent a wave of arousal crashing through her body. She buried her fingers in the satin of his hair when he drew on her, the suction making her whimper. He moved to her other breast, his hands warm and slightly rough against the bare skin of her back as he pressed her into his mouth. The moment of respite let her run her fingers down through his hair to glide along the curving muscles of his shoulders and back. When he scraped the edge of his teeth around her nipple, she dug her fingers into his shoulder blades, arching against him on the exquisite balance of pain and pleasure.

Desire seared through her like tropical sunlight, blinding and hot. She wanted him inside her with a fierceness that unnerved her. Seeking his belt buckle, she dragged her hands down his chest and stomach. She felt the contractions ripple through his muscles wherever she touched him. He straightened away from her, but his gaze was downward, watching her hands on his skin.

As she scrabbled for his belt, her hand brushed against the denim-covered ridge of his erection. A hiss came from between his clenched teeth, and he took the end of his belt from her to unfasten it with one swift jerk. He wrenched the button out of its hole and hauled the zipper down before reaching into his back pocket and producing a foil envelope.

"I'll bet you were an Eagle Scout." Miranda took the condom from him and laid it on the table beside her so she could fumble at the button of her trousers.

"Let me." He opened her pants in two swift movements. "Lie back on the table," he ordered before he worked her trousers and panties over her hips as she arched up. He yanked them down to her ankles while she toed off her shoes.

"Yes," he said, his gaze skimming over her naked body. He shoved the waistband of his briefs down and freed his cock.

Miranda ran her fingers along the hard length of him, pulling a low groan from his throat. Then she ripped open the envelope and rolled the condom on.

He started to push at his jeans, but she shook her head. "I like that look."

His smile was tight. "If you like it, you got it, sugar. Because I sure like your look."

His hands were on her thighs, pushing them wider apart. She leaned back on her hands, slanting her hips up to give him easier access. She kept her gaze on his face, where a sheen of sweat glistened on his forehead. His grip tightened, and she felt the head of his cock against her, pressing slowly into the slippery heat between her legs. "You are so ready," he said.

"Oh, yes," she gasped as he pushed inside, stretching her, filling the hollow ache.

He thrust hard to seat himself fully in her, throwing back his head and growling as she pulsed her hips to meet him. "Yeah, that's good," he said, moving his hands to cup her bottom and bring her forward so his cock went even deeper. The power and intimacy of their joining spiraled down inside her, pushing her beyond just physical pleasure.

"Wrap your legs around me."

She ran her ankles up along the seams of his jeans to lock them together behind him, opening her even more. He moved in closer and pushed in farther. "And now, sugar, let's get to know each other."

With his cock impaling her in place, he traced a line up the indentation of her spine with one finger while he nibbled at the side of her neck. He twined his hands into her hair, using it to angle her head back so he could lick his way down her throat to her cleavage. He released her hair and brought both hands to her breasts, lifting them with his palms and flicking his thumbs over the nipples.

His exploration was slow and thorough, as though he was truly fascinated by her body. She let herself go, reveling in her unrestrained responses to his touch.

Every time he moved, she felt the shift of his hard length inside her and the press of his groin against her wide open thighs, winding the tension tighter and tighter. She couldn't stop him from touching her wherever he chose. And each touch made her pulse around the fullness within. It was so overwhelmingly erotic she almost forgot she could touch him, too.

Somehow she brought her hands up to flatten her palms on his chest, carefully avoiding the dark bruises, so she could savor the slight roughness of his wiry hair, the immovable stone of his pectoral muscles, the living warmth of his skin, and the hard thudding of his heart.

She wielded power over him, too.

At her touch, he sucked in a breath so his abs defined themselves even further. She spread her hands to thumb his nipples and make him moan. He pinched hers, so sparks showered through her. She traced the lines of definition down the front of his hips until she brushed the base of his cock where it was pressed so close to her. He rocked into her as though he couldn't stop himself, sending her arching back as a shock of pleasure seared through her.

"Lean away from me, darlin'," he said, moving his grip to her behind. "Put your feet on the edge of the table."

She braced herself on her hands and bent her knees so her heels rested on the padded tabletop, against her bottom. The new angle of his cock set off another shudder of arousal. He kept his eyes on hers and began to move, withdrawing almost completely before he eased back into her. She dropped onto her elbows as her muscles melted under the sensual assault.

The tendons in his neck drew taut and the heat in his eyes blazed while he drove into her harder and faster. Every time he pushed in, he rotated his hips, grinding against her, ratcheting her closer and closer to orgasm. "Yes," she gasped. "Yes. More."

He thrust and pulled her in sharply, so she was fully open to the friction of his body against hers. The hard, hot pressure set off her climax, her body going rigid as all her muscles seemed to clench at once before exploding in a release so mind-bending she screamed and bowed back, her head hitting the vinyl padding. As she convulsed around him, she felt him go still, his fingers digging into the flesh of her behind.

After the shocks ripped through her, she collapsed so she lay on the table, quivering with little echoing ripples of sensation. Luke was still huge and hard inside her, which made her insides begin to hum with anticipation again, despite her release. She levered her hips up in invitation.

"Are you sure you're ready?" he asked.

She opened her eyes to see him nearly grimacing with the effort he was making to hold on to his control. "So ready."

That blasted his control to bits, and he started to thrust in a wild rhythm. She could feel the brush of worn denim on the backs of her thighs as he pulled her hips up even higher to give himself a better angle. The table bucked in time with his hips, and she could hear it scraping across the floor. Her inner muscles quivered and tightened with the power of his strokes. She lifted her arms over her head to hang on to the top edge of the table.

"You look so hot like that," he rasped, his attention concentrated on her jutting breasts. Her nipples tightened in response.

He drove into her and stayed there, throwing his head back and shouting at the ceiling as he came inside her, his cock pulsing so strongly she could feel it along its entire length.

When the pulsing stopped, he eased his hold on her hips, and she wondered if she would have bruises where his fingers had dug in. He slid out of her and turned away for a moment. When he came back, the condom was gone, and he bent over the table to brace his elbows on either side of her. "You are amazing," he said, his breath whistling through her hair as he rested his forehead on the pillowy surface beside her neck.

She let her heels drop off the table so her legs dangled on either side of his. Now the denim was scraping against the sensitized spot between her thighs. "So are you." Draping her arms over his back, she gave her hips a little grind against him.

"Sugar, allow me a few minutes. You take more out of me than an entire defensive line."

She rotated her hips again, igniting little flares of heat in her belly. "Are you one of those players who doesn't believe in sex the night before a big game?"

He stiffened slightly and she regretted her joking question. Then his body relaxed against hers. "I try to keep my focus on football during the season, but sometimes it's worth making an exception."

"Because I'm exceptional."

He huffed out a laugh. "You are that." And then he was sliding down her toward the end of the table, trailing kisses to her navel and below.

"I didn't mean for you to—"

He put his mouth between her legs, and a jolt of electricity flared through every nerve in her body. She shuddered and hissed and grabbed the edge of the table again as his tongue traced down and inside her, then swirled around her hypersensitive clit. A few more of his touches sent her raging into another orgasm as mind-bending as the one before. He sucked on her until he had wrung every ounce of response from her body.

She lay limply on the table, her legs draped over one end, her arms dangling over the sides.

"Stay here," he said, stroking his hands down her thighs.

She moaned her agreement. It felt as though her bones had melted in the inferno he had generated inside her.

So she stayed, her body slowly easing down from the sensual heights Luke had taken her to, while he rustled around somewhere across the room.

When she finally mustered enough energy to prop herself up on her elbows, he was walking barefoot across the polished wooden floor toward her, his half-unzipped jeans riding low on his hips, a smile softening the angles of his face.

She let her gaze drift over his gorgeousness and saw for the first time the full extent of the bruising on his left side. Guilt made her sit up when he came near enough to touch. She skimmed her fingertips ever so lightly over the dark shading on his skin. "I keep forgetting you're so hurt you can't play. I shouldn't have . . ." She couldn't finish the sentence.

He caught her hand and brought it to his mouth to kiss. "Sugar, I haven't thought about that injury since our dance together."

Blood rose in her cheeks at the reminder of her public loss of control.

He hooked one arm around her shoulders and slid the other one under her knees. "Oh, no," she said. "I'm not going to make it worse by letting you carry me."

She felt his arms tighten.

"Do you want an elbow in your ribs?" she said. "Because I'll do it for your own good."

In one motion, he swung her off the table. "I'm betting you won't carry out that threat." He started walking.

"You called my bluff." Miranda looped her arms around his neck to try to take her weight away from his injured side. The rock-hard muscles of his arms against her bare thighs and back made her skin tingle.

He brushed a kiss on the top of her head as he lowered her feet to the ground in the corner of the gym. "It's not as good as my bed upstairs, but it's better than the floor."

At her feet was a pile of exercise mats, neatly covered with sheets and a blanket that must belong to the massage table. He'd rolled up two white towels into tidy cylinders to use as pillows. Something about the care that went into fashioning those pillows made tears prick behind her eyelids.

He wasn't bundling her off to the limousine; he wanted her to be comfortable. With him. The makeshift bed, the way he treated his fans, his slouching posture in the theater—all the small, thoughtful gestures made her fall a little in love with him.

"That's the nicest bed I've ever seen."

He looked surprised, and she realized she'd been too emphatic. He gave her a wink. "If you get in, it will look about perfect to me."

She knelt and pulled back the blanket so she could wriggle under it. Luke stripped off his briefs and jeans, the flexing muscles in his legs riveting her gaze as he knelt to slip in beside her. He rolled her on her side and spooned himself against her back, his arm lying heavily around her waist. He was so large that she felt engulfed by his body, soaking in the warmth of his bare, sweat-dampened skin pressed against her almost everywhere. Tucking her head under his chin, he let out a long breath. She could feel his muscles go slack in relaxation and wished she could see his face.

Was he falling asleep? Did he expect her to stay here all night?

"You comfortable, sugar?" His voice seemed to vibrate through her where his chest was fitted to her back.

"Comfortable might not be quite the right word."

"Give me the right word so I know if it's good or bad."

"I might need several words." She took an inventory of the happy glow still radiating through her insides, the warmth of him infusing her skin, the feel of his cock nestled against her bottom, and the solidness of his long legs intertwined with hers.

"Would three do it?"

"I'll try." She hummed for a few seconds before going with honesty. "Blown away. Amazed. Uncertain. I guess that's four."

His arm had tightened when she said *uncertain.*

"I'll go with the first three," he said, "but I'm *certain* this is a good thing."

"What do we do next?"

"Well, sugar, we take a little rest, and then we find a better use for these machines than weight training."

She glanced at the nearest contraption. It sported a padded seat with two upright cylinders attached to either side. She was pretty sure you were supposed to put your knees outside the cylinders and squeeze them together to lift the weights cabled behind it. The thought of herself in that position made liquid pool between her thighs. She shifted her gaze away.

His breathing slowed, and she found her eyelids drifting closed, her sated body dragging her down into sleep like an exhausted swimmer.

She came awake to the feel of his cock hard against her bottom. "Am I dreaming?" she asked as her nipples went tight and sent an arrow of arousal zinging downward.

He skimmed one hand over her stomach to where her thighs began, sliding his fingers between them. "If you are, it's the best dream I've ever been in."

He hooked his fingers inward so he could push two partway inside her. His touch against her clit made her gasp and twist in his arms. His cock jerked between the cheeks of her behind. That sent more liquid to bathe his probing fingers, and he pushed farther into her. She lifted her thigh to give him more space.

"You see that weight bench over by the mirror?" His voice rasped in her ear.

She nodded and moaned as he worked his fingers in and out.

"You see that cylindrical cushion at one end? I can adjust it higher, so the bench slants down from it." He flicked her clit with his thumb.

She gasped and jolted against him, tension winding tight, low, and sizzling.

His voice dropped low. "I would sure love to bend you over that headrest and come into you from behind. The padding is thick and cushiony, so you'll be comfortable, I promise. But you can say no and it will be fine."

He slid his fingers inside her and stopped.

She imagined the bench tilted and herself folded over the end of it, feeling the power of Luke driving into her. Nerves sent butterflies fluttering through her stomach. She would be completely exposed and at his mercy. Her body clenched around his fingers.

She nodded.

"I need you to say it, sugar."

She could barely find the breath to speak. "Yes, I want that."

He withdrew his hand. She found herself propelled upward as he pulled her to her feet and led her to the bench. He leaned down to give her a long kiss, their bodies pressed skin to skin from knee to shoulder.

"Hold that thought," he said before he bent to move various pins. She watched the ripple of his back muscles as he changed the position of the bench, and thought again of the sculptures in the museum. Except this one moved from one pose to the next with a gorgeous fluidity that made her toes curl.

When he straightened, his face was incandescent with desire, and he wove his fingers into her hair to give her another slow, sensual kiss. Then he turned her so the tops of her thighs brushed the rounded cushion at the end of the bench. He skimmed his hands around to knead her breasts, snugging himself up to her back. His mouth was on the side of her neck, gently sucking, and his cock was once again nestled against her behind. There was nothing for her to do but dissolve into desire under his hands.

And then he began to press her forward, his chest hard against her back. The nervous butterflies gave a few more flutters as he used his body to bend her over the bench so her bottom curved farther and farther up. But when his cock dragged across the swollen, aching spot at her center, a sun flare of yearning ripped through her, and all reservations evaporated. "Oh, yes," she breathed. "Like that."

He kept going until her face was turned and resting against the heavy padding that cradled her like a pillow. He gave her breasts a last squeeze and pulled his hands away, his callused palms abrading her nipples with delicious friction.

He swore. "Have to get a condom."

She closed her eyes to shut out her surroundings, listening to Luke's bare feet pad away and the clink of his belt buckle when he found his jeans. His feet thudded on the wooden floor, so she could tell he was jogging back to her.

A smile of gratification curled her lips. Then his hands wrapped around her hips, and the smile turned to an *oh* of shocked pleasure as he entered her without any prelude.

He also made a guttural sound of satisfaction as he seated himself within her. When he spoke, his voice was strained. "Seeing you like this, feeling you so wet, it's going to make me come faster than I want to."

He released her hips to stroke his hands over her back, the erotic massage making her inner muscles ripple around his cock. "So hot," he growled.

He started slowly, but she could feel his control break, and then he was driving into her—his breath rasping, the bench shaking, and her own climax building and building as the base of his cock slammed into her over and over again. It was brutal and primitive and perfect.

And it came to a climax as he thrust into her so hard the bench scooted forward. He howled his release, his fingers like a vise on her hips. He stayed buried inside her, throbbing for a long time, before he folded down over her, sandwiching her between his big body and the bench's cushion. His breath was coming in gulps, his chest heaving against her back.

She mewed a complaint as he slid out of her, driving her to the edge of orgasm without taking her over. She felt him work his hand between her thighs. He slid one finger inside her and used another to circle her clit. It took about three rotations to detonate the explosion in her gut. Held between Luke and the bench, she couldn't move, only feel, as her orgasm wrung her muscles into a final delirious release.

Drifting down from the high, she became aware of his forearms braced alongside her shoulders on the bench. He was blanketing her with his warmth but not crushing her with his bulk.

She shuddered through a few more aftershocks, soaking up the full-body contact with him. When she began to feel guilty about the position he had to hold, she said, "I could stay like this all night, but you're doing all the work."

He cupped his hands under her shoulders and unfolded both of them from the bench. Turning her to face him, he brushed a strand of hair away from her face. "You trusted me."

Miranda laid her hand against his cheek, feeling the prickle of stubble on her palm. "Because you can be trusted."

He moved to close his lips over her fingertip, applying the tiniest bit of suction. "I want to devour you," he said, his voice rough like gravel.

"And I want to touch every inch of you." She pulled her finger away from his mouth to follow a tendon in his neck down to the hollow at the base of his throat and then across his clavicle. That's when she noticed an array of scars on his shoulder. "What are these?"

"Surgical scars. Minor stuff to fix up my throwing arm." He took her wandering hand in his and started toward the makeshift bed. "You collect those over time."

She hated to think what a toll the violence of football took on his magnificent body.

He helped her down onto the piled mats and pulled the blanket over them. She snuggled against his chest, facing him this time. "How many times have you been sacked in your career?"

"That's too much math for me to do when you've reduced my brain to pulp."

A glow of satisfaction blossomed in her. She'd had as powerful an effect on him as he'd had on her.

He resettled them so his arm pillowed her head and one of his legs lay crooked over her hip. "I'm feeling mellow enough for another nap," he said, closing his eyes.

Freed of his gaze, she let her eyes roam over the perfection of his face. This close she noticed small scars there, too: one cutting through the outer end of his eyebrow, one at the jut of his chin, and one near his ear. Instead of marring his beauty, they gave it a sexy edge.

In one day Luke Archer had gone from being a giant icon she admired on a billboard to a living, breathing human being. And the truth was, she was lying here naked with him after one day together because she knew this would be her only chance to be so close to him. He would go back to his fame and wealth and football, and she would go back to being an assistant concierge.

"There's something I need to tell you," she said.

His eyelids snapped open.

"It's nothing bad." She stroked her hand down his suddenly tense back.

"Go ahead."

"I didn't do, er, this because you're a famous quarterback," she said. "I did it because after spending the day with you, I liked you as a person. Well, more than liked." She took a breath. "I don't expect anything more, and I won't tell anyone this happened."

Ice formed in his eyes, and his smile turned hard. "So we're back to the concierge code."

Luke knew he should be grateful. The woman in his arms had just said everything he usually wanted to hear. Instead, he was pissed off that she thought he'd screwed her because he was a famous athlete. Or that she'd screwed him because he was a famous athlete. Or whatever she'd just said.

Because she gave him a sense of himself as something other than a football player. She'd said it: she made him feel appreciated as a *person*. But now she was treating him as the quarterback again.

This was ridiculous. Why was he getting bent out of shape because Miranda was making valid assumptions about his intentions? *No rings, no strings.* She was being realistic, and he was being an asshole.

"What if I expect something more?" he asked, using the leverage of his leg to pull her in closer to him.

"You want more from *me*?" The astonishment in her voice fanned the flames of his anger.

He slid his hand down to the luscious curve of her behind and squeezed lightly. "I've made it clear that I've enjoyed today. All of it."

"Yes, but you could have any . . . well, I'm just . . ."

He let her stammer to a halt. "Do you think because you're a concierge I would just screw you and send you home?"

He felt her flinch as though he had smacked her. He who prided himself on never hitting a woman had just lashed out at her verbally.

"I'm trying to manage my own expectations."

"Which are not very high." He moved his hand up her back to twirl a strand of her thick shiny hair around his finger because he couldn't resist.

"I was afraid you might have the wrong idea about me," she said. "I don't usually jump into bed—or onto a weight bench—the first time I go out with a man. You could easily think I was just a—a football groupie."

That defused some of his anger. "Not a chance of that, sugar. No self-respecting football groupie would turn down tickets on the fifty-yard line."

He felt her breasts press against his chest as she sighed.

"Have dinner with me tomorrow night," he said, before all the reasons he shouldn't ask her stopped him.

"Seriously?"

He couldn't decide if happy or astonished described her tone better. "Yes." He tried to see her expression, but she'd angled her head downward on his arm.

"Shouldn't you spend some time with your brother?" Her voice was heavy with regret.

He thought of Trevor's response when he'd invited him to DaShawn's retirement party—*I have nothing to talk about with a bunch of jocks.*

"Trevor's here on business. He's got other things to do," Luke said.

Her softly curved body shifted against him, making his cock start to harden. "Thank you, but it's not a good idea," she said.

That killed his arousal. "Why not?"

He put his fingers under her chin and tipped her head up so he could see her face. Her velvet brown eyes held guilt. "I work here."

"We went out to dinner tonight." He'd been able to just talk, no editing, no worrying about whether it would find its way onto the Internet tomorrow. Not to mention how the candlelight made her lips look full and kissable, while he'd pictured her silky dark hair cascading over her naked breasts.

She lifted her chin out of his grasp but kept her gaze on him. "That was part of the tour."

"I'll get a private room at the restaurant. No one will know." And afterward, well, he had a limo.

He saw longing weaken her resolve and applied more leverage. "Any restaurant in the city. Your choice."

She still hesitated, so he used his final weapon. He leaned in and devoured her mouth in a hot, sensual kiss.

When he finally released her, her fingers were digging into his shoulders, and her eyes were closed. He allowed himself a satisfied smile as he felt how hard her nipples were.

Her eyelids fluttered open, so he could see the haze of desire in her eyes. "You're used to getting what you want."

"Is that a yes?" He waited.

She inhaled, pressing those tight nipples more firmly against him. "Yes, I'll have dinner with you tomorrow." She gave him a seductive smile. "But you have to make the reservations."

Chapter 13

Trevor shuffled into the kitchen wearing flannel pajama pants and a T-shirt. "You were out late last night," he said as he poured himself a cup of coffee.

"Yeah." Luke took a sip of his protein shake. He had already showered and dressed in his film-watching outfit of navy blazer, khakis, and a blue button-down shirt with well-shined loafers. As he'd pulled on his clothes, he'd been relieved to find that his night with Miranda had not aggravated his injuries. In the throes of lovemaking, the bruises had been forgotten, which meant he hadn't been careful about how he moved. Truth was, his body felt more fluid today, so maybe the sex had been good for him. He'd go with that.

Trevor persisted. "I guess your tour went beyond the cultural."

"I went to the ballet." Luke figured that would throw Trevor off the scent.

His brother froze for a moment and then started to laugh. "No, seriously. Where did you go last night?"

"The New York City Ballet. An all-Balanchine program. Those dancers are in shape, man."

Trevor choked on his coffee. "Okay. Say I buy that. The ballet is over at ten thirty, max. You didn't stroll in until way later than that."

"All that dancing made me want to do the same, so I went to Cleats."

"You could have called me."

Luke thought of Miranda having an orgasm in his arms on the dance floor, one of the most intense things he'd experienced sexually, which was saying something considering that he hadn't been involved. That made his cock hard all over again. And made him glad he hadn't called his brother.

"Next time, Trev." Luke took another swallow of the protein shake. "How'd your meetings go?"

His brother looked out the windows toward the Verrazano Bridge. "Not so great."

"Academia is a tough field."

"Don't patronize me," Trevor snapped.

"I was stating a fact. Lots of candidates, few job openings."

"Tell me about it." His brother transferred his gaze to his coffee mug before he looked up. "I know I was supposed to leave Friday, but I need to stay a little longer, bro."

Luke cursed inwardly as he thought of his big, comfortable bed and what he wanted to do with Miranda in it. But he didn't trust Trevor to keep his mouth shut, so he wasn't going to let the two of them get near each other. *"Mi casa es su casa."*

Trevor stared back into his coffee cup. "Jodie told me not to come home until I had a tenure-track job offer. She said she didn't care where it was, but she wasn't going to wait any longer to have children." He plunked down on a kitchen stool. "With my lack of publications, no one is going to hire me at that level."

A bad feeling hit the pit of Luke's stomach. "Not to kick a man when he's down, but why don't you finish that book you've been working on? You've done the research." Maybe his brother had writer's block like that asshole Miller.

"It's not good enough."

"You don't know that." One thing about Luke's career—it was easy to measure it in wins and losses.

"Yeah, I do. Wilson at Art Forum Press says it's publishable, but not groundbreaking."

"You don't need groundbreaking. You just need publishing credit."

Trevor stood up. "Really? You would be happy with an adequate career in the NFL? No, you had to be the best goddamned quarterback in the history of the sport. Shit, Luke, don't be such a hypocrite."

"What you do and what I do are totally different." Luke kept his voice level, the way he did when tempers flared in the locker room. "There's no comparison."

"Damn straight there isn't. You make hundreds of millions of dollars, and I make peanuts. Even if I got tenure at Harvard, I'd still make peanuts compared to you."

Luke wanted to say it wasn't a competition, but that was crap. Everything in his life was about winning and losing. "You're comparing apples and oranges. My career will last maybe another four years. You have the best of yours in front of you."

The truth of it walloped him in the gut.

Trevor snorted. "You've broken every offensive record there is to break in the NFL. When sportswriters argue about who's the greatest quarterback who ever played, your name usually settles in at number one. How do I compete with that?" He threw out his arm dramatically.

"Don't." Luke felt a throb start in his left temple as he said something he hated. "I'm the jock. You're the brain. Our skills are measured differently."

"And valued differently," Trevor said bitterly as he sagged back down on the high stool.

Yeah, their parents had valued Trevor's skills over Luke's. Maybe that's why Luke had worked so hard at football. To prove that it was worth doing.

He grimaced at his own introspection on a morning when he had awakened in a surprisingly good mood, considering he was benched. That was Miranda's doing. And he was seeing her again tonight. "You have any other leads on a job?"

Trevor hunched his shoulders. "A couple of third tier schools in New Jersey and Pennsylvania. They're no better than where I am now."

Luke considered the idea of pulling strings for his brother. He could endow a professorship or something, but it didn't feel right. His brother needed to earn this one on his own or he'd never feel good about himself. "Set up the interviews. I'll get you a car and driver to take you to them. It's a start, and then you can do some groundbreaking research."

"Thanks," Trevor said in a tight voice.

There was no gratitude in his brother's curt word, but Luke needed the conversation to end. "No problem. I have to get to work."

"How about we order Tex-Mex tonight?" Trevor said.

A halfhearted peace offering. "I wish I could," Luke said, "but I've got a commitment."

"Business or pleasure?"

Luke gave his brother one of his patented "none of your business" stares.

"I guess that answers my question."

"How about Thurs—oh, crap, I have a charity thing that night that Doug roped me into. You want to come?"

"Nah. I wouldn't be able to make a big enough donation."

It wasn't worth responding to that, so Luke got up and rinsed his glass before putting it in the dishwasher. As he grabbed his jacket and headed for the elevator, he considered the idea of inviting Miranda to the gala. She'd turn him down. Too public. However, he could wring some pleasure out of twisting Gavin Miller's arm until he showed up and forked over a donation.

He waited until he was in the limo to pull out his phone and dial the author.

"If it isn't the benched quarterback," Miller said in greeting. "I'd offer you one of my books to read in your free time, but there isn't a new one."

Luke had expected the dig at himself, but not the writer's sneer at his own problem. "I can provide you with a distraction. I need to fill a table at a charity gala for foster kids tomorrow night." He reeled off the cause, location, and time.

"I'll send a check, but I'm not in the mood for society right now." Miller's voice was bleak. "No, wait. Get Trainor to bring his mystery woman and I'll come." Now his tone had an edge of malicious glee.

"Bring a date yourself."

"What about you, Mr. All Football All the Time? Will you have a lovely lady on your arm?"

Miranda's face leaped into his mind again, but the prospect of Gavin Miller's presence added yet another reason to keep her away from the evening. "My personal trainer." Elyssa Lauda often acted as his date when he wanted no complications.

"Ah, a woman with a killer body, I imagine."

"She keeps fit," Luke said.

"Let me know what Nathan says." The writer hung up.

He dialed Trainor's cell and got voice mail but chose not to leave a message. He wanted to apply the right pressure to get the CEO there with his date. Luke was curious about her, too.

Once again Miranda drifted into his thoughts. That reminded him of the need to find an alternative location for their after dinner activities. He speed-dialed the Ritz-Carlton in Battery Park.

Unlike his brother, Luke made his own arrangements where women were concerned.

"Miranda, would you please come to my office?"

When Orin's nasal voice came through the phone's speaker, Miranda made a face. She'd been savoring the happy hum of her body as flashes of the night before flitted through her mind. Not to mention the anticipation of sitting across from Luke at a fine restaurant in a few hours. And what would happen afterward. Her nerve endings did a little tango.

The situation was so far beyond anything she'd ever experienced that she couldn't make herself worry about the risk of being seen with Luke. She'd been keeping her nose to the grindstone and holding her expenses down so she could help her brother out. She needed—deserved—this brief, spectacular fling. Her expectations were realistic, as in zero, so why shouldn't she let go just this once?

"I'll be right there," she said to Orin, wondering what it was this time. Probably some complaint from a client because she wasn't at the Pinnacle yesterday. Orin hadn't been happy when Luke had arranged for Miranda to be away the entire day. He couldn't say much because Luke was such a high profile client. But her boss could still take it out on her.

"Close the door," Orin said from behind his desk as she entered his office.

That was ominous. She eased the door shut.

"What is this?" He slapped a folded tabloid newspaper down and jabbed his finger at a photo.

Miranda leaned over to see what looked like an amateur cell-phone picture of herself and Luke standing in front of a Van Gogh painting at the Metropolitan Museum of Art. The headline read: QUARTERBACK CULTIVATES CULTURE WITH CONCIERGE CUTIE. Miranda relaxed and straightened. "It was just part of the tour I took Mr. Archer on."

"You're holding his hand."

She bent again to see that the photographer had captured their hands in a way that highlighted how intertwined they were. A cold finger of concern drew a line down her spine. "I was escorting him to the next painting."

"Do you think I'm a fool?" Orin jabbed at the photo again. "You've got your fingers knotted around his."

Miranda thought fast. "It was camouflage. People were starting to notice Mr. Archer, and he said they were less likely to approach him if he looked like he was on a date." She shrugged. "It worked for a while."

Orin looked unconvinced. "How did the paper find out who you were?"

"Maybe they looked up his residence and checked out photos of the staff. We're all on the website. They're reporters—they know how to track down information."

Orin's eyes narrowed. "Mr. Archer will be very upset."

Now she was on more solid ground. "It was his idea. Do you want to speak with him about it? I'm certain he will reassure you."

"Of course not. I don't want to bother him any further than he already has been." Orin was still huffing, but her confident tone had undermined some of his righteous indignation. "I want your assurance that there will be no further incidents of this nature." He tapped his finger on his desk to emphasize each word. "We do not socialize with our clients."

In fact, there was no rule, written or implied, stating that. "I understand," Miranda said, as nerves squeezed at her throat.

What if Orin found out about tonight's dinner with Luke? Her boss would go ballistic. Maybe she couldn't afford this fling, after all.

"If I receive any complaint from Mr. Archer, we will discuss this further," Orin said.

Luke wasn't going to complain, so Miranda allowed herself a tiny smile. "Of course."

Her boss gave her a look of such venom she nearly took a step backward. Then he turned to his computer. "You may go."

Miranda's knees felt like jelly as she left Orin's office and walked across the lobby to her own. Dropping into her chair, she blew out a breath.

Her boss seemed unusually upset. Was it just envy that she got to spend time with someone famous? Or was it the tip he imagined she was getting?

She choked on a laugh devoid of humor. That would be the ultimate joke, since she had refused to let Luke tip her after their day together. She had to charge him for her hourly working time because it went to the concierge company, but she had stopped the clock when they left the ballet.

She needed to cancel dinner with the quarterback. The moment she thought it, every cell in her body screamed, *No!*

As Miranda's sense of responsibility waged a battle with her desires, her phone rang.

"Hey, Miranda, it's Erik at the Dartmouth."

"Great to hear from you. What can I help you with?" Erik was the concierge at another luxury condo, and they swapped favors regularly.

"It goes the other way this time, sweetie. I just heard through the concierge grapevine that your evil genius of a boss is spreading nasty rumors about you getting involved with clients. He's saying you're behaving unprofessionally. He e-mailed Christine a photo of you and Luke Archer holding hands." Erik gave a whistle of admiration. "Honey, if it's true you're dating him, I am green with envy."

Miranda managed a shaky laugh. "I was giving him a tour of some museums at his request. The whole hand-holding thing was to keep people from bothering him for autographs."

"The media is so irresponsible," Erik said.

"At least they didn't say I was pregnant with Luke's baby."

"Just let them get their hands on another picture of the two of you together and that will be the next headline."

She rubbed her forehead in an attempt to ease the tension headache forming there. "I don't understand why Orin's so bent out of shape over this. Luke Archer just wanted a private tour guide."

"I'll get a little countercampaign going for you," Erik said. "If I categorically deny his accusations, the opinion of the concierge community is going to come down on your side."

Unshed tears clogged Miranda's throat. Erik's offer of support warmed her heart. But it also brought a stab of guilt. She couldn't allow him to deny her involvement with Luke because she *was* involved, no matter how briefly. "You are the best, but I can't ask you to do that for me."

"You're not asking, sweetie. I'm offering."

"That makes it all the more special, but I need to fight this on my own."

"I hate to let that nasty little worm Spindle get away with smearing your reputation."

"He won't." Miranda tried to inject a confidence she didn't feel into her voice. "I'll make sure of that."

"By the way, I have two tickets to *Hamilton* for Friday night, if you could use them."

"I know exactly who would want those. Send them over." She paused. "I just wish I knew why Orin dislikes me so much."

"Because you are so much better at the job than he is. It's not just the clients who prefer to deal with you, it's us concierges, too. You watch yourself, sweetie. And I'll do the same."

Miranda disconnected and sagged back in her chair, staring sightlessly at her computer screen.

She thought of Luke explaining the hieroglyphics to her in his warm Texas drawl, of his gaze intently focused on the Morgan's manuscripts, of his patient willingness to sign autographs for every fan who asked, and of how his skin and muscle felt against and inside her body.

Then she pictured Dennis trudging to the barn before the sun came up to milk the cows so he could make the next batch of cheese with the equipment she was paying for. She thought of Patty growing flowers to sell at her roadside stand to make a little extra money. She thought of Theo's agile brain and the price of college tuition.

A long sigh dragged itself from her throat. Orin's poison was bad enough with that one photo to support it. If the paparazzi caught Luke and her together again, her boss would have proof positive, and he would use it mercilessly.

He could ruin her chances at the head concierge job in the new luxury condo going up. The building wouldn't be finished for another couple of months, which gave Orin far too much time to make trouble for her.

Disappointment filled her with a dull, gray fog.

It was better this way. She was already captivated by Luke. Spending more time with him would just make it worse when he went back to football.

With dragging steps, Miranda got up and shut the door to her office before she dialed Luke's cell phone. When it went to his voice mail, she wasn't sure if she was relieved or disappointed.

The beep sounded. "Luke, I'm very sorry, but I'm going to have to cancel our dinner plans. I have a conflict with work. Thank you for a wonderful day yesterday." She wanted to add something about the pleasure of getting to know him, but decided it could be misconstrued as sexual. Of course, it was, but she left her message at that.

The hours that had been bright with the anticipation of seeing him again now stretched before her in dreary, colorless succession. In addition, the shadow of Orin's ugly allegations had destroyed any joy she might take in her job today.

To cheer herself up, she dialed her favorite resident to offer him the *Hamilton* tickets. At least someone would be happy with her.

Twenty minutes later, a deliveryman walked into her office carrying a vase of sunflowers so large that Miranda could barely see his face behind it. "Miranda Tate?"

"That's me."

The man plunked the flowers down on her desk. "Jeez, lady, that arrangement is bigger than your office."

Miranda pulled a five-dollar bill out of her drawer and handed it to him, turning his grumpiness into gratitude.

Luke had sent her Van Gogh flowers! A sigh of combined delight and regret welled up in her throat. He must have sent them before she left her message.

She pulled off the business-size envelope stapled to the plastic wrapping and ran her finger over the letters of her name in his handwriting. She loved the fact that he hadn't called the florist and dictated the card. He must have had it messengered in.

She opened the envelope carefully and pulled out a single sheet of stationery with the Empire logo at the top. In a bold scrawl, Luke had written:

Dear Miranda,

Yesterday was surprising in more ways than one, all of them good. I figure if you like Van Gogh, you'll like the flowers. I'll find out what other things you like at dinner and afterward.

Luke

Miranda couldn't help smiling, although her pleasure was laced with wistfulness. The last sentence sent a little shimmer of heat through her body. She wondered what "afterward" he had planned.

Now she would never know.

Chapter 14

Luke sat in the darkened room, trying to keep his focus on the video of last week's matchup of the Jaguars and the Buccaneers. But he kept drifting back into memories of the day before with Miranda, and they weren't all about the sex. He remembered moments like when she was impressed with his knowledge of Egyptian hieroglyphics. Or the way she looked at him as though he'd said something smart when he commented on the Van Gogh. And then there was the sex.

"Archer, what do you think?" The coach's voice shattered Luke's mental image of Miranda draped over the massage table, naked and gasping.

"It's my week off. I don't have to think," Luke said.

His teammates chuckled, while Junius looked annoyed. But Luke wasn't worried by the coach. He was more concerned about his own inability to concentrate. You didn't win Super Bowls by daydreaming.

"Fine, how about you, Burns? You got any comments on how to keep Terrance Fairley from knocking the shit out of you and taking the ball away?"

Luke studied the clip as the Bucs' giant linebacker put on a surprising burst of speed to slam into his opponent's star wide receiver, causing a fumble and turnover. Junius cued up another play where the linebacker danced around a guard and a tackle to sack the quarterback. Luke let his lips curve into an evil smile as he flicked a glance at Brandon Pitch. The backup quarterback looked queasy. Luke shifted to test the condition of his bruises and felt the twinge.

Junius showed another play where Fairley flattened a tight end to create a turnover. Luke sat forward. "Can you show that one again, Coach? I might have an idea."

As he was explaining his strategy, he felt his cell phone vibrate in his pocket, indicating a missed call and voice message. As they discussed and refined the counterattack, impatience swelled in his chest. He was sure the message was from Miranda, because the flowers must have arrived by now.

Finally, the coach released them from the film session, and Luke ducked into an empty office to check his phone. Sure enough, Miranda's number came up. He punched in the code to check his messages. As he listened to her regretful recording, anticipation turned to fury. That scumbag Spindle was involved in this somehow.

He gave the metal leg of the desk a good, solid kick before he dialed Miranda's number.

"Luke, thank you so much for the sunflowers," she said before he could speak. "I feel like I'm in Arles with Van Gogh."

He could hear both sincerity and constraint in her voice. "What's the problem with work? I'll fix it with your boss."

There was a beat of silence before she said, "It's a scheduling issue. It can't be fixed."

"Look, I want to see you tonight." The truth of that surprised him. "I'll work around your schedule."

Another moment of hesitation before she sighed into the phone. "One of the tabloids published a photo of us holding hands at the museum, and that's creating some, um, ill will here."

He was right about Spindle. He'd like to unleash Terrance Fairley on the head concierge. "If I guarantee that no one will see us together, would that work for you?"

"How could you do that?" There was a gratifying note of longing in her voice.

"I already have a room reserved at the Ritz-Carlton at Battery Park." He needed to explain that. "Because of Trevor. There's a private entrance we can use." He wasn't going to mention that he'd used it before for similar reasons. "We'll get room service. No photos."

"That's a lot of trouble to go to."

He could hear *no* in her voice, so he laid on the drawl. "You're worth it, sugar. Let me send a car to pick you up at seven. Just an anonymous black sedan. No one will be the wiser."

"I . . . well . . . thank you," she finally said after a pause so long he thought he'd lost her. "That would be nice."

He pumped his fist. "The car will bring you right to the entrance, and my driver will escort you from there. That eliminates the chance of anyone seeing us together."

"I appreciate how careful you're being," she said. "And I feel ridiculous about it."

"It's not your problem, it's mine. Being in the spotlight is not always comfortable for the people around me, so I've found ways to dodge it." He'd also learned to avoid the people who basked in the light reflected from him. Miranda wasn't one of them. He let anticipation vibrate in his voice. "I'll see you tonight."

Luke disconnected and glanced at his watch. He was going to be late for his session with his trainer. Stan would give him an earful, but Luke didn't care. He could block out the abuse as long as he had Miranda to focus on.

A few hours later, Luke changed positions on the seat of the limousine for the third time, trying to ease the soreness his session with Stan had induced. His trainer assured Luke he would feel fine in the morning if he got a good night's rest. But rest wasn't on Luke's agenda, so he had a couple of ice packs strapped to his ribs, and he had swallowed a few Aleve capsules before he left the Empire Center. That would do for now. Once Miranda arrived, he'd forget all about his pain.

An alert pinged on his phone. That was his assistant's reminder that Luke needed to call Nathan Trainor about the gala.

He dialed the CEO's cell number. This time Trainor answered.

"Trainor, I need a favor," Luke said. "I got talked into buying a table at a charity dinner tomorrow night, and I need to fill it up. Miller's coming, so I'm asking you to come, too. And bring a date." He smiled.

"Miller put you up to this." The CEO hadn't gotten where he was by being stupid.

But Luke hadn't, either. "Miller? No, he's just willing to go along with it for a good cause. We're raising money for foster kids in the New York metro area."

"That's not what I meant. He wants to meet my date."

"Hell, based on what Miller says, *I* want to meet her," Luke said. "You work fast, man."

"As I told him yesterday, the meeting is premature." Trainor's voice was tight. "And I have no intention of exposing her to Miller's curiosity."

Definitely not stupid, but protective. "Too bad," Luke said. "The silent auction has some damn nice jewelry, and all the proceeds go to the kids."

Silence instead of refusal. That was a good sign, so Luke sank the hook in further. "There's a listing of the items online. I'll text you the link."

"Did you donate a signed football?" the CEO asked.

Luke could tell Trainor was still on the fence, so he injected an element of competition. "With four tickets on the fifty-yard line. Miller kicked in an entire set of autographed Julian Best books, along with a prop from the last movie."

Trainor laughed at that. "Put me down for a TE-Gen10 3-D printer."

Luke had him now. "Sounds high-tech. So you'll come."

"I'm sure I'll regret it, but I'll ask Chloe if she'd like to attend."

"Chloe. Nice name. I'll text you all the information."

Luke hung up and forwarded the details Doug had sent him about the gala to Trainor's phone. He envied the CEO's ability to bring the woman he wanted with him to the event. He found himself resenting any free time not spent with Miranda.

Because the clock on their time together was running out.

Chapter 15

Miranda walked out the front door of the Pinnacle and spotted the black sedan pulled up at the curb. Refusing to look around furtively, as though she were doing something wrong, she strode across the sidewalk and opened the car's back door to let herself in. When the driver had texted her that he was there, she'd told him not to get out. She'd even worn a long belted raincoat to cover the dress she'd changed into in her office.

She slid into the backseat, breathing a sigh of relief that she appeared to have escaped unnoticed. However absurd, her precautions seemed necessary. Two more colleagues had called to mention the rumors Orin was spreading about her. Miranda slumped back into the leather seat and unbuttoned her raincoat. She'd been foolhardy to take this risk, but when Luke promised her complete privacy, temptation had overwhelmed her good sense.

"Is the heat on too high?" the driver asked.

"No, it's fine." She almost laughed. It wasn't the car's heater that was sending flares of warmth licking through her body.

She smoothed her palms over the skirt of her rose-colored dress. It fit her like a glove without being overtly sexy. She'd fastened a statement necklace of chunky quartz and gold around her neck to add interest to the plunging *V* of the neckline. The high-heeled gladiator sandals in faux snakeskin gave her outfit some edge. She'd taken care with her outfit because she was meeting a man who was accustomed to women wearing high-end designer clothes. In the growing darkness, she wondered if it had been a fluke of time and place that she and the celebrity quarterback had felt such a connection yesterday.

He seemed to think it was more than that, arranging for all this secrecy. Of course, he wasn't used to hearing *no* from a woman or anyone else, so it probably brought out the competitor in him.

The town car wove through the narrow downtown streets and crept into a back alley before coming to a stop. This time the driver jumped out and jogged around to hold the door Miranda had already opened.

She swung her legs out and stood in the pool of light thrown by an ornate bronze fixture over an unmarked door. It reminded her of the back entrance to Cleats, and she had a sudden understanding of the downside of fame—always sneaking into places from dark alleys, through utilitarian doors, dressed in a raincoat or a baseball cap and sunglasses. Ironic that she often arranged such access for her clients.

"I'll take you to Mr. Archer," the driver said, gesturing toward the door.

Miranda waited while the driver knocked. The door swung open, and then she was ushered through a series of hallways, the decor going from white paint and linoleum to wood paneling and ultrathick carpeting. The driver tapped a distinctive rhythm on a double door before turning to walk away down the corridor. Miranda didn't have time to say thank you before one of the doors swung inward.

No one greeted her, so she stepped through into a sitting room decorated in richly textured modern fabrics and paneled in dark wood. Huge windows framed spectacular views of New York Harbor, with the Statue of Liberty raising her glowing lamp above the waves. A mouth-watering aroma of gourmet food floated past her nostrils.

The door closed behind her, and she pivoted to find Luke turning the privacy lock. He gave her an apologetic smile. "I'm sorry about the cloak-and-dagger routine. I didn't want anyone to see or hear me from the hallway. For your protection."

"It was a little spooky," Miranda said, a slight quaver in her voice.

Luke was dressed in charcoal gray trousers that made his legs look even longer than usual, and a dark blue shirt, unbuttoned at the neck, which gave a surprising elegance to his broad shoulders and narrow waist. The dark colors of his clothing made his gilded hair and pale eyes practically glow in contrast. She drew in a deep breath to dampen the flutters in her chest.

"Let me take your coat." He stepped behind her and slipped the raincoat off her shoulders. His breath stirred a strand of hair against her temple, sending a shiver of sensation skittering down her neck. He laid the coat across a chair set by the door and turned, this time with heat warming his blue eyes.

"Now for a real hello," he said, bringing one hand up to splay along her jaw as he angled his head downward to brush her lips with his.

The feel of his strong fingers against her skin, the touch of his mouth on hers, the sense of his body only inches away, lit a subtle flame that licked along Miranda's veins. She stepped into him. As she ran her palms up his chest, he circled her waist with one powerful arm to bring her even closer.

She expected him to intensify the kiss, so she let her lips part, but he lifted his head. "Dinner first. Because once we get started, the food will end up cold."

A wave of apprehension swept through her, dousing the sensual glow he'd just kindled. He was looking at her with intense anticipation, as though he'd been making plans all day.

She didn't know if she could live up to them.

"It smells wonderful," she said, starting to move away from him. His encircling arm stopped her.

He was staring down at her with a frown. "You don't need to worry about Spindle. No one knows you're here except my driver, and he's been keeping my secrets for years."

That drove home how foolish she had been to come. She was jeopardizing her career—and her brother's farm—to see a man whose interest she probably wouldn't hold even through this one evening.

She scanned his face with the distinctive eyes, the sculpted jawline, the thick golden hair—all both famous and familiar from a multitude of photos, advertisements, and television interviews. His head was framed by a window with the kind of view that meant this suite bore a price tag that was stratospheric.

She didn't belong here with this man. She could only disappoint him. "I'm sure your driver is completely trustworthy, but I probably shouldn't have come."

He let his arm drop. "At least have dinner," he said. "I was going to take you to Bouley, so that's what we've got here."

He gestured toward a round table set in front of one of the windows, the reflection of candles and yellow roses glowing against the dark blue of the night beyond the glass. A metal warming hutch stood beside it, along with a silver ice bucket containing a bottle of champagne.

He—or his assistant—had gone to some trouble for this dinner. She was flattered and oddly touched. If this was about sex, at least he was romancing her first.

"I just got nervous." She gave him a genuine smile. "It's hard to get used to the reality of a date with you."

All emotion disappeared from his face. "I thought we'd gotten past that."

"Yesterday we had. Today the shock hit me all over again." She brushed her fingers lightly against the back of his hand. "Oh, my God, I'm touching Luke Archer."

The corner of his mouth twitched upward. "Maybe you should keep doing it until the novelty wears off."

She reached up to comb her fingers through his gleaming hair because he'd given her permission. "So many textures to explore."

He turned his head to kiss her hand. "I'm starting to think you don't want dinner."

She caught her breath as his eyes went hot. "I'm starting to think you're hungry."

He gave her a slow smile, his dimple emerging gradually. "There are all different kinds of hunger."

The dimple and the velvet of his drawl sent desire curling through her. Before she could reply, he walked to the table and pulled out a brocade-covered chair. "Let's satisfy one at a time."

She walked toward him, feeling his appreciative gaze as a physical touch, skimming down her legs to her ankles, then back up over the swell of her hips to her achingly taut breasts and finally her lips. "How do you do that?" she asked as she stepped between the chair and the table to sit.

"Do what?"

"Make me feel like you're touching me just by looking."

"Focus of desire." He pushed in the chair with a smooth motion that made her conscious of his strength. His fingers brushed against her skin as he moved her hair aside with one hand before he bent to press a kiss on the side of her neck. His lips were firm and warm, and she shivered at the contact.

"Focus of desire," she repeated, trying to shake off the haze of arousal he was creating. "It sounds like one of those slogans athletes use to psych themselves up."

He gathered the hair away from the other side of her neck, and she tilted her head in anticipation of his next touch. This time the kiss was lingering. She heard him inhale as though he wanted to enjoy her scent as well as her taste. She felt a slight rough flick of his tongue and shuddered at the streak of sensation flashing down to liquefy low inside her.

He moved his head far enough away to say, "It's just how I do things." His breath tickled her ear.

"It's effective."

She could tell he had straightened and stepped away because the air around her lost its charge. She swiveled to see him pick up the champagne and twist the metal basket off the cork before easing it out of the bottle. He leaned over to fill her flute. "Some people can't handle it."

Miranda wondered if she was one of them.

He seemed to read her thoughts. "You can."

As he sat down, she thought she caught a wince of pain. "Is the bruising still bad?"

An odd expression of relief crossed his face. "Right. You know about it. My trainer Stan says the workout we did today should help, but I'm not feeling an improvement yet."

Miranda thought about their activities the night before and wondered if they had contributed to his discomfort. "Maybe tonight"—she made a vague gesture with her hand—"is not such a good idea for you."

"Sugar, last night practically cured me." He picked up his champagne and raised it to her in a toast. "To us."

"To us." She touched her glass to his with a melodic ding. His toast described exactly what was going on here. The two of them together for one night. Nothing more.

His eyes never left hers as he took a drink of the fizzing liquid. Caught in the laser beam of that gaze, she barely tasted her own first sip.

He took another swallow, and she found her eyes drawn to the strong muscles moving in his throat. Every part of his body exuded power and control.

He reached over to lift the silver cover off the plate in front of her. "Organic Connecticut farm egg. Or you can have chilled Wellfleet oysters." He waved to the oysters on his plate. "There's also sea urchin-and-rabbit salad." He uncovered two more dishes resting on the side of the table.

The delectable aromas wafted past her nostrils as each cover was removed. She closed her eyes to inhale. "I could dine on the scents alone." When she opened them, his gaze was resting on her mouth.

He took an oyster and put it on his plate with a clink of shell on china before passing the rest to her. "We'll eat family style and share everything."

"I've always wanted to do that at Bouley," she admitted.

"Do you have a connection at every high-end restaurant in the city?" Luke took a dollop of sea urchin and caviar before passing the spiny shell to her.

"If I don't, one of my colleagues does. But frankly, your name would get me anything I wanted anywhere in New York City and possibly the whole United States."

He shook his head. "They don't like me much in Boston."

"You ruined their perfect season last year, but they'd still want you at their restaurant, trust me."

"Maybe to poison me." He accepted the other half of the Connecticut farm egg.

"Has anyone ever tried to do that?" She dipped into the sea urchin, nearly swooning at the burst of flavors. "Not poison you, but sabotage your food or something before a big game?"

"Not since college." A look of distaste flitted across his face. "And that wasn't food. Nowadays the team goes into lockdown at a hotel before big games, partly to prevent anything like that."

"The sea urchin is fantastic." She took another bite of the extraordinary dish. "What happened in college?"

He looked away. "They sent a hooker to my room. I still don't know how she got in when the door was locked."

She hadn't meant to bring up dark memories. "You don't have to tell me any more."

His gaze returned to her face. "I told her to leave, and the scene got ugly. She'd been paid a lot to keep me awake all night, and she wanted to do her job. It was my first bad experience with the press."

She imagined him as a young golden boy, still with a glow of innocence even though he was rapidly becoming a star. There was an innate uprightness about him as a man that made her think he would have been shocked by the sordidness of that incident in his youth. "You had to grow up fast."

"No faster than my teammates." The planes of his face angled sharply, all the innocence honed away.

"The spotlight was on you, the quarterback, the glory position. That's more pressure than the others had to deal with."

"It was my choice."

"Do we really understand the choices we make at that age?" she asked.

"What choice did you make that has you looking so unhappy?" He put down his fork to give her his full attention, the intensity of his gaze making her feel as though he could see into her mind.

"Not unhappy. I've never regretted my decision to leave the farm and move here. But every choice seems to bring along its own burden. My parents were baffled by my ambition to leave the country behind and move to a city they find dirty, ugly, and rude." She gestured toward the spectacular view with her fork. "They don't see the magnificence of the architecture, the museums, and the culture. They think what I do, catering to the whims of the very wealthy, is frivolous and unproductive." Her parents' dismissive attitude toward her chosen profession, no matter how successful she was, still hurt way down inside.

He spun an empty oyster shell on the plate, watching it rotate before he looked back at her. "My parents don't know what a two-point conversion is."

"What?" Astonishment made her voice sharp. "Don't they watch your games?"

"They claim they do, but"—his shoulders rose and fell on a sigh—"they're not typical Texans. Football was not on their radar."

"*Not on their radar!* You're the greatest football player who's ever played—"

He gave her a wry smile. "Some would argue that."

She dismissed his interruption with a wave of her hand. "I've read your bio." She didn't care that he knew. "You were bound for glory from high school on. Your parents should have been waving pom-poms at every game."

"My parents thought I came from a cuckoo's egg that got laid in their nest. I was supposed to like books, not balls. Especially not the kind where a bunch of violent, brainless men just run into each other."

She heard the buried hurt in his voice, and it wrung her heart. She wanted to give his mother and father a good talking-to. Even superstars needed their parents' approval. "So let me guess . . . they applaud what Trevor does?"

"They *understand* what Trevor does."

"Wow." She shook her head in disbelief. "They have a son whose talent and success are brilliant to the point of genius, and they can't be bothered to *understand* what he does." Her voice had gone sharp again, and she made an effort to soften it. "I'm sorry. I shouldn't speak that way about your parents."

"No, I appreciate the support." He gave her another wry smile and picked up his fork. "They would disagree with using the word *genius* as applied to sports."

"Why can't our families celebrate our successes without judging them?"

"They think our choices are a comment on theirs."

"Exactly." Miranda found it hard to believe that he shared her experience. She remembered the scene in Orin's office. "Does Trevor feel like your parents do?"

"Yeah, plus being envious." The navy silk of his shirt stretched over the flexing bulge of his shoulder muscles as he shrugged slightly. "I'm not complaining, but everyone sees the trappings. No one sees the things I gave up to get them."

She thought she understood. "Focus of desire. You have to strip away everything else because you can't afford to take your eye off the goal. You set the bar so high that it requires total commitment."

"Funny thing is, I don't remember setting the bar. It was just there."

"Because of who you are." She sighed. "I don't get why there's a problem. We're not hurting anyone else by pursuing our own passions."

"They compare themselves to us and don't like what they see."

"When I see someone doing well, I don't want to tear them down." She leaned in. "I want to work harder so I can get there, too."

"That's the difference between you and me. I want the defensive line to flatten them."

She flushed when she realized she'd been talking as though there was some correlation between her career and his. "I didn't mean to get so earnest."

"No apology necessary. I just had to be honest about myself."

She thought about everything she'd watched him do in the last few days. All the small gestures, his vulnerability to his parents, his protectiveness toward Trevor. All the fame and adulation hadn't warped the bedrock integrity of the man. "You don't see yourself very clearly."

It struck him again that she viewed him differently than others did. "You deal with some selfish, demanding people as clients," he said. "How do you keep from getting cynical?"

"My clients can be challenging, but they're also appreciative of my efforts. I like working in a residential building instead of a hotel because I get to know them, their likes and dislikes, which makes it easier to do a good job. I've grown fond of many of our residents."

He felt a strange twinge of jealousy at the warmth in her voice. Since he never used the building's concierge services, he knew he wasn't included in that group. "What about your boss?"

"Orin's a necessary evil. Our shifts don't overlap much, so he doesn't bother me." Her full lips twisted and her shoulders went rigid. "All right, so coming to work for him might have been a choice I regret.

But the Pinnacle, well, the name says it all. If I want to start my own concierge agency, it adds major credibility to my résumé."

So she had her own ambitions. He wasn't surprised. But Spindle bothered her more than she wanted to admit. "There must be other buildings as high-end as the Pinnacle where the boss isn't such a scumba—er, jerk. He tried to make you look bad in front of me and Trevor."

She finished chewing her oyster before meeting his eyes. He could see her making the same decision he had: to be truthful. "I don't know why he dislikes me so much. I've never done anything to provoke that."

"I'm guessing the clients like you better than him and he knows it. Which takes us right back to what we were talking about earlier."

"He could get rid of me if he would stop trying to ruin my chances of getting another position." She went still. "You're too easy to talk to."

A flicker of gratification banished his jealousy. He sat back in the chair and wished he hadn't when pain wrapped around his rib cage. He swiped the champagne glass off the table and finished the remainder. "So you're looking for a new job?"

Her slim shoulders lifted and fell on a sigh. "I have a shot at head concierge for a new luxury condominium uptown, but I need Orin's reference."

"What about a recommendation from someone else?"

"There are some colleagues who would help me out, but it wouldn't carry the same weight, especially when Orin is running a smear campaign right now."

Now he understood the tension in her shoulders. "What's he smearing you about?"

She looked away. "Just general incompetence. The worst part is that he's sabotaging things that I've set up for clients." When she met his eyes again, hers were lit with indignation. "Making me look bad is one thing, but deliberately making our residents unhappy is something no concierge should do."

Despite her sincerity, he could tell she was trying to deflect him from the smear campaign. Spindle must be using the newspaper photo Miranda had mentioned to stir up trouble for her. "Is it against the concierge code to date a client?"

The champagne sloshed in her glass as she started. "No-o-o-o, not really."

"But Spindle doesn't like it, so he's making your working life hell."

Yet here she was, in a killer dress that made him want to unwrap it from her body and eat oysters off her bare skin. He liked her guts, and he really liked what it said about her feelings toward him.

She squared her shoulders and picked up her fork with a determined air. "Let's talk about something more interesting. Have you sent a document to the Morgan yet? I'm curious to know what you chose."

"My brother started this, so how about I write you a recommendation?" He owed her that much. "You said using my name would get you anything in New York City."

Her lips parted on a sharp inhale. For a moment he saw hope flare in her eyes, but then she shook her head, making the thick, glossy waves of her dark hair ripple. "The problem started well before your brother's issue. That was just something Orin thought he could leverage."

He'd only offered the recommendation out of guilt and because it would cost him nothing, since he'd get Doug to write it. Now he was determined that she should take it. "It's a no-brainer for me. I'd rather help you than most of the people who ask me for things."

"I didn't ask you for it." Her voice was tight.

He laid his drawl on thicker. "And that's why I offered. No strings attached."

"Sorry. Orin has me tied up in knots." She gave him an apologetic smile before she polished off her champagne as well. He refilled their glasses.

"So I'll write the letter."

He got a surprise when she shook her head again. "I'll find a way to get the job on my own." She tried to look impish as she said, "No strings attached." But the worry lingered in her eyes.

"Why?"

She didn't pretend to misunderstand the question. "You don't use the concierge service at the Pinnacle. It wouldn't be a legitimate recommendation."

"I used it yesterday. I can highly recommend it."

She gave a little cough. "Yesterday was . . . out of the ordinary."

He raked his fingers through his hair in frustration. "I know about lowlifes like Spindle. He won't stop until he's dragged you down in the dirt. Take my reference letter, sugar."

Those liquid brown eyes went fiery. "I'm not going to use the influence of a man I'm having sex with, who happens to be so famous I can't even meet him in public."

She jabbed her fork into a piece of rabbit with such force that a lettuce leaf skidded off her plate.

He held up his hands in surrender. "Subject closed, sugar." How had he gotten to the point of pissing her off when he was just trying to help her out? He wasn't used to pushback, and it triggered the competitor in him. "Have another oyster."

She accepted the shell he held out with a wary glance and a flickering smile. "I don't need any extra aphrodisiacs around you." She lifted it to her mouth and sucked the slippery mollusk off the shell.

That sent a wave of arousal straight to his groin. He wanted to lunge across the table and taste the brine of the oyster on her tongue. Instead he gave her a slow smile. "Maybe we could do some dancing after dinner."

Chapter 16

Miranda had to brace herself to withstand the burn in his eyes as he held her gaze for a long moment. She sagged in relief when he smiled and stacked the empty appetizer plates, saying, "Time for the main course."

She felt like she'd been caught in a stormy surf with waves slamming and tumbling her in the churning water. The earlier sense of connection had betrayed her into sharing too much about Orin. Luke's offer of the recommendation had nearly blinded her with temptation for a moment; armed with that, all doors would open. For a short time.

She knew she deserved the head concierge job, but no one else would believe it if she used the famous quarterback's influence. Her abilities would always be in question.

She'd expected him to be relieved when she turned it down, but instead he'd pushed harder. It was the first time she'd experienced the steel behind his drawl. She should have known it was there, but it had shocked her to have all that power unleashed against her.

And then he'd gone back to the seducer in the blink of an eye. When he'd mentioned dancing, she'd been flooded with embarrassment at the memory of her wanton behavior at the club. But the memory had also sent shimmers of excitement rippling through her body to pool in the hollow between her legs. Her appetite for the food had vanished, replaced by her hunger for his beautiful, muscled body.

She glanced up to meet his eyes and nearly moaned at the desire she saw there. He was as hot as she was, but he was controlling it with that famous iron discipline. It was time to see if she could break it.

She picked up a morsel of lobster from the plate in front of her and deliberately nibbled on it while keeping her gaze locked with his. She watched the icy control start to melt as she sucked at the rich, buttery sauce that coated the meat. She put the rest of the lobster in her mouth, letting her eyelids drift closed as she chewed and swallowed it with overt pleasure. Then she opened her eyes and licked her fingers.

His breathing grew harsh. His hands were splayed flat on the cream linen tablecloth.

She picked up another piece of lobster and held it out to him. "Try this."

The table tilted slightly toward Luke, and she realized he was pressing down on it. Very slowly he angled in toward her hand, his eyes scorching. His height allowed him to reach the proffered morsel easily. When he closed his lips around her fingers, the touch of his mouth seemed to travel to her tight nipples. He took the lobster with a sucking pressure on her fingers, and she felt her breath hitch in a gasping sigh.

He swallowed and shoved back his chair. "Dinner's over, sugar."

She'd started this on purpose, but as he stalked around the table, she had a moment of panic. He was a big, sleek predator at the top of the food chain, and she felt like a little brown mouse who was being played with before she was devoured.

But she should have known he wouldn't yank her to her feet and haul her off to the bedroom. Instead, he came up behind her and ran his palms along her shoulders and down her arms to where her hands lay in her lap. He interlaced his fingers with hers and brought her arms back behind her chair, where he cuffed her wrists together in one of his big hands. Her breathing quickened as she felt his strength holding her in place, yet her panic vanished. Now she just waited in delicious anticipation of where he would touch her next.

He surprised her by combing his fingers through her hair. "I like how it looks when it's loose this way."

He took a handful and let it sift down against her neck, the brush of it tickling her so she shuddered in his grip. His fingers went to where the chain of her necklace lay against the side of her neck, and he traced it around to the front, stroking down along the chunks of quartz where they nestled in her cleavage.

"I want to be this necklace, lying against your skin," he said, his fingertips leaving the stones to drift over the upward swell of her breast. She held her breath as his callused fingertips grazed the skin bared by her neckline.

She knew he could see how hard her nipples were through the thin fabric of her dress. She yearned for him to touch them, but she understood the pleasure of waiting, so she let him hold her in place.

He continued his leisurely exploration, his fingers just under the edge of her dress as he dragged them over her skin. Every stroke seemed to move a little closer to the longing at the center of her breasts, and she willed him to thrust his hand all the way under the fabric and relieve the ache.

Did he realize his slow, sensual exploration was winding her arousal tight to the point of exquisite agony?

His breath whistled past her ear, its rhythm becoming more ragged. Suddenly, he reached down and separated her hands, moving them to the bases of the wooden posts that supported the back of the chair. "Wrap your hands around these and keep them there."

She clenched her fingers around the smooth wood, slightly uncomfortable at how the position thrust her chest forward. The awkwardness evaporated as he slid his hands down from her shoulders to cup and knead exactly where she wanted him to, circling his thumbs over her nipples so she surged into his palms and moaned his name. Every circle spiraled in and downward, and she rocked her hips forward to ease the tension there. But she kept her hands locked on the wood.

"That's good, sugar. You hold on tight and let me take you where you want to go."

She felt a tug at her waist as he untied the bow, and her dress fell partway open. For a few moments, her insecurities resurfaced. He was used to the bodies of supermodels.

"It's like unwrapping the world's best Christmas present," he said, pulling on the inner tie to release the last fastening. He drew the fabric of her dress aside, folding it back so the black lace of her bra and panties was exposed. She'd worn her most expensive lingerie.

For a long moment, he didn't move. Her grip on the chair became convulsive as heat coursed through her at the knowledge that he wanted to do nothing more than look at her. She stopped worrying about his previous lovers.

"There's something about black lace that never gets old," he said, his drawl taking on a rasp.

She tilted her head to look up. He bent over her, his hands braced on the arms of the chair, his eyes scalding as they moved over her body. His blond hair framed the planes of his face, and she wanted to pull his head down to feel those perfectly male lips against hers.

He seemed to read her intention, because he shifted to wrap his fingers around hers, the strength of his grip melding her fingers to the posts. "Don't let go, baby."

He slid his fingers under the lace of her bra, and she cried out when his skin touched hers. Sheer need sizzled through her, and she could feel her own moisture soaking the flimsy fabric of her panties. Now he pulled at her nipples, brushing them against the lace she had once thought was silky but that now felt exquisitely rough against her sensitized skin. The near pain gave her pleasure an edge that sharpened the experience of every new sensation. "Oh, God, Luke," she moaned as a satisfied smile tugged at the corners of his mouth.

"Lean forward," he said, thrusting his hands between her and the chair to unhook her bra. "Now let go for just a second." He had her dress and her bra straps off her shoulders and down her arms in one deft motion. Then he returned her hands to their position on the posts.

"I'm going to move your chair," he said, scooting it away from the table as easily as though it were empty.

She felt more vulnerable now that the tablecloth wasn't covering her bare thighs.

But he remained behind her. He took handfuls of her hair and brought it over her breasts, brushing the ends against her like a paintbrush. Instead of edgy arousal, a gentle, tingling pleasure danced over the surface of her skin. It wasn't enough, though.

"Please," she begged. She wanted his hand between her legs. "Please," she repeated, opening her thighs in invitation.

"I never say no to a lady," he said, his drawl thick as molasses. He dropped her hair and reached down to push against the damp lace.

"Yes, there." She pulsed against him. The sleeve of his shirt brushed against her bare nipple and made her hiss as it sent another streak of electricity downward.

He found the edge of her panties and stroked under the lace. "Sugar, you feel like wet satin."

When his fingertip touched the focus of her arousal, she arched up with a strangled scream. The tension in her belly ratcheted a notch tighter. "Inside me. Please. Inside me."

He obliged her, thrusting one finger deep into her as he rubbed his thumb against her clitoris. With his other hand, he massaged her breast, rotating his palm over the center of it to drive her closer and closer to orgasm. He found a rhythm that had her hovering on the verge of finishing as he sent waves of pleasure washing through her, making her writhe in the chair. She didn't have to remember to keep her hands on the wooden supports; she was holding on for dear life.

"Okay, sugar, come for me," he whispered beside her ear. He increased the pressure of his thumb and inserted a second finger into the hot, moist center of her with a hard, swift thrust.

She went absolutely still as she felt the exquisite moment of suspension before she began to fall over the edge into her release. Then he curled his fingers inside her and every muscle in her body seemed to convulse around the detonation within her.

The breath screamed out of her lungs as she bowed upward, her spike heels digging into the carpeting while she rode his hand to another explosion. And another. He found a new way to touch her and triggered one last burst of radiating pleasure before she sagged back onto the chair's seat, her heart beating furiously, her lungs laboring to refill themselves.

He slowly withdrew his fingers, sending little aftershocks of delight rippling through her. "Ahh." She let her head fall back against the chair and closed her eyes.

She felt his breath on her cheek before his lips touched hers ever so lightly, an acknowledgment that she needed time to come down from her orgasm, but he wanted to be there with her.

"You can let go now," he said.

Her fingers were still clenched around the chair posts, the anchors she'd been clinging to as the storm of sensation broke over her. She released her grip, flexing and stretching her fingers.

And then his hands were under her knees and around her back, and she was sailing upward. Her eyes flew open, and she started in surprise as she landed against the wall of his chest.

"Easy," he said, walking away from the table. "We'll be more comfortable on the couch."

He strode to the giant sectional sofa and settled onto the gray cut-velvet upholstery effortlessly, as though he didn't have a benchworthy injury and a full-grown woman in his arms.

His touch was undemanding as he eased her onto his lap, but she felt the rock-hard length of his erection against her bottom. It sent another tremor through her.

"Cold?" he asked, seizing a throw blanket that was folded over the back of the couch and draping the whisper-soft cashmere over her exposed side.

"No, just getting a little extra thrill." She snuggled under the blanket anyway, feeling self-conscious about being nearly naked while he was fully dressed.

He wrapped his arms around her over the blanket, one thumb stroking against her shoulder, the softness of the cashmere caressing her skin. She nestled closer, reveling in all the textures of his body against hers. The heavy silk of his shirt pressing against the side of her breast as he breathed. The warm steel of his thigh muscles covered with fine wool. The bands of his arms encircling her in a shelter of protective strength.

Odd that she felt protected even as his cock pushed against the *V* of her panties, reminding her that his needs had yet to be satisfied. The fact that he had taken care of her with such exquisite attentiveness made unshed tears burn behind her eyes.

She turned her face in to the hollow of his neck, inhaling the fragrance of aroused man and fresh, tangy aftershave. "You smell like Texas," she murmured.

A chuckle rumbled against her ear. "You mean like bluebonnets?"

She smiled, even though he couldn't see her. "Like a hard-riding cowboy."

"You were the one ridin', sugar."

"And it was one heck of a rodeo." She started to shift on his lap, but he held her in place.

"Rest a spell. I like having an armful of warm, satisfied woman."

He seemed content to do no more than sit. Maybe his injuries were worse than he let on. Although he hadn't demonstrated any difficulties with carrying her or bending over the chair to make her come. Memories of how he'd touched her sent tendrils of excitement curling through her all over again. "I want to unbutton your shirt."

There was a moment's hesitation before he said, "Go right ahead. Just don't be surprised at the color of the bruising. It gets uglier as it heals."

She levered herself onto her knees and lifted one leg over to straddle his thighs. The blanket slipped off her shoulders, and his gaze zeroed in on her breasts, making them throb with the desire to be touched. But he raised his eyes and stretched his arms out along the back of the couch, so she had access to the buttons running down the front of his shirt. The expression in his eyes was almost challenging, and the corners of his mouth turned up just enough to bring out his dimple.

It was impossible not to brace her hands on his shoulders and brush her lips over the indentation in his cheek. That brought her aching nipples into contact with his chest, and they both inhaled audibly.

"That dimple is so disarming." She kissed it again. "Not what you'd expect on a rough, tough football player."

"I got it from my grandfather, who was a rough, tough insurance salesman. According to the family stories, it was an effective sales tool with the ladies of the town."

She dragged her hands down from his shoulders and leaned back to flick the first button from its hole. "You should smile more when you're on the sideline. You'd convert a lot of women to being football fans."

"Grinning like an idiot would go over big with my teammates."

She walked her fingers down to the next button, slipping it out before she looked up at him. "It might make your opponents wonder what you knew and they didn't."

"That kind of smile doesn't bring out my dimple."

"Show me."

Right before her eyes, he went from red-hot lover to brutal gladiator with ice water flowing through his veins. His eyes froze to glacier blue while his lips thinned and drew back in a near snarl that held the promise of pain and defeat.

As a shiver of trepidation rolled over her, she was grateful for the lesson. She needed the reminder that behind the molasses drawl and the sexy dimple beat the heart of a stone-cold competitor, willing to do whatever it took to win in a game that was ferociously violent. He had climbed to the top of his world and stayed there for years. You didn't do that by being a kind, compassionate human being. Even if he still wanted his parents' approval.

"I like the other smile better."

The ice in his eyes melted, and the dimple reappeared. "I'd be worried if you didn't."

Relief chased the nerves away. Her Luke was back. She gently tugged his shirt out of his waistband and finished unbuttoning it. "Now I get to unwrap *you*," she said as she bared his spectacular musculature. "Ouch." She traced around the splotches of blue, green, and purple on his side, making sure her touch was gossamer light. "That looks even more painful than yesterday."

"I've had worse." He paused. "It just takes longer to heal these days."

She glanced up to see a shadow darken his eyes, and remembered that even Dennis said Luke's age might be catching up with him. To her, he seemed as unalterable as granite, but maybe he was admitting he wasn't.

He brought one of his hands around to cup her cheek. "You don't have to look so worried, sugar. I'll be back on the field next week."

She feathered her fingers over the vivid bruises again. "I'm just wondering if you should go back so quickly."

"Christ, you sound like Stan." He lifted his hand to scrape his fingers through his hair.

"I'd like to meet him." She didn't want to dwell on his troubles, so she changed the subject by lightly trailing her fingers along the lines and curves of the muscles that rippled under the skin of his abdomen. He sat with his arms outstretched on the sofa, his head tilted back against the cushions, eyes closed.

She watched his reactions as her hands moved over him, noticing when he sucked in a quick breath or contracted a muscle. There were more scars than she had noticed the night before, some small nicks and some jagged slashes. She ran her fingers over those as well, ever so gently, but he showed no discomfort.

Did he keep playing because he had a high tolerance for pain, or did he simply override it by sheer force of will?

She rose onto her knees to trace her fingertips up the powerful column of his neck and along his clean, sharp jawline, burying her fingers in his hair, combing through it so the different shades of blond glinted in the soft lighting. "It isn't fair for a man to have such beautiful hair."

She leaned in to kiss that firm, male mouth, her breasts brushing against his bared chest. A long groan tore out of his throat, and his hands were on her waist, lifting her up and sideways so that she sprawled on the couch. Luke shucked off his shirt and came down on top of her, his knees pushing her legs apart so his erection was pressed against the apex of her thighs.

"You rested?" he asked, letting just enough of his weight land on her so her breasts were crushed against his warm skin. That and the pressure of his cock sent erotic energy coursing through her body.

"You were the one who insisted on a rest period."

His mouth curled into a wicked smile. "I think you just challenged me."

She thought of his warrior face and shuddered. "I would never do that."

He levered himself off her and stripped her black lace panties down over her shoes, tossing them behind the couch. He pulled a condom from his trouser pocket, put the foil packet between his teeth, and unbuckled his belt.

He got the condom on so fast that Miranda simply lay there, mesmerized by the speed and economy of his motions.

Then he was over her again, the head of his cock nudging at the opening between her legs. Very slowly he pushed inside her, so she felt herself stretching around him. She closed her eyes to concentrate on the sensation of being filled in slow motion. It was exquisite torture as she waited for him to seat himself fully inside her, her body craving more, yet wanting to savor what he was doing to it. At last he stopped. She could feel the wool of his trousers brush the tops of her thighs.

She tried to pulse her hips, but his weight held her immobile against the sofa cushions.

"Not yet," he said, picking up on the tiny amount of movement she managed. He interlaced his fingers with hers, pinning her hands down beside her shoulders while he braced himself on his forearms. He rubbed his chest over the hard tips of her breasts, sending bolts of arousal streaking down to where he was anchored inside her. All she could do was tighten her internal muscles in response.

He exhaled sharply. "You play dirty, lady."

"Focus of desire." She squeezed her inner muscles again.

The sound he made was somewhere between a moan and laugh. "Using my own words against me."

The light banter contrasted in a highly erotic way with having Luke's cock buried within her.

"I can't use anything else against you, can I?" She pushed against his immobilizing grip on her hands.

"You're using your whole body against me." Nuzzling the side of her neck, he blew gently on each spot he kissed. She shivered at the hot-cold seesaw. He whispered by her ear, "I can feel every inch of your skin on mine."

"And I can feel every inch of you *in* me," she murmured back.

He gave her a little pulse of movement, as though he couldn't stop himself. It was enough to send flares of sensation through her. "Yes-s-s!"

"Aw, hell, sugar, I was going to take my time, but it's not happening." He locked his gaze on hers and started to move, his rhythm measured but relentless.

She wanted to meet his eyes, to watch the heat build in the pale irises, but the feel of him driving inside her was too powerful. She closed her eyes so she could ride the wave growing within.

He released one of her hands, and she felt his fingers curl around her ankle, bending her leg to put her foot over his shoulder. The position angled her hips so he had greater access. He thrust faster and the tension tightened inside her.

She opened her eyes to see the muscles in his neck corded with effort, his eyes glazed. His focus was inward as he drove both of them inexorably toward orgasm. The sight of him made the furled bud inside her burst into a blossom of sound and heat and motion. At the first clench of her muscles, he drove in hard and went still for a second. Then he howled her name and plunged in again, his climax throbbing inside her. Her muscles contracted and she arched upward, pressing against his body without moving it. He pushed in one more time, going deep, and she felt as though her insides would burst open with pleasure.

She melted back into the sofa cushions as aftershocks vibrated through her. He gently unhooked her ankle and lowered it back to the sofa before coming down onto his forearms with his head resting on her shoulder. His breath rasped fast and heavy over her skin while his heartbeat thundered against her breasts.

She luxuriated in the weight and heat of his body as they lay still joined, tiny shudders of residual satisfaction twanging at her nerve endings.

Superbly conditioned athlete that he was, Luke caught his breath much too quickly, pushing up and sliding out of her effortlessly as she whimpered her objection. "I'll be right back," he said, giving her a swift kiss on the lips.

He stripped off and disposed of the condom as she lay there. Her muscles seemed to have stopped listening to her commands. Or maybe it was her brain that had forgotten how to tell them what to do.

She felt his presence and opened her eyes to see him standing over her, an appreciative grin tilting his mouth. "You look mighty pretty like that." He leaned down to draw a circle around one nipple with his fingertip, igniting her skin. "There's a nice, big, comfortable bed in the next room," he said. "We should use it."

He went down on one knee, and Miranda realized he was planning to scoop her up in his arms again. She put her hand against his magnificent bare chest to hold him away. "I'll walk. Otherwise my conscience won't leave me alone."

"As long as I can walk behind you, I won't argue," he said, taking her hand and pulling her up with him as he rose to his full height.

She started to reach for the throw blanket, but his reflexes were too fast, so he got it first, tossing the soft cashmere halfway across the room. "That would ruin the view." He gave her backside a pat to start her moving. "Why would you want to deprive me of such a pleasure?"

Since she seemed to have no choice, she decided to put on a show. Heading for the bedroom door he pointed out, she let her hips sway as she put one foot directly in front of the other, strutting like a runway model. A quick glance over her shoulder caught him staring down at her behind, so she put even more sashay in her walk.

"You're killin' me, sugar."

"You asked for it."

"I think *you're* askin' for it." His hands were on her bottom, his fingers flexing. "They're so smooth and round. Makes me want to take a bite."

"No tooth marks," she said. "I have to be able to sit at my desk tomorrow."

She sauntered into the bedroom and stopped. The giant bed faced another plate-glass window with a view of the harbor, the lights on various shores flickering over the dark water while several boats plowed steadily through the waves. "Now *that's* an amazing view!"

He came up behind her, wrapping his arms around her waist and resting his chin on her shoulder. "I prefer the closer one."

Smiling, she turned in his arms so she was caged against his chest. "Who knew such a tough guy could be such a flatterer?"

He didn't match her smile. "I don't have to be a tough guy, and I don't have to say anything I don't mean. That's why this is so good."

His words made her heart stutter with surprise and delight. "You're not at all what I expected."

Did he want to know more about her expectations? He looked at her back reflected in the window, the curves of her creamy skin glowing against the dark blue of the outside evening. "Tell me what surprises you," he said.

"Now you're fishing." She looked up at him with a teasing smile on her intensely kissable mouth.

"I want the truth."

That knocked the smile away as she lowered her eyes to where her hands lay flat against his chest. "Hmm," she said.

She felt so small in his arms. He splayed his hand to span her shoulder blades.

After a few seconds, her soft brown eyes came back to his face. "So many celebrities believe other people were put on this earth solely to keep them happy. With who you are and the way you look, there are a lot of people who would jump to smooth your path for you. You never take advantage of that. In fact, you go out of your way to be nice to people who can't do anything for you."

He didn't want praise for his fame or his looks. And the other virtue she ascribed to him was no more than basic human courtesy, something he didn't always receive himself, so he made a point to extend it to others.

"It doesn't make me happy that you find a little simple decency a surprise," he said.

She stared at his chest for a moment before giving him a shy look. "I'm surprised by how generous you are about giving me pleasure when we make love."

"So you thought I'd be selfish in bed?" He was getting pissed off. He'd wanted more.

"Let's just say that someone as extraordinarily good-looking and famous as you are might consider just his presence more than enough."

She must have had some lousy lovers. The thought pissed him off even more, for reasons he didn't want to explore.

Truth was, he liked watching how a woman responded to his touch, how she moved, what sounds she made, which parts of her body were the most sensitive. It was like seeing a play unfold on the field and then taking it in the direction you wanted it to go. It stoked his own arousal.

But he wanted to go beyond sex. "What else?"

That had her avoiding his eyes. He put his finger under her chin and tipped her face up. He'd trade her some real feelings. "I thought being benched would make me bored and restless. Instead, I look forward to getting away from the Empire Center and back to you." He was astounded by the truth of it.

He'd thought she would smile. Instead, her eyes lost their glow, and her mouth turned sad. "I'm glad I could make your time off bearable."

"You've made it a holiday." Suddenly, the time between now and Monday didn't seem nearly long enough. He wanted to explore the bond he'd felt when they were touring around the museums. Taking her to bed might have screwed that up, but the intangible connection had felt so powerful that a physical relationship seemed like the inevitable next step.

He leaned down to kiss the wistful curve of her lips. She responded by clutching his shoulders and running her knee up the side of his thigh so that she was pushing against his half-hard cock.

He sensed an edge of desperation in her reaction and knew she was trying to distract herself or him with sex. Locking his hands under her, he lifted her to wind her legs around his waist before walking to the bed. His bruises howled, but the pressure of her against his arousal submerged the hurt.

As he lowered her to the edge of the mattress, an arrow of intense pain lanced into his rib cage. He straightened with a grunt.

"You have to stop carrying me," she said, her reproof laced with guilt. She smoothed her hands around the edges of his bruises as though she could take the hurt on herself.

"I moved wrong. That's all."

His cock hardened even more as she looked up at him from where she sat, her hands still on his skin and her dark hair streaming over her naked breasts. "You're supposed to be resting."

"Sugar, I brought you over to the bed so we can do just that." He stripped off his trousers and briefs.

She gave a gasping laugh as his erection sprang free. "You don't look like you're ready for a nap."

Her head was at waist level, and he had a vision of her lips wrapped around his cock. He forced it away, clenching his hands into fists to control the wave of desire. But he wanted something different from her.

He knelt in front of her, taking one of her high heel–clad feet in his hand and fiddling with the buckle. He needed some distraction to get himself under control.

"Let me do that," she said, trying to lift his shoulders with her soft hands in an attempt to make him stand. "You're going to hurt yourself again."

He ran his finger along the bottom of her arch, making her jerk and giggle.

"Hey, the handsome prince isn't supposed to tickle Cinderella," she said, the smile back in her voice.

He tossed the shoe over his shoulder. "Good thing it's not made of glass," he said as he unbuckled the other one and sent it sailing as well.

Taking her ankles in his hands, he swung them up onto the bed and climbed in beside her. As she started to cuddle against him, he rolled over onto his uninjured side and propped his head on his hand.

"Now talk to me, sugar."

Chapter 17

Miranda looked adorably confused. He couldn't blame her. He had taken off his clothes, gotten into bed with a naked woman, and told her to talk. Hell, *he* was confused.

"Talk about what?" she asked.

"About you. What you like. What you want."

"That's pretty open-ended." Her tone was wary.

"How about telling me what you would do if you didn't need to earn a living?" Because that was the question on his own mind.

She gave him a dubious glance before saying, "I think I'd be a tour guide for travelers overseas."

Maybe she had missed the not-earning-a-living part. "Money doesn't enter into this, so you don't have to take anyone with you. You can travel by yourself."

"I'd travel on my own first, discover all the most interesting places to see and most scrumptious places to eat, and then share my knowledge." She was warming to her vision. "I like helping other people enjoy things."

"You're a strange one, Miranda Tate." He imagined going on the exploratory trip with her, searching out exotic locales, deciding which sights and food they liked and didn't like, trying out the beds at hotels. It was a damned appealing picture.

"What about you?" she asked. "What would you do if you didn't play football?"

He should have seen that coming, but it felt as though she had hauled back her fist and punched him in the sternum. He rolled onto his back and stared at the ceiling.

Now she came up onto her elbow and brushed her slim fingers around his bruised ribs. "Your injury isn't that bad, is it?"

He fought with himself for another few moments before he said, "No." He rolled toward her again. "I don't have an answer to your question."

"Why is that a problem? You love football, and to say you're good at it would be an understatement." Her brown eyes held puzzlement.

He ran his finger along her arm. "I'm thirty-six."

He saw understanding dawn on her. "You're wondering what to do *after* football." She paused for a long moment, and he watched something that looked like pity cross her face. That should have bothered him, but instead it made him feel less alone.

"Wouldn't you like to coach?"

Everyone assumed that was his next step. He pictured himself standing on the sideline, watching the game unfold when he could do nothing about it. "If I can't be on the field, I don't want to be anywhere near it."

"You could start that art collection we talked about at the Morgan Library," she suggested.

He'd considered that, a lasting legacy of some kind, but—"I'd have to hire experts, take their advice."

She frowned, coming up against the same wall he kept hitting. "There's got to be something that interests you other than football."

He let his fingers drift over the smooth skin of her shoulder again, avoiding eye contact by following their progress. He took the plunge. "Investments. The stock market. Venture capital."

"I can see you being very good at that. It requires strategy and risk taking."

She hadn't laughed or looked shocked, so he confessed some more. "Sometimes I help out my teammates with their investments. I got tired of seeing them get cheated or just fritter away their money."

"You like to help people as much as I do."

"I'd have to learn a lot more, take some tests, get licensed." He smoothed his palm down the curve of her hip.

"And the problem is?"

This was the hardest part. "Studying wasn't my strong suit in school."

She raised her eyebrows. "Don't you memorize all the plays for every game so you don't have to wear one of those wrist thingies?"

"Not the same. I know football like I know the back of my own hand."

She snorted, a surprisingly inelegant sound from such a cultured woman. He liked it. "I've seen those charts with all the *X*s and *O*s. If you can memorize those, you can handle stocks and bonds."

"The study guide for the Series 7 test is three inches thick." He'd taken one look at it and decided he needed to find something else to do for chapter two of his life.

She scanned his face, seeming to peer into the fault lines of his soul with her grave, kind eyes. "If I had a portfolio, I'd hand it over to you without a moment's hesitation. There's no one I would trust more than you to take care of my hard-earned money."

The uncertainty inside him melted away. She'd made it so simple and so clear. He might not be the most sophisticated money manager in the world—yet—but he was 100 percent committed to doing the right thing for anyone who entrusted their money to him.

He wanted to leap out of the bed and do a touchdown dance like DaShawn's famous Cotton Bowl boogie. Instead, he let a grin spread across his face.

"What?" she asked, her lips curling upward in an echoing smile.

"You are a very smart woman." He pulled her against him to plant a loud smack of a kiss on her lips. As soon as the season was over, he'd hire a tutor to get started on the Series 7 material.

"Am I?" A shadow dimmed her smile.

He wasn't having any of her self-doubt, especially not with her soft breasts crushed against his chest. "More than smart. Brilliant. A genius." He slid his hand under the sheet to take a satisfying handful of rounded behind.

"If that's where my genius resides, I'm not flattered," she said, but he heard the tiny gasp in her breath.

All the exhilaration her words had sparked seemed to flow into his cock. He wanted to bury himself inside her and make her feel as good as he did. He slipped his fingers between her legs from behind and made her gasp long and loud.

Miranda lay in the big bed as Luke slept facedown beside her, the muscled weight of his arm heavy over her waist. The steady rise and fall of his back as he breathed was almost hypnotic, while the warmth of his athlete's body soaked into her bones. She felt as wrung out as he looked, but her brain wouldn't stop revving. She stared out the window, only half seeing Lady Liberty's solemn presence as the helicopters and ferries plied their routes back and forth across the variegated dark blues of water and sky.

She knew he'd entrusted her with something private when he'd talked about his parents and then admitted his ambition to be a financial adviser. And his doubts about his ability to handle the examination.

When he'd said he had no answer for his future, she'd felt a wrench of heart-cracking pity. He'd had to cut away everything else in his life to reach this level of success. If he couldn't play football, what was left?

It shocked her to realize how bleak his future must look to him. She didn't want to feel sorry for him.

He'd confided his past disappointments and shared his future dreams with her. His trust was both potent and treacherous, because she wanted it to mean something.

A dangerous longing for an assistant concierge to feel about a superstar billionaire.

Chapter 18

Since he was the table's host, Luke did his best to hide his ferociously bad mood at the charity gala. All he could think about was wasting an evening he could be spending with Miranda.

He was annoyed by her gracious acceptance of the news that he had to attend this shindig without her. If she'd been disappointed, she'd concealed it well behind her unruffled smile. Orin Spindle had better pray he didn't cross paths with Luke anytime soon.

Not that Luke's personal trainer and date, Elyssa Lauda, didn't look stunning in her formfitting sequined sheath. He often brought her to public events because she looked the part. That and the fact that she was gay, so neither of them would get into trouble after a few drinks.

But he wanted Miranda beside him so he could wrap his arm around her waist and pull her warm, curvy body close against him. It had been hard as hell to let his driver take her home to New Jersey in the dark, chilly hours of the early morning. He'd wanted to spin the sheets into a cocoon around the two of them and stay there until the sun blazed through the big window, talking to her, touching her, making love to her.

In the meantime, Miller had resorted to a professional connection for his date as well, bringing his high-powered literary agent, Jane

Dreyer. Jane was using all her persuasive skills to talk Luke into writing his memoirs. So far he'd held firm, but it was surprisingly difficult to say no to the tiny blonde woman with the steely determination of a hunting tigress. Luke recognized a kindred spirit.

He got a brief reprieve from Jane's cajoling when Trainor walked up with the mysterious Chloe on his arm. The CEO looked every inch the powerful businessman in his tailored navy suit, while his companion wore body-hugging blue lace, undoubtedly designer. The dress would look even better on Miranda, with her dark hair and curves. He pulled himself up short as his mind strayed to the specifics of where the dress would touch Miranda.

As she shook his hand, Chloe surprised him by saying, "I'll never forget the eighty-two-yard pass you threw to win the Super Bowl. My heart was in my throat as that ball flew through the air. I'm a great fan of yours." She nodded toward the rest of the room with a smile. "Along with everyone else here, I suspect."

He could see what Nathan liked about this woman. There was a straightforward honesty about her that drew you in. He shook his head with a smile. "There are plenty of Patriots and Dolphins fans here."

He introduced the two newcomers to Jane and noticed that even when he shook hands with Miller's agent, Trainor never let go of Chloe. And she nestled comfortably against the CEO's side. Their body language told Luke all he needed to know about how real the relationship was. The craving for Miranda's presence intensified.

Miller strolled up with Elyssa, triggering another round of introductions. Luke saw the assessing way the writer's gaze traveled over Trainor and his companion. Miller maneuvered himself into position beside Chloe. "So tell me how you and Nathan met. Being a writer, I'm always interested in the backstory."

Chloe had the good sense to look wary before she said, "I worked for him briefly. I'm temping between permanent jobs."

"An office romance, then." The writer's eyes brightened with interest. "So you spent hours in his company and still agreed to go on a date with him. You're a brave woman."

Trainor slid his arm around her waist in a protective gesture. "*Foolhardy* might be a better word. Not to mention the fact that for the first few days of our acquaintance, I had the flu."

His date looked startled by his admission, but she smiled up into Trainor's eyes in a way that made Luke's gut tighten with envy. "And germs make him cranky."

"I'll bet," Luke said, awarding her mental kudos for speaking frankly in intimidating company.

The CEO gave him a hard stare. "Chloe and I are going to take a look at the auction offerings," Trainor said, guiding his date away from Miller's inquisition. "We'll meet you at the dinner table."

"Methinks there's more to the story than Trainor is letting on," Miller said, watching the couple's progress through the crowd of guests.

Luke saw Trainor snag two glasses of champagne from a passing server and hand one to Chloe, his look and posture intimate. "Doesn't matter. That's the real deal."

"There's many a slip twixt the champagne flute and the lip," Miller said. "Based on what Trainor has said to me, it's far from a sure thing."

"Trainor discusses his love life with you?"

The writer chuckled. "Mostly he curses at me for getting him involved in this wager."

"But he hasn't backed out."

"No." Miller turned to Luke. "Having second thoughts?"

"I made the bet. It's done." Miranda slid into his mind again. He didn't like thinking about her and the drunken wager at the same time. It made the reality of what he had bet on too vivid.

"Ah, but this gamble has just begun," Miller said.

Luke had a strange desire to shield Chloe and Trainor from Miller's cynical prying. "How's the writing?"

The writer flinched, making Luke feel a twinge of guilt. "How's the bruising?"

"Healing fast."

"I've heard that's one of your talents. You don't get hurt much, but when you do, you recover at amazing speed."

It was true that Luke didn't have an obvious Achilles' heel. His shoulders and knees were sturdy enough to handle the constant wear and tear of the sport, with only a few minor surgeries. He took very good care of his body, so it mended quickly. But he also played through pain. And not just limped through it, but played full-out without anyone being the wiser. "It's a gift."

"I wonder." Those green eyes of Miller's were damned penetrating. "So the exquisite Ms. Lauda is not the love of your life?"

Luke allowed himself a tight smile. "Just my personal trainer."

"Too bad. She's quite beautiful."

Miranda's velvet brown eyes, her serene, elegant voice, the glossy tendrils of her hair, and the feel of her satin skin floated through Luke's mind. "Never challenge Elyssa to a capoeira match. You'll get your butt kicked."

"I'm a lover, not a fighter," Miller said. "Based on your date, I'm guessing you're not making any progress with our little wager of hearts, either."

"I have other things to focus on during the season." But today at the Empire Center, he had found his mind again wandering to Miranda during the video review. Not just how she felt when she was moving underneath him, but her belief that he could pass the Series 7 exam. He'd ordered the study guide that morning.

He'd also put Doug on the task of tracking down Miranda's dream job. There couldn't be too many luxury high-rise buildings nearing completion in Midtown, and he trusted Doug to zero in on the right one. Luke would take it from there. He was damned if she would work for that puke Spindle any longer than necessary.

"Archer?"

Luke snapped out of his reverie to find Miller giving him an amused glance. "Maybe you're making more progress than you let on," the writer said. "You had a strangely dazed look on your face."

That pulled him up short, since he knew what—or whom—he'd been thinking about. "After a few minutes of your conversation, I zone out."

Miller cracked a laugh. "I like you. Underneath that homespun Texas twang and clichéd dimple is the soul of an ancient pillager." He gestured to Luke's hands. "So why don't you wear your Super Bowl ring?"

"Which one?" He put on his patented "that's all on that topic" smile.

Miller was impervious. "Your favorite one, of course."

"I don't have a favorite."

"Sure you do." Miller's eyes glittered. "It's the one that cost you the most."

"That should be my least favorite." And it would be the most recent one. The Empire had clawed their way into the playoffs and then hung on by their fingernails to make it to the Super Bowl. There had been times when he felt like he was carrying the entire fifty-three-man roster on his battered and aching back. At the end of the game, as he hoisted the Vince Lombardi Trophy over his head, his overwhelming emotion had been relief. He could go home and rest.

Miller disagreed. "The things you work the hardest to earn are the ones you treasure."

Trainor interrupted them as he rejoined the group minus his date. "I need to talk to you privately," Trainor ground out. He swung his gaze to Luke. "Both of you. Please excuse us, ladies." He stalked away from the table, obviously expecting the other two men to follow him.

Miller quirked a smile at Luke. "This promises to be entertaining."

Luke apologized to Jane and Elyssa for leaving them before he strolled after the CEO. Trainor was waiting for them in a small conference room, his arms crossed and a look of irritation on his face. "Keep it up and I'll leave you with empty seats at your table, Archer." Trainor's gray eyes were pure steel as he held Luke's gaze.

"What are you talking about, man?" Luke asked, but he knew he and Miller had been too obvious about their interest in Trainor's companion.

"Chloe's a smart woman," Trainor said. "She's already asked me what's going on." He cut his eyes to the writer. "So lay off the interrogation, Miller."

"Will you tell her about the bet, or will that be our little secret?" Miller was amused rather than repentant.

Luke considered the question himself. "I say keep it to yourself. It might just make her mad."

"Why wouldn't she be flattered to know she won the bet for you?" Miller asked. "By the way, I can see why you chose her. She's got that certain something. Well done."

"You're both getting way ahead of yourselves." Trainor's tone was hard. "I'll take Chloe home right now if you don't back off."

"Hey, talk to Miller, not me," Luke said.

Miller laughed. "You've got it bad, my boyo. I'll behave, if only so I can watch you guard your Chloe like a dog with a bone."

"You're an idiot," Trainor said, his ramrod posture going even stiffer.

Maybe it was a good thing Luke hadn't been able to bring Miranda.

The thought surprised him. Why did he worry that Miller would make Miranda a target? She didn't look at him the way Chloe looked at Trainor. Luke didn't hold her with the possessiveness Trainor showed around Chloe. There was nothing for Miller to pick up on.

With a sigh of relief, Luke settled himself in the back of the limousine as it headed downtown, dancing the stop-and-go tango of New York City traffic. Loosening his bow tie, he popped the stud out of his collar to open it.

Because he was famous, he couldn't take Miranda out in public. And because he was trying to help out his brother, he couldn't take Miranda to the privacy of his own home.

Something was screwed up about this picture.

As the evening had worn on, Trainor's and Miller's presence had made the wager more and more real. Before, it had seemed an abstract concept waiting in the distant future. But the way Trainor and Chloe looked at each other and touched each other was a powerful illustration of what he needed—hoped—to find.

When he had gone to drop some more money in the charity's coffers by bidding on an auction item or two, his eye was caught by a Cartier necklace. It was a gold chain with a tassel at each end clasped at the front with a ring of pink diamonds. He could see it around Miranda's graceful neck, the two tassels nestled just at the top of the valley between her breasts. It would tantalize him as she sat across a dinner table from him, and then he would take off everything except the necklace when they were alone. He'd almost picked up the pen to scribble down a bid, but he realized she wouldn't accept it.

As he stalked into the private elevator to the penthouse, the vibration of a powerful bass beat began throbbing through the car's walls. When the door slid open on his floor, a wave of pounding rock music smashed into Luke's ears.

Luke leaned against the elevator wall and put his hand to his forehead. "Well, hell."

Trevor had decided to have his own party—presumably without the jocks or socialites he scorned.

Luke shoved himself off the wall and into the entrance foyer. If he just walked down the hall, he might be able to get to his bedroom unnoticed. However, he wouldn't be able to sleep with the music at that volume. Maybe he should go to the gym and set up a bed like the one he and Miranda had shared. The memory sent a jolt of arousal through him.

He hesitated a moment too long.

A woman wearing skintight black leather pants leaned out into the foyer. "That you, Leon?" She blinked unfocused eyes at him.

He recognized that glassy look. It wasn't liquor; it was drugs. Anger ripped through him, and he started past the woman, who threw out her tattooed arm. "Hey! You can't go in there."

"I live here," he ground out, giving her one of his cold stares.

She pulled her arm back to her side and cradled it as though he'd hit her. "Don't get pissy. Trev said *he* lived here."

Luke didn't bother to respond. He stalked into the living room and stopped, scanning the bodies gyrating to the blasting music or sprawled on chairs, couches, and even the floor. The sliding door was open to the terrace, and the silhouettes of more guests flickered in the city lights. But Luke didn't care about that. His gaze zeroed in on the white powder scattered over his coffee table while his nostrils flared at the smell of pot. Some empty bowls indicated there might have been amphetamines on offer as well.

Trevor was nowhere in sight. Luke turned on his heel and walked right back out of the living room to the entrance foyer. Spinning left, he jogged down the stairs that led to the gym floor of his complex. Once he'd shut himself in with the exercise machines, he yanked his cell phone out of his pocket and hit a speed-dial number.

"Escobar Security. That really you, Archer?"

"Yeah, Ron, it's me," Luke said, massaging his temples with his free hand. "I need you to clean up a mess my brother has made at my place. He decided to throw a party while I was out, and it's one I can't be at."

"I hear ya. How about Trevor? Do I give him a scare?"

"Wouldn't hurt, but leave him here. He and I need to talk."

Ron whistled. "Based on your tone, he's gonna wish I'd taken him with me."

"Thanks, Ron. I owe you another one."

"You don't owe me nothin', and you know it," Ron said. "But since you'll send me tickets anyway, don't send them for this week's game since you ain't playing in it. I don't want to watch that second-stringer Pitch. Next week is good."

"You got 'em." Luke headed for the elevator as he talked. For the first time all evening, he felt a genuine smile at the corners of his lips. "You're a good friend, man."

"The best." Luke could hear the answering smile in Ron's voice. "I'll call you when it's clear."

Luke disconnected and slumped against the elevator car's wall as he rubbed his palms over his face, thanking his lucky stars for Ron. Escobar had been a defensive tackle on Luke's team at the University of Texas. He'd been good enough to go pro, but he'd chosen to serve his country instead. After a couple of tours with the Army in the Middle East, Ron decided to move into private security, and Luke had bankrolled him. It had been one of the best investments of his life, because Ron had extricated him and more than a few of Luke's teammates from some sticky situations before the police could get involved.

Now, Luke allowed fury at his brother to flood through him. Trevor knew Luke had to stay miles away from drugs of any kind. There could be no whiff of suspicion that the quarterback used any chemical substance to enhance his performance. And illegal drugs were off-limits for so many more reasons. So his selfish screwup of a brother had brought the drugs right into Luke's home.

He wanted to slam his fist into something, but he couldn't take the risk of hurting his hands when he was this enraged. He shoved them into his pockets and muttered a long, creative string of curses.

The elevator glided to a stop on the ground floor. Luke stood in the stationary car, trying to decide where to go while Ron did his job. He needed a corroborating witness to say he hadn't been at his own apartment with the drugs, just in case the press got wind of it. He'd signaled his driver to be at the door, but he needed a destination before he walked out.

There was only one place he wanted to be, and it was a place he should stay away from. If Miranda had to confirm his whereabouts to the press, it would negate all their precautions. But his driver knew where she lived, so the temptation gnawed at him.

He pulled his cell phone out and swiped his thumb over the screen, scrolling to the personal cell-phone number she'd given him.

He shouldn't do this.

He tapped his thumb against the number and lifted the phone to his ear.

Chapter 19

Miranda's phone rang on her bedside table, making her roll over with a groan. The ringtone indicated a personal call, which meant she didn't have to answer it. She stared at the ceiling and debated. As the fog of sleep cleared from her brain, she remembered Luke was going to be out late. Without her.

She grabbed the phone. "Luke?"

"Miranda." She heard a strange mix of emotions in that one word. There was relief but also hesitation.

She shoved the hair out of her face and sat up against the headboard. "Yes, it's me." He didn't say anything, so she filled in the silence. "How was the gala?"

"Gala? Oh, yeah. It was fine." He went silent again. When he spoke, the tone of his voice was warmer. "No, it sucked. I wanted you there with me."

He'd told her he wished she could come when they'd said good-bye much, much earlier that day, but it hadn't carried the raw honesty it did now. Pure joy zinged through her. "I wish I could have joined you. Did all your friends show up?"

"They did. I was surprised."

Miranda pushed a pillow behind her back and settled in more comfortably. "Why would that surprise you?"

"They can be . . . unpredictable."

Luke had told her about the high-tech CEO and the famous novelist he'd recently met at his club. "Did your autographed football bring in a lot of money for the charity?"

"The tickets that went with it did." His tone changed. This time she heard uncertainty. "I need a favor. A big one."

"Of course." She was happy he'd called her but worried about what he might need so late at night. Had his injuries gotten worse?

"Can I come to your place for a couple of hours?"

She straightened away from the pillow in shock. "Now?"

"It's a lot to ask, I know."

"No, no, it's fine. I just wasn't . . . I didn't expect . . . yes, please come here. Do you need my address?"

"No, my driver still has it." Now she could hear the smile in his voice as she called herself a moron. His driver had taken her home this morning. "We're headed for the Holland Tunnel, and there's light traffic. I'll be there soon."

Miranda hurled the covers off and leaped out of bed. Her apartment wasn't exactly a mess since she hadn't spent much time there recently, but she needed to clear her piled-up junk mail off the dining table, stash the recycling bins in the kitchen closet, and get herself dressed in whatever the perfect outfit was to entertain a famous quarterback for a late-night visit.

As she tidied, she mentally reviewed her wardrobe. It was heavy on work clothes and very light on anything else other than jeans. So, jeans. And under them, a lacy bra and panties, just in case.

The buzzer sounded as she was dragging a brush through her hair. She'd gone basic: a tailored cotton blouse over slim jeans and silver ballet flats. With peach silk underneath.

She checked through the peephole, catching only his profile, and opened the door. She nearly gasped out loud. He stood on her stoop in a perfectly fitted tuxedo with the tie loose but still draped around his neck. His tuxedo shirt was open at the throat, so the strong column of his neck was visible. The fine black wool of the tux subtly highlighted the breadth of his shoulders, the leanness of his waist, and the muscles of his thighs. His hair glowed like molten gold under the streetlight.

"You shouldn't look at me like that," he said, his voice a sharp rasp.

"It's impossible not to."

She could swear he moved at the speed of light, because he was in her house with her body sandwiched between his long, hard frame and the back of the door before she could blink.

"I've been thinking about this all night," he said, his eyes blazing down at her before he lowered his head and gave her a mind-bending kiss.

His words were as potent as his kiss. Heat blasted through her at the idea that she'd been in his mind at the gala, and she shifted against him. He drove his thigh between hers, sending a bolt of electric desire zinging through her as his solid muscle hit the sensitized throb between her legs. Her mouth opened under his.

"Now," he said, his voice pure male command. She knew what he meant, because she wanted the same thing.

They tore at each other's zippers as though they'd gone mad. He yanked her jeans and panties down as she toed off her flats. She ripped open the condom he'd pulled from his pocket and shoved down his briefs to roll it onto his erection.

Then she was levitating upward like an autumn leaf caught in a whirlwind as he lifted her off her feet. Bracing her against the door, he shifted his grip to her thighs, opening them so he could thrust up into her, burying himself fully in one motion. "Oh, God, yes, Miranda," he ground out. "This is so good. You are so good."

He held her in place up against the door so he could withdraw and drive into her. It was primal and powerful and made her beg him to do it again. She teetered on an exquisite balance of yearning emptiness and fierce fullness. The contrast made her grind her hips into his for more.

He obliged, moving faster, filling her more completely, until she locked her arms around his neck, closed her eyes, and let him take her wherever he was going. Sensations swirled inside her like a kaleidoscope: the unyielding wood at her back, the controlling grip of his fingers on her thighs, the husky warmth of his breath on her cheek, the wool of his tux on her bared skin, the stretch and thrust of him moving inside her. Her need tightened down in her belly until he flexed his hips at exactly the right angle, and everything inside her burst into a perfect storm of contraction and release and pure, elemental satisfaction. She threw her head back, knocking it against the door, and shouted his name.

Her orgasm ignited his. He drove into her and stopped, suspended for a moment before he pulsed and arched back from where they were joined, her name tearing from his throat.

The force of his climax sent more tremors through her, a ripple of pleasure tugging at already sated muscles. She sighed into him, her head dropping onto his shoulder.

His iron grip on her thighs eased as he let his weight hold her up against the door. His chest expanded against hers when he drew in a long, shuddering breath. "Sweet Jesus," he said. "I'm sorry."

Her eyes flew open and she lifted her head. "Sorry?" She tried to see his expression, but he was resting his forehead against the door beside her cheek.

"I'm sorry I didn't take more time with you." Regret laced his voice.

She let her head drop onto his shoulder again. "In case you didn't notice, I beat you to the finish."

He was silent for a moment before she both felt and heard a chuckle rumble up from his chest. "You're a mite competitive."

"This is a win-win situation," she said. "We both get a prize."

"Sugar, you *are* the prize." His weight shifted and he slid out of her. "I'm going to let you down slow now."

"That's good, because I think my legs might fold up under me."

He eased them both away from the door and set her down on the floor as gently as though she were made of fine crystal. Her knees wobbled, and she clutched at his lapels while he kept his hands firmly around her waist to support her. She looked up to find his pale eyes warm with something she might have called happiness. It transformed his face, gentling the angles and softening his implacable will. "Want me to carry you?"

"Yes, but I'm going to walk," she said, remembering his injury.

He released her and turned away while she scrambled back into her panties and jeans, the lightest touch of the fabric against her still-sensitive clitoris making her suck in a quick breath. She watched Luke zip his trousers, leaving the tails of his tux shirt hanging out.

It was surreal to see this huge, gorgeous man in the midst of her ordinary apartment. She crossed her arms and wondered what to do next. They'd already cut to the chase. "Would you like a drink? Wine? Coffee?"

"I'm good." He glanced around, and she wondered what he thought of her exposed-brick wall, the built-in bookcases she and her brother had spent a weekend constructing, and the scarred but lovingly polished parquet floor. "This is a nice place," he said.

"Not quite the penthouse, but I'm content here."

He walked to the bookcase to examine her reproduction of a Degas horse sculpture before he pivoted to meet her eyes. "It's like you. Warm and elegant."

"Elegant?" She raised her eyebrows and glanced around. Maybe the small Oriental area rug in tones of burgundy and blue was elegant. And the bronze-and-crystal Victorian chandelier she'd found in a consignment shop might qualify. The rest was just comfortable. "It's home."

His expression darkened at her last word. "I shouldn't be here."

"Why don't you have a seat and tell me why?" She wanted to keep him there, so she waved toward the sofa she loved so much. It was upholstered in a subtle, cream basket-weave pattern that she'd found marked down in a high-end fabric store.

He held out his hand. "Sit with me."

She put her hand in his and let him help her onto one of the plump cushions. When he settled beside her, she snuggled into his uninjured side. "*I'm* glad you're here, so why shouldn't *you* be?"

The arm he had draped around her tightened. "Because my brother is an asshole."

"I'm not getting the connection." She felt the tension in his body and rubbed her palm in circles on his chest to ease it, stroking the fine, soft cotton of his shirt.

A sigh expanded his ribs. "When I got home from the gala, Trevor was throwing a party at my place. That was a jerk move, but I could have swallowed it. However, he broke the cardinal rule. There were drugs."

Miranda let all the implications of that circle through her brain. Now she knew why they'd had fast, hard door sex, and why he'd apologized for it. Luke was venting his anger at his brother. "So you needed to get out immediately and find someplace else to go."

"Yeah, where there was someone who would corroborate that I wasn't at the party to take the drugs, in case the press gets wind of it. I have a good friend cleaning up Trevor's mess, so I don't think it will be an issue, but I shouldn't have involved you."

He might be right, but Miranda felt a warm glow of pleasure that he'd chosen her as his refuge.

Before she could say anything, he continued, his tone reflective. "I can't remember the last time I did something I knew for a fact was wrong."

"You're a highly principled person."

She felt him shake his head. "The temptation hasn't been there. Until now." He tipped her face up so their eyes met. "Do you know how damn good this feels?"

"Really damn good," she said.

"I was cranky as a bear about going to that gala without you." He dropped a kiss on her lips.

Miranda felt it all the way to her toes.

"There was a necklace there I wanted to buy you."

She held up her hand. "No more gifts." Knowing he'd wanted to buy her something was enough of a thrill.

"I haven't given you anywhere near what you've given me. You broke me loose. I don't know how—" He fell silent.

"How what?"

"How about a glass of that wine, after all?" he said.

She could tell he wasn't going to finish his sentence for her. "Red or white?"

"Real men drink red wine." His humor didn't reach his eyes. They were shadowed by something she couldn't read.

Before she could get up, he rose to his feet. "I'll give you a hand."

She led the way to her small kitchen. When Luke stepped in, the space seemed to shrink, so she could practically feel the air moving when he did.

Pulling her best bottle of merlot out of the tiny built-in wine rack, she rummaged through a drawer for a corkscrew.

"I'll take care of that," he said.

As she put the wine and the corkscrew in his strong hands, she glanced up at him with a smile. "I was pretty grumpy about not being with you tonight, too."

It took him only a few seconds to extract the cork. "Good to know." His answering smile flashed and was gone as he poured the garnet-colored liquid into the two balloon glasses she set out.

"It's not that I begrudged the charity your presence at their gala," she said. "It's that we have so little time left, I hate to give up even one day."

His glass halted in midair. "What do you mean?"

She shrugged. "You have to go back to football on Sunday. You don't have, um, relationships during the season." She'd read all about how Luke didn't date during football season. She didn't expect to be the exception.

"So you know about that." He finished lifting the glass to his lips and swallowed a slug of wine. "I didn't start out with the intention of getting this involved."

That stung, even though she understood. He had gotten more involved than he expected, which was a backhanded compliment.

"I didn't, either," she said with equal honesty. "Sometimes circumstances weave themselves together to create a moment out of time. And when someone walks into that moment, you can't stop what happens. You just savor it for what it is . . . a strange, wonderful interlude."

"An interlude." He stared down at the wine he swirled in his glass. "Is that what this is?"

"What else could it be?" She'd expected him to be relieved that she knew the parameters of their relationship. So why didn't he look pleased?

He lifted his glass with a smile that didn't come close to warming his eyes. "To interludes," he said, touching the rim to hers. Then he tossed back the entire glass. "Strange and wonderful."

He refilled his glass and met her eyes. "Maybe it could be—" An electronic tone sounded from his inner jacket pocket. "Ah, hell!" he said, reaching inside his tux and bringing the phone to his ear. "Hey, Ron."

Miranda wanted to strangle Ron, even though he must be the friend cleaning up after Trevor. Luke had started to say something about their relationship. Some sort of possibility. *Maybe it could be . . . what?* A dangerous flicker of hope came to life in her heart.

"Thanks, man. I'll send over those tickets tomorrow." Luke's shoulders went rigid. "I'm going to make some things real clear to him."

He disconnected, and drained his wineglass to the bottom. "My friend Ron says the coast is clear. I guess that means I should go."

So he wasn't going to finish their interrupted conversation.

"Stay here as long as you like," she said. She'd welcome any time she could steal with him.

"I have to talk to Trevor."

"What are you going to say?"

He rubbed the back of his neck, his expression grim. "Hell if I know. I was pretty definite about the rules, but he either doesn't listen or doesn't care. Or both."

Miranda saw the hurt in Luke's eyes. For all his confidence and success, his brother's betrayal still wounded him. "It must be hard to be your brother," she said. "Trevor knows that he'll never be as successful as you are."

"He could be, in his own field," Luke said. "He's smart, really smart."

Miranda thought of Trevor's free use of his brother's apartment and the concierge services that went with it. "I get the feeling you've helped Trevor a few times along the way."

"Why wouldn't I when I have the resources to do it?"

"That might create resentment. He feels entitled to take what you offer because you have so much, but he sees himself as a failure compared to you. So he tries to pull you down."

He pinned her with those laser blue eyes. "What would you do if you were in my shoes?"

She met his gaze. "Tell him you love him. Explain how much power that gives him over you, even though you appear to be invulnerable. Hope he rises to the occasion."

"Trev and I aren't big on that kind of talk."

"Maybe this is the time to try it. He wants your attention, so he might respond better than you think." She touched his shoulder in comfort. "You can't force other people to behave in a certain way. All you can do is be true to yourself and hope your brother can respond to that positively. If he can't, maybe he shouldn't be a significant part of your life."

She watched for his reaction, but he had on that impenetrable mask he wore on the football field.

"Cut him off?" Luke asked.

"That would be the most extreme outcome." Miranda hoped she hadn't started something that would damage Luke and Trevor's relationship further.

He stood with his head bowed as he appeared to consider her words. But when he lifted his gaze, his eyes blazed with a hunger that meant he was done with the topic of Trevor. "I don't know why I'm wasting our time together talking about my brother."

He put her glass on the counter and interlaced his hands with hers, pulling her in so he could slant his mouth over hers. She tugged one hand free and curled it around the back of his neck to bring him closer, putting all she felt into the kiss.

He gave her back the same intensity in a long, temperature-raising embrace. When he lifted his head, Miranda wanted to shriek in frustration. His erection was hard against her, and she was liquid with need.

"Tomorrow," he said, his voice husky. "Spend the night with me."

"Yes," she said, her yearning nearly at a point of pain. "Where?"

His voice turned granite hard. "I'm pretty sure I'll have my place to myself again."

"Remember that you love him."

"Sugar, that's the only reason I told Ron to leave Trevor for me." He turned her so that she was snugged up to his side. "Walk me to the door. I don't want to let go yet."

That made her melt into him, even as she thought how glad she was not to be Trevor tonight. There was cold anger blazing in Luke's eyes. She could feel it in the rigidity of his body.

They reached her door, where he tightened his arm in a brief squeeze and released her. "No more kisses to tempt me," he said.

She laid her palm against his cheek. "Good luck with your brother."

He turned the doorknob. "I've always believed you make your own luck, but tonight I'll take whatever you can send me."

And he was gone, closing the door firmly behind him. She jogged to the window and twitched back the curtain to watch him stride across the street to where his driver waited. As he started to fold his body into the backseat of the car, Luke looked back and raised his hand in farewell.

So he'd caught her at the window. Unembarrassed, she waved in return before letting the curtain fall back into place.

A cold, hard lump of panic clogged her throat. Only two more days.

Luke sat back on the car's leather seat and stretched out his legs. "Back to my place."

As the limo glided down the empty street, Luke folded his arms and let his chin sink onto his chest. Trevor should be his most pressing concern, but instead his mind turned to Miranda.

That rule he had about not dating during football season? He had made it, so he could break it. Problem was, everyone knew about it. People would talk, and it would create expectations.

He grimaced. And what about his thirty-six-year-old body? When he was around Miranda, he wanted to touch her. If he touched her, he wanted to make love to her. His body needed rest when he wasn't training. Could he force himself to kiss her good night and go to his own empty bed to sleep?

He muttered a curse.

"Excuse me, sir?"

"Just talking to myself, Brian," Luke said. "I guess that's a sign of my age, too."

"Your age? You're only as old as you feel, and the way you play, you must feel like a twenty-year-old."

Luke shook his head. "Age and treachery can fend off youth and talent for only so long."

Especially when the Super Bowl was on the line.

Could he ask Miranda to give him time, to wait until the end of the season? He shifted on the seat as he considered how to phrase the request. *Look, I'm interested in continuing our relationship, but not until the football season is over. Can we put whatever is between us on hold until then and try to pick up where we left off?* It was only for a few months. She might be willing to do that.

Unless she met someone else. He smacked a fist onto the seat beside him. He had no right to expect her not to see other men just because he was focused on moving a pigskin toward a goalpost.

Maybe she was already dating someone else. She'd called their relationship an interlude. She might consider him just an extended one-night stand before she went back to her other boyfriend.

He was about to pound the seat again but got a grip on himself. That wasn't Miranda. If she were already in a relationship, she would have given Luke the tour on Tuesday and then told him—very politely—she wasn't interested in anything more.

That made his dilemma worse. If Miranda agreed to wait for him, she wouldn't allow herself to start another relationship. Since Luke had no idea what their long-term prospects were, he didn't feel right asking her to put her love life on hold.

He slammed the seat cushion so hard he felt the blow vibrate up his arm.

"What the hell's the matter with you, Archer?" Luke muttered to himself. He stood in his own foyer with his head thrown back and his hands shoved in his pockets, curbing his anger to a manageable level. He didn't want to go in and confront Trevor. He wanted to go back to Miranda and forget about his brother's betrayal. He'd never before hesitated to do what needed to be done. But Miranda's words echoed in his mind. Trevor was not a teammate or a coach. He was Luke's brother, and Luke loved him. That complicated things.

Taking a deep breath, Luke walked into the quiet, tidy living room. It was empty, but the sliding door to the terrace was open, letting in a draft of chill October air. As Luke passed the coffee table, he noticed that the glass top had been wiped to a sparkling clean. Ron was thorough.

Luke stepped out onto the tiles of the terrace and slid the door closed behind him. Trevor sat slumped on one of the rattan sofas beside the glowing embers of the fire pit.

"Go ahead. Rip me a new one," Trevor said, not moving.

Luke sat across from him. "You knew you were screwing with my career."

"Yeah, I suck."

Luke sat forward and laced his fingers together between his knees. "No, you have a lot going for you, Trev. Now get off your ass and use it."

"Says the legend-in-his-own-time billionaire quarterback."

Luke kept his expression neutral, but his anger surged. "I'm not here as some yardstick for you to measure up to. Live your own life. If you do that, I'm here for you." He waited, hoping his brother would respond, but Trevor made no comment. "But when you betray my trust, I draw the line. It's time for you to leave."

"I'll remove my noxious presence in the morning." Trevor's words were slurred. He must have had a hell of a lot to drink.

"Tonight. You tell my driver where you want him to take you. Once he drops you off, I'm done."

Trevor levered himself upright. "It's the middle of the night. Where am I supposed to go?"

"This is the city that never sleeps." Luke gave it another shot. "Why, Trev?"

"Because I heard from your alma mater today, and their answer was no." Trevor glared at him. "I'm so crappy that not even your all-powerful influence at the University of Texas, where they worship the ground you walk on, could get me a job."

"I'm sorry, bro." Luke had told the dean at UT he'd appreciate the search committee giving Trevor a good, long look, but not to hire him if the fit wasn't right. Maybe he should have been more insistent.

His brother sagged back again, his head angling upward so he was looking at the sky. When he spoke, his voice was low. "Sometimes I hate you."

Trevor's words slammed into him like Rodney D'Olaway's massive shoulder.

"No, I hate how you make me feel," Trevor said, correcting himself. "Like a loser."

Now pure rage boiled up in Luke, scalding hot. "So you want me to blow the season so you can feel better about yourself?" He huffed out a snort of derision. "Stop playing the victim."

"You should try being your brother. Ma and Dad are so in awe of you that they can't believe you're their son. I'm just the average kid they had to help with homework and college applications while you were off becoming a superstar."

"Ma and Dad think I'm a mistake, a jock in a family of brains."

Trevor shook his head. "You're dead wrong. When I was fourteen, I overheard Ma talking to one of her friends. Ma said you would succeed at whatever you went after, whether it was a Super Bowl ring or getting elected president of the United States. The best thing she could do was to get out of the way."

Luke's worldview tipped and spun. All those years of thinking his parents favored Trevor because he was more intellectual had been wrong. But his parents had been wrong, too. He'd needed them as much as Trevor had, in a different way. "You get your digs in about my lack of a PhD."

"It's my one puny weapon in a losing battle."

Soul-deep weariness rolled through Luke. "It's not a battle. We're on the same side."

Trevor made a sound of disbelief. "You're the most competitive human being I've ever met. You have to beat everyone."

That was like a pair of cleats stomping on his chest. "Have I ever done anything but help you?"

"Why shouldn't you? You won't miss what you give to me."

"So I don't give you enough?" Luke couldn't believe what he was hearing.

Trevor sat up, only to drop his head in his hands. "I don't know what I'm saying." He raised his gaze to Luke. "I'm out of here."

He pushed himself up from the sectional and stumbled to the sliding door, fumbling to get it open. Luke leaned back and scrubbed his palms over his face. Miranda would probably want him to let Trevor stay until morning, but Luke was too pissed off.

And hurt. Yeah, it hurt to know his brother dismissed what Luke had done for him over the years. It hurt to hear that Trevor thought they were competitors. It even hurt to find out that his parents thought he hadn't needed their help.

Did they think he was made of stone? That they could pound on him, lean on him, take from him without inflicting any damage?

No, they thought he was made of ice.

Chapter 20

Miranda couldn't stop yawning, even though the morning had been hectic. After Luke had departed last night, she hadn't been able to go back to sleep for another hour. Even when she did, she had vivid dreams that involved tuxedos, football helmets, and Luke wearing both or nothing at all.

Today she felt a sense of frantic melancholy. He hadn't contradicted her when she said their relationship was going to end the day he jogged back onto the practice field, so she was desperate to spend as much time with him as possible. Now here she was, waiting for the phone screen to light up with his caller ID.

"I need a distraction," she said to herself, picking up the phone and dialing Patty's cell number.

"Miranda, how did you know?" her sister-in-law greeted her.

"Know what?"

"That I was about to call you. I just brought Theo home from school because he has a fever, and Percy, the new hired hand, has been out sick for two days. So I've been helping Dennis, but now I have to take care of Theo. Any chance you have a day off this weekend?"

"This weekend?" Dismay tightened her throat. "I'm off on Sunday. I could come up first thing in the morning."

"Could you come after work on Saturday? Assuming you're not on the late shift." Patty blew out a breath. "Dennis can barely handle all the milking and cheese making when Percy's here full-time. I don't want him to exhaust himself now that I can't pitch in."

Of course she could . . . if she gave up her chance of seeing Luke one last time. Her conscience battled with her deepest, darkest desires. Of course, Luke hadn't said anything about seeing her Saturday night. She was just assuming, hoping.

"I'll drive up Saturday right after work." Regret seared through her like a hot dagger, but she couldn't leave her brother to face all the farm chores alone. "Can you find another hand for next week, in case Percy is still sick?"

"Everyone around here is coming down with the flu, so it's going to be tough." Patty sighed. "I'm just praying that Dennis and I don't get sick. We both got flu shots, but you never know if those are going to work."

"Here they're calling it an epidemic. Our messenger has spent the last two days running to drugstores, picking up prescriptions for our residents."

Patty groaned. "Well, stay away from unhealthy people, and no swapping spit with anyone. I need you hale and hearty. Seriously, sweetie, you are the best sister-in-law ever."

Patty had no idea of how very saintly Miranda felt at this moment, giving up the prospect of her last date with Luke Archer. However, she did not intend to follow the no-spit-swapping rule tonight. Miranda forced a smile into her voice. "Remind Dennis of that the next time he's giving me grief. Tell poor Theo I'll bring up a Shake Shack treat for him."

"That will cure him faster than all the meds in Doc Redding's office."

Miranda disconnected and grabbed her spotted stress ball out of the drawer. "Stupid cows!" she said, hurling it against the wall so hard it ricocheted back behind her.

That reminded her of Luke catching it when he'd walked in the door, and she lowered her head into her hands with a long, agonized moan. She'd been tormented about only having two more nights with Luke. Now it was down to one.

"It's better this way," she muttered. The more time she spent with him, the more involved she became. This would limit the damage. "Who am I kidding? It stinks."

She got up and closed her door so she could eat her lunch in peace. As she walked back to her desk, her cell phone buzzed. Swiping it up, she checked the caller ID, her heart flipping when she saw Luke's name.

She froze, trying to decide whether to tell him about Saturday night. But he hadn't asked her to meet him. Maybe because it was the night before a game, he couldn't go out, even though he wasn't playing in it. And he'd never answered her question about whether he had sex before a game.

She would wait until she saw him tonight.

She swiped her finger over the phone and said, "I can't look at my front door without thinking of you."

She heard him suck in a sharp breath of surprise, but he recovered quickly. "I can't look at play diagrams without thinking of you. Or at the weight room. Definitely not at the weight room."

Miranda felt the heat rising and melting her insides. "Play diagrams? Really?"

"All those Xs and Os."

Who'd have thought the big, tough football player could see hugs and kisses in a play diagram? "You win."

"Always do, sugar." His drawl was like warm molasses.

She switched to a more serious subject. "How did it go with Trevor?"

His heavy silence answered her before he did. "I threw him out. Nicely."

"Nicely?"

"I told him my driver would take him anywhere he wanted to go."

"Did you talk to him first?"

Another heavy pause. "I tried. He was drunk or high or both. All he did was whine. I've heard that tune before."

"I'm sorry." She said it gently, because there was pain in his voice. He had tried, and his brother hadn't been able to reciprocate.

"I know you don't have long for lunch, so let's talk about tonight." His tone changed on the last word.

"Is that a polite way of saying you need to go?"

"No, I'm benched, so I have all the time in the world. And you know I like to take it slow."

His husky drawl sent liquid heat to pool low in her belly, but she wasn't going to let him have all the fun. "Not last night. You went for it hard and fast." She let her voice drop low. "I like it both ways."

He groaned, and she allowed herself a satisfied smirk.

"Sugar, you better watch out because I'm about to drive back there, lock us in your office, and do it both ways, so you can make up your mind which one you like better."

A vision of Luke storming through her office door with that focused look in his eyes made her squirm on her chair. "Let me know when you're leaving so I can clear my desk off." Now she conjured up the image of herself sitting on her desk with her skirt up around her waist and Luke between her thighs. Her panties grew damp.

"When do you get off work?" His voice was a harsh rasp.

"Six."

"Damn. Five more hours. How do you feel about meeting me at my place? Trevor is no longer an impediment."

She'd wanted that, but now the problems it raised struck her. Luke's home happened to be her workplace. So which one took precedence?

He spoke into the silence. "If it makes you uncomfortable, we'll go back to the Ritz-Carlton."

But she wanted to see his home, to see him *in* his home. "No, it's fine. I was just thinking about logistics."

"Come in the private entrance. The security cameras back there are monitored by Ron's guys, not the building's. Spindle won't know."

It wasn't just Orin. Everyone who worked at the Pinnacle gossiped about what went on in the building. It was like a small town, only vertical. Could she really keep her visit to Luke's apartment a secret?

Maybe not, but she only had one more night with him, and she was darned if she was going to ruin it with second guesses. "What's the code?"

He recited a string of letters and numbers. "Text me when you're on your way." His voice was husky when he added, "I'll be waiting for you in the elevator. We can get started on the ride up."

Memories of being pressed between Luke's body and her door—two hard surfaces that felt entirely different—exploded in her mind. "You don't waste any time, cowboy."

"When the clock is running, you have to keep moving the ball."

Luke lowered his phone with a grin. Tonight was going to be a low-key evening at his home, because he'd planned a blowout of a date for tomorrow.

Saturday, he was going to fly her to the mountains of West Virginia to dine at the Aerie, a restaurant so exclusive he'd had to call in two favors to get the reservations. He had booked a private room so no one could photograph them. And they would have plenty of time to make love as his jet sped them there and back before the game-night curfew.

Since he couldn't ask her to wait for him, he was going to make sure he left a big impression on her. It would make her future dates with other men pale by comparison so she'd still be free when he could come back into her life. At least, that was the plan.

When the phone chimed again, he checked the caller ID and blew out an exasperated breath. How did Gavin Miller know when Luke was in a good mood so the writer could destroy it? "What is it, Miller?"

"And hello to you, too, Archer."

"I'm at work, so cut to the chase."

"What exactly does a benched quarterback work on?" Miller didn't even try to make his question sound like anything other than a barb.

"The same thing a blocked writer works on."

"Bastard. But I walked right into that." Miller's tone was flat rather than angry. "I called to see what you thought of Trainor's Chloe. The real deal or a mere fling?"

"I guess we'll find out in a year."

"And what about you and your pretty concierge? Real or a fling?"

So Miller had seen the photo. "Do you believe everything you read in the gossip rags?"

"I'll be drummed out of the fraternal order of writers for saying this, but a picture is worth a thousand words. You and the lady were holding hands."

"Camouflage. It keeps the autograph hounds away if it looks like you're on a date. She was being paid to give me a cultural tour of New York. I aspire to be as suave as you."

Miller barked out a laugh. "I don't believe a single thing you just said, my boyo. Except the part about my being suave."

Thank God he'd kept Miranda away from the gala and Miller's insatiable prying. "Miranda works for the building where I live. That's all." The lie came easily, even though he was visualizing her in the elevator with her legs wrapped around his waist and her back against the wall as he surged into her. His cock began to harden.

"Ah, yes, that pesky rule of yours about no women during the football season. I thought you might put it on hold while you're benched." Miller injected a question into his tone.

"A week isn't long enough to find the right woman."

"Not a believer in love at first sight, then? All that ice around your heart takes time to melt."

That goddamned nickname. Luke said something unflattering about Miller's parentage.

"Touchy, aren't we?" Miller taunted. "Never mind. I'll go back to trying to cajole Julian Best to come out and shoot a one-liner at his nemesis."

Sympathy pinged in Luke's rib cage. "It'll happen, Gavin. My bruises are healing. So will your muse."

"I'm a commercial hack. We don't believe in muses. We just sit down at the computer and crank out books."

"And I'm just a dumb jock." Luke recognized the edge of anger in Miller's voice at the criticism that was leveled at him. Probably by those who envied his success. "Maybe you just need a vacation. Change up the scenery."

"Tried it. Tried working on a different book. Tried writing nonfiction. It was all garbage, but it doesn't matter anyway. My agent says it has to be Julian Best."

"What about your love life? You found Ms. Right yet?"

"I don't have time. I need to stare at my blank computer screen for ten hours a day. However, your personal trainer is quite lovely."

"You're wasting your time there."

"Ah, I had a feeling she might play for the other side. At the gala, she resisted my potent animal magnetism without any difficulty."

Doug stuck his head in the empty office where Luke sat with his feet propped up on the desk. When he saw Luke was on the phone, he signaled that he would wait outside.

"Miller, I have to get back to warming the bench. I wish you luck, man."

"I don't need luck. I need a goddamned miracle."

Luke hung up and swung his feet down from the desk. "Doug, you want something?"

His assistant popped through the door. "Coach wants you in his office. Said he couldn't get through on your cell phone."

"Any idea what's so urgent?"

Doug shook his head. "I'm just the messenger boy."

"So I won't shoot you." When Doug looked baffled, Luke felt old. He walked out the door with Doug trailing him. "Would you read my memoirs?"

"Heck, yeah! Are you working on them?"

"No. Why would you want to read them? You know me, in the here and now."

"No offense, Boss Ice, but you don't give away much. I'd like to get a glimpse inside your brain."

"Huh. There's nothing special in there." Luke tapped his temple. "It's just football."

"It's football *legend*. You're a superhero to a lot of people." Doug grinned. "Including me."

"You've seen me in my jockstrap. There's nothing heroic about that."

"In fact, I've been offered a lot of money to take a picture of you in your jockstrap," Doug said.

"You're a good guy, Weiss. Maybe I'll give you another raise in six months."

"I'll put it on your calendar." Doug peeled off as they approached Junius Farrell's door.

"Archer, is your cell phone busted?" Junius sat behind his giant desk. "Shut the door, will you?"

Luke swung the door closed and sauntered to one of the oversize chairs in front of the desk to sit down. "No, I was using it."

"You haven't got a wife, so who the hell were you talking to for so long?"

"What did you want to see me about?" He crossed his ankle over his knee and waited. Junius was unhappy about something.

"Pitch." The coach looked around as though checking for eavesdroppers. "You sure the door's closed?"

"Want me to lock it?"

"No." Junius drummed his fingers on the desktop. "He's not ready. I want you to work with him today and tomorrow."

Luke didn't like the sound of this. "Work with him on what?"

"His mental focus. I think he's got the heebie-jeebies about his first game in the NFL. I need you to talk him through those."

For the first time in years, Luke fought an internal battle between his obligation to his job and his desire to please himself. Usually, his interests aligned without conflict, but he'd planned to leave early to get set up for Miranda's visit to his place. And there was Saturday's expedition. Babysitting the rookie quarterback could put a kink in all those plans. "I'll go talk to him now."

"Don't tell him I sent you. He'll think I've lost confidence in him."

Luke rose from his chair. "If you want me to play on Sunday, I'm ready."

"Stan doesn't think it's a good idea."

Luke swallowed the insults he was about to heap on his longtime trainer. "Stan is being conservative. There's no pain when I move."

"Sit down, Luke."

Luke sat, but he didn't relax. Junius's expression was ominous.

"Some people say you're the greatest quarterback ever, and I'm not going to argue with them," the coach said. "You're the face of the New York Empire. When you play, the stadium sells out, no matter where in the country—or the world—it is."

It was Anoint Luke Archer Day and no one had told him. But he didn't like his coach's tone. "Good to know you feel that way."

"But you're not getting any younger."

There it was. The bullet to the heart. Luke felt the tearing impact but gave Junius a nonchalant shrug. "None of us are."

"At best, you can play another—what?—four years. I have to look to the future of the team. I need to bring a new quarterback along." The coach locked his gaze on Luke. "I will never have the opportunity to work with another athlete of your caliber in my lifetime. But Pitch could be good enough. With your help, he might even be excellent."

Junius was trying to play on his vanity. Except he didn't have any when it came to coaching. He didn't want Junius's job. Luke would work with Pitch, but the rookie had to find the mental focus and drive to succeed inside himself. "I'll do my best." Luke stood again.

"He'll never be you, no matter what," the coach said, throwing him a bone.

"We'll see how close we can get him." The coach nodded and picked up a sheaf of papers, so Luke strode to the door and jerked it open.

As he walked down the corridor, fear sent cold tentacles snaking through his chest. One injury and his coach was writing him off. And Junius didn't even know about the shoulder pain.

This week he'd been forced to ease off on training, but next week he would go back at it full throttle. He had to make sure no one thought he was slowing down.

The fear joined with a dark cloud of regret as Luke faced another truth. Somewhere in the back of his mind, he'd been hoping he could play football and keep Miranda in his life, but that was off the table now.

Unlike Pitch, he knew how to focus.

Chapter 21

At 6:10, Miranda stood at the private entrance to Luke's elevator foyer. She drew in a lungful of the crisp evening air and let it out slowly, allowing her mind and body to shift gears. The assistant concierge scheduled for the afternoon-into-evening shift had called in sick, so Miranda had been insanely busy all afternoon. She'd barely had time to change into the clothes she'd brought from home before she bolted from her office to avoid being asked to stay.

She'd spent a lot of time choosing the rose-colored, open-worked lace top and matching camisole that allowed lots of peeks of her skin. Below those were slim jeans and a pair of black stiletto ankle boots. She'd pulled her hair out of its ponytail to hang in long waves over her shoulders.

She inhaled again. Knowing this was her last evening with Luke made it seem important. She wanted him to like her clothes, to know she'd chosen them for him. No, what she really wanted was for him to break his rule about dating during the football season. It was a ridiculous dream, because he'd had some of the most beautiful women in the world in his bed, and he'd kicked them out when training camp began.

She swallowed the stupid tears threatening to clog her throat and typed the code into the security keypad. The lock clicked and she swung the door open. She took two steps into the small marble-lined foyer and stopped.

Leaning against the open elevator door was Luke, looking like a pinup cowboy in a tan Stetson, leather chaps over faded jeans, and tooled-leather cowboy boots. Even better, he wore no shirt, so she could see every muscle of that magnificent torso, as well as the technicolors of his healing bruises.

"Hey, sugar," he drawled, pushing away from the elevator and sauntering toward her.

"Should I call you Tex?" she asked as Luke's slow smile banished all thoughts of future problems from her mind.

"You called me cowboy on the phone."

"Did I?" She was having a hard time even remembering her own name, much less what she'd said earlier.

He stopped scant inches from her, so she could feel the warmth radiating from his skin and catch the fresh scent of his aftershave.

"So you're here to fulfill all my Old West fantasies?" she asked.

"Oh, yeah, and all mine, too." His voice was a low rasp as he threaded his hands into her hair and bent to kiss her, the brim of his hat creating an intimately enclosed space. When she ran her hands over the bare, warm skin of his shoulders, a low groan rumbled in his throat. He pulled his mouth away from hers. "Let's get in that elevator."

He locked one of his arms around her waist and swept her into the walnut-and-brass-paneled space. The doors closed behind them, and Luke flipped a switch before turning to slip her bag off her shoulder and drop it in the corner.

"The elevator's not moving," she said.

"I've got it on hold." He began to unbutton her coat. "I didn't want to rush through your fantasy." He lifted his eyes so she could see the burn in them. "We're taking it slow this time."

"Oh," she breathed as he pulled the coat down her arms and tossed it on top of her purse. Desire was already rolling through her in waves. "I thought cowboys liked to ride hard."

"Hard doesn't have to be fast." His fingers traced along the low neckline of the camisole that showed through the lace. "I like this. I can feel you through it."

The brush of his fingertips against fabric and skin sent little tendrils of sensation dancing over her nerve endings. Such a light touch from such a powerful man. As his fingers glided down to skim over her already-hard nipples, she shuddered, arousal spreading through her like licking flames.

When he slipped one of his hands under the hem of her camisole and around her waist to hold her steady, she decided to take advantage of that tempting expanse of bare, muscled chest right in front of her.

She placed her palms against his pectorals, relishing the way they jumped under her touch. There was a light sprinkle of glinting blond hair over his smooth skin. She found the surgical scars on his shoulder and ran her fingertips over them. Skimming downward, she walked her fingers over the washboard of his abdomen, marveling that this was a living, breathing body and not the carved marble of an idealized statue. Except for one thing. "Your bruises have turned a lovely shade of purplish green." She gently traced just outside the edge of the discoloration. "Do they still hurt?"

"I don't even remember getting hit."

She smiled up into his eyes. "Big, strong football player. Never let them see you wince."

He was serious when he said, "Damn straight." Then he hooked one finger in the waistline of her jeans and pulled her in closer. "Truth is, you have miraculous healing powers in your touch."

"You're just temporarily distracted."

"That's why I need you to stay here. To distract me all night."

God, she wanted to stay. It was her last chance to be with him. But tomorrow was going to be long and exhausting even without the loss of sleep. She wasn't used to the physical labor of farm chores anymore. However, she wasn't going to ruin his seductive mood by telling him about the farm. So she kept it vague. "I have to work tomorrow. Can we spend a few hours actually sleeping?"

Satisfaction gleamed in his eyes. "We'll definitely spend some time in bed."

"I caught the difference between those two phrases." She took all hint of teasing from her voice. "I know how wonderful it is to curl up against that large, hot body of yours and drift off to sleep."

"I'll make sure you get your rest, sugar. But you'll sleep better after some exercise."

With that he took hold of her lace overblouse and tugged it upward, so she raised her arms to let him slip it off. He peeled the camisole up and off, too. Now all that stood between his hands and her breasts was a wisp of cream-colored lace. "This is real pretty," he said, grazing his fingertips along the scalloped edge of the bra, "but it's in my way."

Before she realized what he was doing, he had snaked his hands behind her and flicked open the hooks. He slid the straps down her arms, and the bra landed on top of the growing heap of clothing in the corner.

His gaze dropped to her now-bare breasts, sending a wave of self-consciousness washing over her. Until she saw his expression. Pure, unadulterated want lit his eyes. "So perfect," he said, bringing his hands in to cup her breasts almost reverently. The feel of his palms against the sensitive skin made her breathe out a long, "Aaah." She arched her back to push into his hands, needing more pressure against the aching nipples. He moved so he could circle the tight buds with his thumbs. Lasers of heat sizzled downward to converge in her belly. She moaned and rocked her hips.

He slid one chaps-clad thigh between hers so she could pulse against him. But there were too many layers of clothes between them. She unbuttoned her jeans and ripped down the zipper.

"Oh, yeah," he said, helping her jerk her jeans and panties down to the top of her boots. He knelt to slip the boots off her feet and set them aside as she kicked her jeans away. His gaze laid a trail of heat up her body until he met her eyes. "Let's put those sexy boots back on," he said, holding one out for her to slip her foot into.

As she stepped into the second one, he stood up, skimming his fingers over her legs and hips. "I like spike heels and bare skin."

He backed her into the rear of the elevator and drove his thigh between hers again, lifting her so she was riding him. She nearly came when her wet, aching center ground against the sueded leather covering his leg. She fought down the near orgasm. He'd said he wanted to take it slow.

"How does that feel?" he murmured against the side of her neck as he wrapped his hands around her hips and rocked her against his thigh.

"Like I'm going to come if you don't stop," she panted when the tension nearly crested again.

"Let yourself go. You can have another one." He pressed his thigh upward so it ground against the searing hunger between her legs. She exploded, holding on to the steel of his upper arms as her internal muscles released from their clench of arousal and her body jolted with pleasure.

"Yesssss!" she hissed, her eyes closed and her head thrown back. He tilted her hips to a different angle and the climax smashed into her again. The wash of blazing, luscious satisfaction flooded through her. "Oh, yes!"

As the tremors lessened, she sagged forward against him, still astride his hard, muscled thigh. He wrapped his arms around her and held her while she eased down from the soaring heights he'd taken her to. "So much for slow," she said.

"I love it that you were so ready." His voice vibrated in the ear she had pressed to his chest.

"How about you, cowboy? Aren't you ready, too?" She felt his erection solid and hard against her.

"I've been ready since our phone conversation this afternoon."

She chuckled smugly. "Some things are worth waiting for."

She felt a jump of tension in his muscles. "I want you to keep that in mind, sweetheart."

"Well, I don't want to wait any longer." She pulled his head down to hers so she could kiss him with carnal intent. He shifted so their mouths melded and their tongues glided together. He took her mouth in a foreshadowing of how he would take all of her.

With a groan he tore his lips away from hers and ripped the buckle of his chaps open.

"Too bad you didn't wear just those and nothing else," she purred.

"So you like leather. How about I just unzip my jeans and go from there?" He did that, freeing his erect cock from the denim and yanking a foil envelope from his back pocket.

She held out her hand. When he passed her the packet, she ripped it open with her teeth. The gesture fit this wild, abandoned encounter. Before she rolled it on, she ran her fingers up and down his erection, loving the growl she drew from his throat. She stroked the condom on, eliciting another low rumble.

Before she knew what was happening, he had spun her into the corner, where the handrails that ran around the sides of the car met. He took her hands and placed one on each handrail before pulling her knee high up on his hip and holding it there. "Hang on tight," he said, as he slid his other hand under her bottom and pulled her upward so she was tipped into the corner and braced on her arms.

He bent his knees and came up into her in a swift, devastating motion, making both of them gasp at the contact. It was so good to have him inside her, filling the fiery ache. She braced herself on the handrails, angling her body so he could have easier access.

"That's it, sugar," he rasped, shifting his grip to splay her thighs wider. For a moment, he met her eyes, the blue of his scorching. Then he deliberately dropped his gaze to where they were joined, watching as he plunged into her and withdrew, then drove in again.

The leather of his chaps grazed her inner thighs, adding one more sensation to the build of pressure and motion inside her. Tension knotted tighter and tighter in her belly as he filled and emptied her.

And then he lost control, moving faster and faster until she felt the beginning of her second orgasm. When her muscles tightened, he thrust hard and lifted his head to send her name echoing around the enclosed space as he came. While he pulsed inside her, she went over the edge, feeling the wholly different thrill of climaxing around the delicious invasion of his cock. A sound she didn't recognize as her own wrenched itself from her throat as her insides seemed to melt into liquid bliss.

When he slid out of her, she moaned at the friction against already stimulated nerves. "Easy, sweetheart." He let her down slowly to balance on her stiletto heels. Her arms had spasmed from holding herself up and she tried to shake them out.

"Cramps?" he asked, using his thumbs to push into the tired muscles in exactly the right places.

"That's almost as good as the sex."

"Then I didn't do the sex right." He pivoted away to strip off the condom.

"If that sex was *wrong*, I don't think I could survive *right*." She bent to grab her jeans off the pile.

"No need for those." He flicked a switch, sending the elevator soaring upward. Once again, his gaze scorched down her body to her boots. "I'll keep you warm." He pulled her against him by grabbing her bottom with one hand.

She smacked her jeans against his thigh. "I'm not walking out of this elevator stark naked."

"Why not? It's a private elevator direct to my place, and no one's home but us." His dimple appeared. "I want to lay you down on my big leather couch and kiss every inch of your gorgeous skin." He dropped his voice lower. "And taste you. God, do I want to taste you. Then maybe I'll talk you into bending over the sofa arm and . . ."

"Stop." She put her hand over his mouth. He touched her palm with the tip of his tongue, a silky, damp warmth. His touch reverberated through her, pooling low and sultry.

The elevator glided to a stop, and the door slid open. Miranda peered out into the light-filled foyer of his apartment.

"I swear it's empty," Luke said, amusement edging his voice. He gave her a playful nudge on her butt. "Go ahead. I'll grab the rest of your clothes."

She wrapped her jeans around her torso as she stepped out onto the gray stone floor, her heels clicking against the hard surface. She felt awkward and exposed until Luke came up behind her and wound one arm around her waist, bringing her back against him so she could feel leather, denim, and his bare skin touching hers.

"It's strange walking into your home for the first time without any clothes on. I want to look around, but I feel too . . . naked."

He blew out an exaggerated sigh against her neck. "Naked is good, but I can offer an alternative."

"You can give me my clothes," Miranda said, wiggling out of his grasp.

He put the handful of fabrics behind his back with a grin. "There's something else I'd like you to wear. Make yourself comfortable in the living room, and I'll be right back."

With that he turned and took off down the hall. The chaps outlined the worn denim that cupped his butt so she could see the muscles moving under the fabric. The buckles gave a faint musical chink with each step.

She'd just had two orgasms in an elevator with the most amazing man she'd ever met. If the night ended right now, she could say it was a good one. Instead, it stretched in front of her with all its exhilarating possibilities. Her body hummed with satisfaction and anticipation. She would not think about the fact that this was the end.

When he disappeared through a door, she turned to admire the huge photographs of cowboys hanging on the foyer walls. They were shot as silhouettes against skies of brilliant blue and white or sunset orange and gold. A photo of two cowboys walking side by side, carrying their saddles, drew her closer. One man looked tough and experienced, while the other appeared slight and untested. The older man walked a step in front of the younger, as though he was both leading the way and protecting his companion.

It made her think of Luke and his brother, and sadness for the two men washed through her.

The thud of Luke's boot heels interrupted her reverie. He held up an extralarge plaid flannel shirt. "This will look better on you than me."

"Was this originally part of your outfit?" she asked, turning to slip her arms into the sleeves as he held it for her. The fabric was so soft she knew it had been worn and laundered many times.

"Maybe."

As she pulled the shirt closed in front of her one-handed, he tugged at the jeans she still held against her. "Hey, I'm not sure I want to give those up," she said.

He disarmed her by skimming one palm down her thigh to the edge of the shirttail, where he let his fingertips play over her skin. "I like seeing your legs bare and knowing what else is bare under there."

Little circles of sensation rippled out from his touch. She loosened her hold on the jeans, and he whisked them out of her hand. She needed to remember those athlete's reflexes of his. As she buttoned the shirt, she felt a thrill at the knowledge that the soft cotton now brushing her naked body had also touched his. She wished she could keep it to wear when tonight was just a memory.

She looked up to find his gaze following the path of her fingers down the front of the shirt. He reached out to flick a button free so her cleavage was fully exposed. "Much better," he said, his eyes burning even bluer.

"For whom?"

He traced a line from the hollow of her throat down between her breasts, making her nipples harden. "I'd say for both of us."

She said with only a slight hitch in her voice, "I'd like to see your place first."

"First?" His drawl thickened. "What were you thinking would come second?"

She did her best to look provocative, not something she attempted often. "Both of us."

"If you talk like that, you're going to get the speed tour." He laced his fingers with hers and pulled her toward a doorway across the foyer.

"Just a minute." She planted her boots. "Can you tell me about these photos? Are they from Texas?"

Pleasure overlaid the arousal in his expression. "They're by a Swiss photographer named Hannes Schmid."

"It's ironic that a European would make such great cowboy pictures."

"Not really," he said, his gaze on the silhouette of a cowboy herding horses through dust-laden sunlight. "The Europeans I've met buy into the whole myth of the American West even more than Americans do."

She remembered an elderly Englishman who had visited friends in the Pinnacle. He had asked her to arrange a day trip to Montana to see an Indian reservation. When she explained the distance involved, he'd been hugely disappointed. Pulling Luke over to the photograph she'd been admiring earlier, she watched his face as she said, "This one made me think of you and your brother."

His lips tightened. She'd expected the anger, but under it lay a profound well of pain. "I tried to call him. He didn't pick up."

"Because he's embarrassed about last night." She flexed her fingers against his in comfort.

"Or he's sulking." His voice was flat.

"Did you choose this photo because of Trevor?"

He made a gesture of uncharacteristic uncertainty with his free hand. "The decorator gave me a bunch of choices, and I marked the ones I liked."

So it might have been subconscious.

He stared at it. "One cowboy looks older, tougher. Tired."

"Yet he seems to be both leading and protecting the other one."

Luke shrugged. "Could be."

Miranda reached up and turned his face toward her. "Your brother will figure out how much he would lose if he stays away. And I don't mean luxury boxes and fancy parties. I mean *you*. It's a precious thing, the love of a brother."

"When you say it, I almost believe it." He turned his head to kiss her palm before he took her hand in his. "But Trevor resents me for reasons I can't change."

Luke looked around the foyer with the high-priced art photos hanging on the custom-papered walls. "I didn't go after all this. I just put my head down and worked like a dog at football. I didn't think about how it would affect my family. My friends." He turned his gaze back to her. "My lovers."

"No one believes that success comes with a price. Until it's time to pay." Orin was exacting payment from her now.

"Most people think I'm whining." His face was somber. "Or faking it so I'll look like a regular guy."

She decided to lighten the mood. "I'm afraid you'll never look like a regular guy. It's just not in your genes."

That brought light back into his eyes. "I thought I looked good in my jeans."

"You look even better out of them."

"Lady, you just delayed your tour by an hour or so." He snaked his arm around her waist and hustled her into a huge living room that had one full wall made of glass. She had a quick glimpse of the lights of the Verrazano Bridge before Luke pressed her down on a room-filling sectional sofa covered in butter-soft tan leather. It reminded her of a well-worn saddle.

He took off his hat and knelt in front of her. "Sweetheart, I want to taste you. You good with that?"

His words sent a rush of desire prickling over her skin. It amazed her that he always asked permission. He never assumed that she wanted the same thing he did, and he never used the strength of his body or the steel of his will to compel her.

She looked into his eyes, now on the same level as hers, and marveled at the change from ice to fire. She leaned forward to comb her fingers through his hair, slightly mussed from the Stetson, and let them drift down to his shoulders. As she traced his muscles with her fingertips, she caught the intake of his breath. "I won't say no to a hungry man," she said, leaning forward to brush her lips against his.

Without breaking the kiss, he came forward to push her back onto the cushions. He lifted his head and ran his hands down the front of her shirt, dragging them over her hard nipples to make her gasp, before he palmed her thighs and pushed them apart. She felt a moment's embarrassment as he just stared down between her legs, his eyelids heavy and his jaw tight with the control of a man trying to take it slow.

He moved suddenly, lowering his mouth to lick the sensitive spot he'd exposed. As intense sensation speared through her, she closed her eyes and left thought behind. His tongue flicked and pressed and thrust, making her rock against him as she moaned and gasped, his touch driving fire through every inch of her body.

He hooked his hands behind her knees and pulled her closer to the edge of the cushions, lifting her legs to crook over his shoulders. He slid his big hands between the leather and her bottom, cupping and lifting her so she was open more fully to his mouth. She bucked in his grip as the heat and pressure of his teeth and tongue and lips wound the tension to a fever pitch low in her body.

"Not so fast, sugar," he murmured, the huff of his breath against her highly sensitized clitoris making her buck again. "I want you to feel it all the way into your bones when you come."

"My bones are already sizzling."

"That's what I like to hear." He flexed his fingers into the curve of her backside, curling them into the cleft and making her jump at the extra stimulation. He kept going, sliding one finger into the hot, slick longing inside her from behind.

"Ahhhhhh," she moaned as the satisfaction of finally being filled rolled through her. He withdrew and slid two fingers in, stretching her with glorious pressure. "Yessssss."

"You feel so good," he breathed against her as he pushed his fingers farther inside her. "Like hot, wet silk wrapped around my fingers."

"Please," she said, grabbing the edge of the cushion so she could pulse her hips in supplication. She was almost there.

"When a lady asks so nicely—" He twisted his fingers inside her, the unexpected sharpness of the motion sending a shock wave through her. Then he flicked her clit with the tip of his tongue and set off the explosion that had been building. Her blood ignited, and her muscles wrenched into an orgasm so extreme that she arched upward and clamped her thighs around his head to survive it.

She heard a shriek of near pain and realized it was hers as her insides seemed to shatter and liquefy in the overwhelming release.

He lapped at her as she convulsed, sending her up and over another peak. She could feel her muscles squeezing around his fingers, responding to the penetration with power. She rode the wave until it collapsed into a series of exhausted tremors.

"No more," she whispered as her muscles softened and released.

He eased his fingers out of her and angled forward to slide her knees off his shoulders. As she sagged down onto the cushions, he swung her around so she lay fully on the couch, the shirt bunched up around her waist and her arms flung over her head with spent abandon.

Closing her eyes, she let out a long sigh as pure contentment sluiced through every cell in her body.

She felt his lips on her inner wrist, a delicate brush against her skin. It was so tender, tears burned behind her eyelids. *Luke* was the only word she could muster.

"Too much?"

She rolled her head back and forth on the couch in a strong negative. "Perfect, but mind-blowing. And nerve-blowing. And muscle-blowing."

The couch sank under her, and the leather of his chaps brushed the bared skin of her hip. "You taste as good as you look," he said.

She let her lips curve into a smile, but she kept her eyes shut. The intimacy and power of what he'd done made her oddly shy about meeting his gaze. She was afraid of what she might reveal about how he made her feel.

"You look like you're falling asleep. I promised you a bed for that."

His weight shifted, and she forced her eyes open, putting her hand against his chest to stop him from moving. He was looking down at her with banked desire, his tousled hair falling forward around his face. "I'm not sleepy," she said. "I'm just coming down from the mountaintop."

He feathered his fingers through the hair at her temple. "Take your time on the descent, sugar."

She followed a tendon up the side of his neck. "You are the most generous lover." His pulse beat beneath her fingers, and she marveled at the strength of it.

He gave her a wicked smile. "I've learned that generosity gets repaid in spades."

"So it's pure self-interest on your part?"

"Let's just say that having you come against my mouth and around my fingers is not torture for me."

"Thank goodness! I'd hate to think you'd sacrificed yourself for my gratification."

"Are you sassin' me, woman? Because that is a dangerous thing to do in your position." He ran his hand down her body to the side of her bare behind and gave it a gentle smack. His smile evaporated into a look of such heat she thought her skin might burst into flames.

She tilted her head to check the swell of his erection under his jeans and thought of how it would feel inside her. All the nerve endings she'd thought were too wiped out to respond came roaring back to life. She grabbed his shoulder to pull herself into a sitting position. "Time for me to ride you, cowboy."

"No rush. We have all night." But his eyes went even hotter.

The prospect of what they could do with all that time sent a thrill through her. Followed by another stab of regret that it would be their last.

"But we have a lot to accomplish, so maybe we should get going." She skimmed her fingers down over his steely pecs to circle his nipple.

He started to move, but she scrambled to her feet first. Putting both hands on his shoulders, she used her weight to keep him seated on the sofa. Or rather, he allowed her to keep him there. "My turn to ride," she said.

"You sure you aren't saddle sore, cowgirl?"

Her answer was to unbuckle the waistband of his chaps.

"Yee haw," he said, helping her yank off his boots, chaps, and jeans in rapid succession. He retrieved a condom from his jeans pocket and kicked the pile of clothes away.

As he leaned back against the leather cushions, she luxuriated in the full glory of his naked body, letting her gaze trail down over the mass of his shoulders, across the gilt-dusted planes of his chest, along the laddered ridges of his abs, and past the tower of his cock. She traced along the ridges of his thigh muscles and drifted down his powerful calves to the strong arches of his bare feet planted squarely on the floor.

"Yee haw is right," she said, stunned as always by how beautiful and male he was.

He was watching her under half-closed eyelids. "Darlin', you looking was almost as good as you actually touching me. But not quite." He sat forward and seized the front of her shirt to pull her closer. "This needs to come off," he said, flicking the buttons out of the flannel and shoving it off her shoulders.

His hands were on her breasts, lifting them and rolling his thumbs over the nipples. She swayed on her high-heeled boots as electric desire sparked through her. Seeing her totter, he brought his hands to her waist to steady her, his thumbs nearly touching at her navel.

She stepped forward so she stood straddling his legs. "I think I need to sit down."

He reached for the condom.

"Not yet." She bent her knees and sank onto the steel girders of his thighs, reveling in the feel of his strength under her backside. Taking his cock in both hands, she stroked up and down the hard column.

Luke groaned and let his head fall back on the sofa cushions, closing his eyes. "You have hands like velvet, sugar."

She circled her thumbs around the tip of his erection, making him moan again. When she reached between her thighs and his to cup his balls, his hips pulsed upward and he lifted his head.

"Time for me to do some of the work." He reached for the condom and rolled it on before he gave her a questioning look. "You ready for that?"

Just straddling his thighs had made moisture pool inside her. The thought of being impaled on his cock made her inner muscles clench. To answer him, she scooted her knees onto the couch cushion and braced her hands on his shoulders so she was poised over his erection. She looked into his eyes and smiled. "Spare a horse. Ride a cowboy." Then she sank downward to drive his erection inside her.

They cried out in unison. His hands came to her waist again, this time gripping her like iron bands as he held her there, her legs spread over his lap, her clit grinding against the wiry hair around the base of his cock. The tendons on his neck stood out as he let her absorb him inside her. "You're so sexy," he said, his gaze resting on the swell of her breasts.

His cock seemed to thicken inside her. To see if she could break his control, she squeezed her internal muscles.

He released one hand to give her behind a light slap. She yelped in surprise, but the tiny sting ratcheted her arousal up another notch.

"You did that to bother me, sugar," he said, his voice a rasp.

"Just seeing how long you can hold out."

"Back to the competition," he said. He flexed his hips to shift his cock inside her.

She tightened her muscles again, winding her own tension tighter.

He growled and seized her hips, lifting her upward until he was barely inside her. She breathed out a mew of disappointment, and then he brought her downward as he pushed his hips upward. They slammed together, sending an earthquake of heat and friction shuddering through her. For a moment they stayed there suspended, his cock driven deep. Then his hips dropped and he pulled her up again, leaving her almost empty before he reversed the motions.

"Ahhh, yessss," she moaned, tilting her pelvis so that she forced him even deeper.

"Miranda," he growled. And then he positioned her so he could let loose, thrusting and withdrawing with a relentless rhythm. He went still before he bucked and howled his release, his voice echoing off the glass wall as he pumped and throbbed inside her. He held her there until she felt his cock soften. When he slid out, the slight friction made her moan.

"Now, you," he said, slipping his thumb up inside her while his fingers played her clit.

Her muscles clamped around his thumb as her core went incandescent. She rocked and cried out. He touched her again, and her orgasm pulsed once more before releasing her.

She collapsed over him, her head on his shoulder, barely twitching when he withdrew his thumb. She felt the back of his hand brush against her as he stripped off the condom, eliciting a minuscule flicker of sensation. All she could do was sigh against his neck.

He swiveled them around so he could stretch out on the couch, bringing her down with him.

"Won't this hurt your bruises?" she asked as he wrapped his arms around her back.

"What bruises?"

"Seriously, I shouldn't be on top of you."

He tightened his hold. "You make the best kind of blanket."

His big body radiated warmth like a giant heating pad. "You can't possibly be cold."

"Not yet."

She stopped arguing because she liked the feel of her breasts compressed against his chest and the way his thigh rode between her legs. She enjoyed the ropes of his arms across her back. Her head rose and fell gently with his breathing, and his heartbeat thumped in her ear. His body was so hard that it made her feel very female and soft by contrast. Her muscles were fluid and relaxed, almost as though she had melted over him.

Her eyelids had drifted closed when a loud rumble made her start. "Was that your stomach?"

"Yeah. Ignore it." He sounded embarrassed, which she found funny.

She remembered that she hadn't eaten dinner, either. "I'm a little hungry, too."

"As soon as I can bring myself to let you go, I'll fix us some quesadillas."

She nestled into him again. "You can play football *and* cook. Wow."

"Quesadillas are not cooking. Anyone can throw some meat, cheese, and salsa on a tortilla and heat it up. Mine are only good because my housekeeper, Carmen, makes the salsa and the guac from scratch."

The thought of fresh guacamole made Miranda's stomach mutter.

He chuckled. "It's a chorus." He helped her roll off him and onto her feet.

She turned to watch him rise from the couch in a ripple of muscle and sinew that took her breath away. "You should really let an artist sculpt a nude statue of you."

"Yeah, my teammates wouldn't give me too much grief about that."

She stepped close to him and traced a ridge of muscle in his lower abdomen. "It's just that your body reminds me of the Greek and Roman statues at the Met." She followed the muscle downward. "Only better, because you're warm and alive. And I get to touch you."

She heard the hiss of his breath and lifted her head. He had a strange look on his face, a mixture of disbelief, pleasure, and arousal.

"Why do you see me so differently from everyone else?" he asked.

"I can't be the only one who thinks your body is a work of art."

His gaze followed her finger as she drew it upward along the clearly defined line in the center of his torso. "My coach sees it as a useful tool. My trainer sees it as something to be whipped into shape. Most women see it as—well, let's just say they've never called it art."

"How do you see it?" She couldn't believe he didn't have any idea of his physical perfection.

"Necessary for my job."

Chapter 22

Luke seized her hand and started toward the kitchen. "Let's eat." He swung around as he felt Miranda pulling back against his forward motion.

"I'm not eating naked," she said.

"Well, damn." Disappointment rolled through him as he bent to snag his flannel shirt off the floor. He loved the way her bare breasts quivered as she walked on those spike-heeled boots. He handed the shirt to her with reluctance. As she buttoned it up, he grabbed his jeans.

"Hey, I didn't say *you* couldn't eat naked." Miranda gave him a lascivious smile.

"The chef needs protection," he said as he pulled them on, leaving the button undone so they rode low on his hips.

She dropped her gaze to his crotch. "We definitely don't want to damage anything down there."

Grinning, he wrapped his arm around her waist to hold her against him as he walked them toward the kitchen. Her hair was a riot of tangled waves and smelled like some kind of flowers when he dipped his head to inhale. He splayed his hand over her hip just to have another point of contact with the soft heat of her.

Despite his hunger, he'd wanted to lie on that couch with her hot little body draped over his for the rest of the night. Or until he could make love to her again.

He stopped in front of one of the high stools by the counter and lifted her onto the leather seat, provoking a startled *Oh* from her and a twinge from his bruises. A smile twitched at his lips as she yanked down the shirt his hands had rucked up.

"Stop smirking," she said, but she was smiling back. She crossed her legs and started to pull at one of her spike-heeled boots.

"Let me."

She moved her foot away from his hands. "No tickling."

He easily caught her foot and straightened her leg out in front of her. "Okay, Cinderella." Slipping the boot off her slender foot, he kneaded the high curve of her arch with his thumbs.

"Ah," she said, her head falling back and her eyes closing. "Another talent to add to your long list."

He worked the boot off her other foot and gave it the same treatment. He savored the feel of her skin, the subtlety of her pale pink nail polish, and the little sound she made in the back of her throat, like a cat purring.

"You enjoy being touched."

Surprise showed in her eyes. "Doesn't everyone?"

He thought of several women he'd dated who disliked having their hair mussed or their lipstick smeared. Miranda looked delightfully disheveled and didn't care. She was good with him looking disheveled, too. "You'd be surprised."

She considered that a moment. She did that a lot: listened to what he had to say and thought about it. "I guess not everyone can handle that kind of intimacy. It must be hard to feel so separate from the people you love."

Trevor's comment about their parents flickered through his mind. "It is."

Her expression softened, and she reached out to brush her fingers along his arm, her touch like a butterfly's wings, draining away the tension in his muscles. "It's not a reflection on you. It's a reflection on them."

"And you say *I* have many talents."

"What talent do I have?"

"You give people what they need."

"I'm a concierge. That's my job."

"No, that's just what they want. You go beyond that, to what will make them feel good about themselves."

She fluttered her hands in disagreement. "I'm not any better than any other concierge."

He gently lowered her foot and placed it on the rung of the stool. Going to the refrigerator, he pulled out the containers Carmen had left for him. He'd asked her to make everything fresh today. Three cheeses, freshly grated. Seasoned chicken, thinly sliced. Tender homemade tortillas. Tangy salsa. With the finishing touch of Carmen's perfectly textured guacamole. He reached up to unhook a skillet from the overhead rack.

"Let me help," Miranda said, hopping off the stool to join him by the restaurant-size stove.

"You can grab a couple of Dos Equis out of the drinks fridge, but I'm doing the cooking."

She walked to the undercounter fridge, her bare feet silent on the wooden floor, and bent to bring out two chilled bottles of beer. He took a moment to enjoy the view of his plaid shirt pulled tight over the perfect arc of her rear.

"Opener?" she asked.

He held up his hand, and she carried the bottles over for him to twist off the caps. She tapped the neck of her bottle to his and then tilted her head back to take a hefty swallow with her eyes closed. "That first taste is always the best," she said, swiping the back of her hand across her mouth.

"I like the way you drink beer." He wanted to kiss her and find out how it tasted on her tongue.

Her dark eyes lit with humor. "I guess I should have asked for a glass."

"Not in my house." But she'd surprised him with her gusto. For a lot of things. "Sit yourself back down on that stool and let me get some dinner made."

She trailed a finger down his arm, making his cock twitch. "A quarterback who cooks. Half-naked. If you vacuum, too, my every fantasy has been fulfilled."

He poured oil in the skillet. "Not big on vacuuming, but I can muck out a stall."

"Half-naked?"

"When it's hot enough."

"I'd turn that into a sexual innuendo, but it's too easy," she said, perching on the stool. She tilted her head. "Do you have any idea how tempting it is to lay my ice-cold beer bottle against your gorgeously muscular back?"

He laughed, a full-throated "I'm having a great time" laugh. Something he hadn't done in a while. "Try it and see where I put *my* ice-cold beer bottle on your pretty little body." He let his gaze rest on her and pictured his revenge, heat flashing through him. "I dare you."

"Maybe after dinner," she said, giving him one of her half-laughing, half-provocative glances.

She kept him smiling as he made the quesadillas with extra care. He wanted them to be perfect. The smell of warm, zesty Mexican spices soon saturated the kitchen air.

"I didn't realize how hungry I was," Miranda said as she inhaled. "At least let me set the table."

Luke flipped the last quesadilla on the platter. "Already taken care of. Grab that tray with the sour cream, salsa, and guac, and come with me." He took out two more beers and gestured toward the door to the dining room, letting her go first.

She stopped short as soon as she walked through the door. "Everywhere I go with you, there's an incredible view." She looked up at him, her eyes luminous. "And sunflowers."

Satisfaction warmed him. He'd set up a table for two right in front of the glass wall looking out across New York Harbor. Carmen had arranged colorful Mexican pottery on the table, and he'd ordered the flowers.

"They remind me of our tour." And of her. The warm, vibrant color with its dark, deep center captured her essence. He nudged her gently with his elbow. "Let's eat."

They settled at the table, lighting the candles and dishing out the food. The candlelight shimmered along the waves of her dark hair and danced in the brown velvet of her eyes.

She heaped guacamole on a slice of quesadilla and took her first bite, groaning in appreciation. "Okay, you don't have to vacuum. The quesadillas are enough." She ate another mouthful, then stopped. "Your stomach started this. Why aren't you eating?"

Because he wanted to concentrate on her every movement, to soak up her presence. He decided on the truth. "It's like the strawberries at the ballet. I want to watch your reaction."

A strange, unsettling expression crossed her face. It reminded him of the way DaShawn had looked around the football stadium after the last game he played. Except Miranda was looking at him across the table.

He felt an urgent need to know everything about her. Picking up a slice of quesadilla, he asked in a casual tone, "So, why did you want to be a concierge?"

Miranda stopped chewing. They'd been flirting, bantering, keeping things light. Except for the sex, which was intense. And now he'd asked her a real question. She didn't want that kind of emotional connection with him. It would just make tomorrow more dismal.

But he was impossible to resist.

She swallowed her food and took a sip of beer. "I didn't want to be a concierge. I didn't even know they existed until I came to the city."

That intense gaze of his was locked on her, and his silence told her to go on.

"I studied bookkeeping at a community college, so I got a job in the accounting office of a midtier hotel. One day the hotel manager walked into the middle of our warren of cubicles and yelled, 'Does anyone here know anything about Broadway plays?'" Miranda still read all the theater listings and reviews, even though she could only afford off-off-off-Broadway tickets. "I thought he wanted a suggestion for his family, so I popped up from my chair and said, 'Do you want a musical, a drama, or a comedy?'"

"I can picture that," Luke said, his dimple showing. "You couldn't help being helpful."

"It's a real character flaw." Miranda took another swallow of beer. "He looked me up and down and said, 'Come with me.' Turns out the regular second-shift concierge had shown up for work drunk for the third time, so the manager had fired him on the spot. It was Friday afternoon and he needed a replacement instantly. He handed me phone numbers for three ticket brokers and a list of maître d's at restaurants near the hotel and left me at the concierge desk. Alone."

"Baptism by fire," Luke said.

She'd stayed until midnight and gone home on a high of adrenaline and exhilaration. "I knew I'd found my dream career. The next morning I called the manager and asked for the job."

"And the rest is history."

"Not quite." She'd nearly cried when the manager had told her she didn't have the necessary connections to be the hotel's concierge. "He wouldn't take me on until I offered to work the night shift for free on weekends to get experience and build my contact list."

He sat back, his beer dangling from one hand. The candle flames danced in a waft of air, casting moving shadows over the sculpted contours of his bare torso. "We're a lot alike," he said.

"You and me? How?" She couldn't imagine any parallel between her insignificant career and his fame.

"We go after what we want." He grinned. "You're just more subtle about it."

"Well, I didn't actually tackle the hotel manager, but I begged blatantly." She returned his smile for a moment before getting serious. "Your turn. Why did you decide to be a quarterback?"

"Huh." She'd gotten to enjoy that huff of a response Luke gave when he was thinking about something. "I played a lot of sports as a kid. Ma said I used practices as an excuse to avoid homework." His face softened at the memory. "Truth is, I was good at all of them. But football is the state religion of Texas, so I signed up for youth football as soon as Ma would let me. I was nine."

"And the rest truly *is* history."

His grin turned cocky. "Well, yeah. I had a great arm even then." He shook his head. "But I knew football was my game for a different reason."

His eyes lost their focus as he thought back to his past, to the decisions he had made then.

"In the first official game I ever played, the other kids just followed the ball like lemmings, no matter how much the coach yelled at them to remember their positions. I didn't understand that, because I could see the whole field, see the play unfolding, figure out where the holes would be, who could get open. Coaches call it field vision. For me, it was like being able to slow down time. I got drunk on that power. Craved it." He snapped back to the present. "It's not a talent that has a lot of uses, so I decided to be a quarterback."

She could hear an edge in his voice as he spoke the last sentence, reminding her of his struggle to find a new purpose after football. "I think it will come in handy when you're a financial adviser and the markets go crazy."

"Maybe." He shifted in his chair. "What does that look mean? It's the second time I've seen it tonight."

She'd been thinking about how much she would miss talking to him so honestly, seeing the vulnerability behind the tough, golden image. She didn't hide hers, either. "Just saving up memories."

He went still, and his lips thinned with some inner tension. She might have revealed too much.

"We've got plenty more time," he said. "Tonight. Tomorrow night. Remember, I can make time slow down." His promise vibrated low within her.

She needed to tell him before he short-circuited her brain. "Not tomorrow night. I can't."

He straightened abruptly, banging his beer bottle against the chair arm. "What the hell!"

"Theo's got the flu, and so does the hired man at the farm. I have to go up there to help Patty and Dennis." Her mouth twisted into an unhappy frown.

A raging boil of emotions seared through him. Hollow disappointment, seething frustration, scorching anger. He didn't stop to analyze what underlaid them. "When did you find out?"

"Earlier today." Her gaze met his before she looked down at her plate.

"Would have been nice to know that before I promised my first-born to get a private room at the Aerie." He set his beer down on the table with great care. Now how the hell was he supposed to impress her so much she wouldn't even look at another man for months? A couple of quesadillas wouldn't cut it.

"You got a reservation at the Aerie?" He could hear wonder and guilt in her voice, which mollified him slightly.

"And had my jet gassed up to take you there."

"I'm sorry." Her voice was low. "I didn't tell you because I didn't want to put a damper on this evening. I should go." She stood up.

He pushed out of his chair, his fists clenched as he worked to control his anger. "Stay. Please."

She padded over to him on her bare feet and laid her hand on his arm. The sweetness of her touch made him want to groan out loud. "We both knew this was going to end. It's just ending one day sooner than we expected."

Temptation clawed at him. He didn't want to say good-bye. He wanted to have that rich-as-cream voice surprise him with her different perspective on the world. To tangle his hands in the dark waves of her hair. To make her come in every way he could think of. To curl around her soft, warm presence in his bed. His chest ached with yearning, and he actually lifted a hand to rub at it.

But you're not getting any younger. Junius's words steamrolled through his brain.

"You're right. I'm being unrealistic." He saw a flash of hurt in her brown eyes and knew he sounded like a jerk.

"I thought . . . hoped we could say good-bye on a positive note," she said.

"Yeah, me, too." He grimaced. "It's harder than I expected."

She looked stricken, and he realized she'd misunderstood him.

"Saying good-bye is harder than I expected."

"Oh, good." She shook her head, making her breasts move under his flannel shirt. He stuffed his hands into his jeans pockets. "I don't mean good . . . never mind. I'm not doing this well." She looked him straight in the eye. "These last few days with you have been an experience I'll never forget. I expected a celebrity, but I got to know an incredible human being." Her voice quavered. "I hope I'll see you at the Pinnacle every now and then."

She put one palm against his bare chest, sending a rope of arousal straight to his cock. Raising herself onto her tiptoes, she wrapped her other hand behind his head and pulled his mouth to hers for a soft, sad farewell kiss.

Before he could respond, she broke contact and bolted for the kitchen door.

"Miranda." He followed her.

"Please don't come in here." He could hear tears in her voice from the living room. "This is hard enough as it is."

He stopped in the doorway, his heart contorting in his chest, while she walked swiftly through the room where they'd just had mind-blowing sex.

She gazed around, looking confused. "Where are the rest of my clothes? Just tell me. I'll get them."

That galvanized him into action. "I'll bring them to you. And I'll call my driver."

"I can get home on my own." Her back was still turned, as though she couldn't bear the sight of him.

His anger kicked up again. "What the hell kind of man do you think I am? You're taking my car home."

Without waiting for her agreement, he strode toward his bedroom, where he'd stashed her clothing. It would give him time to think of the right thing to say.

He scooped the little heap of lace and satin off the chair where he'd dropped it, bringing it to his face so he could imprint her scent on his brain. But he could think of no words that would bind her to him.

He strode down the hall to find her standing in front of the elevator, already wearing her jeans and boots under his shirt. Her handbag sat on the floor beside her feet. The thought of her going out into the night without panties made him crazy with both arousal and the desire not to let her out of his sight. But he had no right to feel possessive. It was his decision to let her go.

He held out her clothes, the garments so small he grasped them easily in one hand. She accepted them with a contained dignity. "Would you mind if I take the elevator alone?"

He minded a lot. He wanted to throw her over his shoulder and take her back to his bedroom and make her scream his name as she came underneath him.

"Miranda—"

She held up her hand and swallowed hard. "Nothing more."

"I have to say this." He rolled his shoulders. "A lot of people count on me to be at the top of my game. It takes everything I've got to stay there. I wish it were different."

He saw understanding mix with sorrow in her brown eyes. She nodded as she hugged the clothes to her chest. When she spoke, her voice was shaky. "Would you mind if I wore your shirt home? I'll return it tomorrow."

"Keep it. I like knowing you have it." Stupid but true.

"Thank you," she whispered, picking up her bag.

He reached past her and pressed the button. The elevator door glided silently open, and she stepped into the car, keeping her back to him. She reached out blindly and fumbled at the control panel for a second before finding the right button. The door began to slide closed.

He'd never been at such a loss. His brain seemed frozen—his tongue felt thick and inert. All the clichés he used in interviews skittered through his brain, blocking him from finding anything real to say.

At the last minute, she turned to face him, and he saw the glisten of tears on her cheeks.

"Miranda!"

The door sealed her away from him, and the well-oiled whir of the car's descent filled his ears.

He smacked the wooden panel so hard the impact vibrated into his shoulder. Pivoting on his bare heel, he walked out onto the frigid tiles of the terrace and braced his hands on the railing, staring at the lights of the boats chugging across the harbor. It was too damn cold to be outside bare chested, but he welcomed the punishing slap of the frigid sea wind.

When had he become such an asshole?

Chapter 23

On Sunday morning, the sky outside the kitchen window still showed the glitter of stars as Miranda dropped into a painted wooden chair. She gulped down half a mug of coffee and groaned. Every muscle in her body ached with exhaustion after spending the evening tending to the cows, and last night tossing and turning.

She crossed her arms on the scarred tabletop and pillowed her head on them. Sleep had eluded her because she couldn't stop thinking about her final evening with Luke. Tears welled against her closed eyelids. She'd known the man for less than two weeks. She shouldn't be this upset about their parting.

It was the sex. It created a false sense of intimacy. She felt as though the relationship was much closer than it was. What did she really know about him, anyway?

She choked on a sob.

"I told Dennis to take it easy on you." Patty's voice pulled her out of her self-pity party.

Surreptitiously wiping her eyes on her sleeve, Miranda lifted her head and forced a smile. "He worked twice as hard as I did. I've just gotten soft from all that city living. How's Theo this morning?"

Worry tightened her sister-in-law's jaw. "His temp's 102, but the doc says that's typical of this flu. And kids can handle high fevers better than adults can. I'm putting him in a tepid bath if it doesn't come down when he wakes up again."

"Theo will love that."

Patty snorted at Miranda's sarcasm. "Yeah, baths are not a hit even when he's feeling fine." She grabbed a mug and poured herself some coffee. "Would you like pancakes or eggs?"

"Whatever Dennis wants is fine."

Patty threw her a look. "Your brother's not real picky, so it's up to you."

"Pancakes, then."

"Could you grab the mix out of the pantry?" Patty had pulled a package of bacon from the fridge.

Miranda rose stiffly and hobbled to the pantry door. As she scanned the shelves, a spear of misery lanced through her. Staring out from a bright orange Wheaties box were the pale blue eyes of Luke Archer, his arm cocked back ready to send a football sailing through the air. She couldn't get enough oxygen into her lungs as she stared at the hand curved around the pigskin and remembered how it felt against her skin.

"Pancake mix is on the third shelf down. Grab the syrup, too," Patty said.

Miranda seized the cereal box and shoved it between the Cheerios and the Froot Loops. "Got it," she said as she scooped up the syrup and pancake mix and backed away from the pantry.

Patty gave her an appraising glance. "You okay? You look like you've seen a ghost."

"Dennis always claimed the farmhouse was haunted." Miranda rummaged around for a mixing bowl. "Where is he, by the way? He told me I had to set my alarm for six."

"Probably thought you'd need time to primp," Patty said.

Miranda touched the sloppy bun she'd yanked her uncombed hair into and glanced down at her jeans and long-sleeved thermal T-shirt with a short laugh. "Yeah, I did a lot of primping."

Patty looked up from laying the bacon in the frying pan. "You're lucky. With your big brown eyes and that ivory skin, you don't have to wear a lick of makeup to look gorgeous."

Right now Miranda felt anything but gorgeous.

"Morning, sis." Dennis shuffled into the kitchen. Patty handed him a mug with steam wisping out of it, and he buried his nose in it.

"Burning daylight, bro," Miranda teased as she stirred water and eggs into the mix.

He squinted at the window, where the sky was just showing a tinge of pink. "Not day yet."

Miranda examined the two of them surreptitiously. They both looked tired and drawn, although Dennis had surprising color in his cheeks. Probably from working outdoors in the frosty October air.

Her brother gulped down his coffee and took the whisk out of her hand with a grin. "I'll handle the pancakes. Last time you cooked, the smoke alarm went off, and I don't want to wake Theo up."

"Hey, that was five years ago." Miranda bumped him with her hip.

"And you haven't been near the stove since," her brother said, elbowing her away from the counter.

"Behave, children," Patty said, but she was smiling.

Miranda was glad to see their faces more relaxed, so she carried on with ribbing her brother as they cooked and ate a speedy breakfast. At the back door, they shoved their feet into rubber boots and piled on warm clothing against the bite of the early-morning chill.

Dennis laid his hand on her shoulder. "It's like old times. I miss having you working beside me."

"Me, too," she said, giving him a kiss on his scruffy cheek. Amazingly enough, it was true. There was something comforting about the familiar tasks of forking hay, attaching milking machines, mucking out the barn, and processing the fresh milk. Not to mention that they kept her mind off Luke Archer. She winced as the sense of loss sliced through her again.

Dennis held the door open for her, and she stepped out onto the flagstone path that led through the yard toward the dairy barn. The rising sun's rays angled along the rails of the fence, lining them with light. The cows stood waiting by the barn door, their warm breath blowing puffs of mist into crystalline air. An occasional moo punctuated the dawn birdsong.

Miranda breathed in the cold-muted smell of manure that always hung around the part of the field where the herd congregated twice a day. Not everyone liked the scent, but it was part of her childhood, so she found it soothing.

As they tromped along side by side, the mooing grew in volume. The herd knew that food and the easing of their udders were nigh.

Dennis veered off the path, and Miranda stopped. "What's up?"

He stutter-stepped and headed toward the barn again. "Nothing. Just tripped."

Two more steps and he staggered before going down on his knees.

"Dennis! What's wrong?" She knelt beside him and peered into his face.

"Hell," he ground out between clenched teeth. "I've caught the damn flu."

She pulled off her glove to put her hand on his forehead, nearly snatching it away again. His skin was scorching hot. "Back to the house with you," she said, standing to help him up. She wrapped his arm over her shoulders and supported him back to the door.

Patty was drying dishes and spun around in surprise when Miranda and Dennis lurched into the kitchen. "What's wrong?" she asked, tossing the towel on the counter as she jogged over to them.

"He's burning up with fever," Miranda said. "Help me get him upstairs."

"Stubborn man. I knew he wasn't feeling right," Patty muttered, coming around to the other side of her husband.

"I can walk," Dennis said, slurring his words.

Worry scraped at Miranda's heart. Her brother was leaning heavily on her, which meant he was having a hard time staying upright.

"You're going to have to walk," Patty said, "because we sure as heck can't carry you, sweetie."

Somehow they got him up the steep, narrow staircase and into his bedroom. Miranda helped Patty take off her brother's outer garments and then left her sister-in-law to handle the rest. She didn't think Dennis would appreciate having his sister see him in his skivvies, no matter how sick he was.

She stood outside the bedroom door, pitching her voice low to ask what Patty needed her to do.

The other woman came to the door. "I hate to ask you this, but can you milk the cows by yourself? That's what Dennis would want done."

"Of course." Miranda injected as much confidence as she could into her voice, even though the prospect made her blanch inside. She didn't have the strength or stamina her brother did, and she was out of practice.

"Thank God you're here." Patty gave her a quick, hard hug and turned back to the bedroom.

Miranda squared her shoulders and clumped down the stairs as quietly as she could in the rubber boots. The warm glow of the knowledge that she was helping her family dispelled some of her fatigue. Maybe she wouldn't be as fast as Dennis, but she could get the job done.

Two hours later, she shooed the last cow out of the barn and collapsed onto an overturned bucket. Dennis had updated much of the equipment to make milking less labor-intensive, but she still had to clean the teat cups. After that, she would call Orin to tell him she needed the week off. She couldn't leave Patty to cope with a sick husband and child and a herd of dairy cows while the hired hand was out of commission.

Miranda grimaced. Orin would want his pound of flesh for making him rework the schedule. She pushed up from the bucket and trudged back into the barn.

Now she remembered why she'd wanted to flee to the big city.

"I'm really sorry, Orin, but I need to take the week off," Miranda said. She gripped the phone tighter and waited for her boss to blow up. Instead, there was a long, ominous silence. "I know it's asking a lot, so I'll take night shifts or weekend shifts as a thank-you for anyone you have to call in."

She plucked at the twine of the hay bale where she sat in the weak warmth of the late-morning sunshine.

"I have reached my breaking point," Orin said. "I'm going to have to let you go."

Miranda couldn't stifle her gasp. She'd expected him to berate her up, down, and sideways, not *fire* her.

Her boss continued, and she swore she could hear a note of triumph in his voice. "Your performance has not been up to the standards we require at the Pinnacle. I will give you one week's base pay as severance, which I'm sure you will agree is quite generous."

Technically speaking, he didn't have to give her any severance pay at all, so by some measures it was generous. However, an assistant concierge's base pay was peanuts, since the bulk of her income came from commissions and tips.

"I will also provide a letter of reference, stating your dates of employment here at the Pinnacle. Without mention that you were fired."

That was Orin's way of saying he would not recommend her for another position. Not that she'd expected it.

Somehow she managed to grind out, "I appreciate that."

"And well you should. I could cite you for dereliction of duty."

Hot anger ballooned inside her. "Dereliction of duty" would be going back to New York to indulge the whims of hyperwealthy people

273

while her brother and his family struggled alone. She clenched her jaw to prevent herself from asking Orin what the hell he knew about duty.

"I will have Sofia box up your belongings. You can pick them up when you get back from the farm. Make sure to wash the manure off your shoes before you walk into the lobby."

Her vision went red with fury. "Good-bye, Orin," she said and hit the "Disconnect" button. That would piss him off more than any of the names she wanted to call him.

She bolted up from the hay bale and paced in a circle in front of the barn door, vibrating with frustration and rage.

"That sniveling little scumbag of a worm-eaten dipstick! Useless sack of cretinous goat manure!"

After a few more circles and creative name-calling, she felt the cold, dark hand of panic close around her throat. She couldn't afford to be out of a job. The cheese was what kept the farm financially viable. If she couldn't make the payments on the cheese-making equipment, Dennis would have to sell the herd and the land. Maybe he could keep the house and continue to work for the new owner.

Miranda shook her head. There was no job security in that, nor was there enough income to send Theo to college, even with Patty contributing her garden sales. No, Dennis would have to move. Her parents would be devastated; the farm had been owned by the Tate family for five generations.

She sank back down on the hay bale and dropped her head into her hands. Two days ago, she'd been a well-respected concierge at one of the most exclusive luxury buildings in a city that specialized in them, not to mention dating a gorgeous, elite athlete. Now she sat alone in a muddy paddock in manure-smeared boots a size too large for her with no job and dim prospects of finding another one.

Sometimes life truly sucked.

Chapter 24

"Jesus H. Christ! Get rid of the ball!" Luke smacked his fist against the Gatorade dispenser as Brandon Pitch got sacked for the third time.

The rookie climbed to his feet and shook his head as though dazed, but went straight into the huddle.

"At least he gets right back in the saddle," Luke muttered to himself.

"Archer!" The head coach beckoned him over. Junius slipped off his headphones and lifted his clipboard to cover his mouth. "Pitch is falling apart. At halftime, I want you to grab him and settle him down before he gets hurt so bad he can't stay on the field."

Luke nodded.

"Rookies." Junius stalked off to consult with one of his assistants.

Luke had worked with the young quarterback on the field and off for the last two days. They had reviewed film, discussed strategy, rated opposing players, and done everything else Luke could think of to prepare Pitch to play with confidence. He'd driven the kid hard, because it kept his mind off Miranda. Mostly.

Pitch had major athletic talent, and he had field vision. He'd played college ball in the pressure cooker of Alabama, so he had experience. But the NFL was a whole different level of tough, and the kid was folding like a cheap suit.

He watched the rookie take up his position behind the center. What could he say that would give Pitch the balls he needed to win this game?

An idea struck him, and he strolled over to Dyson "Dice" Fredericks, another former Alabama player. "Hey, Dice, you know anything about Pitch's family?"

"Like what kind of anything?" the defensive tackle asked.

"Like has he got brothers and sisters, and where does he fall in the lineup?"

"Seriously, man? What you want to know that for?"

"Psychology," Luke said.

Dice slanted Luke a look. "You mean, so he gets his act together and wins this game?"

Luke nodded.

"Nah, I don't know that stuff, but Devell would. He and Pitch hang out sometimes."

Luke waited a minute before he moved to stand beside the veteran Derrick Devell. He made it look casual, because Luke never knew when the television cameras would focus on him and the announcers would start speculating on what was happening on the sideline. Luke asked Devell the same question.

"He's got three brothers and a sister. He's the baby, apple of his mama's eye," Devell said. "Not spoiled, though. Good kid. Doesn't expect to be given anything." The man turned away from the field to look Luke in the eye. "You going to get his mind right?"

"Do my best."

When the whistle blew for halftime, the Empire were down by seventeen points. Luke gave Pitch credit: the quarterback walked off the field with his head held high and confidence in his stride. You'd never guess he was bombing.

However, as soon as the team filed into the locker room, where cameras were forbidden, the kid's shoulders curled inward, and he sagged onto the bench. Luke walked over, tapped him on the back, and nodded toward an unoccupied office.

Resignation was written in every line of Brandon Pitch's body as he walked ahead of Luke. As soon as Luke closed the office door, the younger man turned. "You'd be playing better injured than I am in top condition."

"Not what I was going to say." Luke leaned his hip against the metal desk. "Is any of your family here?"

"What? Yeah, my parents and my brothers and sister are all watching me screw up." He smacked the wall with his hand.

Luke wanted to tell him to treat the tools of his trade with more respect, but he needed the kid to focus. "You're the youngest, so you've got something to prove. I want you to forget about everyone else in the stadium—your teammates, your opponents, the fans, the coach, me— and picture your family and what they will take away from this game. You want to give your mom a win to bring home and brag to all her friends about. You want to make your dad's friends buy him a drink in celebration of his son's first victory in the NFL. You want your brothers to sit up and say, 'Damn, Brandon is really something.'"

Because that's what he'd wanted from his family.

He watched Pitch as he spoke every sentence, testing to see what would flip the switch in the younger man's brain. The kid's shoulders were squaring up again, and his hands were closing into fists, but it was the last sentence that lit a spark of steely determination in Pitch's gray eyes. Sibling rivalry was a powerful motivator, as Luke could attest.

Luke straightened away from the desk and rested one hand on the other man's shoulder pad. "You've got all the tools, kid. Now make your family proud."

Pitch nodded before he gave Luke a tight smile. "Aren't you going to tell me I gotta have heart?"

Luke liked the kid's sense of humor. "Nah. I saw you get up after that third sack. You've got the heart covered."

Pitch strode out of the office with his head up. Luke hung back so the other players could get a good look at their quarterback's new attitude. Junius wound up his halftime speech, and with a slap of pads and a clack of cleats, the players readied themselves to head back out on the field.

As Luke joined the procession, Junius came up beside him. "Think you turned him around?"

Luke shrugged. "We won't know until he runs the next play."

"I've been around long enough to know how a winner walks out on the field." Junius swung his gaze from Pitch to Luke. "You could have a real future as a coach."

"Thanks." Junius's comment was not something to dismiss lightly, but all Luke could think about was the Series 7 study guide he'd hurled into the trash after Miranda walked out two nights ago.

After the evening milking, Miranda fumbled off her filthy rubber boots in the mudroom. Slumping onto the hard wooden bench, she braced her elbows on her knees, hanging her head in exhaustion and indecision. She needed a shower, but she wasn't sure she could make it up the stairs just now.

Despite her physical fatigue, she was having a hard time sleeping. The wrench of her parting with Luke dropped like weight onto her heart and mind at night. Now she could add the anxiety of joblessness.

The sound of cheering drifted down the hall from the family room, and Miranda realized that someone was watching the Empire football game.

Did she want to see Luke on the wide-screen television, or would it hurt too much?

"Miranda? Is that you?" Patty's voice echoed down the hallway as her silhouette appeared against the light. "Can I get you some tea or coffee?"

She needed comfort, not caffeine. "How about hot chocolate?"

"You got it," Patty said. "Go on in and watch the game. I'll bring it to you."

Miranda knew she should offer to make it herself. Patty had pitched in at the barn until she needed to go check on Dennis and Theo.

The prospect of getting up and doing it all over again in the morning wrenched a groan from her throat.

Patty stuck her head into the mudroom. "You okay?"

"Just thinking I should go to the gym more often."

"Farming's hard work, especially if you're not used to it. You're doing an amazing job for a city slicker."

Miranda managed to chuckle before she shoved up off the bench and staggered into the kitchen to wash her face and hands. "How are Theo and Dennis?"

Patty had banished her from the sickrooms, saying they couldn't afford to lose their only healthy farmhand.

"Theo's temperature broke an hour ago. I had to change every stitch on him and his bed because they were drenched." Miranda could see tears of relief standing in Patty's eyes. "Dennis is still up at 102 degrees, but we know that's the way this flu runs. They both wanted to watch the game, so I let Theo join his dad in our bed."

"You should be up there with them," Miranda said, coming over to the stove, where her sister-in-law stirred the warming milk.

Patty gave her a wry smile and kept whisking. "I needed a break."

Miranda nodded her understanding.

"The Empire's backup quarterback isn't doing so great." Patty poured the steaming hot chocolate into the crockery mug she'd set beside the stove. "I wish your friend Archer wasn't injured."

"He wasn't happy about being benched," Miranda said without thinking.

"He told you that?" Patty handed Miranda the mug with her eyebrows raised.

Miranda brought the chocolate to her lips to give herself time to think. She took a tiny sip of the hot liquid. "I must have heard it on the radio."

Patty was still watching her. "Luke Archer never questions his coach's decisions in public."

"I guess he told me, then."

There was a moment's silence before Patty took the pan to the sink and ran water into it. "Let's go watch the second half of the game."

Miranda cursed herself for being indiscreet. She was so tired she couldn't think straight.

Following her sister-in-law into the family room, she curled up in one corner of the green-and-blue plaid sofa, dragging a knitted afghan over her lap.

The Empire had just returned to the field, and she found herself scanning the sideline for Luke's golden head. She found him in an instant, despite the baseball cap he wore. She could recognize him just by the set of his shoulders and the shape of his legs, even with the pads distorting their long, muscular lines. He and the coach were conferring as the rookie quarterback, Brandon Pitch, ran onto the field.

"Let's hope Archer gave Pitch what for at halftime," Patty muttered.

Miranda realized she hadn't even looked at the score. She cringed when she saw the Empire's seventeen-point deficit.

"What do you think veteran quarterback Luke Archer said to rookie Brandon Pitch in the locker room?" the announcer asked his sidekick, in an echo of Patty's comment.

"Archer doesn't make long speeches, so I'm figuring something like 'Get your act together and win this game,'" the sidekick responded with a chuckle.

"I think I'd use stronger language than that, after Pitch got sacked three times," the announcer said.

The camera cut back to the sideline and zoomed in on Luke, so close that Miranda could see the cold, focused blue of his eyes in the shadow of the cap's bill. She sucked in a sharp breath at the painful beauty of the face that she would never touch again.

"Miranda, is something going on between you and Luke Archer?" Patty asked.

"What? No." She tried to give her sister-in-law a look of bland innocence. But the ache of loss walloped her in the chest and she choked on a sob. "Not anymore."

"Sweetie, what happened?" Patty put down the bowl of popcorn and scooted over next to Miranda.

"I was an unrealistic fool," Miranda said, clenching her hands around the mug to keep the tears at bay. "I knew he would go back to playing football, but I let myself get involved with him anyway."

"How involved?"

Miranda stared down into the dark, rich chocolate. She'd spent the last two days telling herself it had just been amazing sex and that was what she missed so much. When she was out with the cows, she could even convince herself of that. But now, seeing him again, the yearning reached far deeper than that. "It sounds ridiculous, but I think I fell in love with him."

"Oh, honey." Patty put her arm around Miranda's shoulders. "Every woman on the planet fantasizes about Luke Archer, so it's no wonder you're dazzled by that brilliant glow that surrounds him."

Miranda shook her head. "I've met a lot of celebrities. I'm not that easy to dazzle anymore." She met Patty's gaze. "He's so different from what you see on television and in the magazines."

Her sister-in-law said nothing.

"He loves his brother, Trevor, and gets hurt by Trevor's resentment. He's insecure about what he doesn't know because he's been so focused on football all his life, but he knows more than he thinks. He's an incredibly generous"—she'd been about to say *lover* but stopped herself—"person."

Patty gave her shoulders a gentle squeeze. "That may be true, but since you hang out with the rich and famous, you know they're not like us. They're used to getting what they want without considering the consequences."

Miranda looked away. "I knew the rules. He doesn't have relationships during the football season."

"So why did he break his own rules?"

"He had some bad bruising, so the coach made him take the week off. He's fine now," Miranda hastened to add. "The coach just wanted to give Pitch a chance to play."

"Wrong decision," Patty muttered before she returned to Miranda's love life. "I hate to say this, but it sounds like you were just his entertainment for the week."

Her comment drilled into Miranda. No matter how often she'd told herself the same thing, hearing someone else put it into words made it sound sordid. And true. Miranda winced. "I told you I was a fool."

"That doesn't make it hurt any less."

Patty's sympathy broke the tenuous hold Miranda had on her tears. They streaked down her cheeks and clogged her throat. Her sister-in-law took the mug out of Miranda's grip and pulled her into a hug. "Go ahead and cry, honey. You'll feel better."

Miranda dropped her head onto Patty's shoulder and let all the tension of the week escape with her sobs. It wasn't just Luke she cried for, but her worry about Theo and Dennis, the loss of her job, and her responsibility for the family finances. She let the tears spill out until her body felt wrung dry.

As she lifted her head, a roar came from the television set. "Touchdown, Empire!" the announcer bellowed.

Both Miranda and Patty turned toward the screen as the replay showed Brandon Pitch shaking off a defender and throwing a perfect pass to the open wide receiver. The receiver sprinted the last few yards into the end zone and did a zany dance.

"And it's good," the announcer intoned when the extra point was scored by the kicker.

As Pitch jogged off the field, the camera followed him until he stopped in front of Luke. The two men did nothing more than exchange a nod, but Miranda thought the announcer was correct when he said, "Something happened between Archer and Pitch at halftime. That's them acknowledging it worked."

Patty turned to Miranda. "I can turn this off if it's too hard for you to watch."

It was an intense combination of pain and pleasure. "I can handle it."

"I guess you'll need to get used to it because you'll see him at the Pinnacle," Patty said, handing Miranda a box of tissues.

Miranda had lied about her job, telling Patty that Orin had agreed to give her the week off. Patty and Dennis had enough to deal with right now without worrying about money. "He has a private entrance and a personal assistant, so I rarely see him anyway."

Maybe getting fired was a blessing in disguise. If she were in her office at the Pinnacle, she would imagine feeling his presence even through all those floors between them, remembering how the leather of his couch felt against her bare skin as he knelt and spread her thighs open with his powerful hands. Even worse, she could picture him staring at the giant photo of the two cowboys and feeling the pain of Trevor's betrayal.

"How about we add something to that hot chocolate?" Patty said, standing up and heading for the locked cabinet where they kept a few bottles of liquor. "Think of it as therapy for your aching muscles and your bruised heart."

Chapter 25

The morning after Pitch snatched victory from the jaws of defeat, Luke tried to focus on a new play diagram, but his mind kept returning to his last night with Miranda. It wasn't making him happy. Well, some parts of it were.

When his assistant, Doug, knocked on the office door, Luke tossed the diagram aside with a sense of relief.

"Morning, Boss Ice. Everyone wants to know what you said to Brandon yesterday that set him on fire in the second half."

"You'll have to ask him," Luke said, leaning back in the chair.

Doug cast his eyes skyward in resigned exasperation. "I should have known I wouldn't get a straight answer."

"Then why'd you ask?"

Doug grinned. "I keep hoping I'll trip you up." The grin vanished, and a slight blush climbed his assistant's cheeks as he offered Luke a printout of an e-mail. "Look, I don't mess with your personal life, but this just came from the Pinnacle, and I thought you'd want to see it."

Luke took the paper.

Dear Mr. Archer,

We wish to inform you of a change in personnel in our concierge service. Ms. Miranda Tate
is no longer a part of our team. We wish her
the best of luck with her new endeavor.

We promise that our unparalleled commitment to the comfort and satisfaction of our
residents will continue.

Regards,

Orin Spindle

CEO, Elite Concierge Services

"What the hell?" Luke sat up straight and read it again.

Miranda couldn't have gotten a new job in the two days since he'd
seen her. The memory of how they'd parted slammed him in the gut.
Again.

"Thanks, Doug. You did the right thing giving this to me."

Doug let out a sigh of relief. "You want me to see what I can find
out?"

"No, I'll handle it."

His assistant nodded and left. Luke stared at the e-mail without
seeing it. Miranda shared her office with someone. Stacy? No, Sofia.
He'd start there. He pulled up the number that used to go to Miranda's
desk and got her office mate. After some persuading, Sofia admitted
that Miranda had been scheduled to work Monday morning. Orin
had called Sofia Sunday with the news that Miranda was no longer
employed there, and he needed Sofia to come in.

That was all Luke needed to know. He speed-dialed Spindle's
number.

"Mr. Archer," the head concierge answered. "It's a pleasure. How may I assist you?"

"By telling me the truth about Miranda Tate." He kept his voice low and even and menacing.

"I'm not at liberty to discuss personnel issues with our residents. It's purely to protect our staff members' privacy."

Spindle's prissy self-righteousness ticked Luke off. "No problem. I'll take it up with"—he searched for the name of the building's executive manager and found it in some recess of his brain—"Boyce Schmidt. Nice talking with you."

"Mr. Archer!" Spindle's prissiness was replaced by a note of panic. "That won't be necessary. Ms. Tate has some family matters that need her attention, and she felt a leave of absence would be appropriate."

"Your e-mail makes it sound like she's gone on to a new job."

"In my haste to inform the residents of the change, I may not have phrased my communication as carefully as I should have. I didn't wish anyone to wonder why Ms. Tate was not responding to their requests."

"You're an asshole, Spindle."

Luke disconnected with a disgusted swipe of his finger. Once he'd tracked down Miranda, he'd have Spindle fired. It was time for that nasty little weasel to get what he deserved.

He leaned back in the chair again, debating. Would Miranda tell him the truth if he called her? Would she even answer his call? Miranda's family might not be willing to talk to him, either. They struck him as loyal folks.

No, he needed to get hold of someone else, a neighbor, maybe. He hoped like hell nothing had happened to the nephew. He was a cute kid. Once again he rummaged around the corners of his mind and came up with the name of the town where the family farm was located. Then he started googling and made a couple of phone calls.

Thirty minutes later, he sauntered into the gym and scanned the room. "Hey, Gorman, aren't you from Wisconsin?"

A man with a slicked-back blond ponytail and massive biceps lowered the weights he was bench-pressing. "Yeah. You want some cheese or something?"

"You ever milked a cow?"

"Just because I'm from Wisconsin doesn't mean I grew up on a farm."

"Did you?"

Gorman eyed Luke warily. "I might have."

"Good. I have a friend who needs some help on a dairy farm. I'd take it as a favor if you'd go up there with me tomorrow."

"I've got plans," Gorman said, picking up his weights.

Luke let his eyes rest on Gorman's face.

After a few seconds, the big man sighed. "When and where?"

Luke smiled. "Davis and Shetler are coming, too. We'll see who handles cattle better, Longhorns or Cheeseheads." Luke tapped Gorman's bulging shoulder. "Appreciate it, man."

His cell phone vibrated in his pocket. Pulling it out, he saw Gavin Miller's name and headed for the door as he answered, "What is this, a weekly check-in?"

"I'm bored," the writer said. "Tuesday's your day off, so let's play."

"I play for a living."

"There you go with that punning when I'm supposed to be the wordsmith."

"If you can't do your job, you have to bring in replacements." Luke kept walking down the hall toward his office.

"Low blow, boyo," Miller said with an edge to his tone. "So what's on the agenda for tomorrow?"

"Milking cows."

Miller laughed. "Now that's a unique attempt to get rid of me. You could just say, 'Piss off.'"

"You're not good at taking no for an answer." Luke felt a smile twitch at the corner of his lips. He admired Miller's imperviousness to insults.

"One of my many charms," the writer said. "Seriously, join me for lunch at the Bellwether tomorrow."

"I told you, I have cows to milk."

"I'll call your bluff and join you in the barn."

Luke cursed inwardly. He'd wanted to keep Miller away from Miranda, and now he was leading him straight to her. "You ever touched a cow?"

"I'm from rural Illinois, where farm animals abound."

"You didn't answer the question." He turned into his office.

After a brief pause, Miller said, "I've touched a cow. And a horse. And a lot of sheep and chickens. But don't tell anyone."

Luke was surprised by the ring of grudging truth in his answer. It sounded as though only desperation would force Miller to admit his background. The man must really need a break. "Okay. Meet me here at the Empire Center at eight a.m."

"Who's driving?"

"My pilot. We're taking the chopper."

Miller whistled. "I can't wait to meet your farmer friend."

That reminded Luke of how badly he'd screwed up with Miranda. "My farmer friend may not feel the same way."

Chapter 26

On Tuesday morning, Miranda groaned as she swung open the heavy wooden door to the cheese cave. Her shoulders and arms already ached from attaching the milking machines to the cow's udders, dragging around bales of hay, and shoveling cow manure. The mouthwatering scent of aging cheese wafted outward, so she closed her eyes and just breathed it in for a long moment.

Dennis's artisanal cheeses kept the farm profitable, but they had to be taken to the markets in New York City, where the high-end chefs paid top dollar to list "Tate Farms handmade cheddar" on their menus. Tomorrow was market day, so Miranda needed to load the cheese into the delivery van she'd backed up to the cave. The driver would pick the truck up at 2:00 a.m. and head for the city. At least *he* hadn't succumbed to the flu.

She stepped into the prep room and swung the door shut behind her. The cave was man-made, a cement-lined space Dennis had dug into the side of a hill once he decided cheese was worth the investment. Each shelf-filled room held different sorts of cheese, aging in different ways and for different periods of time. Luckily, Dennis had already sorted and packaged the cheeses that were ready for shipping before he'd been struck down by the flu. All Miranda had to do was lug them to the truck.

"Yeah, that's *all* I have to do." She shed her outdoor boots and jacket and put on the clean overalls and boots required for handling the pristine cheeses. As she was tucking her hair into a net, her cell phone vibrated in her jeans pocket.

She considered ignoring it since she'd just fastened up the coveralls. But Dennis was still feverish, so she dragged the zipper back down and fished the phone out of her jeans pocket. When she saw Patty's name on the screen, she answered instantly. "Is everything okay?"

"No one's died, but I think you'd better get back here to the house right away. Can't talk anymore. Gotta go." Her sister-in-law hung up.

Miranda swiftly toed off the boots and tossed the hairnet and overalls back on the counter. It sounded as though Dennis or Theo—or maybe both—had taken a turn for the worse. That would be bad news when Theo had seemed on the mend, and Dennis's temperature had come down to 101. She shrugged into her jacket and jogged back out to the battered pickup truck she'd parked by the cheese-making shed. Seeing all the gleaming equipment through the window reminded her of her responsibility for the payments, and she felt the weight settle on her already sagging shoulders.

It would be easier to sling hay bales than to carry the financial burden right now.

As the rattletrap old truck crested the hill, she could see the farmhouse. A large green SUV and an unfamiliar pickup sat in the driveway.

All she could think of was that Patty had needed to call the doctor. Terror tightened Miranda's throat, and she slammed her foot down on the accelerator, practically going airborne. Skidding into the driveway, she leaped out of the truck and barreled through the front door and into the hallway. "Patty! What's happened?" she called, not sure whether to go upstairs.

"In here." Her sister-in-law's voice came from the kitchen.

Miranda bolted down the hall and through the kitchen door, where she stopped dead.

The room was filled with people—very large people. But her attention fixed immediately on the man leaning against the counter at the far side of the kitchen, his hands shoved into his jeans pockets, his golden hair glistening in a slanting sunbeam. Joy flooded through her body like a brilliant white light, warming away the morning chill, erasing her aches and pains, sending the corners of her mouth upward in an uncontrollable smile. "Luke!"

Every face in the room turned in her direction. She dialed back her smile and forced herself to look at the rest of the visitors in the kitchen, some seated at the table with mugs of steaming coffee, some lounging against the counters like Luke. Three were obviously athletes. One looked to be a local farmer. The fifth, a lean, dark-haired man with a wicked glint in his green eyes, seemed out of place, despite his jeans and casual jacket.

When she met Luke's eyes again, the blast of joy had faded. He wouldn't have brought all this company if he had planned a romantic reconciliation. She was an idiot to dream of it for even a second. "I wasn't expecting to see you here."

He had straightened away from the counter, his expression unreadable. She imagined that's the way he looked on the football field when surveying the opposition, giving nothing away.

"I heard you might need some help," he said.

She did her best to ignore the weight of all the gazes in the room. "I can't imagine who you heard it from, but it was kind of you to come." She glanced around the room with as much of a smile as she could muster. "And to bring reinforcements."

Why was he here?

He'd made it clear that their relationship was over now that he was back in the game.

Then it hit her: he'd found out Orin had fired her, and he felt responsible.

"I brought a dairyman and a couple of cattlemen," he said, his smile not reaching his eyes. "Kort Gorman here's a Cheesehead from Wisconsin. Greer Davis and Tank Shetler are Longhorns. Kort says he's in charge."

The giant men nodded politely to her before razzing their teammate about his qualifications as a supervisor.

"Oh, and this is Gavin Miller, the writer." Luke tilted his head toward the dark-haired man sipping his coffee. "I'm not sure why he's here."

"You write the Julian Best novels," Miranda said, recognition dawning. He was one of Luke's new friends. "They're fantastic."

Miller's eyes held an odd shadow, but he gave her a charmingly rakish smile. "My compliments on your good taste in literature." He threw a glance at Luke. "Contrary to Archer's assessment, I am quite good around farm animals, so I believe I can contribute."

Patty slid between the men to bring a mug of coffee to Miranda. "They landed their helicopter in Jim Tanner's field, and he drove them over." She nodded toward the farmer before leaning close to Miranda's ear to whisper, "What the heck is going on? I thought you two broke up."

Miranda took a sip of the fragrant coffee before she murmured back, "I have no idea."

"I understand you have a cheese truck to load," Luke said. "Let's get it done."

The unmistakable edge of command in his voice brought everyone to their feet. Now the kitchen walls seemed barely able to contain the mass of colossal shoulders, tree-trunk thighs, and swelling biceps.

Gratitude loosened the tension of wondering how she was supposed to respond to all this. She didn't have to lug all those heavy hunks of cheese from the cave to the van. Tears of relief welled up in her eyes, and she had to blink hard to will them away. "Thank you all," she said, not quite suppressing the slight break in her voice. "This way."

She could feel the farmhouse's hundred-year-old pine floor sag under the heavy footsteps of the men following her down the hall and out the front door. As soon as Luke stepped outside, he took charge, assigning men to vehicles. Then he slid into the passenger seat of Dennis's pickup truck beside Miranda.

She kept her gaze on the steering wheel as she turned the key in the ignition and shifted the truck into reverse.

But the air inside the cab vibrated with Luke's presence. His weight on the old springs of the bench seat made it slant in his direction, so she felt as though she was being pulled toward him. As she twisted to look behind her, she found his gaze turned on her, but she refused to let herself meet his eyes. She hit the gas too hard, and the truck's tires spun on the slippery asphalt before yanking them out onto the road.

Anger scalded her. She was mad mostly at herself, for falling in love with a man she knew damn well she had no business even kissing. But she was furious with him, too, for giving her that blinding moment of hope in the kitchen. It was difficult enough to see him on television. Having him present in this confined space intensified her yearning to the point where it slashed at her like a razor blade.

She slammed the truck into drive and burned rubber again as she headed up the hill. "Why are you here?" It sounded ungracious, but she didn't have the energy to soften it.

"I found out that you lost your job."

She slowed down as the truck bounced on the undulating lane. "My problems with Orin started before your brother's issue."

"It made the problems worse. *I* made them worse."

She sneaked a quick glance at him. His hands were fisted on his knees, and his attention was locked on her. She turned back to the winding road in front of her. She didn't want him here out of pity. "You can stop feeling guilty. I have another job lined up."

"I'm not surprised. You're excellent at what you do."

Her temper flashed. "You don't have to give me a pep talk. I'm not your teammate."

The cheese cave came into sight, and she heaved a sigh of relief. The conversation would be over soon.

"I don't tell my teammates they're good if they're not." She could hear a flicker of irritation in his voice. "Look, I was a—"

"We're here," she said, jerking the wheel around to veer into the parking area. She felt a twinge of guilt when she heard his elbow bang against the door as her sudden turn threw him off balance. She didn't want to give him a chance to undermine her anger. Without the strength it gave her, she would suffocate in the breath-clogging misery of her longing.

She heard him speak her name as she shoved open the door and jumped out of the truck. The SUV pulled up behind them, its doors swinging open to disgorge the rest of the crew. She stepped toward the huge men, feeling like Alice after drinking the shrinking potion. She'd been grateful for their muscular heft until she realized that the three largest ones wouldn't fit into the coveralls Dennis kept in the cheese cave.

She felt rather than saw Luke come up beside her. "Gorman here tells us that we can't all go tromping through a cheese cave because it will disturb the bacteria or something. So we'll create a kind of bucket brigade and pass the cheeses along it," he said. Again, the undertone of command resonated under the Texas twang. "Kort, you handle the van. I'll work inside with Miranda."

"Always quarterbacking," Gavin Miller said, slouching against the SUV's fender.

Miranda looked sideways to see how Luke reacted.

"You wanted to come. You play by my rules," Luke said, his eyes narrowed.

She'd thought that Miller was a friend of Luke's, but their interaction seemed more fraught than amicable.

"I've never been good at that." Miller pushed off the truck.

Miranda pivoted toward the cheese cave, and Luke fell into step beside her. No matter how hard she tried, she couldn't ignore the muscles of his thighs under the worn jeans as he matched his stride to hers. Before she could reach for the big metal handle, Luke had grasped it and swung the substantial door open as though it were cardboard.

She led the way into the changing room, plucking the largest coverall off the wall and picking up the hired hand's boots. "I don't know if these will fit, but give it a try," she said, offering them to Luke. It was the first time she had faced him directly since the kitchen. He took the clothes but didn't move to put them on. Instead, his gaze roamed over her face.

"You look tired," he said.

"I can jog in Jimmy Choo stilettos, but I've lost my cow-milking muscles," she said, trying to ward off his concern with feeble humor. If he was nice to her, she would lose it. So she put up a wall of gratitude. "I really appreciate all the help you brought with you. Especially because it's very strong help. Cheese is darned heavy."

"Miranda, I want to—"

Gavin Miller poked his dark head inside the door. "Heigh-ho, the derry-o, where stands the cheese?"

Luke's eyes blazed with annoyance, but he kept his tone neutral. "We have to suit up."

The writer came inside and glanced around. "I had imagined something more picturesque when I heard the word *cave*."

Miranda stepped into the coveralls and pulled them up. "It's just a cement tunnel dug into the hill. The ground provides natural temperature control."

Luke was cramming his shoulders into the coveralls with difficulty. She stifled the urge to help him work the fabric over the swell of his muscles.

Miranda tucked her hair into the hairnet. "High fashion in the world of cheese making," she said, posing with one hand on her hip and inviting Gavin to laugh with her.

"I'm not wearing one of those," Luke said, eyeing her headgear.

"You wear a helmet to play football," she said, even though she had no intention of forcing a hairnet on him. "It's the same principle."

He shook his head so that his blond hair rippled. "Do you know how much sh—er, garbage they'd give me?"

The writer smiled an evil smile. "Even worse, they'd put it on Twitter."

"Okay, no hairnet," Miranda said. It was the first time Luke had shown any concern about his image. There was some comfort in seeing a tiny crack in his composure. "Try the boots."

He toed off one cowboy boot and shoved an athletic sock–covered foot into the rubber footwear. She heard him mutter a curse as his toes hit the front of the boot while his heel was still inches above the sole.

"We weren't expecting to clothe giants," she said. "You can wear your own boots. Just don't go into the aging rooms."

The relief on Luke's face as he slid his boot back on almost made her laugh out loud. This was an improvement over her mood in the truck.

Gavin scanned Luke, encased in the white polyester fabric like a sausage. "I may have to tweet this myself."

"Go right ahead." Luke's voice held such a threatening edge that Miranda took a step backward. When she caught the look he directed at the writer, she shuffled a few more inches away. This was the man who faced down entire defensive lines on the field. She was glad he was looking at Gavin and not her.

Evidently, the writer didn't want to tangle with him, either. He flung up one hand in a gesture of self-defense. "I don't, in fact, have a Twitter account."

"Can't keep it to a hundred and forty characters?" Luke asked with a lifted eyebrow.

"Can't come up with a hundred and forty characters," Gavin shot back.

"Sorry, man."

Gavin waved his hand in casual dismissal and disappeared out the door.

"What was that about?" Miranda asked.

Luke shook his head. "A bestselling novelist with writer's block."

"Ouch. I wondered why there hadn't been a new Julian Best book in a while." How easy it was to talk to him again. His lips curved in sympathy with Gavin's problem, and she had to force her gaze away to focus on getting into her boots. "Let's move some cheese."

He opened his mouth and then shut it again, silently following her through the door into the holding room.

"Whoa! That's one strong smell," he said.

"You can almost taste the air." Miranda sniffed. She'd come to love the cheese cave's overload of scent.

Luke surveyed the shelves stacked with all shapes and sizes of cheese. "We're going to need more help in here."

"Two of us are enough."

He turned sharply. "You're not going to lift a single chunk of cheese. Just supervise."

"Quarterbacking again?"

"What's the point of having a bunch of athletes here if you don't let them use what God and the weight room gave them?"

She climbed onto a high wooden stool. She was too tired, both physically and emotionally, to put up a fight.

His eyes widened. "You're not going to argue?"

"I'm happy to sit down."

Every line in his face softened as he walked toward her perch. Knowing he was going to touch her and knowing how she would react, she cast around for an escape route, but her back was against a wall, and two shelving units loomed on either side, trapping her.

"Miranda." The low rumble of his voice vibrated through her. "I'm sorry for everything that's happened. I was a real jerk Friday night." He cupped her shoulders ever so gently with his big hands. "Will you accept my apology?"

Shivers of delight ran through her, and her eyelids drifted closed as she savored the feel of his hands on her. Had he asked her a question? Something about an apology. "Yes," she murmured.

"Thank you." She opened her eyes just enough to see him bend his head toward her, so his lips brushed her forehead and then her cheek. Then his grip went tight, bringing her breasts hard against the wall of his chest and sending sparks of pleasure shimmering through her rib cage. He pushed his knee between hers, spreading her thighs around his hips as he moved in close. She felt the ache of emptiness low in her belly and the need to be filled by him.

"I've missed you. Missed this." His mouth slanted over hers, his lips hard and warm and male.

She felt his touch as a blossom of heat in every molecule of her body. Yes, desire pooled inside her, but it was also the sense of being in the right place with the right arms around her. The resonant timbre of his voice, the silky thickness of his hair, the perfectly calibrated pressure of his chest against hers—all danced together and set her heart flipping in her chest.

"Ahem."

A blush burned up Miranda's cheeks and she tried to jerk away, but Luke's grip didn't loosen.

He moved his lips one inch away from hers to say, "Go away, Miller."

"Boyo, I understand you want to win the bet, but it's colder than a mother-in-law's kiss outside."

"So sit in the truck with the heater on," Luke growled.

As much as she didn't want to, Miranda wedged her hands against his chest and pushed. It was a token gesture, since she couldn't budge the quarterback if he didn't want to move. "Luke, they're all waiting for us."

She felt his body give against her palms and he lifted his head. "I really hate your guts, Miller."

"I consider that a compliment from the Iceman."

Luke released her and stepped back. "Suit up, jackass. I'm going to need your help in here."

"Do *you* have a Twitter account?" the author asked.

"With three quarters of a million followers. My assistant runs it, so you're safe."

Gavin disappeared out into the changing room, where they could hear him rustling around.

Something the writer said surfaced through Miranda's embarrassment. "What bet was he talking about?"

"Nothing. A stupid bar conversation." But he didn't quite meet her eyes.

"What does it have to do with me?"

"Miller's a troublemaker. Ignore him."

"Take his advice. He's correct." Gavin slouched into the storage room dressed in a coverall and boots.

Luke gave him one of those icy stares that made Miranda shiver before turning back to her with a warmer look. "Where do we start?"

Her blush subsided as the two men loaded the cheese into containers and hauled them out to the door. Watching Luke's hands carefully cradling her brother's handiwork sent little tendrils of desire winding through her. When he bent and straightened, the too-snug coverall rippled over the shifting muscles of his back and thighs. The memory of how those muscles felt under his skin when he moved over her sent a flood of prickling arousal through her breasts and lower.

As he tramped past her laden with a stack of large cheddar wheels, Gavin Miller gave her a sly look, as if he knew what she was thinking. She yanked her thoughts away from Luke's body and tried to make sense of his behavior toward her. He'd been almost standoffish until the passionate kiss. But even then she'd felt a reluctance in him, as though he hadn't meant to do it.

A surge of power straightened her spine and lifted her chin. Once he touched her, he'd been unable to stop himself from wanting more. That was a rush. But he'd come here just to clear his guilty conscience. When that was done, he would return to the screaming fans, blazing lights, and adrenaline-fueled battles of his first love.

She couldn't compete.

"That's it for the cheese in here." Luke squatted to check the lower shelves.

"I can't believe you finished so quickly," Miranda said, sliding off the stool.

"Many hands make light work." The writer lounged against the doorjamb, his gaze traveling between the two of them.

Luke straightened with that controlled grace she loved so much. "Nice job of pitching in," he said with a nod to Gavin.

"You thought I was just another pretty face."

"I hear there's hay to be stacked in the barn." Luke gestured for Miranda to go ahead of him.

Gavin stepped aside before following them into the changing room.

"Can't say I ever want to wear one of these again." Luke struggled to strip off his coverall. Miranda gave in to temptation and helped ease the fabric off one of his shoulders, her fingers sliding over the swell of his biceps. He seemed to freeze for a moment before pulling his arm free. "Thanks," he said in a clipped tone. "I've got the other one."

Once again Miranda felt Miller's gaze on her. When she met his eyes, he lifted one of his dark eyebrows and gave her a conspiratorial wink. Uncertain of how to respond, she smiled faintly. She found herself torn between liking his impish humor and feeling uneasy about the undercurrents that swirled around him.

When they walked outside, Kort stood by the open doors of the delivery van. "You want to make sure everything looks okay?" he asked her.

Miranda smiled at the blond giant. "You're from Wisconsin, which means you already know more about cheese than I do. So close it up!"

A swirl of activity saw the van locked up and everyone loaded into the two vehicles. As she pointed the truck back down the lane, Luke spoke. "I don't regret kissing you in there because it felt damn good, but it wasn't my intention."

She gripped the wheel so hard her knuckles turned white. "What *was* your intention in coming up here?"

He shrugged. "Farming is hard work, and you're just a little slip of a thing."

His description of her was so sweetly old-fashioned that it chipped away some of the tension.

"I intend to get rid of Orin," he said.

"What are you talking about?" Astonishment made her jerk her gaze around to him.

He was staring forward, with his jaw set and the tendons in his neck drawn taut. "He's an asshole who doesn't deserve his job."

He was riding his white horse to her rescue. She kept her thumbs hooked on the wheel but flexed her fingers wide as the knowledge washed over her like a warm Caribbean sea. Not that his gallantry would do her any good. "Orin owns the concierge service that the Pinnacle contracts with. If he loses the job, every other concierge there does, too."

Luke muttered a curse and raked the fingers of one hand through his hair, leaving it entrancingly disheveled. "You could start a concierge service and hire them all back."

She hoped to do something like that one day, but she didn't have the capital yet. "It's a nice thought."

Luke huffed out a breath but kept his gaze forward. As the heater warmed the air, her nostrils caught his distinctive scent of citrus aftershave and strong, clean male. How did a person smell like strength? She inhaled, bringing it into her lungs and trying to etch it on her memory.

Pulling up in front of the barn, Miranda shifted the truck into park. Without looking at him, she said, "I'm glad you came."

From the corner of her eye, she caught the movement of his head toward her. "I wasn't sure you'd feel that way."

The SUV bounced up beside them. "Thank God," Miranda muttered as she opened her door and got out, shoving her hands into her jacket pockets and swallowing the yearning that was nearly choking her.

She hung back as Luke marshaled his squadron, reciting the tasks Patty had set for them and gauging each man's expertise in this new territory. When he turned back to her, she had herself under control again.

"Okay, I'll give you a tour of the barn," she said, striding toward the gate. Kort leaped forward to open it for her, swinging it out just enough for a human to slide through without tempting the staring cows to make a break for freedom. "You're a real farmer," she said with an approving smile.

"Thank you, ma'am."

The rest of the men trooped through the gate, and Kort latched it closed.

Several of the cows took a few steps toward the group, their soft eyes lit with curiosity.

"That's a nice-looking herd," Kort said. "Calm. Your brother treats 'em right."

"I'll tell him you said so." She started to pick her way across the semifrozen hoof-churned paddock toward the barn door. As she wobbled over a rut, she felt Luke's firm grip on her elbow. A sizzle of pleasure rippled through her, making her skin tingle and her backbone soften.

She wished he wouldn't touch her.

But he steadied her all the way into the barn. When he released her and stepped away, she had the urge to pull him back to her so she could wrap herself in his arms.

"Let's get the feed and hay moved first," Luke said.

He positioned a hay bale where she had a view of the crew and told her to sit herself down and stay there. "If you see us doing something wrong, say so," he said. "Otherwise you're not involved."

With a few brief instructions, he had organized his crew and started the process. The giant football players tossed seventy-pound bales of hay and hundred-pound sacks of feed as though they weighed no more than a medicine ball. It was pure sensory pleasure to watch the flex of their muscles under sweatshirts and jeans.

Luke worked right alongside them, setting the pace. They joked and taunted one another, but they were clearly a team, and Luke was clearly their leader. Even Gavin Miller got absorbed into the group, his laughter floating over the good-humored insults. Miranda basked in the warmth of their camaraderie. It struck her that this was one thing Luke would miss when he retired, this sense of being a crucial part of something larger than himself. Especially since he didn't have this kind of closeness with his own brother.

Her heart ached for him. Knowing this was a dangerous weakness, she jumped up from the hay bale. "I'll go get some drinks. Hot or cold?"

She noticed that everyone, including Gavin, waited for Luke to speak. "I could go for some of that apple cider your sister-in-law mentioned this morning," he said. "Cold, because I've worked up a thirst."

There was a general murmur of agreement, so she jogged off toward the farmhouse.

Patty was in the kitchen, already putting together sandwiches and defrosting homemade soup. "Holy moly!" she said, putting down the bread knife and leaning against the counter. "Maybe I was wrong about you and the quarterback. He brought his teammates up here. To do farmwork." She shook her head in disbelief.

"No, you weren't wrong. He's just feeling guilty," Miranda said, shrugging out of her coat. "Where's the big water cooler? They want cold apple cider."

"Guilty about what? Dumping you? He could change that." Patty went to the pantry and pulled out a large, insulated beverage dispenser.

Miranda still wasn't going to tell her about being fired. "No, it has to do with my job, so I can't tell you."

Patty's eyebrows rose. "I thought you didn't have much contact with him on a professional level."

Miranda gave her a little information. "He has relatives."

"Interesting."

Patty helped her fill the cooler and dug out some large plastic cups. As Miranda zipped up her coat again, her sister-in-law put her hands on her hips. "Guilt may be a powerful motivator, but I don't think that's the only reason he came here in a helicopter. On his day off. With three football players and a bestselling writer."

As Miranda slogged back to the barn, with the cooler in one hand and the bag of cups in the other, she wished she could share Patty's optimism.

Chapter 27

Lunch was a boisterous affair once Patty made her admiration for football clear. The men told war stories about their college days, their rookie years, and their Super Bowl journeys. Miranda was sure the tales were highly edited, but she enjoyed the glimpses into the life of a professional athlete. It became obvious that these men looked to their quarterback for leadership both on and off the field. No wonder he felt so responsible for everyone around him. Sympathizing with the pressures on him was another feeling she preferred not to have, so she banished it to a dark corner of her heart.

At one point Luke looked intently at Gavin and said, "None of this goes in a book."

The writer held up both hands. "The thought hadn't crossed my mind."

"Bullsh . . . crap," Luke said.

"As you know, my keyboard is collecting dust right now."

"You'll break through soon."

Gavin gave a half nod and the conversation went back to football.

When the last roast beef sandwich and homemade brownie had been devoured, Luke stood up. "We've got more hay to stack." He looked down the table at Miranda. "We can handle the rest of the job from here. You stay inside where it's warm."

She didn't want to stay inside. She wanted to be out there, squeezing in memories of the last hours she would spend in his company. She lifted her chin. "I'll help Patty clean up before I come out to check on your progress."

The kitchen emptied swiftly, and Miranda lingered a moment by the window, watching the band of large men stride with athletic grace across the leaf-strewn grass of the yard toward the barn.

"That's a sight that makes your ovaries dance, doesn't it?" Patty said.

Miranda choked, and glanced over to find her sister-in-law gazing out the window over the sink. "I won't tell Dennis."

Patty turned with a grin. "Hey, just because I'm happily married doesn't mean I can't appreciate beauty in all its forms."

"I'll go get the invalids' trays," Miranda said, wanting to avoid any further conversation about Luke. Despite begging from both husband and son, Patty had forbidden them from joining the lunch, saying that giving the football players their germs would be a poor way to express their gratitude.

She jogged up the stairs to find both bedrooms empty. "Where the heck—"

Two figures, one large and one small, came down the hall from the bathroom. "Are you all okay?"

"We're just fine and dandy." Dennis was grinning.

"That was so cool," Theo said, his face bright with excitement.

Miranda narrowed her eyes. "Why were you both in the bathroom?"

"You should know," Dennis said, steering Theo back into his bedroom. "Forced-air heat."

Then she remembered. The heating ductwork for the bathroom came up through the kitchen wall. If you sat by the bathroom vent, you could hear everything that was said in the kitchen as if you were there. "So you heard all the stories."

"Yeah. It was amazing," Theo corroborated as his father tucked him into bed.

"I'm glad." Miranda had felt bad that they were missing out on such an experience. She picked up Theo's tray and followed Dennis into the master bedroom. Putting the tray on the dresser, she started stacking all the dirty dishes on top of it.

"What the hell is going on with you and Luke Archer?" her brother asked as he climbed into bed. "I mean, we have about fifty million dollars of athletic talent working in our barn, not to mention God only knows what Gavin Miller is worth."

Miranda sighed and Dennis looked guilty. "Patty ordered me not to ask you, but I'm your brother."

"He feels guilty because there's been some trouble with my job." Miranda saw the next question coming and trusted Dennis to keep a secret. "Caused by Luke's brother. And that's all I'm going to say about it."

"His brother must be a real jerk."

Dennis's loyalty spread warmth through her. "You're a good brother. But I'm not going to hug you because I can't afford to get sick."

"Yeah, you shouldn't be in here. I'll feel like as big a jerk as Luke's brother if you catch the flu."

"Your fever's down, so you shouldn't be contagious anymore," Miranda said.

"So why wouldn't Patty let me come down for lunch?" he groused.

Miranda picked up the stacked trays and walked to the door. "Because she wanted to ogle all the football players without you there to cramp her style."

Miranda was sitting at the kitchen table with a mug of hot chocolate cupped in her hands, bracing herself as she heard the men's voices approaching the back door. No matter how many people spoke, Luke's rumbling Texas drawl stood out like a flow of sweet, golden honey. She wanted to bathe in it.

A tiny choke of a sob surprised her, and she gulped a mouthful of hot chocolate to wash it away.

She heard the door slam open and felt the clomp of their boots through the floor. Rising from the table, she went into the hallway, where the men were stripping off their coats. "What would you like to drink? Cold or hot cider? Coffee? Tea? Hot chocolate?"

They all requested cider. Except Gavin, who asked for tea. "I've had enough of being quarterbacked for today," he said with a glint in his eyes.

Patty bustled into the kitchen. "I've got fresh peanut butter cookies, too."

The men surged for the kitchen door, but Gavin caught Miranda's wrist and drew her back into the mudroom.

He cast a glance over his shoulder at the empty hallway before he released her and leaned his shoulder against the wall. "Look, I'm the least qualified person on the face of the earth to give advice about relationships. But I couldn't help noticing a certain . . . tension between you and Archer."

She felt a flush crawl up her cheeks. "It's not—"

He held up his hand to silence her. "Clearly, it's not going well, and I shouldn't give him any help with his wager anyway, but you seem like a lovely young lady."

There was that wager again, but Gavin kept on going. "And you seem to be foolish enough to care about him. So let me tell you something that you can use or not—he cares about you, too. He tried to convince us he dragged us up here because he owed you a favor, but I've been watching him all day. He's been like an overwound spring every time you were present. And that is not typical of the famed Iceman."

That impossible-to-kill hope fluttered to life again.

"He's a fiercely hard-driving competitor, my dear, not a man you want to take on lightly. But you've opened up a chink in his armor. If you believe you can be happy with him, you should exploit it." He gave her a shockingly genuine smile.

It was a lot to absorb, but the hope was spreading its wings now. "How?" She swallowed. "He's gone back to football, and I'm just a distraction."

"Ah, I'd come up with a scenario for you, but I suffer from writer's block." The writer straightened away from the wall and strolled toward the kitchen. "I'm afraid you're on your own."

Miranda stared after him, trying to imagine a way to deflect Luke from his firmly held decision to banish her from his life.

However, it didn't matter that she couldn't think of a way to break through the barrier Luke had built, because he wouldn't let her get near him. Every time she found a way to approach, he used his quarterback's skill at evasion to shift away from her. He never made it obvious, but she felt like they were two magnets with the same poles turned toward each other.

It wasn't until Patty's offer of dinner had been politely refused and the men were trooping out to the trucks that Luke stopped in the family room of the farmhouse. It was odd to see his big, golden presence amid the familiar hand-braided rugs, rickety old wooden chairs, and dated plaid upholstery. He seemed both at home and out of place.

Miranda halted, too, shoving her hands into the back pockets of her jeans. Here was her opportunity to follow Gavin's advice.

Luke folded his arms over his chest and stared down at the faded blue-and-red rug. "Your brother has a real nice place here."

"But exhausting. I have to admit that the prospect of moving all that cheese had me on the verge of collapse. Thanks for saving me." She took a step toward him.

He lifted his gaze and she nearly backed up. His eyes were icy pale. "Now that I'm out of the picture, you'll find someone who can take you to a restaurant for dinner without getting interrupted a half dozen times or being hounded by the press. Someone who can talk about art and ballet with you. Someone whose brother doesn't hate him." His voice grew tighter with every sentence. "You deserve that."

She took a deep breath. "What if I prefer someone who comes home bruised and needs the doctor I call for him? Someone who signs dollar bills for blue-haired ladies. Someone who can read Egyptian cartouches. Someone whom I love."

She'd said it.

He flinched as though she'd backhanded him across the face. "It's only been ten days. No one can fall in love that fast."

Now she felt as though he'd slammed his big, football-tossing fist into her chest. "I guess *you* can't."

He shook his head and repeated, "No one can."

She lifted her chin and looked him straight in the eye. "I never thought I'd be saying this to the illustrious Luke Archer, but you sell yourself short."

She thought she saw uncertainty flicker across his face, but it was gone too fast to be sure. "We all have to make choices in life."

That pretty well closed up any chinks in his armor. *Damn Gavin Miller.* She gave it one more try. "You can make different choices in the future."

He looked away, his arms still crossed over his chest. "I owe my teammates my best."

What could she say to that? She let her shoulders sag. "I hope you bring home the Vince Lombardi Trophy for the fifth time."

He stood a moment longer, still not meeting her eyes, before he pivoted to walk out the front door.

Miranda wanted to sink into a heap of wretchedness and humiliation on the floor, but she owed the other helpers a thank-you. She smoothed her palms down the front of her jeans and forced herself to follow Luke outside.

He saved her further embarrassment by walking to the SUV and leaning against the hood while she said farewell to everyone else.

Gavin Miller came up and nodded his head toward Luke. "Look at him."

The quarterback had his legs crossed at the ankles, his arms crossed over his chest, and his face turned away. Every line of his body was a rejection.

The writer leaned down beside her ear. "He's using every ounce of his iron self-control not to grab you and kiss you senseless."

Chapter 28

As the elevator glided upward toward his penthouse, Luke's cell phone pinged with a text message from Gavin Miller.

```
You're an idiot.
```

Luke slammed his boot into the wall, making the elevator sway slightly. The man was like a wasp.

He slid his phone back into his pocket without answering the text. The elevator doors slid open, and he started down the hall toward his bedroom. He needed a shower, and he needed to stop thinking about Miranda.

"Hey, bro." Trevor's voice halted him in his tracks.

Luke muttered a curse under his breath. He rerouted his footsteps into the living room.

Trevor stood in front of the couch, his hands hanging by his sides. He was wearing what Luke thought of as his teaching uniform: a tweed jacket, a white shirt with a funky tie, and jeans. A bottle of water and a half-eaten sandwich sat on the coffee table in front of him.

"I got hungry waiting," Trevor said. He scanned Luke. "You look like you've been in a barn."

"Nailed it."

His brother's expression turned skeptical.

"What do you want, Trevor?"

The other man flinched before he sucked in a breath, his shoulders rising on the inhale. "I came to apologize."

"This isn't a good time." Luke had enough to deal with. He didn't need more whining self-justification from his brother.

Trevor hesitated a moment. "What's going on, Luke?"

"I need a shower."

"Fine. I'll say my piece and get out of your hair." Trevor's hands curled into fists. "I got a job as an adjunct professor on the tenure track at Skidmore."

Luke frowned, racking his memory. "Skidmore. No one from there called me."

"I didn't use your name as a reference." Trevor lifted his chin. "One of my visiting profs from Harvard ended up there. I reached out to her when I saw the job listing. The final interview was today."

"That's real good news, Trev. Congratulations."

"Jodie's flying out to look at houses tomorrow." Trevor dropped his gaze. "I don't know what the hell I was thinking when I called the concierge the other night. Thank God she wouldn't accommodate my request." He met Luke's eyes. "I know how lucky I am to have Jodie."

Envy hit Luke like a helmet to the chest. "I'm glad you two straightened things out."

"What you said to me that night . . . it shook me up. I didn't want to take responsibility for my failure, so I shifted the blame to you." Trevor shrugged. "I guess I figured your shoulders were strong enough to carry it."

Luke sat down and waved toward the sofa behind Trevor.

"I couldn't believe you threw me out. Cursed you with every foul word I could think of," Trevor said, seating himself on the edge of the cushion. "Then I woke up the next morning and realized I'd lost my brother." He looked Luke in the eye. "And that was about the worst feeling I've ever had."

Luke sat back as he absorbed Trevor's about-face. It was like the spreading warmth of a shot of great tequila. "Hardest thing I ever did."

"I've had my head up my ass for too long." Trevor stared down at the hands he had clasped on his thighs. "You don't have to forgive me. I just wanted to tell you that I heard you."

"It's not about forgiving. That's done." Luke wanted to make sure his brother understood. "It's about owning your actions. That's the only way to move forward."

Trevor raised his head. "I'm headed in the right direction now. I want to include you in the journey."

"You got it, Trev. I'm with you all the way." He stood and walked over to his brother with his hand held out. Trevor took his hand and rose to pull him into a brief, hard hug.

As they stepped apart, Trevor grinned. "Man, you even *smell* like a barn. So you weren't busting my chops. What the hell were you doing?"

"It's a long story." The screwed-up mess he'd made crashed into him again.

"I've got all night."

For a split second, Luke was tempted to spill his guts, the way he had years ago when they were close and his brother was the one person he could trust to keep his secrets. But the feelings were too raw, and he'd gotten used to keeping things to himself. "I appreciate it, but about all I have the energy for is a shower and bed." He gripped Trevor's shoulder. "You're welcome to stay here tonight."

"Thanks, but I've got a hotel room already booked." Trevor's smile turned wry. "No more mooching off my older brother."

"It's not mooching if you're welcome."

Trevor gave him a level look. "I know you mean it about staying here, but I need to stand on my own two feet."

"I hear you." Luke walked him to the elevator. As the door slid open and his brother stepped in, he said, "Give my love to Jodie. And come back soon."

He stood, listening to the hum of the elevator as it descended. He wanted to shout at Trevor to come back so he could celebrate the fact that he had a brother again. But Trevor had called the play this time, and Luke couldn't argue with it.

He pivoted to the photograph of the two cowboys walking side by side. Maybe it did remind him of himself and his brother. Miranda had thought so.

And Miranda had made his reconciliation with his brother possible. She was the one who had told him to push past the guilt to honesty. Her support had given him the courage to tell Trevor the truth about how he felt.

Regret and longing clawed at him as he remembered how her face had lit up when she'd walked into the farmhouse's kitchen. She hadn't looked at any of the other people crowding the room, just him. He felt like he'd been sacked in the end zone.

And he'd shut her down. Killed the light because he was afraid of how she made him feel.

He shook his head to stop the pain that pulsed through it. He needed to find a way to get Miranda her job back. Somehow Orin had to go while the rest of the staff kept their jobs. And Luke couldn't be involved, so he needed a front man. He searched his memory and came up with a client name Miranda had mentioned . . . Anglethorpe. He'd enlist them to lead the campaign. Once he got that taken care of, he could focus on football. Be the Iceman again.

He strode out to the terrace, hoping the razor-sharp wind would blow Miranda out of his mind. The Statue of Liberty stretched her arm upward tirelessly, and the distant lights of the Verrazano Bridge winked like the jewels of a necklace against dark, liquid velvet.

The spectacular view couldn't stop him from remembering how beautiful Miranda had looked in her jeans and rubber boots, her hair wisping around her face. The smudges of fatigue under her eyes had made him want to scoop her up in his arms and carry her to a bed.

Except if he'd gotten anywhere near a bed with her, he'd have climbed in and made love to her. He'd barely been able to stop himself from ripping the coveralls off her in the cheese cave, with his teammates—and even worse, Gavin Miller—just outside the door.

Once she got her job back, he would run into her every now and then, hear her satin-smooth voice, watch her lips curve into a smile. Maybe even see her with another man, the one she deserved.

His fingers clenched on the stone parapet so hard that tiny bits of grit embedded themselves in his skin.

"I'm an idiot," he muttered, echoing Miller's text. If he saw another man touch Miranda, he'd horse-collar the guy and break every bone in the hand that had dared to touch her.

Miranda had told him to be honest with his brother. Now he needed to be honest with himself. As he stared down at the corded tendons of his hands, the truth unfolded in his heart like a perfectly executed play-action pass on the field.

He'd felt the pull of something down deep when Trevor declared how lucky he was to have Jodie. Luke had understood his brother, but he hadn't known why. Now he did.

You *could* fall in love with someone in only ten days.

He threw back his head and shouted into the wind, "I love her!"

It felt so good, he did it again, the words whirling away on the currents of frigid air. Yet he felt only warmth soaking through him. Every muscle in his body seemed to relax and stretch and bask in the relief of knowing this was right.

But yelling it alone on his penthouse terrace wasn't enough by a long shot. He owed Miranda the world's best apology. She deserved to see him grovel, after how he'd treated her.

She might just tell him to go to hell.

He frowned as the wind yanked at his hair. He'd thrown her love back in her face. Maybe she was done with him.

Once again he clamped his hands down on the parapet.

He needed to come up with something really good. Something that would prove to her he was committed 100 percent. As an idea formed, he started to smile.

Sometimes fame could come in handy.

Chapter 29

On Friday morning, Miranda's cell phone started a mad vibrating dance on the barn shelf where she'd left it while cleaning the teat cups. She raced over to check the caller ID and discovered it was Erik, her concierge friend. He must have heard she'd left the Pinnacle. She went back to cleaning the milking equipment when the phone rattled again. This time it was Boyce Schmidt, the Pinnacle's manager. Probably some kind of exit interview. Her hands were soapy and the water was running, so she went back to work. When the phone buzzed for the third time, she rinsed her hands and turned off the water. This time the missed call was from her office mate, Sofia Nunez.

What the heck was going on at the Pinnacle?

Erik usually had the best gossip grapevine, so she called him back first.

"Miranda, sweetie, why didn't you tell me about sleazoid Spindle?" he asked.

"You mean that he fired me?" Miranda plunked down on a hay bale. "It's not the kind of thing I wanted to shout from the rooftops."

There was a fraught silence. "You mean I get to deliver the news?" Erik said, his voice throbbing with excitement. "Your scumbag boss has gotten the sack."

"What!" Luke wouldn't have done this after what she'd told him, would he? Although he always warned her that she underestimated his ruthlessness.

"Not only that." Erik's words tumbled out at high speed. "He got sacked for firing you."

It was sounding more and more like Luke had had something to do with Orin's departure. But she couldn't believe that he would jeopardize all the other concierges' jobs.

"*And* they offered all the people who worked for your scurvy boss the opportunity to stay on at the Pinnacle. Sebastian got promoted to head concierge."

"Sebastian will be great." Relief surged through Miranda. No one had lost their job except the one man who deserved it. How had Luke engineered the coup? "How did you hear all this? Never mind."

"Exactly, sweetie. I protect my sources," Erik said. "You need to get on the phone to Sebastian right now. He'll hire you back in a millisecond. And, Miranda, karma's my kind of bitch."

Miranda thanked Erik and disconnected. She needed to return Boyce Schmidt's call first. She hit the number and waited, hope bubbling up in her throat like the fizz of champagne.

"Miranda, thanks for getting back to me." The building manager's lightly accented voice boomed through the phone. "I hope you haven't found another position already, because all of us at the Pinnacle would like to have you back here."

Her brain was having a hard time processing the sudden turn-around, so she hesitated.

Boyce jumped into the silence. "And we'd like to offer you a raise."

"A raise?" She'd be able to make the next payment on the loan for Dennis, no problem.

"You have quite the supporters in the Anglethorpes." Boyce's voice held a humorously rueful tone. "They insist that you are worth your weight in gold. However, we can't pay you quite that much."

Miranda chuckled politely when she wanted to scream with joy. "I'm very grateful to you and to them." The Anglethorpes had done this?

"And you will be reporting to Sebastian Wyndham, our new head concierge. Orin Spindle has left our employ." Boyce's voice was tense with distaste. "We are sorry for any distress he may have caused you."

"No apology necessary. I'm happy to return to the Pinnacle. It's a pleasure to work there."

"Excellent. Please take whatever family time you need, and let Sebastian know when you wish to return. We're delighted to have you with us."

Miranda put down the phone in a daze. The Anglethorpes had swooped down like guardian angels and set her world right. Almost.

Orin's firing would have been enough to make her happy, but getting rehired—with a raise—was beyond amazing.

She couldn't celebrate with Patty and Dennis because they had no idea she'd lost her job. Instead, she leaped off the hay bale and did a crazed victory dance in front of a few startled cows.

Cheers erupted from the family room as Miranda took the bag of popcorn out of the microwave oven and dumped it in a wooden bowl. She'd volunteered for snack duty to get away from the concerned glances Patty and Dennis kept sliding toward her when they thought she wasn't looking. Patty must have told Dennis about her broken-off relationship with Luke.

She also needed to take a break from the Sunday afternoon football game in which, according to her brother, Luke was moving better than he had before his injury.

"He's playing like the old days, like he's enjoying it. He must have needed the week's rest," Dennis said before Patty glared at him and he threw Miranda an apologetic look.

Theo had gone back to school on Thursday, the hired hand had returned to work on Saturday, and Dennis had helped with today's early milking. So Miranda was headed back to New York tomorrow morning to restart her job on the evening shift. Sebastian had been thrilled to hear she was returning, and she'd written the Anglethorpes a heartfelt letter of thanks.

However, even her good fortune on the work front couldn't dull the pain of Luke's rejection. She still suspected he'd been involved in Orin's disgrace in some way, but she would never know for sure.

This was supposed to be her time to relax and unwind, but she'd forgotten about her family's devotion to the Empire. She couldn't ruin their pleasure by refusing to watch the game. They might feel guilty enough to turn it off.

After Luke and his all-star crew left on Tuesday, Patty had turned to Miranda and said, "Well, I was sure wrong. You weren't just entertainment for him."

Miranda had shaken her head. "He came up to make it clear that our relationship is over. He milked the cows so he wouldn't feel too guilty about it."

"He didn't look at you like it was over."

He hadn't kissed her like it was over, either. But then he'd pushed her away and into the arms of an imaginary lover, even when she'd made a fool of herself and told him she loved him. She swallowed to clear the clot of desolation that was stuck in her throat. "Honestly, I don't know why he went to all that trouble. All I can tell you is that he was very definite about ending it. So I really don't want to discuss it anymore."

"I understand, honey. Topic closed." And Patty had kept her promise.

Miranda puttered in the kitchen, refolding the dish towel, refilling the napkin holder, and wiping up a scattering of crumbs from some earlier sandwich making. Then she just stared out the window as the aroma of fresh popcorn wafted by her nostrils. She should take it into the family room before it got cold, but she was having a hard time not watching for the blue jersey with the number nine on it. And when she saw it, despair would fill her up like cold tears.

"Miranda! Get in here! Quick!" Dennis and Patty's voices mingled, their urgency unmistakable.

Abandoning the popcorn bowl, Miranda bolted for the family room, sure that Luke had been injured in some horrible way.

She skidded to a stop, her gaze skittering from the broad grins on her family's faces to the television screen.

Luke's face was front and center, surrounded by a forest of microphones with colorful network logos on them. His damp hair was slicked back from his face, and his pads made his shoulders look so broad he could carry the world on them.

"Thanks for helping me out," he said with a nod to the offscreen reporters surrounding him. "Miranda Tate, I hope someone has fetched you so you're watching this broadcast by now." He paused, his face solemn. "Sugar, I've made some bad calls in my life, but walking away from you was the worst fumble ever. Maybe I don't deserve it, but I'm asking you to forgive me and give me a chance to make it up to you."

A bleak shadow darkened his eyes. "But I'll understand if you can't see your way to doing that." He nodded again. "That's all."

There was a cacophony of questions with Miranda's name repeating throughout them, but Luke reiterated his thanks and vanished into the dressing room, where the reporters weren't allowed at halftime.

Miranda stood staring at the screen. She felt as though she'd been picked up, turned upside down, shaken, and then set back on her feet by a large, blond quarterback. Her head spun, and her heart felt as though it would pound itself right out of her chest.

"You record all the games, right?" she said to Dennis. "Play that again."

She listened to the incredible, unbelievable words, but she also caught the tension in his jaw and the uncertainty in his eyes. Was it because he thought she wouldn't respond, or because he wasn't sure he should say this?

But Patty was whooping and hugging her. "I knew it!" Her sister-in-law pulled away, still holding Miranda's shoulders. "We have to get you there. Dennis, you stay here with Theo while I drive Miranda to the stadium."

"Are you kidding me?" Dennis jumped up from the couch. "Theo and I are coming, too. I want to see my little sis looking happy again."

"Wait, we don't have tickets," Miranda said. "So we can't even get into the stadium. I can't call Luke during the game."

"Why not? He was willing to go on national TV to ask you to forgive him. Leave a message. Someone will answer it." Patty did a little jig before heading for the hallway where the coats hung.

"Didn't that PR lady give you her cell-phone number?" Dennis asked, taking her by the elbow and towing her toward the front door. "Call her from the car. We don't have time to mess around here."

Theo trotted along behind them. "Is Aunt Miranda going to kiss Luke Archer?"

"I sure hope so," Patty said.

"Ew! Football players shouldn't kiss people." Theo shrugged into the jacket his mother held out as they all trundled out the door.

Once in the Subaru, Dennis tuned the radio to the game. The Empire were winning seventeen to seven. Miranda sat in the back alongside Theo, feeling little sparkles of delight every time the announcer said Luke's name.

"He's relentless," Dennis said as the Empire collected first down after first down in their drive toward the goal line.

"Touchdown, Empire!" the announcer shouted.

Patty turned to grin at Miranda. "He's working off the pressure of waiting to find out what you'll say. I predict the Empire win this game big."

Her family took it up as a mantra. When Luke connected on a long pass, Dennis cheered, "He threw that one for Miranda."

When he ran the ball, Patty gave her teasing look. "He was imagining it was you at the forty-yard line."

Even Theo joined in. When the Empire scored again, her nephew shrugged his skinny shoulders. "I guess he scored that touchdown for Aunt Miranda."

Laughter bubbled up in her throat and spilled out with each absurd claim. Beneath her happiness, she knew there were no guarantees that she and Luke could find a way to make things work between them. Despite sharing a building, there was a vast gulf between the world-class athlete and the assistant concierge.

She shoved those thoughts away, refusing to let anything cast a shadow on this moment of pure elation.

By some miracle they hit very little traffic, and soon Dennis was following the instructions Heather had given Miranda when she called. "I hoped you'd get in touch with me," the young PR representative had said. "This is the most romantic thing I've ever seen."

She'd done her job well, because all Miranda had to do was flash her driver's license at the various security guards and they were directed into VIP parking, ushered through the players' entrance, and escorted to a private lounge outfitted with a giant flat-screen television and big cushy chairs and sofas.

Heather joined them there, her face beaming with excitement. She threw her arms around Miranda. "The press has inundated our office with inquiries about you. Everyone wants to know about the mystery woman who got Luke Archer to apologize on national television."

Nerves took Miranda by the throat. She'd been so focused on getting to Luke that she'd forgotten about the difficulties of dating a celebrity, especially one who claimed you in front of millions. "I—what did you tell them?"

"Nothing," Heather said. "It's not our policy to comment on our players' personal lives. This time it was easy, since we didn't know anything about you."

"Touchdown!" Dennis leaped up from the sofa where he and Theo had settled. "That makes the score thirty-seven to thirteen. I call that a rout."

Miranda and Heather turned toward the screen as the Empire kicked the extra point and the clock ran out. Luke headed off the field, unsnapping his helmet as he walked. A blonde reporter in high heels raced out to meet him, but he kept going, disappearing into the swirl of players congratulating one another on the win.

She ignored the chatter of the commentators dissecting the game until she heard her name. "So we have to wonder if Archer's rejuvenated play is the result of a week's rest, or the influence of the mystery woman, Miranda Tate. Or maybe both."

Miranda buried her face in her hands with a groan.

"Don't mind them," Heather said. "They don't really want to talk about anything but football, so they'll get back to the game stats soon. It's just a concession to the ratings, which went through the roof after Mr. Archer's speech." The young woman looked at Miranda. "I guess you know that he's never talked to the press at halftime before."

"Um, well, no." Miranda smiled apologetically. "I wasn't really a football fan. Until now."

A clamor of approaching voices came from outside the door. It swung open and Luke walked in, his helmet dangling from his hand. He slammed the door closed on the crowd following him. Turning, he raked his fingers through his hair and scanned around the room, his gaze coming to rest on Miranda.

She opened her mouth and realized she had no idea what to say.

"I didn't expect you to come here," Luke said, shifting his helmet to the other hand.

"Dennis drove me," Miranda said, gesturing to her brother and his family, who were standing beside the couch. She waved her other hand toward the PR rep. "And Heather got us in." She couldn't tell if he was glad she'd shown up at the stadium. "What you did was pretty dramatic . . . I mean, saying all of that on national TV. So we thought I should be here."

"I wanted everyone to know you're mine," Luke said, still not moving toward her. "No more sneaking around."

Miranda heard Patty let out a long sigh. "Let's give them some privacy," Heather said. Miranda threw her a look of gratitude as Heather shepherded Dennis, Patty, and Theo toward the door. Patty turned and gave Miranda a wink before she stepped out into the hall. The reporters shouted questions, but Miranda could hear Heather turning them aside before the closing door muted the noise.

She couldn't stop staring at Luke as he stood there, his uniform smudged with dirt, his hair dark with sweat, his blue eyes striking above the black greasepaint smeared on his cheeks. He looked like a world-famous, larger-than-life quarterback, not like the Luke Archer who had milked her family's cows. But he was both those people, and she needed to embrace one along with the other if she was going to love him.

She hurried into speech again. "I know it's football season, so I promise not to get in the way of your practicing and watching film."

That seemed to unfreeze him. He tossed the helmet onto a chair and crossed the room in three strides to wrap his arms around her. "Damn all these pads," he said, easing his grip so she wasn't mashed against the hard edges. He smelled of exertion and energy, a potent combination. "I want you in the way. All the time. To keep me balanced. To believe that I can be more. To open up my world."

Miranda cradled his face between her hands, falling into the depths of his eyes. He laid a finger over her lips.

"Don't say anything yet," Luke said. "I want to fall asleep with you in my arms and wake up with you in my arms. I want to find out what makes you laugh and hope I can keep you from crying. But if you do, I want your tears to be on my shoulder."

"You're about to make me cry right now," Miranda said in a husky voice.

His eyebrows drew downward in a frown. "I made you cry on Tuesday, didn't I? You had the courage to tell me how you felt, and I lied because I was afraid."

She was stunned. "Of what?"

"I thought my feelings for you were distracting me. I didn't understand that it was my denial that was destroying my focus. When I finally had the guts to admit that I loved you, everything turned clear again." He dropped his arms and stepped away from her. "I know what you give me, but all I can offer you is this." He swept his hand downward in front of his body. "Myself. Not a very good trade."

Miranda closed the distance between them, resting her hands on his chest pads as she looked up at him, smiling. "What else can we ever give the person we love?" She crumpled fistfuls of his football jersey in her hands and tried to give him a shake. Of course, she couldn't budge him. "You're everything I want."

He searched her face for a long moment, his eyes opaque and unreadable. Whatever he saw there made him crush her against him so hard she could barely breathe. Then he stole what was left of her breath with a searing kiss. When her legs threatened to collapse under her, he raised his head. "You know all those things I said you should do with another man? I realized I'd kill him if I caught you two doing any of them together."

"You mean like talking art and ballet at a restaurant without reporters?" It was hard to remember his words when he turned her veins into rivers of fire.

He ran his mouth along her jawline, sending shivers of desire down her neck. "I'll rent out the entire restaurant so we can talk without being bothered."

"I'd rather stay home and eat quesadillas," she said, yanking the hem of his jersey and his undershirt up to get her hands under them. "In your gym." She had to shove her fingers up under the chest plate of his shoulder pads to feel the sweat-slicked heat of his skin.

He thrust his hands inside the back of her jeans and under her panties to knead her bottom in his powerful grip. "We can't do this now," he growled, his hands contradicting his words as he slid one finger forward to press into the wet heat between her legs.

"I know," she said, her head falling back as he worked his finger in and out of her, sending spirals of arousal into her belly. She scrabbled at his pads, but the straps and buckles were too intricate to succumb to her divided concentration.

"Come for me, sugar, so I know you forgive me," he murmured in her ear, as he slipped another finger inside her.

She ran her hand down the center of his tight pants, only to find a hard plastic shell where his erection should be. He groaned as she tried to shift it. "Sweetheart, that protector is built to withstand being sacked by a three-hundred-pound lineman. You're not going to be able to move it." He increased the rhythm of his strokes inside her. "This is all about you, as part of my apology."

She wedged her hands back up under his pads to hold herself steady. He pushed his thigh between hers so that the movements of his hand had her riding the combination of muscle and pad. Tension wound tighter and tighter within her as the friction fanned her arousal to a blistering heat. When he took her earlobe in his mouth and sucked gently at the small gold hoop she wore in it, the pull of his mouth echoed the pressure of his fingers, shooting exquisitely intense pleasure into her center from above and below. Her muscles clenched explosively around his fingers, and she arched into his body, feeling the bite of the pads and reveling in the edge of discomfort that contrasted with the release of her orgasm. Some fragment of sanity made her swallow the cry of satisfaction she nearly let loose.

"That's it, darlin', let it take you," Luke said beside her ear. He twisted his fingers and sent another wave of hot, melting sensation ripping through her. She nearly choked on the shriek that tried to escape her throat.

"No more," she panted as her muscles clenched and eased again . . . and again, wringing every ounce of pleasure from her highly sensitized nerve endings.

"Until tonight," Luke said, easing his fingers out of her and gently extracting his hand from her jeans. He brought his fingers to his nostrils and inhaled before he sucked the taste of her off them. "God, that makes me want you even more."

She sagged against him as the glow of satiation leached the ability to stand out of every muscle in her body. His arms went around her, and she felt the weight of his chin on top of her head. "Sweetheart, I came so close to letting you go. Miller was right. I'm an idiot."

The writer's name penetrated the fog of postorgasm relaxation she was drifting in. "He told me to exploit your vulnerability."

Luke's laughter rumbled against her cheek. "I'll be damned. The cynical writer played matchmaker."

"He kept mentioning some bet. What was he talking about?"

She felt a tiny shock of tension stiffen his body. "Three drunk guys made a wager on something that should never be gambled on."

"What?"

He hesitated. "Love."

That made her angle her head back so she could see his face. "Are you serious? You don't date during the football season."

"That rule has changed," he reminded her. He led her over to the sofa, dropping onto it and pulling her down beside him. "It was a bad night. My best friend had just retired from football. I knew my time was coming, and I wasn't feeling good about that. Miller got us drunk and we started in on the problem of finding a woman who loves you for yourself and not because you're famous or rich."

"Who's the third?"

"Nathan Trainor of Trainor Electronics." Luke looked away for a moment before meeting her eyes again. "We all bet that we would be engaged by the end of a year. I figured I would wait until after the end of the season and then get to work on the project. Because I'm an arrogant jerk."

She thought about how dark his mood must have been to agree to such a wager, and her heart pinched.

"I want you to know that the bet had nothing to do with today." His voice carried an undercurrent of concern. "Well, maybe it did. It made me think about how limited my life was, so I decided to go on that tour with you. But I'm not here to win the bet."

"Considering how hard you tried to get rid of me, I'm not all that worried. Although you *are* pretty competitive." She smiled up at him to show she wasn't serious.

He didn't return her smile. "I almost asked you to wait for me until the end of the season, but it didn't seem fair to you. I couldn't guarantee that things would work out between us. I told myself if you found someone else, then we weren't meant to be." His eyes went dark. "But I've never been good at sitting back and letting someone else decide my fate."

She touched his cheek. "I would have waited. Gladly."

"That still wouldn't have made it right to ask you." His grip tightened. "You had the courage to tell me how you felt. I needed to make the same commitment."

"I guess we owe Gavin a thank-you," she said. "Although I wanted to strangle him after you walked away."

"He gets that reaction from a lot of people." Luke's tone was wry.

"So, how do you prove you've won the wager?"

He hesitated a moment before shaking his head. "I can't tell you that."

"Can you tell me what the stakes are?"

"When my win is official, I'll let you in on all the details. Before that would be cheating." He looked down at her with a smile as tender as it was hot. "If you really want something, you have to earn it fair and square."

She wanted to melt into him. "You athletes just love your clichés, don't you?"

"They're clichés because they're true." His dimple faded. "When you think about it, *I love you* is probably the world's most overused phrase. But when your heart is in it, those words take on whole shades of meaning you never imagined before." He leaned in to touch her lips with his. "I love you, Miranda."

She smiled against his mouth. "That's one cliché I'll never get tired of hearing."

The kiss went long and intense before he pulled away. "Now you'll get your first taste of what a pain it is to be my girlfriend."

She thought of Orin. "I already have." She looked him right in the eyes. "I need an honest answer from you about something. Do you know the Anglethorpes at the Pinnacle?"

"Never met them," he said, his expression unchanged. "Why?"

"They got me my job back. And I think they got Orin fired."

"Then I like them." He kissed her again. "Okay, sugar, it's time to meet the press. Just to prepare you, there are probably at least a dozen reporters camped outside that door."

"You mean, while we . . . while I . . ." She dropped her head into her hands as heat flared up her cheeks. "They're going to know. I mean, I must look like I've just, er—" She glanced back up at him pleadingly.

"Found out that I love you?" His dimple deepened. "Only I know exactly how I convinced you it was true."

Little imps of light were dancing in his eyes, and Miranda choked on a half laugh, half groan.

He tugged her to her feet and wrapped his arm around her waist like a protective barrier. "Just stare up at me adoringly and they'll leave you alone."

"I know you're joking, but I can do that without even trying," she said, her throat suddenly tight.

As their eyes met, his grew hot. "Don't look like that now or you'll end up naked on the sofa."

"That's not the best way to stop me."

A strangled sound came from his throat before he tucked her against him and marched her to the door. Wrapping his hand around the knob, he looked down at her, his face serious. "You don't have to do this. I can deal with them alone."

"No way, cowboy. I'm never leaving your side again."

As the unlatched door swung open, the explosion of camera flashes barely registered with Miranda because she was locked in a soul-deep kiss with a living legend.

Epilogue

Miranda was still shivering slightly from the frigid air of the February night as she and Luke walked, fingers intertwined, into Frankie Hogan's office at the Bellwether Club. Although she'd been to the club before and met Frankie, Miranda had never been in this room. She was startled by the bright, sleek, glass-and-chrome modernity of the room when the rest of the club was all dark paneling, leather upholstery, and Oriental carpets.

The club's founder rose from behind her desk, her smooth silver hair contrasting with her dark red pantsuit. "Welcome to my lair," she said in her raspy voice with its undertone of Irish. "Congratulations to both of you on winning your part of the wager."

"Thank you, ma'am," Luke said, his drawl pronounced.

Miranda had learned that his accent deepened when he was either trying to disarm someone or when he was more emotional than he wanted to let on. She slanted a glance up at his sculpted face, trying to gauge which it was. He caught her looking and gave her a wink. It still amazed her that this extraordinary man had chosen her. Now she could touch those beautiful cheekbones and that golden hair and all those gorgeous muscles anytime she wanted to. She winked back and squeezed his hand, just to feel the strength of his fingers.

"Well, then, let's see the ring," Frankie said.

Luke lifted their joined hands, turning them so that her engagement ring with its large marquise diamond and its frame of smaller blue and white diamonds scintillated in the light. She loved the shape of the central diamond because it reminded her of a football. Luke claimed it hadn't crossed his mind when he chose it, but she didn't believe him for a second.

"Wait a minute," Frankie said, moving closer and narrowing her eyes. "Is that another ring underneath it?"

Luke's dimple showed, but he didn't answer.

"You son of a gun, Archer. I like your style." Frankie turned to a large cupboard and typed a code into a keypad. The door clicked open and she pushed it farther ajar to reveal an industrial-looking safe. "A different sort of congratulations is in order, as well. I watched you win your fifth Super Bowl. That's damned impressive, even for a member of the Bellwether Club."

"I didn't win it alone. It takes the whole team."

"Spoken like a champion." Frankie chuckled as she swung open the massive door and pulled out a leather portfolio. "However, the whole team doesn't wear a target on their chests."

Miranda silently agreed as she thought of the many times Luke's body looked like a painting of pain with its multicolored bruises. That was the hardest part for her, knowing how battered he was as he jogged onto the field to be slammed into all over again. After the Super Bowl victory, he'd gone out to celebrate with his teammates and then come home to crawl into bed, where she'd covered him with a blanket of cold packs. No one except she and his trainer Stan knew how much he had to endure to win game after game. He said that being able to admit to her how much he was hurting eased the pain. She hoped it was true.

"Here's your stake." Frankie held up a cream vellum envelope with Luke's name slashed across it. She flipped it to show him the back. "Still sealed." She picked up a pen. "As I did with Trainor's, I will mark this 'wager satisfied' and initial it." She did so with a flourish before sliding it back into the portfolio. "One forfeit is left, and judging by his mood, I don't see Miller getting any closer to canceling it."

"He has time," Luke said, but Miranda knew he worried about his friend, who still couldn't write, much less open his heart to a woman. They owed Gavin Miller a debt of gratitude, and Luke felt that keenly.

"Not everyone moves as fast as you do." Frankie's gaze touched Miranda's beringed hand again. "I wish you both joy."

"Much obliged." Luke shook Frankie's hand. His new Super Bowl ring gleamed large on his finger.

Miranda gave in to an impulse and hugged the club's owner. Frankie hesitated a moment but gave her a quick squeeze in return.

"Your fellow gamblers are waiting in the bar where this all started," Frankie said, shooing them out of her office.

Luke walked sedately beside Miranda down the hallway until they passed an open door. Before she knew what was happening, he had pulled her inside the room and bent down to give her a long, hard kiss.

"What brought that on?" she asked when he gave her a chance to catch her breath.

He framed her face in his big hands, his expression solemn. "The envelope reminded me of where I was five months ago and where I am now, and what a difference there is between those places. The night I made that bet, the future looked so grim I was willing to do anything to change it. Now I look forward to all the years I get to spend with you."

She blinked hard to keep her tears away from her mascara.

"That's the power loving you has given me." He shifted his grip to her shoulders. "When I think of how close I came to letting you go . . ." She felt his hands tighten. "That will never happen again."

"I wasn't giving up, either. Gavin wouldn't let me." She put her hand over his heart, savoring the strong beat under the fine cashmere of his navy blazer. "Speaking of Gavin, we'd better get upstairs."

He let his palms glide down over her back to cup her behind through the silk chiffon of her cocktail dress. A shimmer of arousal ran through her, awakening an answering heat in his eyes. "I was thinking of letting them wait," he said. "I can wedge a chair under the door handle, and this couch looks pretty comfortable." He tugged her zipper down and flicked open the hooks of her bra.

She twisted in his arms, trying to grab his wrists, but he was too strong and quick. "When those announcers talk about what good hands you have, they don't know the half of it. You have to stop."

He caught her hands behind her and pushed the bodice of her chiffon cocktail dress down to her waist. Then he bent to suck one nipple into his mouth.

He flicked her with his tongue, and she gasped and shuddered as heat spread through her to focus between her thighs. "Luke! Stop!"

He lifted his head and gave her a wicked grin. "I just wanted a taste."

He loved to do this, get her flushed and disheveled and wanting. He said he needed her to think about him as much as he thought about her. He still didn't believe that he was never out of her mind or her heart.

"How did you get this undone?" she asked, struggling to get her bra fastened again.

"Allow me." He had her hooked and zipped in two seconds flat.

Miranda sighed and checked her appearance in the ornamental mirror hanging over the small fireplace. A swipe of lipstick and she looked respectable in her floating black dress with its dusting of beading. The diamond earrings Luke had given her for Christmas flashed on her earlobes.

He came up behind her and put his arms around her waist and his chin on her shoulder so his gilded hair glowed beside her dark waves.

She let her gaze rove over the perfect planes of his face: the slashing cheekbones, the hard line of his jaw, the arch of his eyebrows, and the pale, blazing blue of his eyes.

"You're so beautiful," he said.

She burst out laughing. "You're much prettier than I am."

He straightened and patted her on the butt. "You're going to give me a complex."

She took his hand and headed toward the door. She loved the way he moved beside her, the thigh muscles under his perfectly fitted gray trousers turning his stride into a visual feast.

"I still can't believe you bet *all* of your Super Bowl rings on finding the right woman," she said in a low voice. He'd told her on the way to the Bellwether Club what his wager had been.

"I felt like I wouldn't want any reminders of football once I retired." He lifted their joined hands and kissed the back of hers. "I wasn't in a good place."

She hadn't understood until tonight just how dark his mood had been when he'd made the wager. Now she felt both the giddy delight and the weighty responsibility of being the one who had snapped him out of it.

They climbed the carpeted stairs and walked into the famous bar where the three gamblers had first met. Gavin beckoned to them from a table set by one of the tall windows. He was dressed in an open-necked black shirt, black blazer, and dark gray trousers. Miranda feared that the color of his clothes reflected his emotional state.

"And here we are," Gavin said as they approached. "Our original number increased by two. Miranda, you look lovely tonight." He kissed her on the cheek before he held out his hand to Luke. "Archer, you look like a football player."

"Miranda, I'm so happy for you and Luke." Chloe Russell, Nathan's fiancée, swooped in for a hug, her rose taffeta skirt rustling. Miranda had met them both at a Christmas party at Nathan's penthouse, and she and the no-nonsense Chloe were on the road to a close friendship.

"Best wishes, Miranda." The tall CEO in his custom-tailored suit bent to kiss her cheek. "Congratulations, Archer. You fooled us into thinking you weren't even in the game until after the football season."

Luke gave Miranda a secret smile. "Life happens when you're making other plans."

"Oh, for God's sake!" Gavin said. "If you're going to spout nauseating clichés, I'm headed for the door."

"Without drinking the 1928 Dom Pérignon?" Nathan said. He picked up the bottle and turned to Miranda. "Vintage Dom has become a tradition at this particular celebration." He filled the sparkling flutes arrayed on the table.

"The ring. We must see the ring," Gavin said, as everyone picked up their glasses. "And I don't mean your Super Bowl monstrosity, Archer. We've already admired that." In fact, Gavin had surprised Luke by hosting a celebratory party at his New York City home. The writer claimed not to be a sports fan, but he had put on quite a gala event.

Feeling strangely shy, Miranda held up her left hand and tilted it so the diamond glittered.

"It's gorgeous!" Chloe said. "May I take a closer look?"

Miranda held her hand out to her new friend, knowing what was coming next.

"Um, Nathan, I think we've been beaten to the altar." Chloe looked at her fiancé with laughter in her warm brown eyes.

"Is that so?" Nathan turned to Luke.

"The clock was running, so I went to a no-huddle offense and called an audible," Luke said.

"We had a family-only service in my hometown church," Miranda said, remembering how intimate and beautiful the ceremony had been in the simple Victorian-era clapboard chapel. Trevor had stood as Luke's best man while Patty had been her matron of honor. Theo carried the ring on a blue-and-gold pillow. "We're planning a big reception here in the city now that football season is over. Of course, we hope you'll all come."

There was another round of congratulations, even warmer this time.

Chloe was examining the rings again. "So, tell me about the wedding band. I sense there's a story there."

The band was platinum, smooth and simple except for the five small stones set in it, alternating diamonds and sapphires. "Luke took one stone out of each of his Super Bowl rings and set them in the wedding band." He'd told her that winning her love was better than all his Super Bowl victories put together.

Chloe guessed something of his feelings. "What an incredibly romantic gesture!"

"You are so damned competitive, Archer," Gavin said. "Trainor beat you to the engagement, so you had to up the ante by beating him to the wedding."

"Since we're discussing weddings, we'd like to invite all of you to ours in October. It will be at the chapel at Camp Lejeune," Nathan said. He smiled down at his fiancée, his whole face softening. "Chloe has taken a liking to Marines."

"I just like the uniforms," Chloe said with a glint in her eye. She turned to Miranda and Luke. "We picked a weekend when the Empire have a bye, so we hope you'll be able to come."

"I appreciate your thoughtfulness, but you don't have to worry about that," Luke said. "I'm announcing my retirement tomorrow." He snuggled Miranda against his side and smiled down at her. "I've got better things to do than toss around a ball."

"I see a white picket fence looming large in your future." Gavin knocked back the rest of his champagne and signaled the waiter for another bottle.

"Going out on top." Nathan nodded. "Smart move."

"Miranda has her own concierge and travel business, which is growing. I'm interested in finance, so I'll be moving in that direction." He broke into a grin. "It will be nice to come home from work without bruises."

"Amen to that," Miranda said.

The incredible thing was that Luke had made the decision to retire without any obvious hesitation. He was eager to do something new, something that challenged him in a different way.

"Got any more surprises for us?" Gavin asked as the waiter refilled everyone's champagne glasses. "No one's pregnant?" He glanced between Chloe and Miranda. "I guess not, since you're both drinking."

"I'd like to propose a toast," Miranda said. "To Gavin. He gave us good advice when we most needed it."

"Gavin?" Nathan said, his eyebrows lifted in surprise.

Gavin waved off the credit. "I simply stated the obvious. Any idiot could see that you wanted each other."

"You told me *I* was the idiot," Luke said. He raised his glass to the writer. "And you were right."

After they drank to Gavin, Luke took Miranda's glass and put it down alongside his own. "We're still on our honeymoon, so I'm taking my wife home now."

He looked down at her, his blue eyes lit with such tenderness that Miranda thought her heart would dissolve. "*My wife*. Only three other words are better." He lowered his head so his lips were a mere breath away from hers as he said, *"I love you."*

DISCUSSION QUESTIONS

1. Both Luke and Miranda are shaped by family relationships. Their parents didn't understand their life choices, and their brothers have become responsibilities, financially and emotionally. Why do our families influence us so strongly, even when the influence might be negative? What positive or negative effects has your family had on you?

2. Luke's celebrity status leads Miranda to assume that he will behave in certain ways, so she's surprised when he defies those expectations. Are certain personalities drawn to the limelight, or does fame itself change people? Why do we assume it is acceptable for celebrities to act differently from normal people? Do you think you would enjoy being famous?

3. What determines a person's worth? Luke is a famous football player, but he struggles with the stereotype that he's just a dumb jock. Miranda is insightful and excellent at her job, but she assumes she's too average for someone

like Luke to consider romantically. Their talents are different but equally important, so why do they both feel lacking at the beginning of the novel? Why do they need each other to comprehend their own self-worth? Do we all seek outside validation?

4. Luke dedicated his entire life to football, forcing his personal life to take a backseat to his career. Can you find true happiness through a job? Are personal relationships more or less important than career success? Can you balance both equally, or does one always take precedence?

5. Miranda and Luke have a "play through the pain" attitude on both a physical and mental level. Is this always a good thing? What are some of the pros and cons of never showing weakness to those around you?

6. Orin Spindle is an unprofessional, spiteful boss, but Miranda is forced to put up with him to retain her job. Have you ever been in a similar situation? How do you handle those who abuse their power over others?

7. If you were in Miranda's shoes, would you have accepted Luke's offer to write a letter of recommendation? She is highly competent at her job and would be an asset to any company that hired her, but she still feels like it would be cheating. Do you agree?

8. Luke is surprised when the curator at the Morgan Library wants a document from him, because he believes football is not cultured enough to fit in with the highbrow collection there. What do you consider "culture"? Is it

possible to predict what will have a lasting impact on cultural history? Is Luke's athletic fame too fleeting to merit inclusion?

9. At first glance, Miranda and Luke seem to have very dissimilar careers and personalities. Do opposites truly attract, or are our hero and heroine more alike than they appear?

10. Gavin Miller is still seeking to win his part of the Wager of Hearts. What kind of woman do you think he will find? Will she be smart and sassy like Chloe, or kind and perceptive like Miranda? What kind of life mate would you match up with the blocked writer?

ACKNOWLEDGMENTS

Writers create their stories in solitude, but it takes an incredible team to turn the story into a book. Many thanks to all of those who have contributed knowledge, effort, and support to this project, most especially:

Maria Gomez, my super editor, whose spirit and enthusiasm make it a joy to work with her.

Jessica Poore, Marlene Kelly, and the Montlake Author Relations team, all of whom are all-stars in my eyes.

Jane Dystel and Miriam Goderich, my marvelously supportive agents, who have helped my career take flight.

Andrea Hurst, my thoughtful, perceptive developmental editor, who knows how to make a book infinitely stronger without ripping it apart.

Sara Brady and Lea Ann Schafer, my capable, conscientious (and entertaining!) copy editors, who catch my mistakes both grammatical and logistical to polish my prose to a high shine.

Jill Kramer, my keen-eyed proofreader, whose painstaking focus and profound knowledge of grammar and punctuation make my book as perfect as possible.

Eileen Carey, the gifted graphic designer who seamlessly combined exactly the right model with exactly the right setting to bring Luke's story to vibrant visual life.

Jeff Theodorou, my brilliant resident football expert, who helped me with terminology, plays, and other details of the gridiron. Any mistakes are entirely my own.

Lawrence Jenkens, professor of art history extraordinaire, who explained the ins and outs of tenure to me.

Rebecca Theodorou, English major turned vet student, who developed the provocative, insightful discussion questions for this book.

Miriam Allenson, Lisa Verge Higgins, and Jennifer Wilck, my critique partners, whose editorial genius keeps me on the right track and pushes me to be a better writer.

Pie, my little gray cat, who warms my writer's garret with her furry, comforting presence.

Jeff, Rebecca, and Loukas, who both anchor me and give me wings. Love you all so much!

ABOUT NANCY HERKNESS

Photo © 2015 Lisa Kollberg

Nancy Herkness is the author of the award-winning Whisper Horse series, as well as several other contemporary romance novels. She has received many honors for her work, including the Book Buyers Best Award, the Maggie Award in Contemporary Romance, and the National Excellence in Romance Fiction Award, and she is a two-time nominee for the Romance Writers of America's RITA Award. She graduated from Princeton University with a degree in English literature and creative writing. A native of West Virginia, Nancy now lives in a Victorian house twelve miles west of the Lincoln Tunnel in New Jersey with her husband, two mismatched dogs, and an elderly cat.

For more information about Nancy and her books, visit www.NancyHerkness.com.

You can also find her on:

Facebook: www.facebook.com/nancyherkness
Twitter: www.twitter.com/NancyHerkness
Pinterest: www.pinterest.com/nancyherkness/
Blog: www.fromthegarret.wordpress.com/